COUNTDOWN TO TAKEOFF

The man behind the big desk sat waiting.

His name was Jeremy Haines, President of the United States. There were those who said he combined the best qualities of his predecessors—Truman's guts, Eisenhower's honesty, Kennedy's style, Johnson's savvy. But none of them had ever faced the kind of decision he had to face today.

The red phone before him rang. The direct line from the Pentagon. Even as he picked up the receiver, he knew what the message would be.

His plane was fueled and ready. His plan was set, no turning back.

THE
PRESIDENT'S
PLANE
IS
MISSING

Robert J. Serling

A DELL BOOK

For Ellin K. Roberts—den mother,
editor and friend

Published by
DELL PUBLISHING CO., INC.
750 Third Avenue
New York, N.Y. 10017

Dell ® TM 681510, Dell Publishing Co., Inc.

Reprinted by arrangement with
Doubleday & Company, Inc.
New York, N.Y.
Printed in U.S.A.

First Dell printing—September 1968
Second Dell printing—October 1968
Third Dell printing—October 1968
Fourth Dell printing—May 1969
Fifth Dell printing—June 1969

CHAPTER ONE

The President of the United States awoke that Monday morning with his usual hangover—fashioned not of liquor but of tensions and worries that sleep had failed to dissolve.

It was this way every morning for Jeremy Haines. With the first stirrings of consciousness, the cares of office snapped to attention and began an immediate march through his tired brain. He shook his head wearily, almost impatiently, as if the gesture would somehow dislodge his troubled thoughts. He looked at the clock on the table adjoining his bed. Seven A.M. His nine hundred and sixty third day in the presidency.

Jeremy Haines picked up the white phone next to the clock and ordered his breakfast. Then he climbed out of bed and donned a robe. Since his wife's death, five years before when he was governor of a Midwestern state, he had acquired the habit of eating breakfast in his bedroom on the second floor of the White House, while he planned his strategies for the day. He could accept this solitude but insisted on company at lunch and dinner. The solitude in the morning seemed to refresh him and prepare him.

He went into the bathroom to shave, examining himself critically in the mirror beforehand in the somewhat worried manner of a middle-aged man searching for any sign of aging. Except for the fatigue that showed mostly in his eyes, the image was not displeasing to either his ego or his concern. At fifty-seven, Jeremy Haines looked ten years younger than his chronological age.

He stood two inches over six feet, without an ounce of excess fat on his slim frame. The only wrinkles on his masculinely handsome face were tiny crow's feet fencing his clear gray eyes, giving him the appearance of a man who had been squinting at the sun all his life. His nose was aquiline, his mouth wide with thin lips. His closely cropped hair was only partially graying, cut so short at the temples that it was impossible to tell where the haircut ended and the graying process began.

He wore rimless glasses for reading, and they gave his rather thin, pinched features a professorial look. A reporter had once described the President as resembling "a husky Woodrow Wilson or a trimmer Warren Harding."

Keeping his hair clipped (he got a haircut once a week) was one of his rare vanities. He thought the near crew cut made him appear younger. Another vanity was a perpetual tan, thanks to a daily fifteen-minute exposure to a sun lamp. The combination made him seem more athletic than he really was. He detested golf and kept his waistline down through religiously regular calisthenics prescribed by an Army physical fitness expert.

By the time he had showered, shaved and donned a charcoal-brown (his favorite color) suit, there was a discreet knock on the bedroom door. That had to be his personal valet, a distinguished-looking Negro who had served three Presidents before Haines.

The valet skillfully and quickly set up the breakfast on a small table. By the coffee he placed the usual copies of the Washington *Post*, New York *Times* and *Wall Street Journal*.

Knowing the President's penchant for breakfasting alone, he performed his last chore—holding the chair for Haines as the tall, stern-faced Chief Executive sat down.

"Thank you, John. I'll be through in about a half hour. Then I guess you can come back and start the packing."

"Fine, Mr. President. I'll return shortly."

The valet left. Jeremy Haines idly stirred sugar in the steaming coffee and perused the top headlines on the *Post*'s front page.

PEKING WARNS U.S. CHINA READY FOR GLOBAL WAR
BOASTS OF VAST H-BOMB MISSILE ARMADA

The President put down the *Post* and picked up the *Times*. Slightly smaller type and only five columns wide instead of the *Post*'s eight, but the headlines were just as alarming.

CHINA AGAIN DEMANDS U.S. WITHDRAWAL
FROM FAR EAST; SAYS NEW ICBM WEAPONS
POISED FOR WAR

Jeremy Haines shuddered inwardly, an emotional rather than a physical chill and one that was immune from the warming effects of the first sip of hot coffee. He turned to the *Times*'s editorial page and glanced over the lead editorial. It was a crisply persuasive argument, couched in the *Times*'s typically calm logic, urging the spending of eighty-five billion dollars on an anti-missile system even if it meant indefinite postponement of all major domestic projects.

He put the *Times* aside and read the *Post*'s lead editorial, mildly critical of his Administration's "thus far ineffective gestures in easing the present world crisis." The *Post* called for a summit meeting with both Red China and Russia and commented that the President's party was using international tensions as an excuse for "treading water on his own long-promised reforms on the domestic scene." The editorial lamented that the Haines Administration evidently had embarked on a "course that is neither guns nor butter" and suggested that the President either make stronger efforts toward world peace or go all out with war preparations.

Haines nibbled at his toast with the slow, aimless mastication of a man eating out of duty, not hunger. Those damned editorial writers, so free with pontifical advice. It was easy for them to criticize from their sacrosanct ivory towers. They never had to soil their minds with the mud of real, massive, sometimes even life-or-death problems facing the President of the United States. Suddenly he realized he was enmeshed in the throes of self-pity and because he was a fair man, an intelligent man, he scolded himself for this sulking reaction to a couple of well-written editorials. A President couldn't afford the vulnerability of being thin-skinned, or he would act to avoid criticism rather than do what he thought best.

And, he decided with an inner chuckle, he had just demonstrated exactly such vulnerability. If the editorials had been dripping with favorable adjectives and gushing forth praise, he knew he would have consigned their authors to whatever category was inhabited by journalists of acu-

7

men and perspicacity. It was this blasted job that reduced a man's skin to the thickness of gossamer. No wonder Thomas Jefferson had called it a "life of splendid misery." No wonder Abraham Lincoln referred to the Executive Mansion as "that damned old house." No wonder James Garfield had confided to a friend, "My God, what is there in this place that a man should ever want to get in it?"

But that was the peculiarly druglike quality of the presidency. Few Presidents actually enjoyed their terms of office, the two Roosevelts being among the rare exceptions to the rule. Jeremy Haines was not really happy. Being human, he relished the trappings of the nation's highest elective post. The heady, delicious savor of being called "Mr. President." The physical luxuries of magnificent planes and cars at his instant disposal. The beauty and dignity of the White House itself, not just a place in which to live but a shrine in which every occupant walked with the ghosts of his predecessors.

Yet for every materialistic and ego-feeding advantage, there were a score of nagging, never-ending pressures. They went beyond the strain of at least one crisis daily, usually coming on top of yesterday's still unsolved crisis. They extended to the demands on his body, such as having to sign his name several hundred times a day. Out of curiosity once, he had kept track of those signatures during an especially busy time and discovered he had affixed "Jeremy Haines" to no fewer than five hundred and seven documents in a twenty-four-hour period. A petty complaint, perhaps, and one that would draw scorn from fellow Americans envying that yearly salary of $100,000, plus a tax-free $50,000 for expenses resulting from official duties and an untaxable $40,000 for travel and official entertainment.

Those same Americans seldom realized that a President's average age at death is five years below the national average, meaning that the mere distinction of being elected carries the dubious bonus of reduced life expectancy. That little statistic, Haines mused, was not cited by the politicians who had urged him to run nor would he have even considered it if it had been brought up when he was deciding whether to run. A man bitten by the presidential bug, afflicted with the uncurable White House virus, thinks only of the honor, the prestige, the challenge and the

8

knowledge that even lackluster Presidents find a place in history books. Not until he is in the White House does he discover that $100,000 a year plus expenses and all the trappings are poor compensation for drudgery, worry and a sense of responsibility magnified a thousand times into a nightmarish ogre.

Jeremy Haines was not afraid of responsibility, or he never would have entertained the slightest notion of trying for the White House. He had been a successful businessman in his earlier years, a kind of career trouble-shooter whose specialty was nursing sick firms back to financial health. He had gone into politics largely because the techniques of curing industrial ailments had assumed a sameness that bordered on the routine. Then there was his older brother, Bertrand, a United States senator, who persistently maintained that Jeremy had a future in public service and urged him to run for governor of their home state. Finally, it was a personal tragedy that had turned wavering indecision into firm resolve.

He had married a college sweetheart, and their union was blessed by an only son. Jeremy Haines, Jr., was killed in the early days of the Vietnam war and it was mainly this that led Jeremy Haines into public service. He served two highly successful gubernatorial terms, the second scarred by the death of his wife from cancer only two weeks before he was to leave office.

In a sense, the fatal presidential bug never really entered his blood stream until fairly late in the actual campaign, when he realized he wanted very much to be President. The decision to fight for the nomination was not so much ambition as therapy for grief and loneliness in bereavement. At that point, entrance into national politics was a diversion from sorrow and unhappy memories, the present and future eclipsing the past.

It was not until he won the election and took up his four-year lease on the mansion at 1600 Pennsylvania Avenue, when he became aware that the presidency was no cure for his own loneliness. In fact it worsened his constant emotional solitude by its very nature. At first he enjoyed the pressuring burdens because they kept him busy. But he was not in office very long before he began to miss more than ever the mutual comradeship he and his wife had shared. Theirs had been a happy, mature, extremely deep relation-

9

ship, one that would have been a perfect antidote for the tribulation of the White House.

He found he lacked, most of all, a true, intimate confidant. Advisers he had in ample supply. Friends too. He was closest to Phil Sabath, a city editor of a major newspaper in his home state whom he had brought to Washington as his press secretary. Sabath had resigned his newspaper job to help him run his campaign, and Haines not only trusted him but liked him as a person. Phil was competent at his job, surprisingly so in view of his relative unfamiliarity with Washington. If he lacked experience in dealing with the journalistic commandos known as the White House press corps, he had plenty of experience in dealing with the somewhat complex person who was Jeremy Haines. Sabath quickly learned the former, and when he did the latter stood him in good stead.

It was thanks to Sabath that Haines gradually evolved a kind of friendly armistice with the press. If Sabath protected the President from reporters, he also protected the President from himself—from his natural inclination to resent criticism, barbed questions, and persistent intrusions into what a President considered private affairs. His press conferences usually were fast-paced, laced with humor and always productive. Like Kennedy before him, Haines had a gift for good-natured repartee and a quick, rapier mind. He was erudite without being patronizing, fluent with no aroma of glibness. Admittedly, he enjoyed his fencing sessions with the press except when he could not avoid bristling at interrogation he considered unfair or childishly petty and unimportant.

"Don't let them get you down," Sabath once told Haines after a particularly rough news conference which had left the President steaming at some of the questioning. "They're doing their job. If I were still on the other side, I'd be asking you the same stuff. And remember, they don't always dream up those questions on their own. A lot of them come from their editors."

Haines had snapped, "I know it's their job but some of them have the subtlety of a hangman. They don't want information, they want blood. They're not out to get answers, they're out to embarrass me. They're not after news, they're after my Administration."

Patiently, wisely and tactfully, Sabath managed to instruct Haines in the mores and morals of the press. Principally, he got it across that a presidential news conference was a Chief Executive's best media for getting his policies and decisions explained to the country and, in turn, getting a feeling of grass-roots opinions from the press.

"Most of the questions they ask," he had reminded Haines, "are the same ones the average citizen wants answered. The men and women attending your press conferences represent nothing but a cross section of America—rural, urban, farm, labor, rich, poor and middle class."

The respect the reporters had toward Haines slowly turned into outright affection on the part of many. The President was considerate, for one thing. Sabath did not have to urge him more than a single time to be reasonable about "the lid"—that moment when the regulars in the White House press room were told that nothing more was expectable that day and they could go home. Some Presidents had been known to use the lid as a means of revenge, keeping reporters around late deliberately even though there was little chance of a news break. Sabath, with Haines's co-operation, tried whenever possible to announce, "The lid's on, boys," no later than 6 P.M.

And where other Chief Executives seemed to take perverted delight in giving insufficient advance warning of travel plans (such as disclosing a departure from Andrews Air Force Base only fifteen minutes before the helicopters left the White House for Andrews), Haines made a practice of even delaying a desired departure time because he knew the press needed time to make its own travel arrangements. He also tried to be punctual, after he saw a group of reporters shivering in the cold at the Andrews ramp area on one occasion because he was almost an hour late.

He could become impatient with the press when, after all these little but important acts of thoughtfulness, the boys inserted needles into his desire for some semblance of privacy. His widower status left him open prey to gossip and rumors. Jeremy Haines was a healthy, virile man who enjoyed female companionship. Rather naïvely, he assumed at first that if the President of the United States wanted to escort a lady to some function it was his prerogative to do so with no public or press outcry.

He once asked the attractive widow of a former senator to attend a Washington Redskins football game. It was almost impossible to see the game itself because of the swarm of photographers hovering around like hungry bees. Haines finally ordered the Secret Service to chase them away. His temper was not improved when the next day's papers were filled with speculation on a presidential "romance."

"I gather," he told Sabath curtly, "that a President isn't allowed to be seen with a woman without those vultures hanging around."

"No, sir," Sabath said with regretful firmness.

"What am I supposed to do for a normal social life?"

"I guess," Sabath admitted, "that a President either puts up with gossip and publicity or he sort of takes the veil."

In time Jeremy Haines achieved a reasonable tolerance toward the inbred inquisitiveness of the press. But the unpleasantness of the football date forced him to retreat more and more into a shell of solitude and almost total devotion to work. Sabath and several Cabinet members suggested that he install some spinster relative in the White House as an official hostess. He adamantly refused, telling them half jokingly that he needed a wife, not a hostess.

So in what still can be a lonely job even for a President with family, Haines used his official duties as sublimation for normal personal pleasures. He substituted memories of the past for the companionship he so badly needed in the present. The inevitable result was a President with an air of aloof yet rather wistful kindness toward the entire White House personnel, numbering more than five hundred persons, all of whom worshiped Jeremy Haines and not a few of whom occasionally felt sorry for him.

He was a strong person, or he would have felt sorry for himself on too many occasions. Fortunately some of the vexations of office helped him to retain his sense of perspective. As had more than thirty of his predecessors, he found that getting mad at Congress easily could occupy enough time to take a President's mind off most personal troubles. He was a forceful Chief Executive, and this automatically put him in frequent conflict with the provincially jealous legislative branch. One of his most difficult adjustments to the presidency was the necessity of getting along with Congress: accustoming himself to its molasses pace, its tendency toward brutally partisan criticism of the executive branch, its self-righteous sensitivity toward any

12

censuring of itself, and mostly its impractical protection of archaic methods and means that preserved obsolescence under the name of tradition.

He liked and admired certain individual congressmen, recognizing them as hard-working and able public servants. But for Congress as an institution he could muster only disdain and disrespect that he kept shoving under the rug of his conscience because he knew legislative support was to a President's program what blood is to a heart.

Capitol Hill, however, with all its foibles, was not the biggest cross on Jeremy Haines's back. Almost from the day he took office the international situation had deteriorated steadily into global sword rattling. He had been elected on a platform largely pledging numerous domestic programs that had suffered mass pigeonholing throughout the Vietnam war. When that conflict ended, in an uneasy, indefinite, Korean-type armistice, Haines assumed he could concentrate on domestic problems. Instead he had to face the growing menace of Red China, emerging more belligerent than ever after a period of internal conflict.

Only three weeks before, he had met with the National Security Council for a briefing on the Dragon's designs. For China had successfully tested an ICBM with a hydrogen bomb warhead and was boasting that the incredibly destructive weapon was now in a stockpile status.

Jeremy Haines had listened with chilling concentration to the Council's report, read verbally by the Secretary of Defense. He and the Secretary of State were the only Cabinet members represented on the Council.

"Possession of the hydrogen bomb by the Red Chinese and the means of delivering it via intercontinental ballistic missile, Mr. President, poses a genuine and serious threat to the United States. The Central Intelligence Agency concurs with this body that a surprise and sneak attack by China on the U.S. is not only within the realm of possibility but even, eventually, probability, and there is no known diplomatic deterrent that seems likely to succeed.

"The CIA also concurs that the Soviet Union in all likelihood would remain neutral in the event of a Sino-U.S. conflict. Neither CIA nor NSC is impressed with the deteriorated state of Soviet-Sino relations with regard to Russia itself being a deterrent to Chinese aggression. Rather, the Soviet Union undoubtedly would prefer to remain

13

aloof during such a conflict, with the obvious goal of letting its greatest rival in the Communist world and its greatest rival in the free world tear each other to pieces. This would enable the Soviet Union to emerge unscathed as the dominant nation in a world decimated by atomic war.

"Following, Mr. President, is the Department of Defense's latest estimates of Red China's missile strength and a revised list of probable priority targets on the Chinese mainland. . . ."

Jeremy Haines could still hear the Defense Secretary's voice droning through the Cabinet Room, dry and yet deadly with its awful implications of the nearness of war. Atomic war. With its horrifying mental image of searing white heat bringing death to millions in the time it would take to scratch one's nose. He thought, impulsively, of his dead son and remembered that when the Vietnam war came to a shaky end he had felt that the blood of Jerry Haines, Jr., had perhaps helped win a respite in the march toward World War III.

A short respite, the President told himself bitterly. The equivalent of a ten-minute break on a hike over an endless treadmill.

His gloomy thoughts were interrupted by a knock on his door and the subsequent entrance of Rear Admiral Luther Philips, the tall but heavy-set White House physician. Philips talked to him casually every day without any formal medical examination, although Haines was aware he was being observed through the critical eyes of a capable doctor looking for the slightest suspicion of an ailment.

"Good morning, Mr. President. Thought I'd stop in for a chat. Any complaints?"

"Not healthwise," the President said. "I can't say the same for my mental state."

"I'm glad I don't have your problems," Philips remarked sympathetically. "You seem a bit tired. Sleeping well?"

"Reasonably well, Luther. Those sedatives have helped. How about yourself? All set for the trip?"

"As ready as I ever am for travel. I leave the packing to my wife and she invariably forgets a few items of importance. Like this time, I'll probably arrive in California minus bathing trunks."

Haines laughed but without real mirth, and Philips worried momentarily whether he had touched presidential

14

sensitivity by mentioning his own wife's packing chores. He was only too well aware of the President's loneliness and that even his innocent remark could have produced pain.

"Well," he said with assumed jocularity that hid his embarrassment, "I imagine you have a pretty full schedule today so I'll be on my way. Surgery at Bethesda Medical in about an hour. Melanoma case. Insidious type of malignancy, melanoma. You're lucky you've got the complexion of a baby. Not a mole on you. One of those little bastards can go bad on you and if it gets under the skin you've got big troubles. . . ."

Philips halted his medical discourse, remorsefully recalling too late that the President's wife had died of cancer. Two unnecessary reminders of the past in the course of a brief conversation. Great. Just great. He flirted briefly with the idea of apologizing, then decided on diversionary tactics instead. "Mr. President, before I go let's take your blood pressure. Don't believe I've checked it for a couple of weeks."

"If it's up," Haines said with a trace of dry humor, "blame it on the Senate Appropriations Committee. What those gentlemen did to the Airport Aid bill yesterday was castration, not economy." He dutifully removed his coat and rolled up both sleeves, surreptitiously eying the doctor's face to see if it would display any expression of medical solicitude.

Philips completed the examination with professional dispatch and smiled his approval. "Perfectly normal. I'll wager you're in better shape than I. Remarkable that a man with all your burdens can keep his pressure down."

"High boiling point," Haines explained. "Luther, tell me something. Are you one of those physicians who believe in letting a patient know exactly where he stands?"

The doctor's eyebrows furrowed into a near frown. "Such as telling him he had a fatal disease? Something like that? Mr. President, I—"

circumstances. Most of all, on the patient. You have to judge how he'll take it. I've had those who insisted they be told the truth and then came apart at the seams. Dammit, now you've got me curious. What prompted you to ask me? You know something I should know?"

Haines shook his head. "No. As I said, I wasn't asking in the medical sense. I was trying to draw something of an analogy, I suppose."

"The patient is the nation," Philips deduced sagely. "And I take it you're wondering how much you can tell your patient without causing panic. Such as how close we are to war."

The President nodded.

"I'm just a doctor and I don't presume to go around giving a President advice on anything but how to stay healthy. Do what you think is best."

"That," Haines observed wryly, "belongs in the same innocuous category as medicine's recipe for a cold. Take aspirin, drink fluids and get plenty of rest. I guess I'm searching for a miracle drug and you hand me an aspirin plus a few platitudes."

"The simple remedy is often the best," Philips said. "Speaking of getting some rest, a vacation trip is the finest medicine in the world."

"Palm Springs, for example."

"Palm Springs is an excellent example. Provided you could leave some of your problems behind. Which you can't."

"Which, unfortunately, I can't. By design or accident. Like the bathing suit your wife will forget to pack. I wish life were that simple."

"I wish, for your sake, the presidency were that simple," Philips said. "Well, time to favor the Naval Medical Center with my august presence. I'll . . . I'll see you around, Mr. President."

"Very soon, I trust," said Jeremy Haines. "Thanks for stopping in, Luther. I enjoy your visits. Make sure you're back here no later than nine-thirty this evening. As my airline friends would say, I prefer on-time departures."

"You're asking a lot if you want a physician to be on time for anything," Philips observed. "However, make it a presidential order and I'll obey."

"In my capacity as Commander-in-Chief, I'll make it an

16

order. And in your capacity as a rear admiral, I expect you to follow orders."

"Ay, ay, sir," Philips acknowledged with mock graveness. He was about as nautical as a Kansas farmer. He waved and left, pleased to hear the President's laughing farewell, and he marveled anew that Haines could muster a laugh in these harried times. What a magnificent man he was. No wonder he was beloved, not only by his associates but by most Americans no matter what their party affiliation.

There was something about Jeremy Haines, the doctor was thinking, that instilled in others a confidence akin to the warm, unquestioning security of the father image. He seemed a kind of political patriarch who might have been Ben Cartwright translocated from the Ponderosa to the White House. Haines had been elected by a considerable margin after a campaign in which he succeeded in establishing what each presidential candidate must sear in the minds of the voters—an easy-to-grasp image. A personality that automatically produces a reflex of trusting acceptance, whether it be confidence, affection, respect or a merger of such qualities. In the case of Jeremy Haines, the political pundits decided he won the presidential election because he had created an image of a man who combined Eisenhower's aura of patriotism above politics and Kennedy's gift of inspiring eloquence. And in the presidency, Haines also achieved those essential qualities of persuasion and leadership. He persuaded because he was a leader, and he led because he could persuade. A man of wise, firm kindness rather than saccharine sympathies.

He remembered the first time he had met Haines, one week before the new President's inauguration.

They had quickly established ground rules. Philips would see the President once or twice daily and meanwhile could continue his surgical duties at Bathesda Naval Medical Center. The President would have a routine physical examination every month and a more thorough checkup twice a year.

"Are you the kind of patient who follows a doctor's advice?" Philips had asked.

"I'm a sensible man," Haines had replied. "That's the closest I'll come to making you a flat promise."

"Fair enough."

"But there's one department in which I might find it

17

difficult to accept your advice, Doctor," Haines said with a poker face as the meeting ended.

"What's that?" Philips wanted to know.

The President-elect eyed the doctor's rotund figure. "Weight reduction," he murmured.

Since that first introduction, Philips' favorable impression of Jeremy Haines had grown into a quiet, solid friendship. It would have pleased the doctor to know that at this moment the President also was thinking of him with affection. Philips was one of a handful of people whom Haines trusted implicitly. If there was one negative quality the presidency had embossed on Jeremy Haines's personality, it was cynicism. Mostly cynicism toward motives. He was never quite sure what might lie behind a proposal, a suggestion, a request or an objection.

He found himself examining others as he would look at an iceberg, knowing that only one third appeared above the surface. Politics was the usual motivation and he could never quite bring himself to regard politics with anything but cynicism. Carefully controlled cynicism, naturally. He could not have become President if he had not been skilled in the art of politics, which in its purest sense is merely the art of compromise. He knew he could not be an effective President without practicing that art, yet he was never truly happy in the exercise. He relished with enormous, grateful pride his role as a nation's leader, but he resented his necessary second role as a party's leader. He had to be two men and he did not have much respect for one of them—the one who had to deal with fawning, wheedling, grasping politicians. Who had to wink at their hypocrisy, ignore their power-oriented ethics, and tolerate the narrow-mindedness of their purposes.

He accepted the inevitability of this double existence, this dual-personality, Jekyll-Hyde facet of the presidency, as had so many others before him. But he occasionally chafed under its overly frequent collisions with his own simple code of ethics—black vs. white, good vs. evil.

That was the trouble with more than just the presidency, Haines mused. There were few simple, this-is-right and this-is-wrong answers. Even war. War was stupid and wasteful. But war sometimes had to be fought, and avoiding it by any means could be as destructive as fighting it. And how many Presidents had been faced with that dilemma?

Every one of his five immediate predecessors, Haines ruminated, had served at least partially through some kind of armed conflict in which American blood was shed. A sad commentary for a nation and a world which thought it had found peace when the guns of two world wars were stilled.

Now there were hands on the triggers again, or perhaps buttons this time. Jeremy Haines sighed in mental weariness and left the room to walk to his office in the West Wing. He passed the valet, who asked if it would be all right to finish the packing.

"Sooner the better, John. There's a list on the top of that big bureau in the bedroom. Just follow that."

"Yes, Mr. President." The valet entered the President's private quarters and began to remove the breakfast dishes. He interrupted this task long enough to glance at the headlines of the papers the President had left behind. He shook his head at the alarming words on the front page of the *Post* and turned the paper over to read what was below the fold. One headline caught his eye.

PRESIDENT FLIES TO CALIFORNIA TONIGHT
Haines Leaves for Indefinite
Vacation at Palm Springs

"Man," the valet said out loud. "I'd sure like to be going with him."

CHAPTER TWO

Gunther Damon awoke that Monday morning with the vaguely unpleasant recall to reality that always seems to follow a Sunday.

The feeling of disappointment lasted only as long as it took to shake the fog of sleep from his mind. For Gunther Damon loved his job at the Washington Bureau of International Press Service. He was the bureau's news superintendent, a title he had acquired a year ago in lieu of a promised raise.

He hauled his slim yet muscular frame out of bed and viewed with renewed satisfaction his new, tastefully furnished efficiency apartment in the Bethesda high-rise. It had the absolutely essential components of a confirmed bachelor's quarters, such as an excellent hi-fi and a well-stocked liquor cabinet, along with an enormous collection of books, most of which he actually had read.

It was typical of him that his first thoughts were of the office and what problems might have to be solved in the next seven or eight hours. No one could predict news with complete accuracy, but a good wire service executive seemed to develop an instinct for anticipating the unexpected. And Gunther Damon was good, whether the need was for careful advance planning or for spur-of-the-moment improvisation. He kept the latter down to a minimum because he was so adept at the former and this made him invaluable to IPS, the smallest of the three wire services and the one with the sparsest manpower resources.

Some men think best while sitting on commodes. Damon's fondest moment of meditation was during the shaving process. Between the first insertion of a fresh blade and the final splashing of after-shave lotion, he could map the day's campaign for his troops—ten copy editors, thirty-eight reporters, six dictationists, three office boys, nineteen teletype operators, three teletype mechanics and the five "special writers" Gunther kept referring to as "our prima donna division."

It was one of those specialists who occupied Damon's early musings as he scraped the stubble off his face. The IPS aviation editor, Rod Pitcher, normally covered all presidential arrivals and departures at Andrews Air Force Base. Any forty-dollar-a-week copy boy could have phoned in a landing or take-off time. Tonight's, for example, would be transmitted on IPS wires mostly so the Los Angeles bureau would know when to staff the Palm Springs arrival. But Pitcher knew airplanes and Damon liked to assign him to Andrews on the one-in-ten-million chance that something would happen to Air Force One on take-off or landing.

Up until two months ago Pitcher had been the ideal wire service reporter, namely a man who never beefed at extra night work. The metamorphosis had occurred with his marriage to an American Airlines stewardess, transforming Mr. Pitcher into a typical newlywed who blackly resented anything that took him away from his bride after 6 P.M., and causing confirmed bachelor Damon to observe sourly —and with only partial accuracy—that "marriage has ruined more goddamned good reporters than the Press Club bar."

And, Damon knew, Pitcher would object loudly to covering *this* presidential departure—at the unusual and ungodly hour of 10 P.M. The aviation writer, like the science, religion, political and general feature specialists, was ineligible for overtime. It was either Pitcher or about ten dollars in overtime pay drained from the Washington Bureau's tight budget. The alternative was to send someone from the undermanned night desk.

Pitcher it would be, Damon decided. He'd give Rod a Friday off sometime as repayment. Let the lovesick bastard gripe and bitch for a change. Pitcher was somewhat spoiled, anyway. He got more free junkets than anyone else in the office and it was widely rumored that at Christmastime Pitcher asked the airlines to send his annual presents to his home so the rest of the IPS staff wouldn't see *all* the embarrassing loot.

Having reached this eminently satisfactory decision—a subconscious reprisal against Pitcher's recent tendency to

21

goof off—Damon suddenly started wondering exactly why the President chose a late night departure. Press Secretary Phil Sabath had explained at yesterday's regular 4 P.M. briefing that the President had many things to do before leaving on a badly needed vacation.

"Like what?" IPS senior White House correspondent Malcolm Jones had asked impertinently.

"Quite a bit of last-minute paperwork and study of various reports," Sabath had answered. "Stuff he doesn't want to take with him to Palm Springs. As I've explained to you guys before, he's going for a rest—repeat, rest. God knows, he needs one."

Made sense, Damon was thinking. Except there was something that bothered him about that take-off time. It would get Air Force One into Palm Springs around midnight West Coast time or even later. That would make it a rather tiring trip for a man so obviously worn by the demands of the presidency that his fatigue sometimes showed perceptibly in photographs. Which in turn poured additional nourishing water on Gunther Damon's inbred seeds of suspicion. It was not like Haines to take a vacation in the middle of worsening international affairs. True, every President carried both office and duties in his pocket, no matter where he was. Maybe the trip was designed to ease general concern over Red China, Damon speculated. A sort of "things aren't so bad that I can't take some time off" soothing sedative for public, press and stock market.

Damon shared with the majority of his colleagues their large quota of esteem for the man who was President of the United States, and it was a quota in inverse proportion to the lack of esteem they possessed for the man who was Vice President of the United States. This largely explained Damon's hazy, undefined concern about the Palm Springs flight. Not the trip itself, but the expressed reason for it— fatigue and the need for a rest.

In the eyes of a distrustful newspaperman, official explanations too often turned out to be camouflage. Damon had only to think back to the persistent denials that FDR was ailing, or the famous Eisenhower stomach upset that wound up as a major heart attack. If he wanted to go back further in history, there was the incredible cover-up of Wilson's incapacitating stroke.

Because he desperately wanted to believe that the President merely was tired and really needed a vacation, he put his misgivings aside temporarily, a bank deposit of incredibility to be drawn on later if circumstances warranted. After all, he reasoned, Haines hadn't looked like a sick man when Damon saw him up close two weeks before, at a White House reception for the Washington press corps. A little tired, perhaps, but that was to be expected. Maybe the vacation story was legitimate after all.

This chain of more optimistic deduction took Damon through the concluding application of English Leather on a face remarkably unlined and youthful, belying his forty-five years of age. He had always looked younger than his years. At twenty, as a cub reporter, he had grown a mustache to add a semblance of maturity. The mustache departed the scene five years later but Damon had since managed to offset his baby-faced appearance with rule-riveted discipline governing a traditionally unruly wire service office. When Gunther Damon chewed out an errant staffer, his five feet eight seemed to swell to six feet. He was simultaneously fair and tough. He was a good editor because he had curiosity, imagination and integrity, virtues which he had managed to implant in most of his staff. Typical of most good wire service executives, he was not a particularly smooth or accomplished writer himself. But he could tell good writing, would encourage good writing and above all he had the ability to prune, revise or organize ordinary copy into stories that were simple without being condescending, dramatic without straining for effect, hard-hitting with no tinge of biased editorializing.

Like so many experienced Washington correspondents, he had acquired a professional personality that emerged as an incongruous mixture of cynicism and idealism, suspicion and enthusiasm. He was an instinctive crusader blessed with an equally instinctive sense of objectivity. He was, in brief, an excellent example of that journalistic breed known as the wire service editor, a man of unappreciated and underpaid competence. If wire services were the infantry of the newspaper world, men like Gunther Damon were their top sergeants—crafty veterans who knew how to cajole, wheedle, soft-soap, inspire and occasionally frighten men of lesser ability into performances beyond their supposed capability.

23

His own by-line rarely appeared on an IPS wire. He was a director who could strain a superb performance out of a lackadaisical actor, yet not be able to deliver a line of his own. A maestro who might mangle his own playing but still could weld a collection of average musicians into a majestic orchestra. A teacher capable of infusing others with genius without being close to genius himself. He could teach a man how to write a taut story without the fat of padded, adjective-laden verbiage. To use words that painted pictures and gave off real odors. To transmit excitement without screaming or shouting.

He was modest and therefore touched with a modicum of insecurity which he kept hidden under a cloak of brusque authority and staccato decisions. His top writers never knew that he sometimes envied them; they were too busy complaining about the occasional surgery he performed on their precious copy. He could have been an excellent writer on his own, but he had lived too long on a diet of what other people wrote. If he had ever tried a novel, the characters would have been no deeper than sweat on skin. Speed, brevity, clarity were the cornerstones of a good wire service report. It was a one-dimensional, superficial kind of topical literature because it had to be. Because it could not be slowed down any more than the world and its events could be slowed down.

If he occasionally succumbed to envy of others, it was a fleeting emotion with no vestige of self-pity. He liked being a newspaperman too much to indulge in that weakness. From boyhood, his heroes and his idols had not been athletes or soldiers or statesmen. The names he had worshiped were Zenger, Greeley, Pulitzer and Bennett. His bibles were the great newspapers and wire services. He still possessed the book his father had given him a long, long time ago, a history of journalism on whose flyleaf his parent had inscribed:

"To Gunther on the occasion of his 14th birthday, from one who can merely quote the words of Henry Ward Beecher—'that endless book, the newspaper, is our national glory.'"

He had stayed a bachelor, rationalizing that marriage would have made him a schizophrenic, with divided and incompatible loyalties. He knew he would use IPS as a crutch for every tension, every difficulty, every misunderstanding that normally occurs in a marriage. And he knew he could not keep Gunther Damon, the husband, separate from Gunther Damon, the IPS boss. Other newspapermen had happy marriages, he conceded, but they lacked his all-consuming dedication to his job. International Press Service was his wife, his mistress. He funneled all his sense of responsibility through the single channel that was the wire service. And while he was frequently lonely and dissatisfied, he made enough feminine conquests to delude himself that sex was better if it were varied.

Gunther Damon dressed, his last act being the affixing of the jaunty bow tie he invariably wore to work. He drove out of the high-rise complex onto the curving Washington Beltway, that sixty-six-mile sash around the capital area, across the Cabin John Bridge into Virginia and then down the George Washington Memorial Parkway. It was a pleasant, tree-lined trip seven miles longer than the most direct route between Bethesda and downtown Washington. Damon preferred it because it was easier with no traffic lights most of the way and far less traffic after 9 A.M., and because it gave his active mind an additional opportunity for advance inspection of the day's forthcoming problems.

He was wheeling peacefully along at the legal fifty-mile limit, all windows down on this hot early September day, when another sliver of suspicion pricked his thinking process. Malcolm Jones had told him Air Force One would not be carrying the usual press contingent—one man each from IPS, UPI, and AP, plus network pool reporters.

"We'll have to go on the press charter," Jones had informed him. "I don't know exactly why—Haines usually likes to have a few regular reporters around on a long flight. But Sabath says no soap this time."

This announcement hadn't bothered Damon at the time. Now it suddenly invaded his thoughts like the first sign of an unwanted cold. It nagged him, bothered him, disturbed him. He hoped again that the President was not ill.

The Vice President of the United States awoke, that Monday morning, acutely aware that his speech last night before the General Federation of Tax Accountants had laid an egg capable of hatching a dinosaur.

Vice President Frederick James Madigan's mediocrity ex

tended even to his physical appearance. It was not that he had unpleasant features or obvious physical faults. He simply looked so nondescript and average that the newspaper cartoonists complained he was impossible to caricature.

His nose was slightly large but not in the Roman category. His jaw didn't resemble something hewed out of granite, but it wasn't weak either. He had a pleasant smile but it wouldn't dazzle anybody. At the age of forty-nine he had the suggestion of a potbelly but he was by no means fat. He was five feet nine, which speaks for itself. His eyebrows were his only distinguishing facial feature—they slanted southward, like an oriental's turned upside down. Yet the reverse slant was not pronounced enough to give him that sympathy-attracting look of perpetual melancholy, the appearance of a martyr always on the verge of justifiable tears. In brief, his face had all the warmth, personality and individualism of an amoeba.

He also was a man cursed by a sensitiveness that recognized his mediocrity. This added up to a sense of gnawing frustration, because Fred Madigan wanted desperately to be liked and, more important, respected. He was more tolerated than liked, and he was seldom respected.

Take last night's speech. It was typical Madigan oratory, saturated with platitudes and empty pomposity. Which, as a matter of fact, described the Vice President. A columnist had once compared Madigan's mind to "a vast desert, occasionally invaded by a covered-wagon cliché."

The speech had been written by Madigan's administrative assistant, who called the VP "chief" and kept his job mainly because he was one of the few people in Washington who could make Madigan feel important. Like the VP, he was well-meaning but armed with a vaporous intellect. He had turned over the speech to Madigan with enthusiastic confidence born of ignorance.

"It's a nut-twister, Chief," he had announced. "Hard-hitting and a great joke to open up with."

Because Madigan himself could not recognize a well-written speech if it walked up and bit him, he shared his AA's opinion. Until the delivery itself. The great opening joke lay down and died, recipient of what is dreaded most by comedians and politicians alike—a few chuckles generated solely by politeness. Ditto the speech. The applause was perfunctory to the point of being insulting. Naturally the toastmaster was generous with his praise—"a fine speech, Mr. Vice President"—and a number of delegates (not many, but a few) had approached Madigan to offer congratulations.

"Excellent talk, Mr. Vice President."

"Thank you very much."

They reminded Madigan of small boys approaching the crestfallen players of a losing pro football team to ask for autographs regardless of their ignominious fall from hero status. Fawning people, themselves inconsequential, who would go home and brag, "I met the Vice President." He knew it was his office, not himself or what he had said, that generated even a modicum of worshipful attention. Now that it was over, he realized he had—as usual—talked too long and had said nothing. That he could realize it was one of his few virtues. That he never could do anything about it was one of his numerous faults.

Now he lay in bed, trying to dredge a few pebbles of satisfaction from last night's failure. After all, it was a rather uninspiring audience. What the hell could you say to a bunch of tax accountants that could raise blood pressure and prompt wild cheering? He had praised their profession as "vitally important to the well-being of the American people," which was more than the dull bastards deserved. And he had come out solidly, unequivocally and foursquare for honest tax law enforcement.

The Vice President sighed loudly enough to wake his wife, curled like a relaxed kitten in the twin bed four feet away. Only Hester Madigan was more of a cat than a kitten. A voluptuous, slithering, stalking, black-haired woman three inches taller than Madigan, she had the knack of catering to his starved ego. In private she called him "lover" and she was one of those females who could simulate wild, runaway passion so skillfully that her husband fancied himself a sexual swordsman. Actually he was no better in bed than he was on a speaker's platform but Hester Madigan was an ambitious woman who had married him principally because, as a then congressman, he knew so many important people. At times she wondered if she had made a mistake but when Madigan won the vice presidential nomination—more or less by accident, as a compromise candidate who offended nobody—she knew

27

she would stick by him. After all, Hester Madigan told herself, there wasn't anything but the health of Jeremy Haines separating her from the status of First Lady.

"Good morning, Freddie lover," she cooed.

"Good morning, dear. Sorry I woke you."

"It's time I was getting up anyway. Come over here and cuddle for a little while."

Madigan dutifully climbed into the conjugal bed and cuddled as ordered. Normally, it would have taken practically nothing to seduce him. But he still was upset over that damned speech. Then he happened to consult his wristwatch, which he wore to bed as habitually as he wore pajamas.

"Jesus, Hester, it's eight forty-five. There's a Cabinet meeting at ten."

"How long is he going to be in California, Fred?"

"Damned if I know. A couple of weeks, I suppose. He never takes me into his confidence."

The last was said with open bitterness and Hester Madigan knew why. Haines treated her husband with deference and even a certain amount of affection. But it was almost amused, tolerant deference and affection. The kind a brilliant, sophisticated man would bestow on a rather backward younger brother. Haines liked Fred Madigan, but he knew him for exactly what he was. He had been a machine-elected congressman originally, a hack politician with all the intellectual depth of a shyster used-car salesman. The trouble was that Madigan knew exactly how the President felt toward him.

It was not from the instinct of a man with a vast inferiority complex, but from what the newly nominated Haines had said to his face the night the party leaders decided to break a strangling, bitter deadlock over the ticket's second spot. Madigan had been summoned to Haines's room after the fourteenth roll call left the two vice-presidential favorites virtually tied, each unwilling to throw in the towel, and with Haines reluctant to exercise the presidential candidate's prerogative of choosing his running mate.

The party's national chairman greeted Madigan bluntly.

"Fred, those two bastards won't give in. We've been talking it over and we figure you'd make a good compromise choice. They're both willing to accept you just so the other guy won't get it. Would you take the nomination?"

Madigan, his heart pounding, tried valiantly but failed completely to look modest. "If the party wants me, I'll take it. Provided I'm acceptable to Jeremy."

Haines, who perhaps had been drinking a bit beyond his normal intake under the now ended strain of his own nominating battle, stared at the little politician with a look that came close to being sardonic. "I'll be honest with you, Fred. You aren't my choice by a long shot. If anything should happen to me, I wonder if you'd be up to the presidency. But you've been loyal to the party, you're a hard worker and we could do worse. I just want you to know where I stand. So now will you take it?"

Ambition wrestled with a flash of anger at Haines's bluntness. Hurt pride collided with political avarice. "Jeremy, I appreciate your frankness. You have what I've always given the party—total loyalty. If you still want me, I accept."

The men in the room applauded. Haines's stern face relaxed into an ingratiating grin. When Jeremy Haines smiled it gave the effect of Mr. Hyde transforming back into Dr. Jekyll and it even achieved the miracle of melting Madigan's inner resentment. The presidential candidate got to his feet and offered Madigan his hand in a gesture of natural, easy graciousness.

But those few moments had been the last when Madigan felt gratitude and friendship toward Haines. When he got over the excitement of sharing a ticket that had an excellent chance of winning, and a possible future beyond his rosiest dreams, he remembered Jeremy's sharp judgment of him.

"If anything should happen to me, I wonder if you'd be up to the presidency. . . ."

That was three years ago. He remembered those words every time he saw Jeremy Haines. They eclipsed Haines's friendliness, his efforts to treat the Vice President with dignity—especially before others. He remembered them at Cabinet meetings, when the President would ask his views on policy matters and issues with respect that seemed genuine.

His wife was snuggling closer, following her subtly clever pattern (never comprehended by Madigan) of sending him off to something important like a Cabinet meeting with his libido satisfied in such a way as to inflate his ego. She murmured, "Just a few minutes more, lover . . ."

But he still remembered Haines's indicting, cutting words even as he held his wife in his arms. Always within his consciousness were his self-confessed inadequacies, his ineptness, his shallowness. Yet he could not prevent what now came leaping into his mind.

He wished the goddamned plane would crash.

Colonel Marcus Henderson, commander of Air Force One, awoke that morning and did what most airmen do on the day of a flight. He looked outside to see what the weather was like.

The pungent, pleasant, tantalizing odor of freshly brewed coffee came from the kitchen where his wife, just beginning to swell with her fourth pregnancy, already was busy. He shaved, showered, put on slacks and a sport shirt, and sat down at the breakfast table. He was one of those homely men whose verile masculinity masked such features as a big nose and jug-handle ears.

"Morning, honey. Kids gone to school?"

"Yes, thank God. I'm glad I let you sleep. They were positively obnoxious this morning. I swear your youngest son should be drafted."

"At seven?"

"Wait till I tell you what he did. He . . ."

She rambled on about their youngest son's latest transgressions, but Henderson hardly listened. As usual, before a presidential trip, his mind was crammed with what had to be done before take-off. Flight planning. Inspection. Crew briefing. And then there was that call from Sabath last night.

"Marcus? Phil Sabath. Thought I'd tell you the President will be sort of *hors de combat* tomorrow night. He wants to stay in his compartment the whole trip and get some rest. Just by himself. Tell the crew that applies to everybody—including the stewards."

"Hope there's nothing wrong, Phil."

"Nothing wrong. He just wants complete privacy. There won't be any reporters aboard this time, either. They're all taking the press charter."

Not like Haines, Henderson thought after the press secretary had hung up. The President was a friendly man who often liked to wander around the cavernous hulk of Air Force One. He particularly enjoyed sitting in the cockpit jump seat, puffing a pipe and watching the crew work. He would do that for about half an hour and then saunter back to the forward passenger compartment where the bulk of the passengers parked on a presidential flight. Secretaries. The regulars from the White House press corps. Maybe a few congressmen trying to act blasé at the honor of being aboard Air Force One.

Haines would stop and chat with every one of them, but longer with the reporters. Not in any public relations sense, but as Kennedy and Johnson had done before him, to draw from their sharp, inquisitive brains what few underlings would tell a President of the United States. Haines, Henderson knew, had enormous faith in their basic honesty. The President admired them all as intelligent, capable men even when he disliked what they wrote or asked at news conferences. It had been an awful shock the first time he inquired of Malcolm Jones what the IPS man had thought of a certain policy speech.

Jones half smiled, a curious mixture of wryness and sadness.

"Frankly, Mr. President, it was bullshit."

Haines's jaw dropped, but then the President burst out laughing.

Like his predecessors, Haines quickly learned to differentiate between the newsmen's professional performances and their personal beliefs, which occasionally involved a chasm wider than the Pacific Ocean. This was why he liked to talk to them on long flights, when they were off duty and discarded their roles as gadflies, hatchet men, hair shirts and lofty representatives of both the free press and the public conscience.

They, in turn, were not a little awed and pleased when a President asked their views, opinions and even, on occasion, their advice. Sometimes, they discovered later, he even took the advice.

Henderson a few times had listened to the presidential-press banter aboard Air Force One with something akin to awe. The Air Force was the most informal of the services, but he still could not get used to banter that often challenged presidential dignity. He would no more talk to a

President the way Jones and others did than he would have told Curtis LeMay to go screw a turbine.

He would miss the irreverent press himself on this trip, but Sabath had given him a logical explanation. He still wondered if the President was ailing. He hoped not. The thought of calling Frederick Madigan "Mr. President" was appalling even to a political eunuch like Colonel Marcus Henderson.

Senator Bertrand Haines, brother of the President, awoke that morning and went immediately to use the downstairs phone so he would not disturb his still sleeping wife.

He cradled the receiver on his shoulder, dialed 456-1414, and between the clicks and the first buzz managed to light a hasty cigarette.

"White House."

"The President, please. This is Senator Haines."

"Good morning, Senator. One moment."

The interoffice dialing system rang the President's bedroom phone twice before Jeremy Haines's deep, beautifully modulated voice answered.

"This is the President."

"Morning, President, sir. This is your older brother. How the hell are you?"

Jeremy chuckled. Bert followed the rigid protocol of addressing the Chief Executive only in public. In private he went to the other extreme, burlesquing that protocol "just to keep you from getting too damned pompous."

Actually, they were more like casual friends than brothers. They did not have the close family, political and intellectual relationship enjoyed by the Kennedys. They were of the same party, but this mutual association might as well have been membership in the same country club. Bert was impulsive, loudly garrulous, earthy where Jeremy was cautious, soft-spoken, innately dignified. Bert was liberal out of fashionable convenience instead of conviction. Liberalism to Jeremy was a religion with toughly elastic rules that could be stretched slightly for occasional, absolutely necessary expedience, but never near the breaking point. Bert regarded compromise as a logical alibi for surrendering a principle. Jeremy erected a steel wall between compromise and principle; he might be forced to move the wall back a few inches, but it was always there.

32

Physically, there was only a superficial resemblance in build. Jeremy was three inches taller and two years younger although this chronological difference was deceiving. Bert looked at least ten years older, thanks mostly to his snow-crusted cranium.

"Bert, I'd appreciate your stopping in here before the chopper leaves for Andrews."

"No problem. You all set?"

"John's packing now. Cabinet meeting at ten, and my appointments list has more people than a Russian novel. But I'd still like to say good-by to my brother."

"Fair enough," the senator observed. "But remember, I've got a reservation on that nine o'clock flight to Boston."

"It won't take long. Just a few things I want to talk over with you. How did your fishing trip sit with the wife?"

"She's resigned to my disappearing into the wilds of Maine every year about this time. But you know Ruth— she's a good sport. She knows I need a vacation as badly as you do. By the way, any idea yet how long this Palm Springs trip will last?"

"Probably not more than a week, Bert, but I'm not sure yet. I'll let you know the return time."

"Okay, Jerry, see you tonight."

The click of the disconnect was a good ten seconds old before the President of the United States hung up his own phone. At that particular moment he felt very close to his brother. A deep, emotional closeness he had not felt since they had been children. Plus a vague, intangible sense of regret that it had taken this long.

Gunther Damon rode the elevator to his office on the seventh floor of the National Press Building. It stopped on 3 to disembark a couple of United Press International reporters, with whom Damon had exchanged nods in somewhat the same coldly formal manner as enemy soldiers swapping salutes during an armed truce.

It had always rankled Damon that the IPS quarters on the seventh floor had once been occupied by UPI, before the latter moved to more luxurious and larger space on 3. He liked the convenient location of the Press Building, but working in an office discarded so eagerly by an opposition wire service as cramped, obsolete and hopelessly inadequate was like wearing hand-me-down clothes bequeathed by a condescending relative.

He had argued loud and long with the IPS bureau manager, Stan DeVarian, against the move to the Press Building as something akin to degrading.

"The rent's reasonable, Gunther," DeVarian had said patiently. "Hell, I know it was too small for UPI but it's bigger than what we have now and it's the largest office available for the dough. Besides, when the building gets through renovating that seventh floor, you won't recognize it."

The renovation *was* impressive, Damon had to concede. The once dingy, dark corridors were brightly lit and modernistically paneled. The IPS office itself had indirect lighting, air conditioning, and DeVarian—much to the total surprise of the entire staff—had wheedled an extra four thousand dollars out of the penny-pinching New York headquarters for new desks and chairs.

Putting the ancient IPS typewriters on those desks was roughly like wrapping a burlap sash around a mink coat. The contrast, however, pretty well described IPS. Being the smallest of the wire services and definitely not well heeled, it was always half starved, in both physical equipment and manpower. A typewriter manufactured in 1946 squatting on a brand-new desk was poignantly symbolic. Or a reporter with a background largely of sports writing having to cover a suddenly summoned press conference on economic policy, because the man who normally would have gotten the assignment was staffing a Civil Aeronautics Board hearing. Which, in turn, should have been handled by the aviation editor, who had been sent, under duress, to a meeting on urban transportation problems.

Improvising, shuffling personnel, plugging one hole only to find news pouring out of another left unguarded—that was Gunther Damon's world. He sometimes marveled himself that his adaptable, versatile, generally uncomplaining staff could perform as efficiently as it did.

He entered his world at exactly ten o'clock, to be greeted by the rhythmic chatter of thirty-odd teletype printers pounding away, their keys marching across the yellow paper like tiny robots.

Les Butler, the day editor, a tall man with perpetually sleepy eyes and languid movements, looked up from his copyreading. "Hi, peerless leader. Get your coat off. We got troubles already."

Damon grunted unhappily and hung up his seersucker coat. "I need coffee before I solve problems," he said. "Have you flipped yet?"

"Nope. Waiting for our prime sucker."

Every morning Damon and the day desk matched coins for the honor of buying coffee. They flipped until all but one coin was heads or tails. The odd man lost, Damon being the odd man an average of five out of six times.

Today he was lucky. Sam Foley, a red-haired deskman of massive proportions and the gentle disposition that comes so naturally to many big men, finally pitched heads against four tails and reached resignedly into his pocket for a crumpled dollar bill.

"My wife tells me this morning the kid needs braces on his teeth," he said sorrowfully. "Now I lose my first flip in three weeks. I should have stayed in bed. Where's Custer?"

"Custer" was the early-trick copy boy, a full-blooded Sioux youth studying law at George Washington University at night. His full Christian name was John Badlon but Rod Pitcher had dubbed him "Custer" the first time he learned of his Indian background.

"He's in the can," Butler said. "Be out in a minute. Gunther, we got a call from the Chicago *Clarion* a little while ago. They're screaming because we missed covering that ICC hearing yesterday."

"What ICC hearing?"

"The one on the railroad merger. They said they expect full coverage today."

"Well, tell Barney McGrath to handle it. ICC's on his run."

"I did. Barney says he's tied up at Justice all day. They're expecting something to pop on the Crime Commission report any hour."

"Oh hell," sighed Damon. "Better call the Hill and see if they can spring a regional guy. What time's the hearing?"

"Starts at two."

"Okay, if the Crime Commission report comes out this morning, Barney can get over to ICC this afternoon. Tell the House staff to have someone stand by just in case."

"The House, peerless leader, will be most unhappy," Butler said.

35

"The House has lots of company," Damon murmured. "Anything else?"

"This message from Louisville."

Butler handed the news superintendent a strip of yellow teletype paper.

WA

CLIENT ASKS WHEN IS PROMISED THREE-PART SERIES ON OCEANIC EXPLORATION EXPECTABLE?

LV

"What'll I tell them?" Butler asked.

Gunther Damon sighed. "Give 'em an evasive answer," he suggested. "Tell 'em to go screw themselves."

Butler laughed.

"Dammit, Joe Tyler's still down in Miami for that medical conference," Damon said. "We can't do anything about that series until he gets back."

Butler slipped a sheet of copy paper into his typewriter and rapped out a message to Louisville.

LV

RE RQST FOR SERIES, SCIENCE ED ON OUTA TOWN ASSIGNMENT. WILL ADVISE ON SERIES SKED SOONS RETURNS MON.

WA

"I liked your first answer better," Butler observed as he handed the reply to the B wire operator.

"The day I leave IPS," Damon said, "I'm gonna put a message to that effect on the A wire and address it to all clients."

He walked over to his own desk, tucked away in a corner of the newsroom, and began opening the mail which Custer had stacked neatly next to his typewriter. Nothing exciting. A note from the New York feature editor suggesting five special projects, each of which would have earned a magazine writer at least $750 and which Damon would parcel out to his own staff to be researched and written (for free) whenever they could find time. A couple of invitations to cocktail parties and the usual collection of handouts hopefully addressed to a top editor like Damon instead of just IPS. He threw away all but one, which contained a possible science feature idea. This he marked with Joe Tyler's initials. When Custer finally brought him his coffee, he asked the copy boy to put the handout in Tyler's mail slot.

His next chore was to examine the overnight report for the first editions of today's afternoon papers. He got no further than the first story out of Washington, because it suddenly reminded him of his earlier, unexplainable uneasiness.

(PRESIDENT)

BY MALCOLM JONES
IPS WHITE HOUSE CORRESPONDENT

WASHINGTON (IPS)—A CABINET MEETING (10 A.M. EDT) WAS THE ONLY ITEM ON PRESIDENT HAINES'S AGENDA TODAY AS THE CHIEF EXECUTIVE PREPARED TO LEAVE FOR A PALM SPRINGS VACATION.

HAINES WAS EXPECTED TO BRIEF THE CABINET ON THE RAPIDLY WORSENING RED CHINA SITUATION, MARKED BY ANOTHER ANGRY ACCUSATION FROM PEKING THAT THE UNITED STATES WAS PLOTTING WORLDWIDE AGGRESSION.

THE PRESIDENT'S DECISION TO PROCEED WITH A LONG-NEEDED REST, HOWEVER, WAS SEEN BY DIPLOMATIC OBSERVERS AS INDICATING THAT THE ADMINISTRATION IS NOT CONVINCED RED CHINA IS READY TO PULL THE TRIGGER FOR WORLD WAR III.

HAINES'S ANXIETY TO GET SOME RELAXATION AT THE PALM SPRINGS RESIDENCE OF HIS CLOSE FRIEND, INDUSTRIALIST THOMAS KENDRICKS, UNDERLINED THE PRESIDENT'S ADMITTED FATIGUE. WHITE HOUSE PRESS SECRETARY PHILIP SABATH, IN FACT, TOLD NEWSMEN YESTERDAY THAT NO REPORTERS WOULD TRAVEL ON THE PRESIDENTIAL AIRCRAFT TONIGHT, EXPLAINING THAT THE CHIEF EXECUTIVE "WANTS TO START RELAXING THE MINUTE THE PLANE TAKES

Damon finished reading Jones's story and postponed checking the rest of the overnight layout. He walked over to the day desk where Butler was editing some copy from the Senate. "Les, anything from the Cabinet meeting?"

"Not yet. Jonesy said he'd phone in a first lead on the overnighter soon as it breaks up. He doesn't think there'll be much, though. Whatever Haines tells them will be off the record."

"Brubaker might talk. He usually does."

Harvey Brubaker was the Secretary of Transportation, a perpetually smiling man who loved most of all to see his name in the papers and cultivated reporters rigorously and almost indecently. A year ago, when he held his first news conference following recovery from a mild heart attack, he had embarrassed the usually unembarrassable press corps by confiding the intimate circumstances in which he had been stricken. The boys had a time deciding whether to use this delicious tidbit, and finally indulged in self-censorship more to protect Mrs. Brubaker than her free-talking husband.

"I doubt if Brubaker will spill anything this time," Butler said. "Jonesy heard that Haines really chewed him out for leaking that maritime subsidy proposal."

"How about Madigan?"

"Hell, Gunther, he's so scared of Haines he wouldn't go to the men's room without White House permission."

Damon nodded. "I guess you're right. When Jonesy finishes dictating, tell him I'd like to see him whenever he can get away. There's something that bothers me about this Palm Springs trip. I keep thinking that maybe Haines is more than just tired."

Butler was surprised. "Jonesy didn't sound alarmed and you know our Malcolm—he can smell something wrong before the can's opened."

"Yeh, I'm probably wrong. But I'd still like to see him. That reminds me, where the hell is Pitch?"

Butler chuckled and it came close to being a lewd chuckle. "He called in just before you got here. Said he overslept. And don't ride his ass, Gunther. If I was married to that doll of his, I'd never get to work."

38

"I don't begrudge him his sex life," Damon growled. "Only when it's on IPS time."

Pitcher arrived five minutes later, wearing an obviously new suit and the first shirt without frayed cuffs Damon had ever seen on his aviation editor, a small, wiry man with a youthful crew cut.

"I'll say this much for marriage," Damon commented. "It sure as hell improved your neatness. You're a little late, Pitch."

"Sorry, Gunther. I was working on my novel pretty late and I overslept. Nancy didn't have the heart to get me up."

Damon, like Butler, had a strong suspicion that Nancy and not the novel was the source of tardiness but he let the alibi stand unchallenged.

"Pitch, can you catch Andrews tonight when Haines leaves? I know ten o'clock is a cruddy time, but I'm strapped for bodies."

Pitcher's face fell, an instant disintegration that collapsed contentment into annoyance. "Aw hell, Gunther, I told Nancy I'd take her to a movie tonight."

"Take her tomorrow night, Pitch. I really need you or I wouldn't ask. Tell you what—you can have all of Friday off. Give you a long weekend with the bride."

Pitcher's dour face reconstructed itself.

"That's a deal," he said happily. He marched off to his desk and began his workday in typical fashion—reading the newsletter *Aviation Daily* to see (1) what he had missed yesterday and (2) what he might swipe out of it today.

That personnel dilemma solved, Damon finished reading the overnight report and managed to turn out four business letters before Stan DeVarian came in. He and Stan had a daily conference on staff and problems, most of them revolving around the inevitable conflict between DeVarian's hamstrung budget and the increasing demands of news clients. The latest edict from New York had been a moratorium on replacing employees who were fired or resigned, which had thrown Damon into a frustrated rage.

Stan informed him today that the "reduce staff through normal attrition" order had been modified.

"We can transfer men from the line bureaus as replacements," DeVarian said. "We just can't hire new personnel here above the rank of dictationist. Happier?"

"It's better than nothing," Damon said sourly. "What

happens to the line bureaus that send us people? They're as understaffed as we are."

"They'll hire at the bottom of the Guild scale—something we can't do because we need more experience."

Considerably mollified, Damon emerged from DeVarian's office in time to hear Evelyn Strotsky, the switchboard operator, call out, "White House bulletin," in the dulcet tones of a Marine drill instructor.

That would be Jones's fresh lead on the Cabinet meeting. Damon parked himself behind Lynx Grimes, the young dictationist on the receiving end of what Jones was phoning in. Gunther was torn momentarily between watching her typing and peeking down her low-cut blouse but professional interest won out over carnal instinct. Jones himself, as predicted, had not come up with anything startling.

Bulletin
1st day lead President

Washington (IPS)—President Haines held a 90-minute cabinet meeting today prior to departure for Palm Springs, Calif., and an extended vacation for the crisis-weary Chief Executive.

more

"Anything hot?" Butler wanted to know.

"No. It's not worth a bulletin. Wait till he finishes a few more paragraphs. You can move it out as an urgent. Keep it tight unless he has some good quotes."

"Right."

Damon's eyes moved back to the dictationist's clattering typewriter, pausing en route to glance again at the open blouse. Lynx was a Vassar graduate willing to endure the lowly status of dictation for an eventual chance to become a full-fledged reporter. She was a quiet, rather solemn girl with a plain yet somehow sexy face, slim hips and long, shapely legs. Damon had hired her seven months ago, partially because her first name fascinated him, and regretting at the time his self-imposed ban against dating girls under his command.

He felt a rebirth of that regret right now but pushed it aside instantly as Jones's smooth, off-the-cuff verbal composition rolled into Miss Grimes's ears and off her fingers onto the typewriter. That was the White House man's forte, the ability to dictate a breaking story without the luxury of time in which to organize, write and edit it. Some wire service men never could do it, and few had Jonesy's consummate skill.

The rest of his output was a brief rehash of the overnighter, plus a paragraph describing the Cabinet members as "sober-faced and non-committal as to what was discussed."

Damon went back to his desk and had resumed work on correspondence when his phone rang.

"Damon."

"Jonesy, Gunther. Les said you wanted to see me."

"Yep. You coming in?"

"Wasn't planning to. I want to get home and finish packing. Christ knows how long he'll be in Palm Springs. Is it absolutely necessary?"

"No, I guess not. Jonesy, is Haines sick or something? I don't like this complete privacy crap and no reporters on his plane."

"He's fine far as I know. Tired, that's for sure. But no sign Sabath's trying to cover up anything. This business of not wanting us on his bird—doesn't surprise me at all, Gunther. Don't forget LBJ and Kennedy didn't always take us. Besides, there's one big advantage to using the press charter."

"What's that?"

"The airlines are a helluva lot more generous with their liquor service."

Damon laughed. "Well, you've made me feel better. Same arrangements at Palm Springs as before?"

"Yep. We'll be at the Pioneer Hotel. That's five miles from Tom Kendricks' little shack. The usual setup—Sabath'll brief us every morning and I have a hunch this'll be more or less of a vacation for yours truly."

"It'll be a pretty expensive vacation for IPS," Damon noted dryly. "That advance you drew—five hundred bucks. Try to bring some of it back."

"If I don't, my expense account should win the Pulitzer prize. So long, Gunther. Be home in about an hour if you need me."

Damon did feel better. He began the task of reading the rest of the overnight report, oblivious to the din of the teletypes that could have been the heartbeats of a sick world.

CHAPTER THREE

At eight that night Colonel Marcus Henderson walked into Andrews Operations.

The duty officer greeted him with a grin that told Henderson most of the paperwork already was finished. Otherwise, the duty officer would have been wearing a harassed frown bespeaking cruel overwork, unreasonable demands on his valuable time and a silent plea for forgiveness.

"Crew and passenger manifests all ready, Colonel," he beamed. "Also weather and the Monster has three flight plans for your inspection."

"The Monster" was Henderson's own sobriquet for the giant computer that digested data from the United States Weather Bureau's mammoth complex at nearby Suitland, Maryland. The en route weather, including upper air winds and temperatures, were fed into the computer along with Air Force One's planned fuel load, gross take-off weight and gross landing weight.

In his early Air Force days, it would have taken Henderson at least thirty minutes to work out a single flight plan. Now the computer analyzed in half that time, for the Palm Springs flight, eight different routings at a common altitude, worked out thirteen different flight plans for each of the eight routings at appropriate altitudes, and then boiled down these one hundred and four plans into the three best.

If Henderson had been an airline captain, he would have picked the route and altitude involving a delicately balanced combination of such factors as safety, comfort and economy. As commander of Air Force One, the latter category was not quite as important although Henderson dutifully considered it. Now he was studying the Monster's suggestions for tonight's flight, row upon row of hieroglyphics that had tumbled out of the computer. An hour earlier he had talked with the Federal Aviation Administration's Air Traffic Control for a preliminary outlook, after which he had phoned Andrews to request alternate flight plans for flight level forty-three thousand.

In his own computerized eyes and brains the conglomeration of abbreviations and numbers in front of him were translated easily and instantly into fuel consumption, empty weight, fuel and payload on ramp before take-off, airways, check points and cruise Mach number—the closeness to the speed of sound. All of which he weighed and balanced in his mind before he handed two of the flight plans back to the duty officer.

"Dahlgren Three looks like the best," he said. "Get me an ATC clearance at forty-three thousand. Hi, Sam."

The last was addressed to a stocky major, copilot Samuel Foster, one of the five flight deck crew members assigned to Air Force One.

"Colonel Henderson, sir," Foster acknowledged with mock formality. "And what have the gods aloft decreed for us tonight?"

"Looks routine. Forty-knot headwinds. Plenty of thunderstorm activity over Arizona. That should be below us, though."

"What's our level?"

"Forty-three. I filed for Dahlgren Three. We could swing farther north but the headwinds aren't quite as strong on our route."

"Sounds fine. The usual crew?"

"We won't have a man from Air Traffic Control aboard this time. Otherwise, the usual."

Henderson read aloud from the crew sheet, skipping his own and Foster's names.

"Flight engineer, Captain Falk; navigator, Lieutenant Eldridge; radioman, Captain Warneke. Stewards, Sergeants Russell and Carvelli. Security guards, Sergeants Larson and Jervis. Jervis? That's a new one."

"Just transferred from Air Police at Edwards, Colonel," the duty officer volunteered. "Good man. Top security clearance. Henzey's on emergency leave—his father's ill."

"When Jervis reports, be sure and tell him I'll hold crew briefing at 2130. If he doesn't know where it is, take him by the hand and lead him there."

"Yes, sir."

"Sam, I'm going to inspect aircraft. Be in the hangar if you need me."

"Right. By the way, I hear we got a light load."

"Wouldn't be surprised. Lieutenant, let me have the passenger manifest."

Henderson looked over the manifest handed him by the duty officer, then gave it to Major Foster, whose eyebrows raised to half staff. The manifest read:

> The President.
> The White House Press Secretary, Mr. Sabath.
> The President's personal secretary, Miss Nance.
> The President's physician, Rear Adm. Philips, USN.
> Mr. McElhenny, Secret Service.
> Mr. Hudson, Secret Service.
> Mr. Bramley, Secret Service.

"Only seven," said Foster. "And three of 'em are Secret Service. Wonder why? Christ, there's room for the whole bloody press corps."

"Ours not to reason why." Henderson smiled. "See you at briefing. When Sergeant Jervis comes in, go over the emergency procedures with him."

"To be assigned to this airplane, he's already had them shoved down his throat and up his butt," Foster reminded the colonel.

"So insert them into his navel," Henderson said.

The commander of Air Force One strode briskly over to the huge hangar where he was accosted immediately by one of the four armed guards on duty twenty-four hours a day. The fact that the air policeman knew him as well as he knew his own father didn't deter the guard from inspecting Henderson's ID badge. The AP brought his tommy gun to port arms.

"Pass, sir—and have a nice trip."

"Thanks, son. Everything in order?"

"Yessir. Beautiful ship, ain't she?"

"That she is."

And that she was, Henderson thought as he stepped inside the hangar and looked up at the ten-million-dollar symphony in gleaming aluminum, with the presidential seal just under the cockpit windows. Yes, sir, one beautiful ship—and one beautiful goddamned flying bitch no matter what the aeronautical experts decreed.

For Marcus Henderson, down very, very deep in his airman's heart and soul, hated this magnificent product of the Amalgamated Aircraft Corporation because he didn't quite trust it.

Jeremy Haines worked well past seven-thirty in his oval office, signing routine legislation and dictating routine memos to Judi Nance. When the last of the dictation was finished the President tapped tobacco into a well-smoked pipe and lit it. The chocolate aroma wafted into the air and curled into the secretary's nostrils. She smiled as she closed her dictation pad.

"I've said it before and I'll say it again, Mr. President. That tobacco is too sexy for the White House."

"You can keep on saying it, Judi. Telling a man his tobacco smells good is like telling a woman she's wearing the right perfume. Looking forward to the trip?"

"Who wouldn't?" Miss Nance asked. "Palm Springs— and I gather not much work to do."

"Not much," Haines said. "All packed and ready?"

"Yes, sir."

"Well, better get something to eat, Judi, before the chopper leaves. And be back here by nine-thirty."

She rose and started toward the door, only to turn around suddenly and stare directly into the sharp gray eyes of Jeremy Haines.

"Mr. President."

"Yes, Judi?"

She paused, forbidden familiarity struggling with female sympathy. "God bless you, sir," she finally blurted.

The President nodded, a wordless gesture of gratitude. She had been gone only a few minutes when the red phone on his desk labeled "Pentagon" tinkled discreetly and rather quietly for a direct line to the Joint Chiefs. Haines always expected it to clang.

"Yes?"

"General Graham, Mr. President. That message from the Alaskan Defense Command you were waiting for—it's in."

"Read it."

Haines listened to the communication. "Thank you very much, General."

46

"Good night, sir."

The click of the phone at the Pentagon end echoed in the President's ears. His pipe had gone out and he relit it. His fingers drummed nervously, impatiently on his desk and he decided to have a martini before his brother arrived.

Colonel Henderson climbed the steep, swaying hangar ramp parked by Air Force One's forward door, conscious when he reached the top that he didn't use to puff that hard. Climbing airplane boarding ramps, he thought, was an embarrassingly accurate barometer of a pilot's aging process.

At the top of the ramp, he looked down the hundred-and-seventy-six-foot fuselage, at the aft-mounted engines and towering T-shaped tail. He never could get used to the sheer physical size of Amalgamated's Condor, twenty-three feet longer than the Boeing 707 which it had replaced as the queen of the presidential aircraft fleet. A replacement which had not been to Henderson's liking.

The replacement was as much a matter of political expediency as of aerodynamic judgment. Amalgamated's brass had contributed substantial funds to Haines's campaign. When the Air Force sought funds for a supersonic presidential transport as the Boeing's logical successor, Congress had balked at the thirty-million-dollar SST price tag. The Condor was a compromise choice, almost fifty knots faster than the 707, but in addition to the speed factor there was the debt the party owed to Amalgamated, which was having trouble selling a large subsonic aircraft to the airlines. Amalgamated finally wound up with a fat contract for forty Condors in a military cargo version and tossed in a presidential configuration as a bonus.

Its basic design, Henderson conceded, was sound. The four aft-mounted engines and T-tail gave it a marked resemblance to Britain's VC-10. The Condor, he also admitted, handled like a fighter compared to the 707—but this was the chief reason he inherently mistrusted the plane. It handled almost too easily. The Boeing's hydraulic boost system, for example, operated at a pressure ratio of three thousand pounds per square inch. A movement of the Condor's yoke sent pressure of four thousand pounds per square inch through the plane's massive control system, activating the ailerons and elevators like power steering

47

on a heavy automobile. Power steering, Henderson worried, that seemed to lack feel of the road. The Condor was a dream to fly ninety-nine per cent of the time, and most pilots would have put this figure at one hundred. The minority, such as Henderson, considered these particular hydraulically boosted controls a shade oversensitive.

His misgivings were more of a wispy state of mind than a solid objection, a vague uneasiness at rare times instead of factually based criticism. Maybe, he told himself, he was just one of those pilots who fell irrevocably in love with a certain airplane and refused to admit the virtues of the newer birds—as if such admission were unfaithfulness and disloyalty to an old friend.

He started his walk-through inspection in the roomy cockpit and proceeded back toward the rear.

Crew berths for overseas flights when Air Force One carried relief pilots.

The communications area, consisting mostly of a huge console looking like something out of a science fiction movie. Most of this electronics gear was transistorized to save weight, including the radio teletype that could be patched into the Kremlin-Pentagon hot line or even the UPI, AP and IPS news printers in the White House. Next to the radio teletype a coding machine for handling incoming classified matter.

The main cabin, about the only conventional-appearing space on the plane. Two-abreast, airliner-type seats with a thirty-passenger capacity. The seats were pale green, the cabin walls a soft beige. At the head of the cabin, on one side a lavatory and on the other a galley. At the end of the main cabin, a lounge area with a television set. As on the predecessor Boeing, the seats faced rearward—not for safety (no one had ever proved that rear-facing seats were safer in a crash) but to provide the semblance of an auditorium or large conference room if the bulkhead dividing this area from the presidential quarters was removed.

Henderson was at the bulkhead now, an easily detachable plastic structure with a large door in the center. He opened the door and entered the really plush area of the plane.

There was the kidney-shaped desk first used by President Johnson and transferred, at Haines's request, to the newer Air Force One. A big, comfortable swivel chair in back of the desk, resting flush against the cream-colored cabin wall. The desk was a rich walnut and the chair likewise, but upholstered in aquamarine that matched the sofa lounges and swivel lounge chairs scattered rather haphazardly throughout this section. Three phones were on wall racks, used by presidential staff members if they wanted to contact their White House offices.

Suspended from the overhead rack was a color television set—which seldom worked very well in flight—and Henderson noted with satisfaction that the small coffee tables placed strategically near the lounge sofas and chairs had vases filled with fresh-cut flowers, plus matchbooks bearing the gold presidential seal and the inscription "Air Force One."

A larger galley and a lavatory were next. Henderson opened a galley compartment and smiled approvingly. There were several cans of chili—Haines's favorite in-flight meal. All Presidents, the colonel mused, seemed to have culinary idiosyncrasies. Kennedy had to have his soup on a flight. LBJ always wanted tuna salad and cream cheese sandwiches placed aboard. Now there was Haines and his chili. Henderson also opened the compartment marked "liquor" to make sure it was stocked with bourbon, scotch and martini miniatures.

The galley inspection over, he looked back over the presidential quarters and thought that, as usual, the twelve-man cabin maintenance crew had done its superlative job. Everything was spotless, including the dark blue rug that stretched the length of the plane. He entered the final bulkhead door bearing the presidential seal, and gazed around the President's private office, lounge and sleeping quarters.

This area was almost as large as the lounge space he had just left. Another, more conventional work desk, bearing two telephones—one white, the other red. The latter was an intercom to the cockpit, not that Haines used it much. Not as often as LBJ, Henderson recalled, who would call the flight deck at every change of altitude, wanting to know what was going on. The white phone was hooked to the communications console.

The commander knelt and lifted the blue and gold bed-cover on the President's berth. Under the bed was Air Force One's only parachute—added to the emergency equipment

49

at the suggestion of the Secret Service back in the days of Eisenhower, who had 'chutes for himself and any members of his immediate family aboard. Henderson privately considered this a useless precaution. If something went wrong at the normal cruising altitudes, it would be impossible to open the plug-type doors for a parachute jump unless the cabin were depressurized. And this would require activating the auxiliary oxygen masks, placing a portable mask over the President's face, strapping an oxygen bottle on his back, and shoving him out of an exit accompanied by prayers that he wouldn't suffer a heart attack or lose the mask on a jump involving thousands of feet.

If he had to jump from a lower altitude, Henderson reasoned, it still would be risky for any man the age of a President. Besides, no Air Force One commander wanted the responsibility of deciding when such a jump would be necessary. In ninety-nine cases out of a hundred it would be safer chancing an emergency landing, staying with the plane. Of course, if there were fatal structural failure, like the loss of a wing, the 'chute would have to be used to save the President's life. But if a wing went, the plane probably would be in a spin generating centrifugal forces that would make an airborne exit nearly impossible.

But the parachute was there, just the same and just in case. Along with life jackets for every seat and four life rafts in the event Air Force One, even on a domestic flight, had to come down in water. Henderson pulled Haines's single chute out from under the bed and checked it, as well as he could externally, for correct packing. It was repacked before every presidential flight, just one more precaution to protect the life of Air Force One's most important passenger.

Henderson walked back through the cabin, stopping briefly to make sure all lavatories were equipped with fresh soap, clean towels and toilet gear. His inspection finished, he climbed down the steps, returned a guard's salute and went back to Operations where he told the duty officer it was okay to roll out Air Force One and start fueling.

"Where's Major Foster?" Henderson asked.

"In the snack shop, sir."

That was typical of Foster, who never seemed to get enough to eat. Henderson once accused him in jest of taking a sandwich to bed with him on his wedding night,

50

and Sam had confessed getting up at 1 A.M. on that occasion to order something from room service.

Well, let the major indulge in his one vice. Henderson opened his flight kit and took out the Jeppesen Standard Instrument Departure (SID) chart for the Andrews area. The Dahlgren Three routing was a convenient verbal condensation of a far more complicated transcontinental flight plan, involving careful vectoring through the Washington airway complex via various radio navigation points and rigid altitude restrictions before climbing to the assigned cruise level and hitting the jet airways. Henderson found Dahlgren Three and refreshed his mind on its details.

". . . via Andrews 187-degree radial to Dahlgren intersection. Cross Brooke Vortac 071 degrees at or below four thousand. Cross Dahlgren intersection at or above nine thousand, then via Herndon direct to Brooke Vortac . . . J8 to Louisville, J78 to Palm Springs. . . ."

Henderson folded the map, checked his watch and told the duty officer he was going to the crew briefing room. Here he would go over once again, complete with oral quizzing of individual crew members, the emergency procedures that were part of every presidential trip. Dull, repetitive, already memorized, but still essential. If something went wrong, there wouldn't be time to open a manual and prod anyone's memory.

Rod Pitcher took his wife along on tonight's Andrews assignment. Nancy had seen presidential departures before (it was part of his courtship, impressing her enormously with the way he passed by the Secret Servicemen, casually flipping open his wallet to display his White House credentials). But she never failed to get a thrill out of what to her husband had come to be an outright bore. The twelve-man honor guard (she was halfway disappointed when Rod told her their rifles were empty, because they were there to honor and not to guard). The moment of excited anticipation when the helicopter from the White House whirled into view and squatted ten yards away from Air Force One, disgorging the President and his briefcase-carrying retinue. She was even freshly proud of Rod when he would pick up the field phone importantly, hamming it up slightly for her benefit, and give the desk the wheels-up or touchdown time.

Nancy Pitcher was a tiny, extremely pretty girl whose

wide mouth was the only discordant note in her otherwise perfectly arranged face. Yet even her mouth did not detract from the over-all picture. It gave her a sensuous air, a hint of latent nymphomania parked incongruously in the middle of sweet young innocence. Her honey-blonde hair was tossed with practiced carelessness over one eye. Her skirt, as they drove, had sneaked above her dimpled knees and who could blame Mr. Rodney Pitcher for thinking disloyal thoughts about Mr. Gunther Damon and his stinking night assignments?

They pulled into the parking area reserved for the press, the right sun visor on their car lowered to give the air policeman on duty a glimpse of the IPS card clipped to the visor. The glimpse, in truth, was unnecessary because the airman by now was most familiar with both Pitcher and his automobile. Nancy didn't know this, however, and the lowering of the visor was just one more item of propaganda he felt was needed to convince her steadily that he was, indeed, an Important Man.

Air Force One was parked beyond the wire fence erected some twenty yards in front of the Andrews terminal building. A fuel truck was just pulling away, having completed its job of feeding the Condor with 22,256 gallons of JP-1 kerosene. The fuel had been pumped into the tank truck and sealed twenty-four hours earlier. When Henderson ordered fueling to start, an Air Force specialist had drained about a gallon from the truck and analyzed it for purity and the proper amount of water and octane. The fuel truck itself had been under armed guard since receiving its load for the flight.

And now the Condor sat docilely under the temporary floodlights hauled out for every presidential night departure, a drowsy beast of burden waiting to be prodded into powerful, pulsating life. The thin block letters U N I T E D S T A T E S O F A M E R I C A gleamed above the long line of cabin windows, stretching almost the entire length of the fuselage. One of the stewards, slightly impatient, peeked out of the open rear fuselage door where the President would enter. The two security guards, pistols strapped to their sides, stood at the foot of the boarding steps conversing quietly.

"Why isn't there a sign on the plane saying 'Air Force

One'?" Nancy inquired as they approached the fence. "I always meant to ask you that."

"Air Force One is what Air Traffic Control calls any plane carrying the President," Pitcher explained. "It's Air Force One no matter what he uses—even a little Cessna would be Air Force One if the President was aboard."

Rod left his wife on the terminal side of the fence and walked through the gate after opening his wallet to the poker-faced Secret Serviceman stationed there. The field phones—one each for the three wire services—were only a few feet past the gate. In the old days the press phones were thirty yards past the fence, on the very fringe of Air Force One's boarding area. LBJ had ordered them removed entirely, for unannounced reasons (the newsmen suspected that it was the Secret Service's idea), forcing the reporters to use pay phones inside the terminal. Haines had relented to the extent of reinstalling the phones close to the fence, but still considerably distant from the presidential aircraft.

Likewise, Johnson had eliminated the traditional honor guard early in his Administration. Haines had restored it, but only for daytime arrivals and departures; there was no honor guard tonight, much to Nancy Pitcher's disappointment.

"Press plane left yet?" Pitcher asked the UPI man.

"About forty-five minutes ago, they tell me."

"Who had it?"

"United. With a DC-8, they needed that much of a head start. Haines might still beat 'em in."

Pitcher picked up the phone marked "IPS" and dialed the office—subconsciously resentful, as usual, that both the UPI and AP had direct lines to their offices and didn't have to waste time dialing. Bill Utely, the night editor, answered.

"This is Pitch, Bill. I'm checking in at Andrews. Has he left the White House yet?"

"The chopper just took off."

"Okay, I'll phone back when he's airborne. Hi, Mike."

The last was addressed to the Andrews public relations officer, Captain Michael Jenkins, who was present at Air Force One movements mostly to protect tardy wire service reporters. If they arrived too late, Jenkins would phone their offices. The newsmen liked him, even though his qualifications for dealing with the press consisted of a subscription to the *Evening Star* and a one-time stint selling ads for the Air Force Academy magazine. The boys kidded him because he had trouble identifying types of aircraft showing up at Andrews. He rode with their verbal punches, laughed at their jokes, and few ever found out that he had been decorated three times for bravery in Vietnam.

It took the helicopter only ten minutes to make the flight from the White House 'copter pad to Andrews. A Secret Serviceman got the word that the chopper had left at almost the same time that Pitcher did and waved toward Air Force One. Colonel Henderson, his leathery face halfway out an open cockpit window, nodded.

"Start three and four," he told Captain Falk.

"Three and four," the flight engineer said laconically.

The turbines on the side of the jet farthest from the fence stirred into life, whining softly at first and then building up an ear-torturing, screaming crescendo. A ground crewman unhitched the umbilical cord that linked the air-conditioning truck to the cabin, climbed into the truck and drove away.

A controller in the Andrews control tower pressed a microphone button.

"Attention, all aircraft. Andrews will be closed to traffic from now until fifteen minutes after Air Force One has departed. Stand by on this frequency for your clearances. Repeat. All aircraft . . ."

The reporters were looking skyward.

"Here he comes," the AP man called out.

Out of the blackness appeared the winking red anti-collision lights of the White House helicopter, the sound of its own engines smothered by the howling turbines on Air Force One. The chopper approached closer, hovered momentarily, then with bulky dignity sat down to the right and rear of the giant Condor. Now the noise of its power plants joined with those of the jet for a few seconds, subsiding as the pilot cut his throttles. The huge blades, gleaming under the floodlights' glare, slowed down and stopped. The 'copter's door opened and small steps fell forward on their twin latches. An Army sergeant emerged, scrambled down the steps and stood stiffly at attention.

The newsreel and television network cameras whirred.

Out of the chopper came the presidential party. The President was the first one out. The cameras focused on his tall figure and trailed his short, quick strides toward the waiting jet. His graying hair looked almost metallic in the artificial light, plainly visible under the homburg Haines always wore on trips.

The security guards at the foot of the loading ramp stiffened and saluted as the President mounted the steps and disappeared into the softly lit cabin, followed by the burly figure of Sabath, Miss Nance, Rear Admiral Philips—dressed in civvies—and the three Secret Servicemen assigned to the flight.

The two guards ran up the stairs when the presidential party was aboard, one of them grasping the inner handle of the huge cabin door and swinging it shut. The engines on the left side loudly responded to Henderson's "Start one and two" command.

"Confirm our clearance," Henderson told Major Foster.

"Request clearance," Foster said to the tower.

"Air Force One, cleared for taxi to Runway 19 Left. You are cleared to Palm Springs Airport via Dahlgren Three, repeat Three. Herndon transition. Jet 30 to Front Royal, then flight plan route. Maintain flight level two-three-zero, transponder code two thousand. Contact Departure Control on three-six-three-point-zero."

"Air Force One," Foster acknowledged.

Henderson advanced the throttles and the Condor, trembling slightly like a human being afflicted with nervous anticipation, waddled from the ramp area.

Ahead of her was an Air Force pickup truck, a big sign reading FOLLOW ME hanging on its rear. Like a little poodle leading an elephant, the truck preceded Air Force One to Runway 19 Left. Overhead sputtered the rescue helicopter, carrying parachutists trained in fire fighting. If there was an accident resulting in fire, the crash 'copter would disgorge its personnel and then hover over the wreckage, its blades fanning the flames away from the fuselage. Moving slowly down Runway 19 Left were two fire engines and a crash truck, part of the protective convoy.

The Condor poised on the runway threshold, an Amazon pausing to catch her breath before a long sprint into battle. Air Force One began to roll.

Pitcher dialed.

"Night desk, Utely."

"Pitcher. Hang on. Just a second. Okay. He's off at ten-oh-two."

"Ten-oh-two," Utely repeated. "Thanks, Pitch. Go on home."

"I'll do just that."

He was walking toward his car, Nancy on his arm, when something jogged his brain.

"You go ahead," he said. "I've got to ask Mike Jenkins something."

Before she had a chance to say anything, he was trotting back toward the terminal. He found Jenkins outside the snack shop, sipping a Coke. "Mike, it just occurred to me. Where was the base commander tonight? He usually sees the President off."

Captain Jenkins shook his head.

"Not tonight," he said. "The White House called this morning and said it wouldn't be necessary for General Blackwell to be here. Which was fine with General Blackwell. He's got a poker game at the Officers' Club. Why?"

"Just curious," Pitcher said. "You know me—I come unglued at anything that doesn't follow routine. Good night, Mike."

On the way to his car, Pitcher decided the absence of the base commander was not worth phoning in.

Air Force One swam through a thin overcast, her 360,000-pound bulk appearing as a tiny blip on a radar screen in the Washington Traffic Control Center at Leesburg, Virginia.

"Air Force One to Washington Center."

"Washington Center, Air Force One. Squawk ident."

"Roger, identing."

Henderson pushed the transponder button that automatically put an "AF-1" and a "230" on the ground radar screen next to the Condor's blip. This was the so-called Alpha Numerics system by which flights and their altitudes were identified on ATC radar screens. In the old days, radar could not distinguish the altitudes of targets. The new identifying transponders were hooked to the altimeter and thus the radar beacon aimed at an aircraft picked up not only its identity code but its height.

"Okay, Air Force One. We have you in radar contact at twenty-three thousand. Continue your climb to flight level four-three-zero. Your transponder code is two-one-zero above twenty-four thousand. Over."

"Air Force One, roger."

The blip crawled across the green radar screen, like a bug heading for suddenly glimpsed food.

"I'm glad that's over," the Leesburg controller remarked to the superviser standing behind him. "I always get the jitters handling that bird."

"Just another airplane," said the supervisor—mainly for the purpose of relaxing an awed trainee observing the operation. "But I'd hate to get a seven-seven-zero-zero from him."

"What's that?" the trainee asked.

"Memorize it well, chum. Seven-seven-zero-zero is the transponder code for an emergency if he loses radio contact."

Air Force One streaked through the night, unerringly glued to the invisible aerial tracks that were high-altitude jet routes J8 and J78.

It had picked up J8 at Front Royal, Virginia, where J8 intersected with J30 from Washington, and flew on a slightly south-westerly course carved into six segments representing the Air Traffic Control Centers along its planned route.

The Indianapolis Center took over as the speeding Condor neared Charleston, West Virginia. Indianapolis handed the flight over to Kansas City Center on J78 just past Evansville. Another jurisdictional hand-off to Fort Worth Center near Oklahoma City. Albuquerque Center assumed control beyond Liberal, Kansas, and would monitor Air Force One until J78 knifed across Prescott, Arizona. Finally the Los Angeles Center, taking Air Force One by its gentle electronic hands, would help it down the airway steps into Palm Springs.

Position reports every fifteen minutes . . . "Air Force One, estimating Amarillo at . . ."

Transponder identification at Center hand-offs . . . "Air Force One, this is Albuquerque Center. Squawk ident, please . . ."

"Air Force One, identing."

All routine.

The door of the private presidential compartment was closed. Judi Nance stirred uncomfortably as she napped on a couch in the rear lounge. She became half awake every time the Condor pitched slightly in mild turbulence, wings flexing slightly like coil springs on an automobile passing over a little road bump.

Two of the three Secret Servicemen were asleep. Sabath and Rear Admiral Philips played gin rummy with the two security guards.

Behind the cockpit, Captain Warneke, the radio officer, hooked the radio teletype into a news circuit so he could pick up some baseball scores.

FINAL AMERICAN NEW YORK 8 WASHINGTON 3. WP HUNTER, LP . . .

Captain Warneke, a never-say-die fan of the Senators, kicked one foot in a gesture of angered exasperation. His shoe touched the padlocked briefcase parked under the communications console. Inside were the War Codes, to be used if the airborne President had to order the ICBMs and B-58s winging toward an enemy.

Baseball scores and War Codes.

All routine.

Major Foster rang a steward on the intercom.

"Any chance for a sandwich and some coffee, Sergeant?"

"Yes, sir. Ham and swiss okay?"

"Fine."

The Condor bucked and trembled momentarily, absorbing the jabs of turbulent gusts. Marcus Henderson disengaged the auto-pilot, adjusted the trim to his liking, and gripped the yoke firmly.

"Air Force One, this is Albuquerque Center."

"Air Force One."

"Informatively, radar is picking up a big squall line seventeen miles northwest of Winslow and moving southeasterly at a very rapid pace. A TWA flight reports unable to get on top of it at forty thousand."

"Albuquerque, did TWA give any turbulence report?"

"Affirmative, Air Force One. Moderate to severe."

"Do you think you could vector us around it?"

"Negative, Air Force One. Unless you want to be vectored about a hundred miles to the south. It's a big bastard, if you'll pardon our language."

"Okay, Albuquerque. We'll turn on our radar and see if we can pick our way through."

Henderson activated the weather-warning radar, setting

58

the range to one hundred miles. The scanning line re-
volved slowly, reflecting the sweep of the nose antenna as it
searched ahead for telltale turbulence.

"Nothing yet," Henderson remarked. He looked at
Foster, peacefully munching his just-delivered sandwich.
"When you finish that goddamned sandwich," the commander added with a touch of sarcasm, "keep your eyes
on that scope."

"I can do both at once," the major said placidly. "I'm
ambidextrous." He hunched over the hooded scope.

In the darkened radar room of the Albuquerque Center,
a controller watched the blip of Air Force One move
steadily across his screen. The watch supervisor picked up a
phone connected directly to the Los Angeles Center.

"Los Angeles, this is Albuquerque. We'll be handing Air
Force One off to you a little later than expected. He's got
some thunderstorms ahead of him and he'll probably have
to slow down a bit."

"Thanks, Albuquerque. Keep us posted."

"Roger."

All routine.

The Condor swept westward, swimming along in its huge
cocoon of protected airspace. The jet trembled and pitched
again, this time with more emphasis and prolonged duration. Henderson used the intercom and told the answering
steward to put on Sabath.

"Phil, we've got some weather ahead of us. Is the
President asleep?"

"Yep. He's in his room."

"Well, somebody should go in and make sure he's
strapped in even if he's in bed. I'll leave it to you."

"Okay, Marcus."

Henderson reached above him and flicked the FASTEN
SEAT BELTS sign with his left hand. His right hand fondled
the throttles, moving them back ever so slightly. With
typical, inbred caution, as much a part of him as his uniform
and his heart and his mind, he opened his flight bag and
took out the Operating Manual of the Amalgamated Condor. He already knew what he was looking for but he still
consulted the printed figures—Recommended Turbulence
Penetration Speeds.

All routine.

Foster peered at the radar scope, adjusting it now down to the fifty-mile range.

"Storm cells ahead," he said quietly. "Try two degrees left."

Henderson gently turned the yoke. Foster brought the range down to twenty-five miles. The Condor was bucking harder.

"Any holes?" Henderson asked.

The major squinted, frowned and then sighed in an airman's progressive surrender to the inevitable.

"Solid. Not even a sliver. How about climbing above it?"

"God knows how high the sonofabitch is. It isn't supposed to be this high. But we'll try. Albuquerque Center, this is Air Force One."

"Albuquerque Center."

"Our radar shows no path through that squall line. We'd like to climb above it if possible. Any traffic?"

"Negative, Air Force One. You're cleared to climb. Please advise your altitude when you level off."

"Roger. Informatively, we're approaching Winslow and climbing."

The yoke came back, sending hydraulic fluid coursing in a split second through the Condor's tubing toward the tail. The massive elevators moved. The Condor began to climb.

All routine. . . .

The Albuquerque controller was watching the blip. The little white blur seemed to waver, then slid off to the left.

"Al, something's wrong with Air Force One," he called out.

The watch supervisor hurried to the radar set and stared in horror as the target kept skidding toward the edge of the screen.

Faintly, with awful suddenness, like a plaintive cry for help out of the night, there appeared by the rapidly slipping blip the letters "AF-1."

Followed instantly by four figures.

"7700."

The blip went off the scope entirely. The transponder code faded.

"Holy Mother of God," breathed the controller.

"Try to raise him," snapped the watch supervisor.

"Air Force One, this is Albuquerque Center. Do you

read us? Air Force One, we've lost radar contact. Please acknowledge if you read us."

The scanner on the screen swept its three hundred and sixty degrees, probing in vain for a target. It circled three more times before the watch supervisor could force four words out of his constricted throat.

"My God," he whispered. "He's gone."

CHAPTER FOUR

Arthur Klockenheimer, known to his IPS comrades as Klocky, was a man blessed with infinite patience, considerable ability and an understanding wife. All were of immense importance in his job as assistant overnight editor, also known as the graveyard shift or lobster trick on other posts requiring an 11 P.M. to 7 A.M. schedule.

The patience was a weapon against the ire of reporters who swore that the overnight employed a careless butcher knife instead of a deft scalpel on their brilliant prose. As inevitable as the sun rising in the east was the anguished morning bellow from some IPS man: "Jesus Christ, look what the overnight did to my story!"

The required ability meshed neatly with the desired patience. A wire service overnight report is largely concerned with preparing copy for the first editions of afternoon papers. Thus it deals mostly with news of the previous day because news is scarce between midnight and 7 A.M. This, in turn, means the overnight is hard pressed (1) to get a fresh angle on stale news and (2) to try to compose copy that will stand up through part of the current day.

Mr. Klockenheimer's difficulties with both his colleagues and clients were compounded by the IPS overnight desk in New York, which had a psychopathic aversion to any story running over three hundred words. Unfortunately, the IPS overnight copy from Washington was filed first on a private teletype to New York, which relayed it back on the main news wires. This meant that Washington's output ran a daily gantlet through New York's hatchet men, who invariably slashed down to their three-hundred-word yardstick by the simple process of chopping off the bottom paragraphs.

"The stupid chowderheads would cut Shakespeare," Klocky once complained to Damon.

"Shakespeare occasionally deserves to be cut," Damon commented. "Hell, reducing wordage isn't our beef—it's the way New York does the reducing. Not many stories are worth more than three hundred, but I agree with you. Those guys use a ruler instead of a pencil."

Klockenheimer's immediate supervisor was the overnight editor, Frank Jackson, who came in at 5 P.M., quarter-backed the organization of the report, and departed about 1 A.M.—leaving Klocky in charge of the entire overnight staff. This usually consisted of one Roger Melville, a lanky, eager and woefully inexperienced rookie fresh out of Missouri School of Journalism now learning even more under the Klockenheimer School of Journalism.

"Roger will be a great wire service reporter someday," Klocky had explained proudly to Damon. "He's not afraid to wake up a Cabinet officer at 4 A.M. with some asinine query."

Klocky loved the overnight trick. He was a pudgy man in his late forties, with shaggy gray hair. His working hours were generally quiet, with only a fraction of the pressures that afflicted the day and night staffs. His schedule was not exactly conducive to a normal home life, but his wife never complained. She went to bed when he went to work, and was up getting their four children off to school when he came home. While he slept, she did the housework and this gave them most of the late afternoon and early evening hours together. When, on rare occasions, she would mention that he didn't see much of the children, Klocky would remind her that the overnight differential—which earned him an extra fifteen dollars a week—was paying for a helluva lot of life insurance including some educational policies.

"Besides," he added, "I'll live longer than I would if I was working in that day-side boiler factory. Nothing ever happens on the overnight."

Nothing did, usually.

Until this particular heartbeat of history.

When, at precisely 4:38 A.M., EDT, Roger Melville had to put down the sex novel titled *The Wife Swappers* which he had swiped from the copy boys' drawer and answer the phone.

"IPS, Melville."

"This is the White House switchboard. Please stand by for a conference call."

"It's the White House," Roger informed Klockenheimer. "Says they've got a conference call. What's a—"

Melville's question was choked off by the look on Klocky's face as he picked up his own phone. It was a weird conglomeration of concern, anticipation and puzzlement.

"IPS standing by," Klockenheimer said. Then he stared at his youthful assistant and muttered, "The first time I heard a White House conference call, it was the day FDR died. I was just a punk cub. I remember—"

The White House switchboard broke in.

"UPI ready?"

"Ready at UPI," said a voice.

"AP?"

"Here."

"All right, please stand by for Mr. Spellman."

It must be something big, Klockenheimer thought. Newton Spellman was assistant White House press secretary, Phil Sabath's able underling. Spellman's voice invaded the IPS editor's mental roll call of the awesome possibilities, such as a presidential heart attack or maybe even war. He was totally unprepared for what the voice was about to say —or even the voice itself. It was not that of the dapper, mercury-tongued Newt Spellman with his rapier repartee and dry humor. This was the voice of a man slugged groggy by shock, grief and disbelief in something that had to be believed because it was true. It was a hoarse voice, pitched two octaves lower than usual, so much lower that Spellman's New York accent was the only way Klockenheimer could recognize it.

"This is Newt Spellman. I'm going to read a brief announcement. There's no point in asking any questions when I'm finished because this is the only information we have right now. There will be a press conference at the White House at 7 A.M., at which time we hope to have more details. If you're all ready, I'll begin."

Klocky snapped at Melville, "Put on a headset and take this down."

The youngster donned the nearest headset. His long, tapering fingers poised over the typewriter. His own heart was thudding.

"IPS ready."

"UPI all set."

"Ditto AP."

Spellman cleared his throat nervously and coughed twice. The effort seemed to brace him. His voice was more normal as he began to read.

"The White House announced today that Air Force One, the presidential aircraft, disappeared off a radar screen at the Albuquerque Air Traffic Control Center at two thirty-seven this morning, Eastern Daylight Time. All efforts to contact the plane have failed. The last communication advised that the flight was climbing to avoid thunderstorm activity. It's last known position was some forty-five miles east of Winslow, Arizona. A search is underway by Air Force units from nearby bases. Further information will be disclosed as soon as it is available."

Newton Spellman cleared his throat again. "That's the end of the announcement," he added almost apologetically.

"Wait a minute, Newt," UPI broke in. "Do you know his fuel exhaustion time?"

"About an hour from now. The Air Force is computing the exact time. I'll phone you later when I get it. Or maybe you'd all better send someone over."

"That 7 A.M. press conference," Klockenheimer asked. "Who's going to be there besides you?"

"General Coston of the Air Force. Federal Aviation Administrator Bettway. That's all I know of right now."

"Newt," said the AP with typical AP caution, "do you mind if we phone back and verify this conference call? You know—gotta be careful of hoaxes."

"I wish to God," said Newton Spellman slowly and distinctly, his voice cracking just a shade at the end, "that it was a hoax."

Melville tore what he had typed out of the machine and handed it to Klockenheimer. The editor paused only a second before making his command decision.

"The hell with a verification call," he said, turning to the lone operator on duty. He swallowed once, with difficulty, and then spoke the one word that paints goose pimples on the hide of every wire service man, from copy boy to brass. This and what was to follow would go on no private wire to New York. Its five letters would be punched on the A wire's direct keyboard. No time to wait for it to be put

65

into the usual perforated tape that runs through a teletype transmitter at a uniform rate of sixty words a minute. No time to wait with *this* word.

The operator slammed down the small key that broke off a murder trial story coming out of Chicago. He held the key down to make sure the wire was clear. Then he hammered out Klocky's dictation.

FLASH

WASHINGTON—PRESIDENTS PLANE MISSING

"Get Damon and DeVarian on the phone fast," Klocky ordered Melville. His stubby fingers were sprinting over the keys of a typewriter.

Bulletin

Washington (IPS)—The giant jet carrying President Haines to a California vacation disappeared off a radar screen early this morning and all efforts to contact the plane have failed, the White House announced today.

more

Too long, Klocky thought as he handed the bulletin to the operator for transmission on the A wire. The hell with it. Get the facts out first and never mind the fancy stuff. A deadline every minute. That was the wire service creed. Literature under pressure—that was the wire service boast. But the literature would have to come a bit later when they knew more. Right now, facts as fast as possible. And the pitifully few facts were pouring from his typewriter in a torrent of terse, crisp writing.

add plane, washn x x x today

Assistant White House Press Secretary Newton Spellman made the startling disclosure in a conference call to the three wire services. He said the big Amalgamated Condor was being tracked by radar at the Albuquerque Air Traffic Control Center when it suddenly disappeared from the screen shortly after the pilot had radioed he was climbing to avoid a thunderstorm.

The text of Spellman's announcement:

more

"I've got Damon," Melville told Klocky as the latter whipped the add out of his typewriter and handed it to the operator with only a cursory pause for copyreading.

"I can't talk to him now. Just brief him on that announcement. He'll know what to do. Tell him we need manpower but quick."

Melville looked a little hurt at Klocky's unaccustomed abruptness.

"He says he can't talk right now, Mr. Damon. All we know is what I just read you. Klocky says he needs some help."

At the other end of the line, Damon smiled wryly.

"I'll bet he does," he said. "All right, Roger—this is what I want you to do. Call DeVarian at home. Then get hold of Rod Pitcher and—let's see—better check the work schedule and phone whoever's on the day desk later today. Tell 'em all to get down there on the double. Tell Chris Harmon to go directly to the White House—we'll staff State Department with somebody else."

"Gotcha," Melville said.

"Don't hang up. Call Mrs. Strotsky and give her the home phone numbers of every dictationist. Tell her to call them and get their asses down there. Her too. Don't waste time giving anybody a complete newscast. Just supply the gist of what's happened and tell everybody to move. One more thing, when you get our Senate guy—you know, Warner Goldberg—have him go right to Madigan's apartment and stick with the Vice President until further notice. After DeVarian, better call Harmon first, Goldberg second and Pitcher next. Then the rest of the list. Okay?"

"Okay."

"Good boy. Tell Klocky I'm on my way."

Damon hung up. The busty blonde who had been sharing his bed was wide awake, her eyes two big question marks.

"Is it something important, Gunther?"

He looked at her, half regretfully because he was feeling horny again, and half in irritation because she represented a decidedly minor problem in the midst of a major crisis.

"President's plane apparently is down somewhere," he said. "Look, I've got to get to the office. I'll leave you five bucks and you can take a cab home whenever you feel like it. Sorry, Janie, but I don't have time to take you myself."

"Sure, Gunther. I understand." Then she added hopefully, "If you want, I'll come back tonight and cook you supper."

Damon shook his head.

"Janie," he said, "I have a feeling I might not be home for a week."

When the telephone jangled impatiently at Fred Madigan's house, he was dreaming that Hester had slapped Jeremy Haines's face at a Cabinet meeting. It being a dream, he did not challenge her illogical presence at that august assembly. The persistent ringing finally jarred him back to reality.

He stumbled out of bed and groped his way in the darkness toward the hall telephone in their Georgetown apartment. Always considerate of Hester, he remembered to shut the bedroom door and only then did he turn on a light so he could find the phone without crashing over furniture.

"Hello," he muttered sleepily.

"Mr. Vice President, this is Bob Davenport at Secret Service. We've got some bad news."

"Bad news?" Madigan was wide awake instantly.

"Yes, sir. The FAA has just told us Air Force One is overdue. We thought we'd better advise you."

"Overdue?" Madigan asked incredulously. "You mean it's crashed?"

"We don't know yet, sir. There's been no contact with the plane for an hour and we're afraid it's down. They're searching around Winslow, Arizona. The White House asked us to keep you informed."

"This is terrible," Madigan said. "What should I do now?"

"Just stay put, sir. We've got two additional agents on the way over to your apartment."

"Additional agents? What for?"

The Secret Serviceman paused as if he was having trouble disgorging the words, and also in disbelief that the Vice President had asked the question.

"In case . . . in case the President is dead, sir."

Only then did the awful import of the moment dawn on Frederick James Madigan. In the same dawning of truth, there was a flush of abject shame as he recalled wishing for exactly what seemed to have happened. He was not an evil man and even as he thanked Davenport and hung up he said a silent prayer for forgiveness.

The bedroom door opened. Hester stood there, sensing that something had happened and confirming it with one look at her husband's face—taut, gray with shock, frightened.

"Fred? What is it?"

"My God, Hester. They think the President's plane has crashed."

She moved to him and took both his hands in hers. He loved her too much to see through the mask of simulated concern that had dropped over her face. He put his arms around her and hugged her as if the contact would give him strength.

"For God's sake, Hester," he blurted in an instinctive surge of honesty. "I don't want to be President. I'm not fit to be President."

"Nonsense, darling. Just take what comes and do your best. And remember, I'll always be by your side, helping you however I can."

She spoke those lines in a low, dramatic voice that would have sounded artificial on a bad soap opera. But her words penetrated Madigan's befuddled mind with a ring of absolute sincerity, inspiration and comfort. She had said what he wanted to hear, what he had to hear, and in his overpowering gratitude for this lovely, understanding woman it completely escaped him that her eyes were bright, excited.

Command authority passed swiftly from Arthur Klockenheimer to Gunther Damon the moment the news superintendent entered the office.

The room already was crackling with half-suppressed excitement. Pitcher was there, rummaging through the contents of a thick manila file folder marked AIR FORCE ONE —PRESIDENTIAL FLIGHTS. Sam Foley had reported, three hours ahead of his normal schedule. Lynx Grimes, looking slightly disheveled with no make-up and bloodshot eyes (she had been notified an hour and a half after sending a date home), was taking dictation from Chris Harmon at the White House.

Damon felt a throb of sympathy toward Klocky, who glanced wearily up from his mounting mountain of copy and greeted him with a fervent "Thank God, I'm glad you're here."

"Who's dictating?"

"Chris. Fuel exhaustion time will be at two minutes after six. The seven o'clock press conference has been moved from the White House to the FAA auditorium."

"Sam, start doing a new lead based on that fuel exhaustion. We'll bang it out at exactly six-oh-two. Wrap up everything we've got so far. That should hold us until the seven o'clock shindig."

Foley nodded, calm as usual in the middle of crisis. He was the kind of deskman who would remain unperturbed if he was handling a story on his own impending death. Damon walked over to where Pitcher was scribbling notes from the Air Force One file.

"Pitch, we're damned close to fuel exhaustion time. You think there's much hope for that plane?"

"It's down, Gunther. It has to be."

"That's what I'm afraid of. We'll start sounding the voice of doom the second we get the word on the fuel. What the hell are you doing?"

"Looking up some stuff on the history of Air Force One."

"Good idea, Pitch. Bat us out a good sidebar on anything that's ever happened to a presidential plane. We oughta have another on that Condor. Maybe you'd better do that one first."

"I did one when Haines first got the plane. Lemme do the history piece and maybe Roger can rewrite my old Condor stuff. It's right here."

"Okay, I'll give it to Melville. Be sure and include the time when Johnson had that Cuban bomb threat just before a flight—all the security precautions they had to take. This damned thing could turn out to be sabotage."

Pitcher finished transcribing his notes and began to write, beating on the keys with his two forefingers in the fashion of so many newspapermen who never took the time or had the time to learn a touch system. He told of the only previous difficulty encountered by a President on an air trip—Franklin Roosevelt in the old DC-4 newsmen had dubbed the *Sacred Cow*. On a flight during World War II carrying FDR to Malta, the DC-4s wing flaps refused to come down. The plane had to be landed fifty miles an hour faster than normal, with Secret Servicemen bracing themselves around the President and hoping they themselves could survive long enough to carry Roosevelt off the *Cow* if she crashed.

The story went on to recall a routine flight by Lyndon Johnson to a Democratic fund-raising dinner in Miami. It was turned into a nightmare of tension when the FBI relayed to the Secret Service a tip that a Cuban pilot would try to ram or shoot down the presidential jet. The Boeing that normally was used as Air Force One was yanked off the trip and replaced by another 707, without the presidential seal and with all the markings including the aircraft serial number painted out. Fighters flew a protective cover above the transport and the landing was made at Palm Beach instead of the announced destination of Miami. The return trip involved a secret take-off at dawn from Homestead AFB. Possible sabotage, Pitcher added, would be a prime target in any investigation involving a mishap to Air Force One.

Pitcher then went into brief descriptions of the predecessor aircraft used by Presidents. The *Cow* flown by FDR and Truman. Truman's DC-6 christened the *Independence*. Eisenhower's Constellation, the *Columbine*. And N-26000 —the Boeing that had served both Kennedy and Johnson. He also noted that the last plane to be called "Condor" was a twin-engine biplane transport flown by American and Eastern in the late twenties and early thirties. For background purposes, he dwelled heavily on the history of the First Air Force One.

. . . but the *Cow*, oldest, slowest and least plush of any of the presidential planes, was the most unusual. For one thing, it was the first aircraft to be designed and flown for a President of the United States.

Its fuselage number was 78. Its factory serial number was 7471. It entered the Douglas assembly line in Santa Monica, Calif., in October 1943—at first identical to the 77 DC-4s that had preceded it down the assembly line.

But one day that month a classified telegram was flashed to the Douglas plant. Fuselage 78 was removed from the regular assembly line and taken to a heavily guarded area. Workers quickly noticed that an unusual number of inspectors were on hand to watch Fuselage 78 metamorphose into a real airplane.

They also were curious about some unique blueprints which called for installation of a battery-operated elevator in the rear of the plane.

The elevator plus the special furnishings and private stateroom were, of course, expressly designed for President Roosevelt. The elevator was more than an item of convenience. It was the brain child of the Secret Service, which told Douglas that on previous air trips involving conventional planes it had been necessary to construct bulky, no-step ramps to aid the polio-crippled President in deplaning and emplaning.

Such ramps, the Secret Service felt, were a dead giveaway to FDR's presence and in wartime this was intolerable. The elevator would make it not only easy to lift the President from ground to cabin level but would also eliminate the telltale ramps.

On June 12, 1944, AF-7451 officially became a member of the armed forces and also became the first airplane in history to be assigned to the White House. The Army tried valiantly to pin the title of *Flying White House* on AF-7451, but reporters began calling it the *Sacred Cow* and the less-dignified name stuck. . . .

Pitcher wound up with the observation that, "from the *Cow* to the Condor, presidential planes have had one thing in common—they have been the most scrupulously maintained, rigorously inspected and carefully flown aircraft in the world, which makes today's events even more incredible and unbelievable."

The hands on the bureau's big electric wall clock moved inexorably toward forming the vertical line between the 6 and the 12.

A red light at the bottom of the clock glowed, a spot of carmine marking the hour. Sam Foley put a cigarette in his mouth but left it dangling from one corner, unlit.

The light went out. Damon cursed softly, under his breath, and it was more like a prayer.

The second hand crept just past the 12.

Pitcher had just finished typing his concluding lines when both the incredible and the unbelievable became confirmed reality.

The hog-caller tones of Evelyn Strotsky's voice boomed through the office. "Bulletin, White House!"

A dictationist's typewriter began clattering. Damon stood over his shoulder, hand poised ready to tear out the paper the second the youngster finished.

Bulletin
   precede plane

   Washington (IPS)—The White House announced today that the fuel exhaustion time for the President's plane was reached at 6:02 A.M. EDT and the aircraft was presumed down somewhere in rugged Arizona mountain terrain.

more

Damon yanked and in almost the same motion was back sitting in the center slot of the half-moon news desk, stylus pen playing rapid hopscotch over the copy. He crossed out the "more" and handed the bulletin to the operator. In front of him was Foley's new lead, pegged to what Chris Harmon had just phoned. Damon nodded in mute satisfaction at Sam's opening paragraphs, wrote "urgent—A wire" at the top and began feeding the pages—"books" in wire service terminology—to the insatiable printer.

Urgent
   3rd lead plane

   Washington (IPS)—The President's jet disappeared over Arizona today while on a routine vacation flight to Palm Springs, Calif., setting in motion the grimmest, most massive search for a missing aircraft in history.

   The White House announced at 6:02 A.M. EDT that the fuel on the giant Condor, only recently added to the presidential air fleet, had to be exhausted. The last known communication from the plane pinpointed its location at 45 miles east of Winslow, Ariz.

   In that final message, Air Force One reported it was climbing to avoid a thunderstorm area. . . .

"Pitch!" Damon summoned the aviation writer without

looking up from Foley's story. Rod already was standing by the desk, having just handed Klocky his sidebar.

"Right here, Gunther."

"Hop over to FAA and help out with that news conference. Evelyn, break into that White House dictation a minute—I wanna talk to Chris."

Damon's fingers tapped an impatient, nervous tattoo on the desk. His phone rang. "Damon, Chris. As soon as you're finished, catch the conference at FAA. I'm sending Pitch over too. I'll get somebody to the White House as soon as I can—maybe Spartan if he hasn't left town yet on his vacation."

Al Spartan was the second IPS White House reporter. His own overdue vacation, which started the previous day, had been approved when Haines's trip was announced. Nothing is duller than the White House beat when the President is out of town, and Damon had figured on covering the run with one of his smarter if less experienced men.

"You don't have to call Al," Harmon said. "He just walked in. Says he heard the news and you can give him his vacation later."

"Tell him thanks—and there'll be a few days added on, compliments of IPS," Damon said gratefully. This, he thought, was so damned typical of most of his staff. They griped, bitched, complained, moaned and cussed at IPS' parsimonious policies. At being outnumbered by AP and UPI most of the time, one IPS man being expected to compete successfully against two UPI and four or five AP reporters. But when a major story broke, they were like old firemen smelling smoke, wading into the coverage with the esprit de corps of a gang of Marines. At this moment, he was sentimentally proud of his troops and then the fleeting wisp of sentiment evaporated under the heat of what had to be done.

"Evelyn—has Goldberg checked in at Madigan's yet? Goddammit, did he walk over there? Put him on as soon as he calls."

The newsroom was filling up. Mobilization, wire service version. The teletypes never paused in their incessant pounding, beating out their uneven yet peculiarly rhythmic cadence with the cacophony of tribal drums.

A copy boy brought Damon a message off the C wire, a

74

private teletype line between the Washington and New York bureaus.

GD/WA
   FYI U BROKE TWO MINS AHED AP BUT ONE BEHIND UPI ON FLASH. POUR IT ON.

                                                    JT/NY

"JT" stood for Jules Tamborello, the New York overnight chief. Damon was used to New York's habit of sending unnecessary pep talks when all hell was breaking loose. He was trying to decide whether this one required a polite or a nasty answer when the operator manning the B wire tore off a message from Little Rock and handed it to him without comment, a faint smile of anticipation on his face. He was rewarded instantly as Damon scanned the message.

WA
   CLIENT ASKS GOOD COVERAGE SMORNING CAB HEARING ON PROPOSED NEW AIR SERVICE TO VARIOUS COMMUNITIES IN EASTERN ARKANSAS.

                                                    LR

Gunther Damon uttered, with exquisite emphasis and justifiable exasperation, that one word of profanity reserved for certain people, occasions and situations.

By coincidence, Rod Pitcher and Chris Harmon arrived in separate cabs at the Federal Aviation Administration Building almost simultaneously. It was a pleasant surprise for Harmon, who had never been inside the FAA. Like most reporters overly used to their own beats, walking into a strange government agency was the equivalent of entering a foreign country for the first time.

The IPS State Department staffer had the build and facial characteristics of Walter Pidgeon and the operating techniques of a New York City homicide detective. The combination came in handy at State, where dignity and digging were twin requisites. He could be and often was mistaken for an ambassador at some diplomatic function. He also had enough tipsters, blabby officials and outright stool pigeons scattered throughout the department and diplomatic corps to keep the DOS press officers in a constant state of confusion. When Harmon quoted some "high diplomatic official," his source could range from the Secretary of State to a minor attaché at the Luxembourg Embassy.

"Where's the conference?" he asked Pitcher.

"Auditorium on the third floor."

"Why are they holding this at FAA?" Harmon wondered as they entered the building, showed their press credentials to a guard and headed for the elevators to the right of the marble reception desk.

"It's an aviation story mostly, I suppose. At least at this stage. And this auditorium will hold quite a mob—which I expect they'll get."

There *was* quite a mob even at this hour of six thirty-five. The two hundred and ten blue-upholstered seats were filling up except for the last two rows. The aisles were littered with cables and cameras of the television networks, their crews jostling impatiently for the most advantageous positions and occasionally glaring at newsreel and wire service still cameramen trying for the same positions.

"Grab us a couple of seats," Pitcher said. "I'll go find Charlie Alexander and make sure we've got a phone staked out."

"Who's Alexander?"

"He runs FAA's Public Affairs Office. It's just down the hall. I'll be right back."

Pitcher found Alexander in his office. The balding FAA official wore the twin badges of a man who had been summoned to work too early—sleepy, slightly bloodshot eyes and a Band-Aid on his chin from a hasty shave.

"Morning, Pitch. And before you open your mouth, you can use my secretary's phone—it's already got a 'reserved for IPS' sign on it."

"Thanks, Charlie. Looks like a bitch, doesn't it? Got anything new?"

"You know as much as I do. We'll hand out a transcript of the ground-air communications at the press conference but there isn't a damned clue in it."

"Except that he was going into thunderstorms," Pitcher suggested.

"I can't imagine a thunderstorm bothering either that crew or that plane," Alexander replied.

"Who'll be at the conference?"

"General Coston, the Air Force Chief of Staff. Bettway, of course. Secretary Brubaker—"

"Brubaker? He wouldn't know a Condor from a Piper."

Alexander grunted with the resignation of a man who has bowed to an unpleasant inevitability.

"You said it, I didn't," the FAA man growled. Alexander privately shared the press corps's opinion of this particular Cabinet officer. Harvey Brubaker was an expert on urban transportation problems and, unlike his predecessor, paid only lip service to the problems of aviation except when they involved ground transportation.

"Will Brubaker be running the show?"

"Bettway'll preside. I suppose the Secretary will get into the act somehow."

Pitcher laughed. "Disloyalty becomes you, Charlie—in this case."

Alexander shook his head sadly. "Just between the two of us, Pitch, the people I hate worst in this town are congressmen who open their fat yaps on subjects they know nothing about, and Uncle Harvey, who also fits that description. I guess we'd better get to the bloodletting."

Pitcher found that Harmon somehow had grabbed a couple of seats near the front. He sat down, whispering, "Phone's staked out—there's an IPS sign on it."

"Fine. If anyone says anything worth a bulletin, why don't you run with it and I'll backstop you here."

Pitcher nodded. The principals in the press conference drama were filing onto the small stage facing the auditorium seats. Charlie Alexander stepped to the podium and adjusted the PA microphone in front of him to his own height.

"Gentlemen, may I have your attention, please?"

The noisy room quieted gradually like a school class coming reluctantly to order at the command of the teacher.

"Gentlemen—and ladies—I'm Charles Alexander of the Federal Aviation Administration's Public Affairs Office. You all know why you're here so I won't waste time on preliminaries. I'd like to introduce the men up here with me. Mr. Harvey Brubaker, the Secetary of Transportation. General Robert D. Coston, Chief of Staff, United States Air Force. Mr. Newton Spellman, Assistant Press Secretary, White House. And now I'll turn this conference over to Mr. Frank Bettway, Administrator of the FAA."

Bettway was a small man with a gamin face, its pixielike

qualities rescued from what seemed to be an easygoing personality by his pale blue eyes. They glinted from behind his square-cut glasses, and it was said around the FAA that one cold stare from those eyes could dismantle an erring employee with the swiftness of a lie detector demolishing an alibi.

"I'll begin by briefing you on what is known as of 6:45 A.M.," Bettway started out. "The transcript of communications between Air Force One and its last ground contact, the Albuquerque Center, is still going through the mimeograph machines. Copies will be handed out at the conclusion of the press conference. I can tell you now, however, that there was definite evidence the aircraft encountered some kind of serious emergency."

The room stirred with visible interest and tension.

"First, there was the abnormality of lost radar contact. The target blip, as we call it, moved off the radar screen until it disappeared entirely. Second, while the communications were normal and gave no hint of trouble, Air Force One did send an emergency message just before the Center lost contact."

Now the auditorium was gelatin-silent.

"There appeared on the radar screen, just before the target slipped off the scope, the letters 'AF-1,' followed by the numerals '7700.' For those of you unfamiliar with the transponder systems used in Air Traffic Control, most aircraft today are equipped with transponders. These intercept a radio beam aimed from ground radar stations at target planes. The beam is bounced back to radar after picking up an automatic identification code which identifies the aircraft and also transmits its altitude.

"In the case of a scheduled airliner, the code transmits the assigned flight number along with the current altitude. In the case of the President's plane, the designation 'Air Force One' would show on the radar screen. Transponder identification is accomplished by the simple process of the pilot pressing his transponder button upon request by Air Traffic Control.

"However, in addition to the codes for flight numbers, every airborne transponder incorporates an emergency signal in the event a pilot cannot transmit through normal radio channels. That signal is seven-seven-zero-zero, which was the last thing we received from Air Force One. Its significance, the nature of the emergency encountered, the reason why the commander of Air Force One felt it necessary to send the code, all are unknown at this time.

"As you will see from the transcript, the only possible hint of potential difficulty was the pilot's request to climb from his assigned altitude of forty-three thousand feet to avoid thunderstorm activity in his path. That request was granted instantly. The last verbal communication from Air Force One, prior to the emergency code signal, was that the aircraft was approaching Winslow, Arizona, and climbing.

"I will now throw open this meeting to questions."

Pitcher glanced hastily at where the AP and UPI men were sitting and cursed softly. Two of them already were heading toward the rear of the auditorium, notebooks in hand like swords carried by charging soldiers. He hated to leave the press conference at this point but that disclosure on the emergency signal was hot.

"They're running with that transponder stuff," he said to Harmon. "I'd better phone in a bulletin."

"Go ahead," Chris replied. "I'll catch this till you get back."

Pitcher was racing out the door as the first question came from a New York *Times* man.

"Mr. Bettway, could you give us any details on what's being done to find the plane?"

"I'll turn that question over to General Coston," the FAA chief replied. "General?"

Coston had achieved what apparently lies in the exclusive province of doctors, high-ranking military officers and airline stewardesses—the ability to look wide awake and freshly scrubbed with virtually no sleep the night before. A stocky man with a florid complexion, white hair and the usual kaleidoscope of campaign ribbons below his silver wings, he rose and somehow managed to march rather than walk to the podium.

"I think it's safe to call this the most intensive search and rescue mission on record," he began in a surprisingly soft voice.

"The search primarily is under the direction of the Air Rescue Service of USAF, which administratively is assigned to the Military Air Transport Service. Aircraft from three ARS groups are at this moment being deployed from Air Force bases at Ellington, Texas; Lowry at

Denver, and from Hamilton, California. Assisting in the air search activities are planes from the following Air Force installations—Luke, Williams, Nellis, Edwards and Holloman.

"Also being utilized are aircraft from the Naval Air Station in San Diego. The search mission is under the overall command of the Hamilton ARS unit, with field headquarters established in Winslow. Approximately seventy-five helicopters are engaged in the operation, but fixed-wing aircraft are being used as well. I would say that the total number of military aircraft involved is about two hundred. These do not include Civil Air Patrol planes from CAP units in Southern California, Arizona, New Mexico and Nevada. The latter, plus equipment from the Forest Service, add up to at least another hundred aircraft."

"How about ground search, General?" asked the Washington *Evening Star*.

"These are almost too numerous to tally. State police, local police and sheriff units from Arizona, California, New Mexico and Nevada. The Army is sending all available mobile ground forces into a hundred-square-mile area approximating Air Force One's last reported position. I was informed just before arriving at the FAA that the Army units alone will approach more than ten thousand men with approximately five hundred vehicles, including half-tracks capable of moving over pretty rough country. Both air and ground units, I might add, are carrying special communications and survival equipment, along with complete medical facilities. Every helicopter, for example, has medical supplies aboard and personnel trained in first aid."

A UPI reporter asked, "Can you tell us anything about the terrain where the plane might have gone down?"

"Rugged," said General Coston with devastating simplicity.

"Does that mean a forced or emergency landing would have been impossible?" the Washington *Post* wanted to know.

"No. There are many areas where an emergency landing might have been made, just as there are areas where no such landing would be possible."

"Would you say that the lack of any communication from Air Force One since fuel exhaustion time eliminates the possibility of an emergency landing?" the *Post* pressed.

"It reduces the possibility," Coston said dryly.

The press paused to digest that remark.

"General," said the AP, "do you think the plane has crashed?"

Coston put his words on a delicate scale of military caution before answering.

"Naturally, we have not and will not give up hope that the President and all aboard have survived but that, for many reasons, have been unable to communicate their, uh, circumstances."

"In other words," the AP man snapped, "it has crashed."

The general stared at the reporter as if wishing he could file insubordination charges.

"That Air Force One has crashed is a very unhappy possibility," he said finally. "But this does not mean there is no hope of finding survivors. All crashes are not fatal. Weighing in favor of optimism are such factors as the skill of the crew, the structural strength of the aircraft with its many safety features . . . I believe the chances of finding the President and his party alive are at least as great as finding, uh, some fatalities."

Pencils and pens scribbled away frantically in a couple of hundred notebooks.

The New York *Times* again. "General, wasn't Air Force One equipped with a crash locator beacon? I'm referring to that device which I understand can be ejected from a plane in trouble, and that it automatically sends a locating signal."

"Affirmative. There is such equipment on Air Force One, as well as on many of our planes. It is catapulted from the rear of the aircraft either manually or automatically on impact."

"I take it," the *Times* said, "that no such signals were sent this time or the plane would have been located by now."

"That's a pretty good assumption," Coston conceded.

"Could I ask why?"

"You can ask, but I can't give you a definite answer. The beacon hasn't always worked as well as we hoped. Most of its failures have been traced to severe impact damage which prevented catapulting and did not permit the sequence of transmitting operations to get started. Manual activation, of course, would depend on the condition of the flight crew."

"I'd like to ask Mr. Bettway," said a reporter from the

Kansas City *Star*'s Washington bureau, "if the FBI has been called into this business."

"Yes," Bettway said. "Or at least the FBI has been notified and presumably is ready to enter any subsequent investigation if necessary. I forgot to mention, by the way, that I have just received a call from John Taylor, the president of the Air Transport Association, who advised me that telegrams have gone out to all scheduled carriers asking their flight crews to be on the lookout while flying over the route followed by Air Force One."

Chris Harmon caught Bettway's attention by waving his hand.

"If the plane has crashed, what agencies or agency would be in charge of the investigation?" Harmon inquired.

"I'd like to answer that," General Coston said quickly. "All presidential aircraft are assigned to the Air Force, including the Condor. So the Air Force would have investigative jurisdiction over any accident or serious incident. But the Air Force would welcome the assistance of the Department of Transportation's air safety experts."

Secretary Brubaker, sitting rather forlornly off to one side, lunged at this remark with the eagerness of an actor picking up a cue for his only line on an opening night. He quickly stepped forward to the bank of microphones.

"Speaking for the Department of Transportation, gentlemen," he said with a smile totally out of focus with the occasion, "I can assure the Air Force of our complete cooperation. As you know, when the Department was organized during the Johnson Administration, the CAB's very able Bureau of Safety became part of the DOT's National Safety Board. The Bureau stands ready and willing to offer the Air Force all possible aid. However, speaking for myself as a member of President Haines's Cabinet, I have not despaired of our leader's safety."

Brubaker hesitated, as if he wanted to say more now that he had the center of the stage, but he could almost feel Bettway's steely eyes boring twin holes in his back. He sat down, sublimely confident that he had given his boys some juicy quotes.

His boys got back to Bettway and the general with alacrity, having dismissed Brubaker's juicy quotes as an unwelcome interruption. Pitcher and his two competitors sailed back into the auditorium at this point, drawing sympathetic glances from colleagues who didn't have to match wire service demands for speed.

"Did I miss anything?" Rod asked Harmon.

"Not much. A halfway admission that it's probably crashed—which is fairly obvious. If nobody else heads for a phone, I'll hold up until this is over."

Nobody was heading for phones at this point. A UPI reporter raised his hand.

"General Coston, could you speculate on what might have caused the emergency that prompted that . . . that transponder signal?"

"No, sir, I can't. It's too early for any speculation. We haven't even found the plane yet."

This prompted a question from Pitcher.

"General, the only possible clue is the report that Air Force One was climbing to avoid thunderstorms. Would you care to comment on the stability of the Amalgamated Condor in severe turbulence?"

Coston stared suspiciously at Pitcher. His reply was made with tiptoeing care.

"The aircraft was thoroughly tested and met or surpassed all military and civil airworthiness requirements for the transport category," the general replied. "I might add that Colonel Henderson, the command pilot of Air Force One, was exceptionally skilled as well as exceptionally cautious."

The Los Angeles *Times* representative managed to raise his voice above a volley of voices. "General, will the Pentagon be the chief source for further developments or will future announcements come out of FAA or the White House?"

This prompted a brief huddle, from which Newt Spellman emerged to call the signals. "To facilitate your own work and keep all information flowing from a single, readily available source, it has been decided that the White House will make all future announcements," Spellman said.

Brubaker looked disappointed. Alexander whispered something to Bettway and the FAA chief nodded, grabbing a microphone stem.

"I'm informed that the copies of the communications transcript are ready for distribution at the door, together with biographies of the Air Force One crew and the passenger list, if any of you haven't obtained the latter material. Frankly, General Coston would like to get back to work and so, I suspect, would all of us. I'll entertain one more question. You, sir."

It was a Chicago *Tribune* reporter. "General, is there anything you haven't told us yet which might indicate the possibility of sabotage?"

"Nothing whatsoever. When the, ah, plane"—he nearly said "wreckage"—"is found, all possibilities that might have contributed to the emergency will be considered. Sabotage naturally will be included."

Several reporters clamored for attention, but Bettway, Coston and Spellman broke up the press conference by the simple expedient of leaving the platform and ignoring questions hurled at them as they moved up the aisle. Brubaker trailed behind them and actually succeeded in easing their departure by stopping to answer some of the nearest questioners. By the time they realized he had nothing new to offer, the trio had escaped.

Pitcher and Harmon hurried to their staked-out phone. En route, Chris asked what prompted the question on the Condor's stability.

"Just something I heard from a couple of airline pilots," Pitcher explained. "They told me they wouldn't fly that plane from Newark to Kennedy in a bad thunderstorm."

CHAPTER FIVE

Early Tuesday morning, Frederick Madigan was riding to his office in the Executive Office Building adjoining the White House, that ancient architectural monstrosity which had once housed the State Department within its walls of gingerbread stone.

As the Vice President, he always was accompanied by a Secret Service agent but now he was enormously self-conscious at the presence of no less than three in the limousine. Two sat on either side of him and the third was in front with the chauffeur.

Madigan thought he saw the outline of a gun under the suit jacket of the agent on his left and he actually thrilled to the import of these silent men, their lives pledged to his safety and protection. He also was enormously flattered and not a little excited, emotions which prompted renewed twinges of guilt but which were still not quite strong enough to quell the excitement.

He hoped the agents did not notice this inner tug of war between conscience and the delicious anticipation of a politician about to take stage center. For the time being, anyway, Hester had effectively eliminated his doubts and fears. Right now, he wanted to be President of the United States.

For a moment he considered asking the agents if they minded his stopping off at a church so he could say a prayer for the President's safety. That also should impress the reporters who had interviewed him briefly at his apartment and were now following him to his office in taxis. There were a couple of photographers in that group, too. . . .

No, Madigan decided. It was bad enough to feel no real sorrow for what had happened, to put on an act of phony concern, without adding sacrilege on top of those sins. But he was not about to abandon the phony act, either, so he dropped a mask of unadulterated sorrow over his face for the benefit of the agent to his right and murmured, "I cannot believe it. I just cannot believe it."

"No, sir, neither can I," the agent said, accomplishing a masterpiece of double-entendre that fortunately went over the Vice President's head.

Madigan's first deed on arriving at his office was in the category of political diplomacy. He called Bertrand Haines's office to express his concern, grief and unyielding confidence that the senator's brother was safe. Only Bert Haines was not in.

"I'm sorry, Mr. Vice President," the senator's secretary informed him, "but Senator Haines left on a plane last night for a fishing trip in Maine. We're trying to locate him now but you know the senator and his fishing—as usual, he wouldn't tell anybody exactly where he could be reached."

"I just wanted to pay my respects and tell him I'm praying for the President's well-being," Madigan said. "If Mrs. Haines calls, please tell her my thoughts are with the family."

He hung up. Nothing more to do except wait. He would have to preside over the Senate at noon—a chore he detested and dreaded—but that was several hours away. Oscar Bartrum, the administrative assistant, popped his head in to announce that the outer office was filled with reporters.

"Tell 'em I'll be out as soon as I finish talking to the White House," Madigan said, wishing at the same time that the White House would call him. Well, it wouldn't hurt to ask Newt Spellman if there was any news of the plane. He dialed the Executive Mansion himself and was told Mr. Spellman's line was busy, with four other calls on hold.

"This is the Vice President," he said in a tone he hoped was authoritative without being too demanding. "Tell Mr. Spellman I'd appreciate his phoning me as soon as possible."

"Yes, sir, I'll put your message ahead of the other calls."

"Thank you." He had time only to light a cigarette when the harassed Spellman returned his call.

"Just wanted to know if you've heard anything yet," Madigan said. "Nothing new? Well, this is a terrible blow to all of us. You know how I must feel, my boy—it's like sitting on a keg of dynamite. Thank you, Newt. I appreciate those words more than I can say. And I would be grateful if you'd keep me advised. Good-by."

The suspense, thought Madigan, was torture. No sir, nothing to do but wait and—he figured he'd tell the reporters—pray. Wait and pray, that should be a good line. He had enough objectivity left in him to wonder wryly if any of them would remember that story about the ailing President Woodrow Wilson and the Senate delegation that came to visit him, headed by Wilson's mortal enemy, Henry Cabot Lodge.

"Mr. President, the Senate is praying for you," Lodge was supposed to have said.

"Which way?" Wilson asked.

Which way was he praying for Jeremy Haines? Madigan asked himself. Again, a few dregs of decency still were in his coffee grounds of conscience that stubbornly refused to be rinsed out of the cup. What kind of a monster was he, wishing for the death of a nation's leader? A man the people had chosen for the presidency. What demon of desire could turn a well-meaning, God-fearing Christian like Fred Madigan into a putrid glob of uncontrollable ambition? Did he really hate Haines that much? Or was it simply the lure of power and prestige and a place in history that only death could bequeath him? A prize that had to be inherited because Frederick James Madigan knew he never could earn it on his own. Yes, he hated himself for his dirty dreams, but he could not prevent the dreaming. And there was Hester. She would be *so* proud. . . .

So what if he wasn't an intellectual giant? Neither was Harry Truman, and he turned out to be one hell of a President. That's whom he would model himself after. The Average American thrust suddenly into Greatness. Rising above his limited capabilities by the very challenge of the nation's needs in a time of crisis. Humble as Truman had been, yet strong and assertive. Truman had said something about feeling that the whole world, the sun, the moon and the stars had fallen on him when Roosevelt died. Yet he had shown guts from the moment he took office. The Hiroshima decision. The way he stood up to Stalin and wouldn't back down in Korea. The typical Little Man transformed into a giant by Fate.

President Madigan. "Mr. President." Hell, it didn't sound so unreal, so impossible, so ridiculous, after all.

Fred Madigan mentally began to compose what he would say to the press when the word came from somewhere in Arizona.

Only there was no word from Arizona.

The ubiquitous helicopters growled their noisy treks across the baked and barren desert, rotor blades lifting sand and dust and tumbleweed into tiny whirlpools. The choppers poked inquisitively and hopefully into gulches and canyons. They hovered expectantly over mountaintops and their crews peered into dingy scrub foliage and thick forests alike until eyeballs ached.

Overhead, the armada of higher-flying search planes criss-crossed the skies in a prearranged grid pattern, looking mostly for the telltale glint of sunlight on metal. The helicopters and the small Civil Air Patrol planes, more efficient in a "low and slow" mission of search, had the best chance of finding Air Force One. That they were having difficulties was not surprising. Aircraft have remained missing for so long that, when wreckage finally was found, the occupants were skeletons. And the Arizona landscape includes virtually every variation of terrain capable of swallowing up the evidence of an accident.

Tuesday, the first day of search, produced nothing. Madigan stayed in his old office after a brief session at the Senate, torn between flashes of anxiety that the worst had happened and a private admission that the worst was what he secretly wanted. By the end of the day he was willing to settle for an end to the suspense no matter what the end involved. His phone rang incessantly, the calls ranging from expressions of sympathy to inquiries on what the Vice President *really* knew about the missing plane. The latter pleased him because it was nice to think that some people assumed he was on the inside of all developments, but they also bothered him because he realized he didn't know any more than his callers. It renewed his old feeling of inferiority.

An army of reporters descended on search headquarters in Winslow, clamoring for news that was pitifully unavailable. One fact they were not given was a classified order by the Joint Chiefs of Staff placing the Strategic Air Command on a war alert. At a score of hidden underground installations, grim-faced technicians stood by their deadly ICBMs and prepared to push their buttons of death. They could take no chances, nervously aware that the President's plane might have been shot down or sabotaged as an opening salvo for World War III.

Editorials and official reactions from around the world took on the semblance of a mass prayer for Jeremy Haines's safety. Only Peking and Moscow remained silent and this fed the rumors, nourished the jitters and ballooned the fears of the stunned nation.

For the news of Air Force One had flared against a backdrop of blackening world tensions. If the average American felt like invoking God's help for his President, he also was inclined to beseech deliverance from whatever evil force might have forged his President's peril. The world held its collective breath, but the United States had its collective fingers crossed. The possibility of catastrophic tragedy was shocking by itself, but adding suspicion and fear to sorrow was enough to fray the nerves of a panic-susceptible public.

The stock market, so sensitive to anything as minor as a presidential head cold, skidded in the worst downward spiral since 1929.

A reporter at search headquarters heard from what he later termed "responsible sources" that the Air Force had found the wreckage but was sitting on any announcement because mysterious, unexplainable marks were on the metal. He had picked this up from an off-duty airman in a Winslow bar and, frustrated by the lack of hard news and fortified by a couple of drinks himself, he filed a story. The result was a wave of flying saucer reports and a demand by the American Committee for Truth about UFOs that the government admit Air Force One had collided with a spacecraft from another planet.

There still was optimism as the first day of search ended, although the optimism was of the whistling-by-the-graveyard variety. But on the morning of the second day the headlines began to sag into such banners as HOPE FADES FOR PRESIDENT. The stock market continued its nose dive and Frederick James Madigan mentally continued to rehearse what he would say to the press after he was sworn in.

The search itself gave Stan DeVarian and Gunther Damon a chance to regroup their bleary-eyed forces. The White House now had to be staffed twenty-four hours a day and Damon, over DeVarian's mild objection, had insisted on assigning a man to stay outside Vice President Madigan's office or apartment at all times.

"We can get somebody there in a hurry when the plane's found," DeVarian pointed out. "My God, Gunther, by the time this is finished our overtime will look like the national debt."

"In a hurry won't be fast enough, Stan. Every additional minute that plane's missing adds up to a new President. He'd be sworn in immediately—and it could be at four o'clock in the morning. The story's in Arizona right now, but the second they find that plane it'll move right back here. Which reminds me, let's get Jonesy back to the White House. We've got plenty of manpower covering the search. Half the LA bureau and the whole Phoenix bureau."

"I suppose you're right," DeVarian agreed. "But Jonesy might balk. I talked to him last night—he called me from Winslow."

"Balk? For Christ's sake, why?"

"It was his idea to go from Palm Springs to search headquarters. When I asked him if he didn't think he should come home, he said he wanted to stay there until they found the plane. Then he started to cry, Gunther. So help me, he was crying like a baby."

"It figures. He went to pieces right after Kennedy's funeral—remember? And he thinks a helluva lot of Haines. Or should I say thought? But, dammit, a White House reporter stays with the President. And that very shortly will be, God help us all, Frederick J. Madigan. Not Jeremy Franklin Haines. So our Mr. Jones belongs right here, not out in the middle of a desert looking for his hero."

"I agree with your king-is-dead, long-live-the-king concept," DeVarian said softly. "But Jonesy's a very sensitive, emotional guy. Let him stay in Winslow, Gunther."

Damon spat out a four-letter expletive and then relented. "Okay, I'll let sentiment conquer my better judgment. He won't be in Winslow very long anyway. They oughta find that plane any time now. It has to be *somewhere*."

The Vice President was thinking that, too, as the hours of futile search stretched into the second day. And so were the three men sitting in his pine-paneled inner office, richly furnished with huge leather easy chairs and a small but thoroughly equipped bar. This private sanctum and the use of a limousine were the two items Madigan liked most about being Vice President.

His just-arrived, early morning visitors were Wayne Verdi, the House Speaker; Matt Parrish, the Senate majority leader, and the Chief Justice of the United States Supreme Court, the Honorable Harrington Van Dyke. It was 7:30 A.M., an hour which underlined the urgency of their meeting.

Parrish got right to the point. He was a man with a pipe-cleaner frame, a cadaverous face and an enormous shock of untamed sandy hair that gave him the general appearance of an animated floor mop. The press gallery considered him the greatest compromiser since Henry Clay, a genius at legislative wheeling and dealing. He did the Administration's dirty work on the Senate side, scrounging votes with techniques that ranged from blackjack viciousness to powder-puff flattery. Ironically, he had never felt real warmth toward a President who was his intellectual and political equal, but he had always been fond of Fred Madigan, who was neither. He had asked Madigan for this meeting because he was convinced Haines must be dead, and he was anxious to have the Vice President fully prepared for what was to come. Wisely, he suspected that the thrill of assuming the presidency had blocked any comprehension of its consequences.

"Fred, we've got to face some unpleasant facts," Parrish said in his rather unpleasant, rasping voice. "The President must be dead. At any second, you could be sworn in. That's why we've got to do some advance planning."

"We may be burying him a bit prematurely," Madigan said. "There's always a chance, Matt. . . ."

"Baloney. That plane couldn't have been lost this long without the worst happening. Wayne agrees with me and so does the Chief Justice. We've got to get moving."

The Chief Justice nodded ponderously. Harrington Van Dyke was the kind of man who must have carried himself with dignity at the age of five. As John Foster Dulles years ago had prepared himself for the day he would become Secretary of State, so had Van Dyke consciously and deliberately prepared himself for the nation's highest judicial post. The Supreme Court had been his goal the day he decided to become a lawyer.

"Matt's right, my friend," Van Dyke said in a deep, resonant voice that could have emerged from an organ. "The next time that telephone on your desk rings, it might be my duty to administer the oath."

Madigan said nothing. His brown eyes blinked, with just a trace of moisture.

"And those are my sentiments, Fred," said the Speaker, a small man whose Cyrano nose dominated a face that would have been totally homely except for Verdi's eyes—deep-set and doelike. "I just hope you're emotionally and psychologically prepared to take over. There will be a joint session of Congress within twenty-four hours. You'll have to hold a press conference immediately. You should be at the Pentagon or the State Department right now getting briefed; I doubt if Haines has ever taken you into his complete confidence, has he?"

Madigan shook his head.

"Well, that's the more reason why you should start preparing yourself."

The Vice President finally propelled some words out of his mouth. "I still think we're being premature. I just finished talking to Newt Spellman and—"

"He's heard something?" Parrish asked quickly.

"No. About forty or fifty false alarms. I guess some of the search planes are seeing wreckage when they spot a jack rabbit."

"Then we—"

"Wait a minute," Madigan interrupted the majority leader. "Spellman told me something I never knew before. Something we've got to consider even if they find that plane with no survivors."

"Like what?" said Verdi.

"It carried one parachute—for the President to use if jumping was the only way to save his life."

The three men stared at the Vice President as their minds digested this revelation.

"My God," Parrish said. "Haines may be wandering around somewhere in the middle of Arizona, miles from civilization. He could be lost for days or even weeks."

"You gentlemen are forgetting one thing," Van Dyke interjected. "When they find the plane, all they have to do is count the bodies and identify them. It will be easy to ascertain if the President used the parachute."

"Provided," Verdi said, "that the bodies aren't burned beyond recognition. Nevertheless, Fred, the finding of the plane should remove most of the uncertainty. Your course, barring unforeseen developments, still is plain."

"Still except for that one little unforeseen possibility," Madigan said.

"And that is?"

"Suppose he did use the parachute."

Captain Kelly Ormsbee of Midwest Airlines always bid the Los Angeles–Washington run for an entirely non-aeronautical reason.

He was an avid student of history, and he never could get enough of the nation's capital and its sightseeing bargain basements. The flight he usually commanded left Los Angeles at 9 A.M. California time, arrived in Washington at 4:30 P.M., and the return trip didn't leave Dulles until five the next afternoon.

This always gave Ormsbee almost an entire day to prowl around the city. He had visited the Smithsonian no less than eighteen times and Mount Vernon twelve. He had seen Congress in session, attended committee hearings, watched the Supreme Court at work, and thanks to a newspaperman whom he had known in college, he even got in to see a presidential news conference.

He did not confine his interests to political history, either. He was a walking encyclopedia on the Indian wars and any flight taking him over Arizona featured brief cabin PA lectures on the Apache nation that had once ruled the land flashing under their wings. He was as familiar with such Apache chiefs as Mangas Coloradas, Victorio, Cochise, Geronimo and Chato as he was with the lives of American Presidents. In fact, on this sunny Wednesday morning, he was letting First Officer Bill Culbert fly the Los Angeles–Albuquerque leg so he could deliver one of his discourses on the greatness of the Apache tribe, with its courage and fierce pride. Plus the belief it might take his passengers' minds off the Air Force One story.

"The present Fort Apache Indian Reservation is a few miles to the south," he was telling the passengers. "Unfortunately we're on jet route J78, which runs a bit too far to the north for us to see the reservation area. On the right side of our aircraft, however, are the famous Pink Cliffs of Arizona . . ."

Culbert, who in spite of himself always got interested in what his captain was saying, instinctively glanced out the cockpit window on his side as if he were one of the curious passengers. In that second of automatic reflex, just before he turned back to his controls, his eyes caught a glint of metal far below.

"Kelly, I just saw something. Sunlight on metal, I think."

"Turn her a bit. Maybe I can spot it."

The 707 banked. Ormsbee shook his head. "Whatever it was, I missed it."

"Maybe we'd better take another look, Kelly. When we left LA, they still hadn't found that plane yet. Maybe . . .'"

"Hell, it could be anything. A tin roof on a farm shack for all we know. But I'm not taking any chances. We on the Albuquerque Center frequency?"

"All tuned."

"Albuquerque Center, this is Midwest 74. We've spotted what looks like reflected metal. We're twenty miles east of Winslow on J78. Request permission to go down and take a closer peek."

"Midwest 74. There is no traffic below you. You are cleared to descend. Squawk ident for your present altitude, please."

"Identing."

"Okay, Midwest 74. Keep us advised, will you?"

"Will do. Seventy-four out. Take her down, Bill. I'll tell our customers what's happening."

Culbert put the 707 into a steep, descending turn as Ormsbee pressed the PA mike button.

"Folks, don't be alarmed at this turn and our descent. We've sighted something that may be a piece of aluminum below us. As you know, the President's plane is still missing and, just to make sure, we're going down to take a closer look. This may delay our flight a few minutes but I'm sure you understand the importance. We'll keep you posted. Thank you."

The descent from twenty-eight thousand feet was not abnormally fast, but Ormsbee told the flight engineer to reduce cabin pressure slightly so the passengers would feel no discomfort. "I'll give you thirty degrees flap," the captain said to Culbert.

They found nothing on the first pass, screaming over the Pink Cliffs at three thousand feet from east to west. Culbert was disappointed and embarrassed. If his eyes had played tricks on him, this little excursion would cost the airline about seven hundred dollars in extra fuel consumption.

"I could have sworn I saw something Kelly. I'm sorry."

"Don't give up. Let's make a pass from west to east. Maybe we can pick up that same shaft of sunlight. If it is the plane, it must be buried under God knows what or the search planes would have seen it by now. You might have caught the reflection at just the right angle at just the right minute. You look and I'll fly. Give me full flaps after we make our turn."

They completed a one-eighty and swept over the jagged terrain, wild and primitive in its unsullied beauty. Two thousand feet, now. Ormsbee closed the throttles until the air speed dropped to only one hundred and fifty-five knots. The 707 literally was crawling now.

"There it is!" Culbert's voice was almost a shriek.

"Yeah, I saw that flash of light. We'll go around again. Did you see anything resembling an airplane?"

"Negative. Just the reflection."

On the next pass they found more than the reflection. At the foot of a cliff, impaled about halfway down a clump of tall, thick trees, was a large chunk of aluminum. They had to make two more passes before they got a good enough glimpse for Ormsbee to give Albuquerque the word.

"Albuquerque Center, this is Midwest 74. We may have something. It appears to be a fairly large chunk of a horizontal stabilizer. Off a T-tail, too. Should we stick around?"

"Midwest 74, any sign of other wreckage?"

"Negative. Just the one piece. It's in a bunch of trees at the base of a cliff. You've got to be right on top of it before you can see it."

"Stand by, Midwest 74. We'll contact search headquarters. Suggest you fly a circular pattern around the area until we can get some instructions. What's your altitude?"

"We're at two thousand and we're gulping fuel. Can we circle at five, please?"

"Cleared to climb to five, continue your pattern. Stand by."

Albuquerque reported back in less than three minutes, although to Ormsbee and Culbert it seemed like thirty.

"Midwest 74, Albuquerque Center. There's an Air Force helicopter and two Civil Air Patrol planes en route to your present location. Search headquarters requests that you stay in your area and when you spot 'em, lead them to the wreckage. The search planes are on this frequency to facilitate air-to-air communications. Acknowledge."

"Roger, Midwest 74. And we have one of those CAP boys in sight right now."

"Thanks, Midwest 74. We hope this is it. Good show. Let us know when you're ready to resume cruising altitude and course. Over."

"Midwest 74."

Ormsbee informed the passengers of the situation, and added he assumed they wouldn't mind too much if the flight stayed around a few minutes longer while the search planes identified what appeared to be aircraft wreckage. They led a CAP Cessna over the clump of trees and listened while the CAP pilot told Albuquerque, "Looks like it's part of a large aircraft but we'll let the chopper make sure."

The helicopter arrived a few minutes later and hovered directly over the trees. The voice of its pilot echoed metallically on the Albuquerque frequency.

"If you airline guys are still listening, you deserve the first word. It's most of a Condor's horizontal stabilizer. We are shifting to search headquarters frequency. Many thanks, Midwest."

Captain Kelly Ormsbee, who loved history, had just helped make it.

They still had to find the rest of Air Force One and this took them another two hours. It was a mile and a half from the portion of stabilizers sighted by the airline crew, strewn, torn and twisted, over the bottom of a deep gorge. The first helicopter to find it radioed the reason why it had taken so long to learn Air Force One's fate.

"Most of the wreckage is buried under mud and silt," he advised search headquarters. "That storm must have washed half of Arizona's soil on top of it."

"Any sign of life?"

"Negative, sir. No survivors as far as we can tell. Can't see any bodies, for that matter. The gorge is pretty narrow but I think we can get down to the surface. Stand by."

Every man at headquarters had the strange experience

of feeling relief mixed with dread. They slumped into chairs or paced aimlessly and restlessly around the room.

"Search headquarters, this is Air Force chopper 32. We're at the bottom."

A hundred eyes were fixed on the radio set.

"We see a couple of bodies. Nobody could have lived through this mess."

The Air Force general in charge of search operations grabbed the microphone away from the sergeant handling communications.

"This is General Dunbar. Are you damned sure there are no survivors?"

"General, this bird is in a hundred thousand pieces. If anybody walked away, he'd have to be Jesus himself."

"The bodies . . . what kind of shape are they in? Are they identifiable?"

"Mac's out looking at them, sir. They appear to be badly burned. Here's Lieutenant McCorckle now, General. I'll put him on."

"McCorckle, sir. I could find only two bodies. They're in pretty bad shape. I . . . I couldn't see anything of the President."

"Go out and look again, McCorckle. McCorckle?"

"This is the other pilot, General. McCorckle's outside. Getting sick."

The general stifled an oath and instead clucked sympathetically. "I know it's rough, son, but we've got to know if the President's dead. Keep looking until we get some rescue equipment there."

"I hope you have some mountain climbers handy, sir. This gorge is two hundred feet deep and almost perpendicular."

"We'll get 'em if we have to. Stay there until further orders. Major Bogley?"

"Here, sir." A lean, sober-faced officer approached Dunbar.

"Where's that FBI disaster team? They'll have to go to work on fingerprints if things are as bad as those pilots say."

"The FBI men already are boarding choppers, sir."

"Good. Well, you can pass the word to Washington. No survivors. Wait a minute. Better make that 'no apparent survivors.' And call in the press."

Vice President Madigan got the word from Newt Spellman at 2:30 P.M. Washington time, "the word" being strained through a sieve of accumulated tension and fatigue. Spellman had not been home for two days and had managed to grab only a couple of two-hour naps at his office in that time.

"What do you think I should do now?" Madigan gulped. "Am I supposed to take over or what?" Spellman stepped quickly into the breach that divided the Vice President's mild panic from his firm desire not to let panic seep out into the public view.

"I think, sir, it's best for you to come immediately to the White House. General Coston's already here, talking to search headquarters. Any further word will be given to him first almost directly from the crash site itself."

"If you think I should, I'll come right away."

Spellman hesitated a second, then decided he might as well prod Madigan into assuming at least partial authority for some of the more delicate and difficult details. "One more thing, Mr. Vice President . . ."

"Yes?"

"If I may take the liberty, sir . . . I'd like to suggest that you ask the Chief Justice, the Cabinet and the congressional leaders of both parties to join you at the White House."

"Newt, don't you think that would be a little presumptuous on my part?" Madigan said rather curtly and even sharply. "Particularly the Chief Justice. Dammit, I'd feel like a ghoul. They haven't found the President's body yet and may not for some time." That, Madigan added to himself, was *just* what Harry Truman might have said. Maybe he liked the sound of "President Madigan," but nobody was going to know it until he put his hand on that Bible.

Spellman was properly and diplomatically apologetic. "Sir, I don't believe anyone could accuse you of being presumptuous if you did what I suggest. To tell you the truth, the reporters are bugging me about some of the legal ramifications. And I figure it would be a good idea if you and Chief Justice Van Dyke could talk to them."

"Legal ramifications? What legal ramifications?"

"Well, sir, as you indicated yourself, the President's body might not be found for quite a while. The press wants to know, to put it bluntly, if it's necessary to have the . . . the corpus delicti, so to speak . . . before you can be sworn in. They're pointing out there are no precedents for this situation . . . nothing like this ever happened before."

"They're right about that," Madigan said grimly. "Well, okay, Newt. But I've got a little better idea. You call the Chief Justice and tell him I suggested he meet me at the White House. That way, it doesn't look as if I'm, uh, pressing. How's that strike you?"

"All right, sir. And the congressional leaders?"

"I'll have Oscar phone all of them so you don't have to bother with anyone but Van Dyke. I know you're busy and pretty upset, my boy."

"Thank you, sir. I appreciate your understanding and your cooperation."

Madigan thought, as he hung up, that Spellman sounded a little sarcastic. Supercilious Jew. He buzzed on his intercom for his administrative assistant, who entered almost immediately as if he were attached to a rope the Vice President had yanked suddenly.

"Yes, Chief?"

"Oscar, call the majority and minority leaders on both sides. Also the Speaker. Tell them—wait a minute, ask them —to join me at the White House in one hour. Make it, let's see, two forty-five. You can tell them we're all meeting with the Chief Justice to discuss some, ah, legal ramifications. And by the way, Oscar . . ."

"Yes, Chief?"

"I take it you won't mind being the new presidential press secretary?"

CHAPTER SIX

The legal ramifications totally escaped the heartsick men working at the desolate crash site.

General Dunbar, who regarded the press with the same degree of suspicion he would have displayed toward a visiting delegation from the Soviet Air Force, at first refused to let reporters into the area. Their bellows of anguished rage were heard—via frantic calls to their Washington bureaus—all the way to the Pentagon. Dunbar, in turn, was told by General Coston to amend his decision at least to the extent of allowing some press representation at the scene.

"Goddammit, Bob!" Dunbar exploded. "We've got enough troubles finding wreckage and bodies without a bunch of newspapermen tramping all over the place. And those TV guys—the bastards'll try to take over the whole operation!"

"I know you can't let them get in the way," Coston said soothingly. "But they've got their job too. We've discussed the problem here and we think there are two alternatives. Let them appoint their own pool representatives, not more than four or five men, and we'll allow these pool reporters to remain at the crash site. Or we'll take the whole bunch of them to the scene just once, give them a chance to see what's going on and what the place looks like, and then make them stay at search headquarters. If they pick the latter, we'll promise to keep them informed via a press liaison officer of anything we find. How's that sound?"

"There's a third alternative," Dunbar snarled. "We can tell them to go to hell."

"That we can't do, Bailey. Call a press conference and lay it on the line. They can choose themselves between a permanent pool or a one-shot visit."

Dunbar, with misgivings, called in the reporters at his Winslow command post. He was a huge bear of a man built along the lines of a pro football tackle with bristly, close-cropped hair.

"I'll give it to you guys straight," he said gruffly. "Washington says there can be *some* coverage at the crash site. I've been ordered to give you a choice between two arrangements—we'll take three guys in plus one TV cameraman, let them stay as long as they want, and they'll pool whatever develops with all of you back here. Or you can all make one trip into the area, watch for about an hour and return to search headquarters where you'll receive briefings on whatever develops. It's up to you."

There was an unfriendly silence at first, then a mushrooming murmur of protest climaxed by Malcolm Jones raising his voice above the others.

"General Dunbar, speaking for IPS, we'd never accept either alternative unless you can give me some compelling reasons why we should."

The question gave Dunbar the opening through which he fired his carefully mustered argument.

"I'll be glad to give you a few compelling reasons, all of you. One, that plane is scattered over a couple of hundred yards of mud with most of the wreckage and bodies buried. The gorge is long but narrow. There isn't room enough for our guys to work if we let fifty or sixty reporters and a bunch of cameramen wander around. Second, this entire operation has only two purposes—to find and identify the body of the President and those of the others, and to find out what the hell went wrong with that aircraft. To fulfill those purposes requires a carefully planned technique of systematic searching and plain digging. Anyone at that site who isn't directly engaged in the aforementioned systematic operation is just getting in the way. And, third, there was classified material on Air Force One—such as War Codes. I'll admit none of you are likely to be Commie agents, but I wouldn't let my own mother get a three-second look at some of that stuff. Have I made my point, Mr. Jones?"

Jones was silent briefly as he digested what for Bailey Dunbar was a full-blown speech.

"General, could you leave us for a little while and let us talk this over among ourselves?" he said finally.

"I'll give you fifteen minutes," the general replied.

He came back in exactly fifteen minutes to find the room

still noisy with protests but markedly less in volume and number. Jones was the press spokesman.

"General Dunbar, we haven't exactly taken a vote but I think the majority is willing to go along. We'll take the pool arrangement."

"Okay. Who goes on the pool?"

"One man from each of the three wire services. The networks will flip a coin for the pool cameraman, and he'll also shoot for the newsreels. We would, however, like assurances that the Air Force will set up some kind of communications facilities so the pool reporters can get all developments to headquarters as fast as possible."

"Can do. Any questions? No? All right, flip that coin. My helicopter leaves in five minutes. And for you lucky guys going—brace. You're going to poke your noses into a corner of hell."

Malcolm Jones, a bull-necked man in his early fifties with homely, rather simian features, had spent twenty-seven years in newspaper work. In that time he had covered fires, murders, wars, revolutions, suicides, tornadoes, hurricanes, riots and a presidential assassination. He had approached this assignment with the gnawing dread of a combat soldier advancing into the teeth of a well-protected machine gun emplacement. His uneasiness was more than merely a matter of fearing a gory scene of death. He feared even more the implications of what he was about to see, the knowledge that it meant the swearing in of another President minutes, even seconds, after the news was flashed to Washington. An oath of office solemnly administered to a man who would immediately assume awesome authority and massive problems, neither of which he was equipped to handle.

Being senior IPS White House reporter had given Malcolm Jones a deep sense of personal contentment. He was one of those relatively rare men who actually enjoy going to work every morning. Most Washington newsmen have something of an indefinable feeling of gratitude about their work, a kind of privileged satisfaction at their closeness to history and those who make history. Nowhere does the term "Fourth Estate" carry more esteem and prestige than in the nation's capital, for the Washington press corps literally comes close to being a fourth branch of government—an informal, unofficial, unwritten part of the traditional check-

and-balance relationship among the legislative, executive and judicial wings. For occasionally the press corps makes its own news and its own history with its indefatigable tools for digging into the camouflaged soil of corruption and deceit.

But Malcolm Jones's attitude toward his job transcended the natural pride of a Washington correspondent. He had enough normal conceit to relish his daily contacts with the famous, the frequent invitations to fire his interrogative darts on programs like *Meet the Press,* the enormously satisfying egocentricity of having the President of the United States address him by his nickname of Jonesy.

His proximity to presidential personalities, however, went far beyond the mere nourishment of ego. More than the majority of his colleagues, he had grasped the awesome loneliness of their exalted positions, their goldfish-bowl environment—a constant exposure to criticism, an unending vulnerability to massive mistakes as well as cruel gossip. He had come to recognize what most Americans cannot conceive in their almost blind worship or hatred of a President, namely that Presidents are only men with the emotions, sentiments, weaknesses and strengths of any human being.

Where the average citizen tends to paint a President with either the shining colors of Godlike virtue or the black hues of Satanic evil, Malcolm Jones dipped his own paintbrush in a colorless, transparent oil of total objectivity. He merely looked at a President through a window he kept clean, instead of trying to paint the window with his own prejudices.

He was first assigned to the White House in 1948 when Harry Truman won a second term on his own. He liked and, more important, respected every President he had covered but this did not make him a subservient reporter living off the personal prestige of a glamorous assignment. Rather, it made him a better reporter because his respect was a kind of tolerance that tempered an inclination toward affection with sharp awareness of presidential faults.

Thus, he could admire Truman's immense courage and simultaneously cringe at his propensity for putting political cronies into jobs they could not handle. He had chafed under Eisenhower's vacillating but he had real admiration for Ike's integrity and his somewhat vague but enlightened concept of liberal Republicanism. He had come close to worshiping Kennedy for his wit, intelligence and youthful enthusiasm, yet he refused to tag JFK with an automatic mantle of greatness simply on the basis of an uncompleted first term. He found in Lyndon Johnson the ruthlessness, the political killer instinct that Kennedy lacked and might well have been able to utilize. He had considered LBJ vindictive and bad-tempered at times, but he also warmed to his personal loyalty, his very real sentimentality and his astuteness at political infighting—the latter a quality, again, that Jones wished JFK had possessed in more ample supply.

Jeremy Haines, in Jones's view, was a rare combination of his four immediate predecessors. Truman's raw guts, Eisenhower's idealism and intelligent conservatism, Kennedy's intellect and courage, and Johnson's political shrewdness, all were imbedded in the mind and conscience that made up the being of Jeremy Haines. And only the Lord could tell what was imbedded in the mind and conscience of the man who would have to replace him.

Those thoughts were unnerving for a man about to gaze on the graveyard of Air Force One. But Malcolm Jones found he still was unprepared for the sight below, as the security guards posted around the rim parted to let him peer over the edge.

The wreckage resembled the carcass of some huge animal, almost totally devoured, the chunks of eviscerated metal strewn haphazardly around like slabs of rotting entrails. A brontosaurus torn apart by a tyrannosaurus, thought Jones, and the scene indeed was one of primeval savagery. The bottom of the gorge might have been straight out of a Jurassic landscape and the remains of the Condor seemed to be something a paleontologist could decipher more easily than an aeronautical engineer.

It was obvious that Air Force One's final resting place was a one-in-ten-million shot. If it had hit a few yards to either side of the gorge's rim it would have been discovered almost immediately. As it was, the Condor must have plunged almost vertically into the relatively narrow pit, squeezing its bulk into the opening like an arrow shot skillfully into a funnel.

Helicopters had managed to airlift a few small tractors into the gorge and, by attaching makeshift plows to this equipment, the rescue party had achieved what amounted to miniature bulldozers. But most of the searchers were working with shovels, digging into muck that already was beginning to crust in the Arizona heat.

"Jesus," said the UPI man simply.

Dunbar watched the reporters' faces, half in sympathy and half with the patronizing disdain of a military man inured to anything in the line of carnage and death.

"There's a semblance of a trail down to the gorge," he said as if to take their minds off what they were seeing. "You'll need gauze masks. Sergeant!"

"Yes, sir."

"Bring us four masks from that medical truck."

"Why the masks?" Jones asked.

"Sanitation, mainly. Sensitivity next. The stench is pretty bad. Ever smelled burned flesh?"

"Yeah," said the AP man. "In Korea—I used a flame thrower on some Gooks and I could smell the results for weeks. I even dreamed about it."

"You'll probably dream about this for weeks," Dunbar assured him. "Here are the masks. You don't have to wear them right away, but put 'em on as soon as we hit the bottom. Ready? Okay, let's go."

His weekly eighteen holes of golf had not conditioned Jones for what the general had charitably referred to as a trail. It started at the north rim and wound laboriously down to the bottom, a pitted scar gouged into the side of the gorge. Dunbar may have been pure Air Force but the reporters suspected he also was half mountain goat. They were puffing after the first twenty-five yards, while ahead of them Dunbar edged his way gingerly but steadily, occasionally glancing back to make sure none of his charges had fallen off. He stopped halfway down to give them a rest.

"Christ, I didn't know I was this much outa shape," the UPI man panted.

"A more apt observation," Jones said, "is how the hell we're gonna get back up. Going down is bad enough."

"Why couldn't we have taken a 'copter down?" AP grumbled.

"A chopper will take you back up," the general promised. "We're flying them down only when they carry essential personnel or equipment. They kick up too much of a ruckus over a small area. We did take that TV pool man

105

down because his cameras were too bulky. If you guys are rested, we'd better get going."

The odor of charred flesh invaded their nostrils the moment they reached the bottom and the UPI man murmured through his mask, "I think I'm gonna get sick."

"You'll get used to it," Dunbar grunted. "Just so you won't step on anything important and know what the hell you're looking at, I've assigned a bright young shavetail to stick with you."

Jones was nettled. "We can find our own way around, General. We don't need any goddamned sightseeing guide. Sounds like a little bit of censorship and—"

"Don't get your bowels in an uproar, Jones. I told all of you back in Winslow there's security stuff involved. Lieutenant Kermit's job is to make sure you don't stumble on anything that's supposed to be classified. But he'll also help you with any questions you might have—and he's been told to answer anything. Satisfied?"

"Yes, sir." The "sir," Jones suddenly realized, was purely inadvertent and almost automatic. There was something about Dunbar that bred respect and discipline even in a newspaperman.

They found Kermit, a tall blond youngster with somber eyes but an easy smile that was more of an unerasable grin. It gave him the appearance of a photographic composite in which the upper facial features of one man have been grafted to the lower features of another. The lieutenant was talking to a burly, gray-haired civilian when Dunbar and the reporters approached. Kermit saluted.

"Lieutenant," Dunbar acknowledged with a cursory return salute. "May I present Mr. Jones of IPS, Mr. Runnels of UPI, and Mr. Castle of the AP. These are the gentlemen representing the press pool. Has the network cameraman gotten down yet?"

"Yes, sir, he's already shooting. Captain Powell's with him. General, have you met Mr. Quincannon of the DOT's Bureau of Safety? This is General Dunbar, in charge of the search and rescue operation."

"Glad to know you, Quincannon. I heard Washington was sending you out to help us. Bring any of your boys?"

"A full team, General. We landed at Winslow yesterday and came right to the scene from the airport. Our top men on structures, power plants, systems and operations. We're all at your disposal. I've already conferred with Colonel Slattery—he's heading the Air Force investigative group—and we're ready to cooperate to the fullest."

Jones decided that Quincannon, being a civilian, might prove to be a more lucrative source than the Air Force.

"Mr. Quincannon, can you brief us on what you've seen thus far? Body identification? Any clues? Any indication of what might have happened?"

Quincannon glanced suspiciously at the general, his eyebrows raised in a mute question as to how far he could go and how much he could say to the press. Dunbar nodded.

"Give them anything you've got," he said. "Matter of fact, I could stand some expert briefing myself. I'm a search and rescue man, not a crash investigator."

Quincannon sat down on a nearby rock, like a scoutmaster about to instruct a group of youngsters on wild-life flora and fauna. He wiggled the toe of one mud-crusted boot into the ground, like a pitcher digging aimlessly at the mound before delivery.

"Well, I suppose you're most interested in the people aboard. First, we haven't found the body of the President. But for that matter we haven't found anybody as far as positive identification is concerned. All the occupants were badly burned. Some bodies aren't even whole—just a collection of torsos, arms and legs. A few are in better shape, but not for identification purposes. The FBI disaster squad is working from fingerprint files and dental charts—that's about the only way to do it. And frankly, I've handled crashes where there was no identification possible—like one of the Electra crashes in 1960. There wasn't anything remotely resembling a human corpse among the sixty or seventy persons aboard. This isn't quite that bad, but it's not going to be easy."

"How many, uh, bodies would you say have been found?" Runnels asked in a voice that was more of a series of gulps.

"So far, we've found five in relatively intact condition. But by that I mean there's a semblance of the right number of arms and legs. Individual facial characteristics have been completely obliterated by fire. We think one of these is a woman, the President's secretary, I believe, but even this isn't sure."

"Any idea when we might get some word on identification?" Jones said.

"You'll have to ask the FBI boys that. The fingerprint and dental charts were flown here only about an hour ago. Naturally, they're working on the President's first of all. In that white tent over there, by the way. I wouldn't advise your peeking inside. It's pretty rough."

"I'll be happy to waive my press privileges," the AP's Castle said fervently.

Jones figured they had milked Quincannon dry on the distasteful but all-important subject of identification. "How about the plane itself? Any theories on what happened?"

"Well," Quincannon replied, "the aircraft impacted in an almost vertical position—a straight dive in. It's too soon to tell whether there was any fire before she hit the ground. All the wreckage appears to be concentrated in a relatively small area inside the gorge, which means the plane was reasonably intact at the time of the crash. With one important exception, as you already know. Part of the tail section was found in a wooded area a few hundred yards from where the airliner crew spotted the first wreckage."

"Which means," Jones put in, "structural failure."

"It appears so. Our structures people and similar experts from the Air Force already have examined the tail section. The damage does not resemble anything suggesting metal fatigue. Rather, the breaks indicate stress overloads beyond design capability."

"In other words," the AP man said, "it broke up in that thunderstorm."

"That," said Quincannon firmly, "is merely a possibility. A strong possibility but still a theory requiring further investigation and proof."

"Aw, come on, Mr. Quincannon," Reynolds said with uncealed exasperation. "That plane was in a bad thunderstorm and you've just told us the tail fell off. What more evidence do you need?"

"Something more solid than circumstantial evidence. I've been in this business too long, young man, to accept anything at face value. I'll admit—off the record—that it looks as if Air Force One was torn apart by storm turbulence. But offsetting this is a contradictory fact. Namely, the Condor is an exceptionally strong aircraft. Structural failure because of turbulence is apparent, but at the same time it's also illogical."

"What else would be logical?" Jones asked.

"God knows. Loss of control in turbulence could lead to excessive attitudes which, in turn, could cause structural failure. It's happened before on jet transports. Northwest lost one over the Everglades for just such a reason, in 1963, I believe. A jetliner crash near Tokyo a few years ago also was attributed to loss of control. But here again, we have a possible cause which is negated by a diametrically opposing fact. The behavior of large, swept-wing airliners in severe turbulence caused enough concern in the past to prompt improved crew training and better techniques for recovery in turbulence. We haven't had a really serious turbulence incident for several years. And it goes without saying that the pilots on Air Force One were the equal of or even superior to airline crews."

"You used the phrase . . . I've got it in my notes somewhere . . . yeh, 'the breaks indicated stress overloads,' " Castle said. "Have you examined the tail section for any signs of sabotage—like an explosion? Or are you completely satisfied that the tail came off because of stress?"

"Not completely. The examination of this section has been preliminary. We didn't find any obvious traces of something like dynamite, for example. And as I said, the breaks were of the type associated with stress overloads. They were not what you'd normally find, say, in metal that had been deformed by an internal explosion with all the forces directed outward. But nobody can discount the possibility of sabotage. There are probably fifty or a hundred different ways to blow up an airplane. And some of them, for all we know, conceivably could leave no traces that an explosive substance was used. However, and this is again off the record, I personally doubt that sabotage was involved in this case."

"Why?" blurted Lieutenant Kermit, apparently forgetting in his absorption with Quincannon's discourse the foreboding presence of a general.

The safety expert hesitated with the inbred, inherent reluctance of any good crash investigator to commit himself publicly. He and his breed were men to whom the obvious was a blood-red flag of warning against hasty assumptions. He finally decided to pass the buck to Dunbar.

"As I said before, the Air Force is running the show. I'll leave it up to the general here if he thinks it's okay to discuss this, ah, aspect."

"Go ahead," Dunbar snapped.

"Well, one of the elevators was found a good two miles from this gorge—"

"The elevators move a plane up or down?" Jones broke in.

"Correct. They are part of the horizontal stabilizer structure—the part which forms the upper portion of the so-called T-tail. Now, the horizontal stabilizer section sighted by the airline pilots retained the other elevator but in a badly damaged condition. This may have been from impact force, but a preliminary examination indicates that this elevator also failed. It did not separate from the main stabilizer, but it probably was inoperative."

"So what happens if one or both elevators fail?" Runnels asked.

"The probable sequence is that the aircraft would pitch violently forward, almost like a man at the end of a suddenly released rope. A fatal dive would result. There would be no means of controlling attitude."

"No way to pull it out of the dive?" Castle interpreted.

"No way on God's earth. The last resort of a pilot would be to try to bring up the nose by applying full power. We've found all four engines and, while they haven't been examined yet, I'll wager they were developing full thrust at impact. Futilely, as you can see."

"Getting back to sabotage," Runnels said. "Couldn't an explosion of some sort have ripped off those elevators? Maybe they came off when the whole tail section went."

Quincannon shook his head.

"The phrase 'tail falling off' is misleading," he explained with impersonal calmness. "Actually, what separated from the main fuselage were the horizontal stabilizers and part of the rudder structure, not the entire tail section. The fuselage itself must have been fairly intact when it hit."

"How can you tell that, with all this mess?" Castle wanted to know.

"The engines. The Condor has four aft-mounted power plants, as you know. They were fairly close together when they were dug up. This would indicate they were still on the fuselage at impact, and if this were true, I doubt if there would have been any in-flight breakup of the cabin. This is why I doubt the sabotage theory."

His audience was silent, each man mentally painting his own picture of what it must have been like in the last few seconds of the Condor's death throes. The awful eternity of a ninety-second plunge to inevitable oblivion. It was Jones's next question which brought them back to the less emotional realities of the living present.

"Did Air Force One have one of those cockpit voice recorders? One of those gizmos which is supposed to record the last conversations of the crew?"

Quincannon nodded, frowning. "It had a voice recorder, and it was found along with the flight recorder which depicts such data as speed, altitude, gust forces, direction and so forth. But unfortunately both devices were badly damaged by both impact and fire. We found them only an hour ago and they're already on their way to Washington for analysis. I couldn't tell you now what information we'll get from them."

"I thought they're supposed to be immune to crash damage," Castle said.

"They're supposed to be," Quincannon said with a note of bitterness in his calm, rather sleepy voice. "But it doesn't always work out that way. In this case, maybe we were expecting too much. One of our structures men told me a little while ago he estimated that Air Force One must have impacted at about four hundred miles an hour. Don't use that figure" (the reporters already were scribbling this down) "—it's an off-the-west-wall guess of just one man."

"It's a hell of an interesting guess," Jones half protested.

"I'd still rather you not use it at this stage. Later, we'll be able to give you a fairly accurate estimate of impact speed. If you men have no further questions, I'd like to get back to work. General, I think Colonel Slattery would like to see you."

"I'll go with you," Dunbar said. "Lieutenant, escort these men around for a while. I'll see all of you later."

"Brusque bastard, isn't he?" Runnels observed—judiciously waiting until the general was out of hearing distance before offering this appraisal.

"I think in about a half hour I'm gonna be pretty brusque myself," Jones said. "Or awfully nauseous. Okay, Lieutenant. Lead on."

For a full hour Kermit took them around the crash site. The cruelly twisted metal that had once been a ten-million-dollar airplane was bad enough. The Condor had dug a huge pit, about thirty yards wide and five feet deep, when it struck the ground. Most of the wreckage was concentrated in this area, Kermit told them, but the impact and instantaneous explosion had hurled bits of metal hundreds of feet away.

"The bodies too," Kermit added laconically. "They found a couple of arms and a torso about seventy yards away."

It was the sight of the bodies that sickened the reporters. Only they were not bodies. Merely stumps of blackened flesh, looking for all the world like abnormally large, over-cooked roasts. The rescue workers were dumping them in big rubber blankets and carrying them to the white tent serving as the identification center. The newsmen's gauze sanitation masks filtered out the odor somewhat, but the sight of the charred remains was worse than the smell. Runnels and Jones both became ill, feeling no shame as they regurgitated from their heaving stomachs what they could never regurgitate from their minds.

But they stuck with it because they were newspapermen covering a story. They stumbled around the mud, taking occasional notes and staring with glazed eyes at the chunks of wreckage that ranged from one huge wing to tiny shreds of metal. Some parts already bore yellow identification tags attached by technical experts from the Amalgamated factory that had built the Condor. "Station 215," one said. "Hydraulic tubing, station 146," another tag read. They meant little to the three reporters, who stood behind one group of the manufacturer's representatives and watched curiously as they consulted a huge sheaf of blueprints, conferred briefly, and then affixed another tag. After they moved over to another piece of wreckage, Jones leaned down and read the tag they had just written.

"Cabin wall lining, rear lounge, station 280." For no particular reason, Jones shuddered.

Incongruously, they were touched mostly by the few un-damaged items they saw. A blue and gold matchbook with the engraved words "Air Force One." A coffee cup. A man's shoe, laces still tied, which Jones picked up to examine on the ridiculous, farfetched chance it might have some identification marks inside. A copy of *Time,* only the edges slightly marred by fire, the wind in the gorge gently riffling the pages like the unseen hand of a ghost. Finally, a mud-spattered girdle that must have belonged to Judi Nance. Jones, feeling that he had somehow intruded on the privacy of the dead, wondered if it had been torn from her body or out of a suitcase, and then scolded himself for yielding to ghoulishness.

"I've had enough," he announced suddenly to the others. "Let's go find General Dunbar. We should be getting all this stuff back to Winslow."

Dunbar was emerging from the identification tent as they walked up. The general's face was pale and his lips were tightened in a thin line, as if he had them sewn together to keep from vomiting. He merely nodded. A tall man in khaki trousers and shirt came out of the tent behind Dunbar, who introduced him. "This is Ed Davis of the FBI Disaster squad. These three gentlemen are the press pool, Ed. They might have some questions."

"Any identification yet, Mr. Davis?" Castle asked.

"Like the President?" Runnels added hastily.

"One," the FBI man said. "Rear Admiral Philips. It's pretty positive, from fingerprints and dental charts. We're still working on some others, with the help of some people from the Armed Forces Institute of Pathology. Might have something in a few minutes if you'd like to stick around."

"General, we should be getting back to Winslow or phoning something to the others if you can set us up some communications," Jones said. "Then we can come back here and stand by for further identification news."

"It's your decision," Dunbar said. "Kermit, take them over to the communications center. But if you guys would rather fly back to Winslow, we can call a chopper."

The three newsmen conferred briefly. Then Jones spoke for the trio. "Castle and I will phone in the hard news—the Philips identification and what Quincannon gave us. Runnels will fly back and do a pool eyewitnesser on what we've seen. If that's okay with you, General, we're ready."

"One thing you might like to know," Davis informed them. "It's pretty hot inside that tent and we've been considering taking all the remains to the city morgue in Winslow. But General Dunbar says the Air Force can drop us a ground air-conditioning unit which'll make it bearable."

"It should be here any minute," Dunbar promised. "Bonanza Airlines over in Phoenix is loaning us one of theirs."

"That's a pretty big piece of equipment," Jones said.

"We've got a chopper than can carry a small tank," Dunbar said with a trace of pride. "Not inside, of course, but with steel cables and a suspended net."

By the time Jones and Castle had finished dictating to Winslow, alternating from their notes, they discovered much to their surprise that they were hungry. Kermit took them to the Army field kitchen set up on the fringe of the gorge where they greedily downed sandwiches and coffee.

"I thought I'd never want to eat again," Castle marveled. "Christ, I was starving. What now, Jonesy?"

"Guess we'd better go back to that FBI tent and stay put until they find and identify Haines's body. That's what everyone's waiting to hear—including, I fear, our beloved Vice President."

"Yeh," said Castle, who wanted to give Jones the impression he was savvy on political personalities. The AP reporter was from the Los Angeles bureau and, like virtually every wire service man, he secretly (and sometimes publicly) yearned for a transfer to Washington.

They were finishing the last sip of steaming coffee when Dunbar strode up.

"Thought I'd get some java myself," the general said. "How's it going?"

"Fine," Jones replied. "We're finished phoning. Anything new on identification?"

Davis told me to tell you there should be something any time now. Wait till I get this coffee down and I'll walk over with you."

He never got to finish the coffee. An air policeman came running up.

"General Dunbar," he panted, "you're wanted back at the FBI tent on the double."

Dunbar put down the coffee cup. "What's up?" he barked.

"I don't know for sure, sir, but I think they've found the President's body."

114

Jones and Castle paced impatiently outside the identification tent for what seemed like hours. All they knew was what Dunbar had told them following a hasty briefing Davis gave the general, in private, after the trio had sprinted to the tent.

"It isn't definite until they get through with the prints and dental charts," Dunbar warned them. "But they did find a body under a pile of mud and some wreckage. It could be that of the President."

"Why do you think so?" Jones asked. "Clothing? Facial characteristics? Build?"

Dunbar shook his head. "This one's burned like the others. All we know is that it's male. But the people from Condor took a look at the wreckage on top of this body. They said it was part of the President's private stateroom."

"Whew!" That was from Castle, who ejected the whistle with the automatic reflex of a man unable to stifle a cough.

The two reporters were torn between unwillingness to leave the tent area and their natural instinct to phone in what they already had.

"We should call Winslow, Jonesy," Castle argued. "Jesus, man, it's worth a bulletin—just the fact that they *think* they've found Haines"

"Maybe," the more cautious and experienced Jones reasoned. "But we might be jumping the gun, and if it turns out not to be Haines, we'll have created a hell of a lot of excitement prematurely. You saw that wreckage and all the bodies, Castle. Scattered and sprayed all over this Godforsaken gorge. The way that plane hit, one of the pilots could have been tossed all the way back to the rear. Or the President's body could have been flung forward as far as the cockpit. Let's wait."

They waited. And waited. And waited some more. The occupational hazard of a newspaperman. A kind of death watch over history about to happen. Mounting tension, nerves stretching taut to the point of preferring the worst if it would only take place.

They smoked enough cigarettes to give a whale lung cancer, throwing most of them away only half consumed. They watched the two tent entrance flaps that mercifully hid what was being done inside, as if their concentrated stares could propel Dunbar and Davis outside.

The general and the FBI man did come out after a half

hour, instantly erasing the newsmen's eager anticipation with Dunbar's "We just wanted a smoke."

"We're still checking," Davis said. "On this one body, I mean. We have established tentative identification on three others in addition to Admiral Philips. Miss Nance, Mr. Sabath, and one of the Secret Servicemen—Hudson."

"That should increase the chances of the other body being that of the President," Jones suggested.

"And how do you arrive at that conclusion?" Davis said.

"I've ridden on Air Force One many times. Those people you've identified—the doctor, Miss Nance, Phil Sabath—they invariably ride in the rear of the plane. So does the President. If their bodies were in good enough shape to identify, it stands to reason so is the President's. Because he would have been in the rear too. You've already said this body was found in the private stateroom."

"Well," said Davis, "your assumption is logical. But logic doesn't dictate in this case. The fingerprints and dental charts do. And we'd better get back to same. Perhaps I'll have something pretty soon."

"Pretty soon" turned out to be nearly two hours later. In that time Castle went over to the communications center and gave Winslow the additional identifications plus the cautiously worded revelation (Jones had extracted a promise to be *very* tentative in phraseology) that another body was being examined "with some evidence that it might have been found in an area of the plane which the President was known to frequent on a flight."

Castle ran all the way back to the tent, an unnecessary burst of energy because Jones still was pacing restlessly outside. They smoked and talked languidly for another hour, and Jones had just started to tell the younger AP man what it was like covering the Kennedy assassination when the tent flaps parted. Out came Dunbar and Davis, their faces wearing twin masks of fatigue and sheer puzzlement.

"Was it the President?" Jones almost shouted.

Davis shook his head. His tanned forehead was furrowed. Dunbar looked at the reporters, his expression curiously sympathetic as if he were about to break bad news to the anxious relatives of a dying man. "Come over here a minute, you two—I don't want that air policeman to hear this."

They followed him like dutiful children trailing a father to the woodshed. Ten yards from the tent, Dunbar turned and faced them.

"This is off the record until I can contact Washington for clearance," he began. "Understood?"

They nodded.

"Okay. The FBI got real good fingerprints off that body. They checked them with the file fingerprints of every person on the plane still unidentified, including those of the President. They checked the President's dental charts with the teeth on the body in question. They checked those teeth with the charts of everyone else on Air Force One. Negative, down the line."

"What do you mean, negative?" Jones said.

"I mean," Dunbar answered slowly, spitting out each word with the emphasis of a jabbing forefinger, "that the body we thought was the President's isn't that of anyone who was supposed to be on that plane."

CHAPTER SEVEN

General Coston brought the word in person to the White House late Wednesday afternoon, taking a helicopter from the Pentagon's landing strip to the 'copter pad on the south lawn of the Executive Mansion. Madigan's meeting with the Cabinet, congressional leaders and Chief Justice Van Dyke had just started when the Air Force chief of staff was ushered into the Cabinet Room in the Executive Wing.

They knew something was up before he opened his mouth. His expression was that of a man carrying a terrible secret inside him, so unbelievable that he could not prevent its import from seeping to the surface and registering near panic on his face.

"Mr. Vice President, Mr. Chief Justice, gentlemen. I didn't phone first because I felt you all should hear this development simultaneously. I've just received word from General Dunbar at the crash site that a body was found which apparently didn't belong on Air Force One. The body of some unknown person. Its fingerprints did not match those of the known passengers and crew members."

He paused to let his disclosure take root in their brains.

"What makes it even more mysterious," Coston continued, "is evidence that this particular body was in or near the President's private stateroom when Air Force One crashed. And before going on, I'd like to ask on behalf of both the Air Force and the FBI, does anyone in this room have the slightest idea who was on that plane who was not listed on the passenger or crew manifests?"

He looked at his audience. Every face was registering a blend of surprise and shock. Not a person spoke.

"Then let me ask this. Does anyone know whether the aircraft made an unannounced or unscheduled stop, where another passenger might have been picked up? Did the

President indicate or hint or actually tell any of you such a stop would be made?"

Again he was greeted by total silence, until Madigan finally mustered life into his vocal cords. "It seems to me, General, that the Air Force itself should know whether any stop was made."

"Agreed," Coston snapped. "We're almost one hundred per cent sure that plane never touched ground between Andrews and Arizona. It made the right position reports and on schedule, and it's damned unlikely it could have landed after one of those reports, taken off again and still made the next position report on time. For that matter, it was being tracked by radar all the way across the country. I had to ask you about the possibility of such a stop, though, because it seems to be the only explanation even if it's farfetched and damned near impossible."

"How about a stowaway?" asked Secretary of Transportation Brubaker.

"Negative. We've already put the security guards assigned to Air Force One's hangar through a meat grinder. Nobody but a ghost could have hidden on the plane before it left."

Secretary of State James Sharkey, a small man who looked about as much like the Hollywood version of a Secretary of State as Fiorello La Guardia resembled a ballet dancer, had another idea. "General, how does the count of bodies compare with the total number who boarded the plane?"

"We've established identification on only four persons thus far, Mr. Secretary. Admiral Philips, Miss Nance, Mr. Sabath and one of the three Secret Service agents. That was the count as of twenty minutes ago. We may never get identification on everybody, which means we may never get a precise body count. There were seven passengers and nine crew members. The fingerprints and dental charts of all sixteen aboard were flown to the crash site. Eliminating the four bodies already identified, the fingerprints and teeth of our unknown passenger didn't match any of the remaining twelve."

A White House secretary slipped into the room at this point and whispered something to Newt Spellman. "General, your office is calling you," Spellman said. "Use that phone over there."

Coston picked up the phone. "General Coston. Yes, go ahead. . . . You checked carefully? Thanks."

He hung up. "Gentlemen, an Air Force photographer filmed the boarding process at Andrews the night the plane left. We've just examined the films. They show exactly seven passengers going up those boarding steps, including the President. And if you'll pardon my language, I'd sure as hell like to know who the eighth person was and where he came from."

"So would we," murmured Speaker Verdi.

Madigan gratefully heard Van Dyke ask the question the Vice President wanted answered but didn't want to ask himself.

"I take it there's still no word on the President's body," said the Chief Justice.

"No, sir."

"General," Secretary of Defense Michael Tobin said, "wouldn't it have been possible for an extra crew member to be aboard? Maybe Colonel Henderson allowed some officer or even an enlisted man to hitch a ride or something —without telling anyone. That would explain the mystery body."

"Mr. Secretary, I've known Marcus Henderson for twenty-two years. He wouldn't have let his own father get on that plane without listing him on the manifest. He operated Air Force One by the rules, and the rules don't allow unlisted passengers or crew members."

"Well," Madigan finally spoke up, "I'm afraid this is going to prolong the uncertainty. The next question is whether we tell the press—or have they already been told, General?"

"Not exactly, sir. Dunbar told me two wire service men at the scene—IPS and AP—were advised of the unknown body but on an off-the-record basis pending clearance. Frankly, I'd like to pass the clearance buck to the people in this room. It's too hot for the Air Force."

"Hot" was the word for it, Madigan thought. He had the impulse to make the decision himself, à la Harry Truman forcefulness, but uncertainty surged ahead of the impulse and instead he turned to Matt Parrish. "What do you think, Matt?" he asked almost plaintively.

"I think we'd better discuss it further," Parrish said. "The papers'll read everything into this from a Commie plot to a mad assassin. Mystery body! My instinct tells me to sit on it for a while. How the hell do we know this character didn't have anything to do with the crash?"

"I agree with Matt," Secretary of State Sharkey said. "It's quite possible there's a direct link between this, ah, unauthorized person and what happened to the plane. Which would—"

"Possible but not likely," Coston interrupted. "We're pretty sure Air Force One broke up from extreme storm turbulence. Your unauthorized passenger, as you put it, could hardly have been responsible for a thunderstorm."

"The Air Force," Parrish said sharply, "is going to have a slightly rough time explaining to Congress and the public how turbulence could wreck the President's plane. A brand-new ship, supposedly well tested—the finest product of this nation's aeronautical genius. This mystery man could give you a little alibi which you bloody well might need."

Coston had to clamp a mental strangle hold on his tongue to keep from reminding Parrish that the Condor's purchase had not been the Air Force's idea, and that its acquisition stemmed directly from congressional refusal to buy what the AF wanted—a supersonic transport.

"Senator," he managed to answer with a modicum of courtesy, "we're as anxious as anyone else to know what happened to Air Force One. I assure you, sir, we're looking for explanations, not alibis."

"We're getting away from the subject at hand," Madigan spoke up. "Is it the consensus here that we do not release this information to the press at this time? Does anyone have a different idea?"

"I think we should release it at once," Secretary of Labor Nelson Gilbert said quietly.

"It'll probably be in Drew Pearson's column tomorrow, anyway," the Chief Justice remarked dourly. "You can't sit on anything like this—and it's better to make the announcement from the White House than let some reporter or columnist leak it."

"Precisely," the swarthy, heavy-set Labor Secretary said. "If we try to suppress it and it comes out anyway, it'll have just the effect Parrish fears—a lot of wild speculation and rumors."

"The speculation and rumors are inevitable no matter how it's disclosed," the majority leader snorted. "But suppose we do it this way—let's sit on it for a few more hours, anyway. By that time, maybe General Coston here will have more bodies identified, perhaps all of them, and we'll have a better picture."

"A better picture of what?" demanded Gilbert. "General Coston has told us there was a body aboard that plane which didn't belong there. We owe it to the American people to disclose every aspect of the investigation."

"Let's do a little more investigating before we do the disclosing," Parrish said. "There must be some explanation for that body. General, I assume you're leaving no stone unturned to find the explanation. Although it's obvious Congress will have to look into this tragedy before we're finished."

This time Coston could not stifle his long-festering disrespect for politicians, and this politician in particular. The supercilious, hypocritical sonofabitch. Talking about a congressional investigation at this stage—as if the Air Force was either incompetent or trying to hide something or both. If the Air Force had all the money it spent flying lawmakers around for free, it could have bought a presidential SST instead of that damned Condor, he thought bitterly.

"I repeat, Senator Parrish," the general said with such slowness that his anger was evident, "we're doing our utmost to solve this matter—and that includes the body as well as the accident. But that's why I came here today, because there's no ready explanation and I was hoping somebody in this room could shed some light. I'm only too sorry they couldn't. With your permission, Mr. Vice President, I'll get back to my office."

Madigan looked pleased at this gesture of respect. "Thank you very much, General. I'll keep you advised of our decision on this press matter. Until you hear from me, tell your people in Winslow to keep it under wraps."

"Yes, sir." The general left, his resentment against the majority leader still lingering in the air like an unevaporated jet trail.

"I'm in favor of doing what Matt suggested," Madigan said. "Let it ride for a few hours. Anyone object to that? All right, I guess it's time to face a somewhat more important problem. Namely, do you want me to take over unofficially or what?"

The Chief Justice cleared his throat, more to draw attention than to oil his vocal cords. "Legally, Mr. Vice President, there is considerable justification for your assuming the presidency on a temporary basis. Until the President's body is found and identified beyond question."

"The revised constitutional amendment on succession?" the Defense Secretary asked.

"Right. As you gentlemen already are aware, it provides that if the President becomes ill or incapacitated to such an extent that he is unable to perform the duties of office, he may designate the Vice President as the Acting President until he is fit to resume those duties. Or the Vice President himself could declare himself Acting President if the President were for some reason unable or unwilling to make such a designation—in the case of mental illness, for example."

"The amendment doesn't seem to fit this situation," Madigan pointed out. "We don't have a sick or crazy President. We don't even know if we have a President."

"True," said Van Dyke, "but the legal authority still is there. Under the law, you could designate yourself as Acting President while Haines is missing. If he's found, and alive, he'd resume office."

"Suppose," queried the bone-thin Defense Secretary, "Haines is found alive but is, well, not quite himself. That isn't a farfetched possibility, considering all the unusual aspects of this business—the mystery body being a prime example. God knows what happened aboard that plane, or what we'll find out eventually."

"The hypothesis you suggest," Van Dyke said rather ponderously, "is that the President would be incapable of assuming his duties but would be unwilling to let Mr. Madigan continue as Acting President. In that case, the law provides that a special congressional commission adjudicate the conflict between the two men, with the aid of proper psychiatric advice."

"I don't think any, uh, conflict would arise," Madigan said hastily, even as Haines's never-forgotten appraisal of the Vice President's governing abilities sailed through his mind.

"That's not the point," Van Dyke said. "The major problem facing us is that the country cannot be without a President, no matter what the circumstances. The precedents are overwhelming. Eisenhower had an informal take-over agreement with Nixon after his first heart attack. Kennedy and Johnson had the same agreement. And so did Johnson and Humphrey. They all recognized the absolute necessity of the continuance of the office. The constitutional amendment merely legalized those informal agreements and spelled them out further to cover all possible exigencies."

"It's still difficult for me to announce to the nation that I'm Acting President before anyone knows whether Haines is dead," Madigan argued. "It seems presumptuous."

"I can only reiterate what the Chief Justice has told us," Speaker Verdi said, gazing directly at the Vice President. "It is imperative that the country not be without a President for another five minutes. Good God, Fred, suppose Russia or Red China launched an attack while we're sitting here. The President of the United States would have to order retaliation. Or, in this case, the Acting President. So let's get on with it. This is no debating topic and no time for personal feelings and being a nice, modest, self-effacing guy. Does the Cabinet agree?"

The Cabinet nodded as one man, with a few verbal murmurs of consent.

"There should be an immediate press conference called," Parrish decreed. "Fred, do you want me to make the announcement, or should the Chief Justice?"

"No," said Frederick James Madigan. "I'll make it myself."

He did, within the hour, and after the press conference he moved right into the oval room with its cream-beige walls, the room that had served as the working quarters for every President since Theodore Roosevelt. Madigan had been here several times, but the big room seemed to have acquired new proportions of size and awesome dignity.

The office, located in the West Wing, was bright and cheerful even without the sunlight of this pleasant September afternoon. The shafts streamed through the twelve-foot french windows, illuminating as if by a spotlight the Great Seal of the United States woven into the huge, grayish-green carpeting.

Madigan was escorted into the room by Newton Spellman. He sat down behind the President's massive desk, noticing instantly the combined pipe rack and tobacco humidor on the left side and the strangely disturbing fact that the pipestems bore the teeth marks of Jeremy Haines.

It gave him the uneasy, unreal feeling that this was not an office used by a living person but rather a carefully restored museum section.

Even the eighteen-button telephone console on the desk seemed more ornamental than electronic. Madigan fingered a couple of the buttons, touching them gingerly in the manner of a child reaching out toward fire. "I guess I'll need to be checked out on this contraption," he said. "Do you know what all these buttons mean?"

"Not all of them, sir. The emergency ones you should know about first. That red one is the maximum security button. It's a special line that scrambles the President's voice. The person being called hears nothing but gibberish unless he has an unscrambling button at his end. The red button is hooked to the war room at the Pentagon. You can talk to any military base in the world on that line via the war room, including SAC headquarters in Omaha or NATO."

"And the amber one next to the red?"

"That's a direct line to an Army switchboard. The switchboard can connect you instantly with any Cabinet member and the heads of certain agencies. The CIA, for example, or the Joint Chiefs and so forth. Both those colored buttons are linked to the Pentagon's war room, by the way. The others, well, maybe I'd better let Mrs. Hahn fill you in on them. That's her button there."

"Mrs. Hahn? Oh yes, the woman in the outer office."

"Yes, sir. She'll be your personal secretary. Very efficient person."

"Fine," Madigan said, although the word came out cloaked with nervous uncertainty. He glanced around the room, awed anew by the Stars and Stripes and the purple and gold flag bearing the presidential seal directly behind the massive desk.

"This desk—must be seven feet long," he remarked as he caressed the ornate wood scrolling. "Looks like something one of my pred—uh, like something picked up at an auction. Where did it come from, Newt?"

The question strained Spellman's credibility. The man was about to take over the presidency and he was asking about a piece of furniture. Well, the press secretary assumed charitably, Madigan probably was just nervous and needed a bit of small talk.

"It's from the timbers of a British warship," Spellman recounted. "When the ship was scrapped, Queen Victoria had some of the wood made into this desk and sent it as a gift to Rutherford Hayes. Every President used it until FDR, who apparently didn't like it and ordered it put in storage. Mrs. Kennedy found it hidden under a piece of cloth on the ground floor and President Kennedy had it moved to the Executive Wing. It originally was in the Lincoln Room on the second floor when that room was used as a President's study."

"Very interesting," the Vice President said with sincerity. "I imagine there's a lot to learn about this place. Historically, I mean. You seem well versed."

"It's sort of a hobby with me," Spellman explained. "Sir, would you like to take a little tour of the White House before you settle down to work? I know you've been here many times, but I'd be glad to show you around."

"I don't think so," Madigan decided quickly. "Not today, anyway, Newt. Haines showed us around quite a bit a couple of weeks after he was inaugurated—not with your historical commentary, I must admit. I think I'd rather get to work. You'll be handy in case I need you?"

"Just down the corridor, Mr. President. My button is this one."

Madigan wanted to call Hester right away, but when he buzzed Mrs. Hahn she informed him that the Secretary of State was waiting to see him. He had forgotten Sharkey had requested a private session after the Cabinet meeting.

"Send him right in," he told her, wondering how at this stage he could manage to look busy. He wished there were some papers on the desk so he could riffle through them in a show of executive zeal, but Sharkey's immediate entrance made any such ridiculous subterfuge unnecessary.

"Jim, I'm glad to see you," Madigan proclaimed, getting to his feet and coming out from behind the desk to shake the Cabinet official's hand. Sharkey didn't bother to sit down, but placed a bulging briefcase on a nearby chair.

"Mr. Vice President, I won't detract from your valuable time. I've taken the liberty of assembling a few classified documents and reports I felt you might want to study. Sort of a written briefing, as it were. There's one in particular, a report from the National Security Council and CIA on China's current intentions. You were on a speaking trip,

126

as I recall, when it was orally presented to the President about three or four weeks ago."

"Yes," Madigan confirmed, "I was sorry to miss that Council meeting. And I'm afraid the President didn't have time to brief me on it after I got back." The last was delivered in the tone of sad but brave resignation mothers have been known to use when an offspring hurt their feelings. Sharkey ignored Madigan's unsubtle whining, took a half dozen volumes and folders from the briefcase, and left them on the presidential desk before departing.

Madigan's next visitor was Frank Corris, the White House appointments secretary, who already had compiled a list of assorted congressmen, politicians and others seeking audiences the following day. It approximated the passenger manifest on a transcontinental flight, and it took more than an hour for Corris and the Vice President to compress it down to reasonable proportions. More difficult for Corris, that is. Madigan was eagerly ready to see almost anyone who asked.

"My God," he marveled after they agreed on seven appointments of fifteen minutes' duration each, "do this many people want to see the President every day?"

"Not quite this many, sir. But enough to occupy an entire day if you don't draw a few lines. And if you don't mind a little advice . . ."

"Go right ahead," Madigan assured him.

"Well, make every caller stick to that fifteen-minute schedule. Otherwise, he'll stay an hour or more if you'll let him."

"I'll remember," Madigan promised. "Uh, President Haines . . . did he . . . uh, does he schedule as many as seven appointments?"

"Limit of five, usually," Corris said huskily, avoiding the use of either past or present tense. "If there's nothing else, sir, I'll get back to my own office."

He left hurriedly without even waiting for Madigan to answer. The Vice President was slightly nettled at this rudeness and made a mental note that Corris might have to be replaced along with Spellman. It never penetrated why Corris departed so abruptly. Madigan had failed to see the tears welling up in his eyes.

Spellman returned to ask if it was all right to put the lid on.

"The lid?" Madigan asked.

"To tell the reporters nothing more is expectable today," Spellman said.

"How the hell should I know?" the Vice President demanded. "Frankly, I'd like to go home myself." The press secretary had unwittingly reminded him of an unexpected problem. Namely, who told the Acting President when to go home?

"I don't know of anything that might come up, sir," Spellman said. "Of course, we might get something out of Arizona at any time."

"Well, do I have to stay around for that?"

"No sir. I was going to stay anyway and I can handle any announcement. I'll contact you, naturally, before I give anything out."

"That'll be fine, Newt," the Vice President said gratefully. Nice boy, Spellman. Maybe Oscar could have some other good job around the White House. Corris' perhaps. Newt certainly knew his way around and he was most obliging. "Oh, before you go out, Newt, would you put those classified reports on that chair away where they'll be safe? I'll get to them tomorrow."

Spellman dutifully took the material out of the way. Madigan felt slightly guilty but he rationalized that he was too tired to read classified documents, even that important-sounding one on China's current intentions. He'd have to get to that one first. But he was tired, and now it was time to go home to Hester. The anticipation of telling her about his first few hours in the White House shucked his weariness like husk stripped from an ear of corn. Tomorrow should be quite a day. Maybe the biggest day of his life.

Hester wanted to go with him to the White House Thursday morning but for once Madigan's nuptial spine stiffened sufficiently to say no to his wife. He realized that Hester wandering around the Executive Mansion might smack of poor taste. And anyway, he didn't want her to sense what he had to admit to himself, that the White House still awed him. It would have even if he had been a full-fledged President and his oath of office already recorded for posterity. In his present status, he felt more like an interloper.

He had the good sense to tell his chauffeur to drop him at the Executive Wing, adjoining the main structure, instead of the normal entrance on the North Portico. Newton Spellman was waiting for him by the White House police captain's desk just inside and to the left of the big reception hall. It was 7 A.M., but already a horde of reporters and cameramen were jammed around the huge circular table on which were deposited hats and a few topcoats.

"Good morning, Mr. President," Spellman said respectfully but not without a taint of sadness. "Good morning, Mr. President," was the rather subdued mimicry of most of the press corps. Madigan came close to preening but decided to be modest and democratic.

"Good morning, Newt. Morning, boys. I guess 'Mr. Acting President' would be a bit too awkward so how about making it 'Mr. Vice President' for the time, uh, until we hear something from Winslow. Any questions before I get to work?"

The reporters were pleased at the prospect of an informal press conference, so soon after the formal news conference of last evening when Madigan announced he was assuming office temporarily under authority provided by the Constitution.

"Any late word from Arizona, Mr. Vice President?" one reporter asked.

"Nothing, I'm sorry to say. You'll be advised the minute we hear of a single development." They should know what he knew, he thought with the smug satisfaction of a man newly entrusted with a secret.

"There is one thing I haven't had a chance to brief you on, sir," said Spellman, this time neatly walking a tightrope between the presumably correct but distasteful "Mr. President" and the lesser designation. "I've already told the press they've now identified the bodies of the other two Secret Servicemen, both stewards and one of the two security guards."

"That leaves just two unidentified," Madigan said. "One guard and the President."

"Plus the flight crew," Spellman prompted.

"Oh yes, the pilots and so forth. Well, as I told you last night, General Coston believes some of these may never be positively identified. The important thing is to find the President, of course. I must re-emphasize what I said last night to you fellows, there was a parachute on the plane and we still have hopes that somehow the President might have used it and is safe."

"Wandering around some Arizona desert?" another newsman postulated.

"There's a lot of room for wandering," Madigan agreed, "but we have the Air Force's assurance that virtually every foot of that state is being searched. Now I think you'd better let me get to work. Gentlemen, good morning for now and I hope you'll join me in continuing to pray for the President's safety."

He hoped he had sounded and acted like a man with his hands firmly on the tiller. He was angry at himself for being nervous. Maybe, when he could drop this damned "Acting" stuff, he'd be more at ease. Right now he had a strange reluctance to act decisively. Constitutional authority or not, he still was in a weird kind of limbo, armed with the trappings of a President and even legalistic power, yet without the magic wand of that oath of office so solemnly sworn on the Bible.

The call he was most anxiously waiting for came through shortly before 10 A.M. Mrs. Hahn, primly proper and in Madigan's somewhat jittery state a bit standoffish, politely advised him, "General Coston is on the line."

Coston's message was brief, rimmed perceptibly with concern, and just another downward push on Madigan's yo-yo of selfconfidence. "Mr. Vice President, I've just finished talking to General Dunbar in Winslow."

"Proceed," Madigan said in what he trusted was a sufficiently commanding voice.

"Dunbar says they've identified the second of the security guards and the body of the radio officer, Captain Warneke. Identification will be impossible for the rest of the flight deck crew, as far as burial is concerned. Their bodies are in bits and pieces—there isn't anything left to identify."

"But the President," Madigan demanded. "How about the President?"

"Sir, there's no sign of the President's body."

"Maybe," Madigan suggested almost in desperation, "he was riding up front, in the cockpit. Then his body would have been in as bad shape as the pilots'."

"Not very likely, sir. We know Air Force One was heading toward some bad weather. Henderson would have sent the President back to his own quarters. He wouldn't have wanted him in a jump seat. Besides, it's already been in the papers that the President intended to stay in his stateroom the entire flight. Sabath was quoted to that effect."

Madigan sighed unhappily, aware that he still was imprisoned by the sentence of uncertainty imposed from the minute the plane was reported missing. "Well, thank you, General. I suppose—"

"One more thing, sir. We're sure Mr. Haines didn't jump. We found what was left of an unopened parachute near where our mystery person was located."

Only at this moment did Fred Madigan realize that he had been clinging subconsciously to that parachute as a last refuge, a final hiding place before he had to step into the new world of responsibility he both wanted and feared. But it had been a false refuge, no hiding place at all. What had been merely uncertainty was now bewilderment. Even the emotional strain of waiting for Haines's body to be discovered and identified was a simple, easily acceptable interlude compared to what Madigan now faced. And what the entire nation and world faced.

"General," he said with one more effort at clinging to fading logic, "that body *must* have been Haines. It had to be. The FBI must have made a mistake."

"No, sir. There was no mistake. They've checked those fingerprints exactly seven times. Also the teeth. Plus another bit of evidence, sir, which hasn't been given to anyone yet. The pathology men working with the FBI say the body was that of a man somewhat shorter than the President. They aren't absolutely sure, but they're willing to bet on it."

"So now where are we?" It was more of a plea than a question.

"I don't know, sir. I'm completely baffled. We've got one damned good possibility and it leads to a thousand question marks. The President may not have been on Air Force One."

"Then," Frederick James Madigan breathed, "where is he?"

The 11 A.M. news conference called by Madigan that same day fell somewhat short of General Coston's thousand question marks, but not by much.

It was an ordeal for the Vice President who, after all, did not know any more than the men and women doing the

131

asking. At Newton Spellman's suggestion, he was flanked by the director of the Federal Bureau of Investigation and the head of the Central Intelligence Agency. Their presence gave him a certain amount of moral support although they felt as helpless as he before the reportorial barrage.

Madigan began by reading a prepared statement (Spellman's composition). The statement alone would have sent half the room sprinting for telephones except that the news conference was being televised. The wire services were monitoring it on TV sets in their own offices, moving a running account on their teletype circuits without waiting for the press conference to end. Television literally had reduced some reporters, especially the wire service men, to the status of mere actors at major news conferences. They were there to ask questions, not handle the story.

The prepared statement was brief; Madigan read it in a low voice with obvious nervousness.

"The Air Force has advised me there is a possibility that the President was not on board Air Force One when it crashed in Arizona. All efforts to locate his body have failed, although these efforts are continuing. In the meantime, personnel from the FBI and the Armed Forces Institute of Pathology have identified the bodies of six of the seven passengers known to have been on the aircraft, plus five of the nine crew members. The crew members whose bodies have not been identified include the commander of Air Force One, Colonel Henderson; Major Foster, the copilot; flight engineer Falk and navigator Eldridge."

He was interrupted at this point by a volley of attempted questions and a forest of raised hands. "Just a minute," Madigan said with a show of impatience and anger, "let me finish reading this. I told you at the start there would be no questions until I've read this statement."

He cleared his throat and resumed in a stronger voice.

"The body of a seventh passenger was found in an area indicating that this person was riding in the rear of the aircraft when it crashed. However, repeated attempts to identify this body have been fruitless. Its fingerprints and dental charts do not correspond with those of President Haines. The Air Force is at a loss to explain the presence of this unknown person on the aircraft. This presence is the source of the tentative belief that the President may not have been aboard."

Madigan paused as if he were expecting renewed clamor from the reporters. There was none. Instead, there was a foglike stillness. The Vice President again cleared his throat and continued.

"The remains of a parachute, located under the berth in the President's private stateroom, were found in an unopened condition. This precludes the possibility that the President might have evacuated the aircraft when it encountered the still undetermined difficulty which resulted in a fatal crash."

Now Madigan's voice rose, gaining confidence from the very drama of the moment.

"I have asked the director of the FBI, assisted by the Central Intelligence Agency, to conduct a full investigation into all aspects of this mysterious situation. This investigation will include such possibilities as an impostor, sabotage, kidnaping or a combination of said possibilities. The Air Force will continue to investigate, on a separate basis, the cause of the accident itself. In that latter area, the Air Force will be assisted by personnel from the Department of Transportation's Bureau of Safety with the added co-operation of all federal agencies as required."

Madigan paused again. He had reached the part of the prepared statement which Parrish had insisted be included and it was the part Frederick Madigan relished the most. His voice was boulder-firm, and he read the words with the slow emphasis of a drumbeat.

"As the Acting President of the United States, I want to assure our friends throughout the free world, as well as the potential enemies of that free world, that I intend to continue the policies of our beloved President. Those policies are aimed at resisting aggression and preserving freedom. We, and I speak for all agencies of the federal government, intend to solve the tragedy that occurred in Arizona, and the apparent disappearance of our President, with dispatch and thoroughness. The American people should feel concern, but not panic. Sorrow, but not hopelessness.

"I ask my fellow citizens to reserve judgment, quell suspicion and refrain from hasty appraisals while this unfortunate matter is being investigated. If whatever fate has befallen President Haines is proved to be the result of an international espionage plot, the United States will take appropriate action. Until we determine that fate, however, it

133

is imperative that all Americans display patience, firmness and unbounded confidence in our investigative agencies.

"This," added the Vice President, "concludes my prepared statement. I will now entertain questions."

(From the official transcript of the press conference, as recorded by the Capital Stenographic Service)

Q. "Mr. Vice President, is there the remotest chance President Haines might have staged a disappearance himself, for some unknown motive?"

A. "No. Not without letting his closest associates know about it. Including myself. It is unthinkable. For that matter, what possible motive could he have had."

Q. "Has the Air Force's investigation of the crash revealed any sign of sabotage which might be connected with that body?"

A. "None whatsoever. General Coston has told me that all the available evidence to date points to a break-up in severe turbulence. The possibility of sabotage will be considered as part of the investigation, but there's nothing as of now to indicate that the plane was blown up."

Q. "Mr. Vice President, this business of an impostor. A great many persons saw the President board Air Force One the night of the crash. Would you care to comment, sir, on how an impostor could have gotten on the plane? Or arranged such a deception? And for what reason?"

A. "I don't have the slightest idea. The still and motion pictures taken of Air Force One's departure show seven passengers boarding, and one of them was Jeremy Haines—or his exact double. To carry out such a fantastic deception would have involved many persons who certainly would have come forth by now and disclosed the truth."

Q. "But those persons who might have recognized a double from close up can't come forth now. They were on the plane. They're dead."

A. "General Coston has advised me that all persons

134

who had close contact with the President before boarding have been questioned. They are positive it was Jeremy Haines who deplaned from the helicopter and boarded Air Force One. These included the pilots of the helicopter and the Army sergeant acting as a security guard on the helicopter."

Q. "Mr. Vice President, could the plane have stopped anywhere en route to Palm Springs and picked up this extra passenger?"

A. "According to General Coston, this would have been an impossibility. The plane was seen on radar screens up until the time of the crash."

Q. "Could there have been a stowaway, sir?"

A. "Again, the Air Force has assured me nobody could have gotten on the plane without being detected."

Q. "Mr. Vice President, you said the investigation would include the possibility of a kidnaping. Have you or anyone else received any kind of a ransom note—either from somebody here in the United States or from abroad? Any inkling of who might have perpetrated a kidnaping?"

A. "I said kidnaping was only a possibility, one of many things to be checked out. We have no evidence at all that a kidnaping actually took place. No ransom notes or anything like that."

Q. "Has Senator Haines been able to provide any clues as to the disappearance of his brother?"

A. "If you can find Senator Haines, I wish you'd ask him. He's somewhere fishing in the middle of Maine. We have the Maine State Police and forest rangers trying to locate him, but so far to no avail. He could be at any one of a hundred lakes. He did not tell his office specifically where he was going. All we know is that he left for Boston the night of the crash. Anyway, I doubt if he'll be able to throw much light on the matter."

Q. "Mr. Vice President, is there any reason to suspect

135

the Red Chinese or Russians for what has happened?"

A. "We have no reason to believe this. Naturally, until the entire mystery is solved, some kind of espionage plot will be one area of suspicion. Just one more thing to be investigated."

Q. "Mr. Vice President, if this turns out to be a Commie plot, what would the United States do?"

A. "Whatever is necessary."

Q. "Whatever is necessary for what, sir?"

A. "Well, that depends on what happened to the President. If he's alive and being held in some kind of international blackmail scheme, we'd do whatever had to be done to get him back safely."

Q. "Suppose, sir, Red Chinese agents had somehow kidnaped Mr. Haines. Would the United States accede to any ransom demands?"

A. "That depends on the demands."

Q. "Well, suppose the demands were as farfetched and drastic as trading the President's safety for pulling our troops out of Far Eastern bases, for example? Or even disarmament?"

A. "We'll cross that bridge when we come to it. I might comment at this point that my answers have to be hypothetical because your questions are based on hypothetical, uh, situations. I must emphasize again that we're as much in the dark as you are. I could stand up here all day and speculate but it wouldn't do anybody much good. I'll answer one more question and then I'd like to end this press conference. You over there, with the maroon tie."

Q. "Mr. Vice President, how long do you anticipate your status as Acting President will last? I mean, if Mr. Haines remains missing for a long time, would you be sworn into office?"

A. "Your question is very premature. I have every hope that our President will be found alive and well and that all elements of this tragedy eventually will

136

be explained. Until that time I shall continue to carry out his policies and act as I think he would want me to act. To the best of my ability."

The senior White House correspondent of UPI said, "Thank you, Mr. Vice President," and the horde of newsmen broke for telephones and offices. A reporter from *Time,* leaving at a more leisurely pace, remarked to a representative of the London *Daily Mail:*

"You know, the poor bastard sounded just like Harry Truman."

CHAPTER EIGHT

Gunther Damon usually went to the National Press Club on the thirteenth floor at 3 P.M. daily, Monday through Saturday, and when he went out the bureau door the staff did not have to glance at a watch or clock to know it was precisely three o'clock.

Four hours after the momentous Madigan news conference ended, he told Custer to get him a sandwich from Bassin's. This was an ominous sign to the staff. Any such departure from the norm usually meant that Gunther Damon was upset and/or angry. In the past, Gunther's ordering lunch from Bassin's had preceded such bureau-shattering events as removing Tom Prather as head of the Senate staff, firing two copy boys on the same day and—the staff had never forgotten that black occasion—posting a notice on the bulletin board that receipts had to be obtained from cab drivers and turned in with expense accounts.

Today it was Sam Foley who heard Damon call out "Custer," and with misgivings watched him give the copy boy a dollar bill. Sam clung briefly to the forlorn hope that maybe the news superintendent had merely sent downstairs for cigarettes. This was demolished when Custer sailed by the switchboard and announced breezily to Mrs. Strotsky, "I'm gonna get Mr. Damon a sandwich, Evelyn. Do you want anything?"

"Oh-oh," Foley whispered to Les Butler. "Our leader just sent out for food. Condition Red."

"May mean nothing," Butler assured him in a whistling-by-the-graveyard tone of voice. "He didn't go out yesterday, either."

"Yeh, but yesterday they found the plane and Madigan took over at the White House. Nobody got out for lunch all day. Not even DeVarian. The press conference is all cleaned up. Gunther could have gone out to eat if he had wanted to."

"We shall see what we shall see," said Butler philosophically.

The staff held a collective breath while Damon gloomily munched a chopped liver on rye and sipped meditatively on what passed for coffee from the office vending machine. He still had the paper coffee cup in his hand as he approached the news desk.

"Lousy coffee," he complained. "It tastes like emulsified engine oil."

Foley brightened up considerably. Maybe Gunther just wanted to denounce the coffee. Or fire the vending machine.

"Very bad," Sam agreed cheerfully. "Uh, how was the sandwich? Didn't you feel like going to the club?"

"No, I've got too much on my mind. The club's no place for newspapermen today, anyway. The barflies have probably located Haines in thirty-four different places with a hundred and thirty-four explanations of how and why he got there. Where's Pitch?"

"FAA," Butler replied, wondering if the aviation editor had committed some nefarious deed.

"Evelyn, get Pitcher at FAA and tell him to come on in unless he's fielding some earth-shaker. Is Jonesy back from Winslow?"

"He called from home thirty minutes ago," Mrs. Strotsky volunteered. "Said he wanted to shower and shave and then he was going to the White House."

"His plane landed a couple of hours ago, Damon," Butler said. "Tell you the truth, I expected he'd ask for the rest of the day off. But he said he wanted to come downtown anyway. He didn't sound happy about being pulled away from the crash site."

"Call Jones and tell him to come straight here instead of the White House, Evelyn," Damon ordered. "And get me Colin at the Pentagon. I'll take it at my desk. Christ, I think I'll order a new vending machine."

"What's up?" Foley said after Damon walked away.

"Damned if I know," Butler muttered. "Sounds like some kind of a conference. Pitch, Jonesy and Chet Colin. Aviation, White House and Pentagon. Something to do with the Haines story, that's for sure."

It *was* a conference, it *was* about the Haines story, and it was held in DeVarian's office, which was the only place in the IPS bureau providing any privacy. DeVarian himself was there, chain-smoking as usual and occasionally blinking at the three summoned reporters from under his bushy eyebrows with a kind of vague, detached paternalism as he let Gunther run the show.

It was not from any lack of ability that DeVarian relegated so much authority to Damon. At one time the IPS bureau chief was regarded as a superb deskman and a skilled writer in his own right. But now he was a human buffer zone between his overworked staff and the harsh but frequently necessary demands of New York. His mind was a delicate set of scales that skillfully weighed budget resources against client pressures, manpower limitations against news commitments.

He and Gunther Damon complemented each other as a ship's captain needs a dedicated, efficient executive officer. He was cautious where Damon was likely to be impulsive. He could be tough where Gunther occasionally would slip into softheartedness, and yet—as he had been when Jones wanted to stay in Winslow—DeVarian sometimes assumed Damon's tendency toward leniency when the news superintendent got his back up.

In his relations with the staff, he was somewhat aloof but this was not entirely the result of his sitting on the pedestal of authority. Stan DeVarian was rather shy, hesitant in speech and unable to loosen himself into casual social informality—unless he was feeling his liquor. On such occasions he was likely to do a 180-degree personality turn and become "one of the boys"—in DeVarian's case, the equivalent of a dignified collie who suddenly decides to romp with some puppies. His inebriation alarm clock was the sudden rendering of his college Alma Mater song, a sure sign at a staff party that the bureau chief had just passed the alcoholic point of no return.

Chet Colin, the only IPS man stationed at the Defense Department, was the last to arrive for the meeting— "Probably," DeVarian kidded him, "because you forgot where the office was." It was a standing bureau joke that Colin had to introduce himself to his colleagues when he made one of his rare visits downtown, about once every three months. He dressed impeccably and he talked the same way, in a soft Boston drawl with letter-perfect grammar.

Damon inspected today's sartorial splendor with as much awe as amusement. The tall, graying Pentagon reporter was wearing a bright red weskit under a handsomely tailored charcoal-gray suit, a neatly folded handkerchief peeping from the breast pocket. Damon shook his head. "Chet, somehow you always make me feel like a kitchen sink full of dirty dishes."

"The trouble with most men," Colin lectured, "is that they buy clothes foolishly—they go for price instead of material and tailoring. So the second time they wear a suit, it looks five years old."

"I paid fifty-five dollars for this one," Pitcher said defensively. "I think—"

"I think it's time to drop the subject of wearing apparel," DeVarian said crisply. "Gunther, this conference was your idea, so take over."

Damon lit a cigarette and inspected his three warriors, noting that Jones looked both weary and depressed.

"I've asked you here to tackle this Air Force One business because I think with some concentrated, old-fashioned digging IPS might be the one to solve this whole mystery. Not only for the biggest exclusive in history, but as a public service. Until Haines is found, alive or dead, this country is going to be one screwed-up collection of anxious, bewildered citizens.

"Now we seem to have two possibilities. One, the President was aboard that plane and his body is still somewhere in the gorge or at least in the immediate vicinity. If that's the case, we also know there was an extra passenger on Air Force One for reasons as yet undetermined. But the second possibility becomes more of a probability the longer the President's body stays missing. And our second possibility is that our unknown extra passenger wasn't an added starter but somebody posing as the President, again for reasons as yet undetermined. Each of you operates in a specialized field and so each may be able to contribute a few pieces to the over-all jigsaw puzzle. What I'd like to do this afternoon is review what we know and get some ideas on where we can start planting our spades. Okay?"

Pitcher and Colin nodded. Jones just gazed at the news superintendent.

"Okay. First, the business of the unknown body. If we can find out who this was, we'll probably have our foot inside the door. All we have right now is that the fingerprints and dental charts don't correspond with those of Haines or anyone else on the plane. Jonesy, when you were out at the crash site, were you told anything else about that body which hasn't been made public?"

"Only one thing," the White House reporter answered. "Dunbar said the pathologists figured he was shorter than the President. That, plus the fingerprint and teeth evidence, convinced them it couldn't be Haines. The height business was off the record. I take it the Madigan didn't let it out at the press conference today."

"No, he didn't," Damon confirmed. "But it still doesn't give us much to go on. Pitch, you saw Air Force One take off. Are you positive it was Haines who got on that airplane?"

"I guess I'd almost swear to it. Remember, it was night and I was about twenty or thirty yards away. But I saw his gray hair, well, let's see—there was the homburg he always wears. The way he walked. And he was tall."

"Did you see his face?"

"No, not exactly. Not at that distance. I mean, I could see his face but not well enough to distinguish his features."

"So he could have been a double."

Pitcher chewed on that for a minute. "Golly, Gunther, I suppose it's possible. But . . ."

"If you're going to take this double or imposter theory seriously," Jones interrupted, "there's one large hole in it."

"Which is?" Damon said.

"I just told you the mystery body was that of a man shorter than Haines. Pitch says the man he saw go aboard Air Force One, presumably the President himself, was tall. Like Haines."

"Well," Damon conceded, "I'll admit there's a hole but there's got to be some explanation to fill it. Maybe we should concentrate on Haines instead of that damned body. For example, where is our President? Why hasn't he come forth? Assuming he's not dead, and I have a hunch he isn't, just where the hell could he have gone and why? Is he seriously ill, insane, or what? Has anybody thought to check Camp David?"

"Camp David's out," Jones said positively.

"Why?"

"Because Jeremy Haines hated that place. Remember, Gunther? He had it closed up right after he took office. Nobody knew exactly why. Haines said it was to save money but that wasn't the real reason. It didn't cost that much to keep open. Haines just took a dislike to it and refused to use it."

"I still think it should be checked out. Jonesy, why don't you run up there tomorrow and see if there's any sign of life?"

"Okay, but at ten cents a mile on my expense account, you'll be wasting IPS dough."

"I'll risk it," Damon said genially. "Colin, I figure you might hit some pay dirt if you do some digging into the backgrounds of the crew. This may sound wild, but I've got a hunch somebody who was part of that crew sneaked or smuggled our mystery man aboard. I know the Air Force says it's impossible, but this whole thing is impossible to begin with. And for all we know, there may have been a link between the mystery man and the crash itself. Pitch, why the vigorous shaking of your crew cut?"

"Because I don't think there was any mystery about the crash. That plane came apart in turbulence. Everything points to loss of control which led to elevator failure when the pilot tried to recover. I've got a half dozen old CAB accident reports in my files which fit this crash right down to the last comma."

"Pitch is right," Jones said thoughtfully. "That's what we heard at the crash scene too. And this gives me an idea—maybe one little piece we could fit into your jigsaw puzzle."

"I'd welcome a piece the size of a pinhead at this point," Damon said.

"It's just about that size. In fact it's only a theory, a kind of vague idea. I'll bet that whoever thought up Haines's disappearance, if it is a disappearance, didn't count on one thing."

"Which was?"

"That Air Force One would crash."

"Quite a theory," DeVarian said. "But it isn't any more logical than another theory. Namely, that the crash was part of a disappearance plot."

"And the thunderstorm also was part of the plot?" Pitcher asked.

"Don't go overboard on that thunderstorm," Damon warned. "You've been telling me for years not to speculate on the causes of air crashes. That things aren't always as obvious as they seem. Maybe there wasn't any connection between the accident and the mystery, but it's damned hard for me to write off the crash as just a coincidence."

"Getting back to my role as the Sherlock Holmes of the Pentagon," Colin said. "I seriously doubt if all the digging in the world would uncover anything unusual or suspicious about the crew. Henderson, Foster, Falk—they were the finest officers you could find anywhere. They flew by the book and they lived by the book."

"There were nine crew members on Air Force One," Damon reminded him. "They all weren't in the cockpit. How about the stewards? The security guards?"

"Every man was a veteran on the presidential aircraft assignment," Colin said. "All but one. A Sergeant Jervis was new. This was his first trip."

"So look into this Jervis, Chet."

The Pentagon reporter sighed, in the manner of an adult about to explain a simple problem to a child. "Gunther, I assure you the Air Force and the FBI must be turning that boy's life story inside out simply because he *was* a new crew member. I couldn't come close to matching an FBI investigation. Be reasonable."

"He's got a point, Gunther," DeVarian said. "You've also got to assume Jervis had a complete security check before he was assigned to Air Force One."

"In this story," Damon argued, "we can't assume anything. Sure he had a security check. So have a few other people who turned out to be spies, murderers or perverts."

DeVarian shook his head. "But, as Chet said, the FBI must be reviewing his security clearance. It undoubtedly is for every person aboard that plane. We can't expect Colin or even a whole platoon of reporters to dig the way the FBI or Air Force can. And even if we had the manpower, they'd just be duplicating the official investigation."

"So what do you want us to do, Stan? Drop the whole thing? Sit around on our butts waiting for the official handouts?"

"No," the bureau chief said patiently. "But you've got to

144

recognize our limitations, Gunther. Let's concentrate on areas where we won't be duplicating official efforts."

"There is no such area," Damon said firmly. "Look, I'm not trying to be unreasonable. I don't expect Chet or anyone else on this staff to compete with the whole Air Force and the FBI. But if we don't do some digging on our own, we'll just stay on the sidelines waiting to be spoon-fed what the Administration is willing to parcel out. Probably in driblets. And we don't have any guarantee the press will be told the truth. Not the whole truth. This could be the most incredible story in the history of journalism. It could involve anything and everything—sabotage, kidnaping, murder, insanity, espionage, even sex. I say we've got to do more than cover it. We've got to solve it—or try to. That's the word you've all missed—try. I know it's a long shot. I know you could spend a year on just this one assignment and not come up with anything. But we can try, dammit, we can try. There's too much at stake."

Jones looked at the news superintendent with an expression of reluctant admiration. "You should have been a football coach, Gunther. After that speech, I'm ready to go out and stop a locomotive with my bare chest. Okay, I'll drive up to Camp David tomorrow and start snooping."

"I'm all fired up too," Pitcher announced. "There's only one trouble. I don't know where I'm supposed to start."

"Second the motion," Colin added. "Or do you still want me to look into the life and times of Sergeant Jervis and the rest of the crew?"

"Frankly," Damon admitted, "I can't really tell any of you where to start. That Jervis suggestion was just a shot in the dark. Let's get back to the main problem—where Haines might be if they can't find his body. For example, how about Russia?"

"Russia?" DeVarian asked incredulously. "What would he be doing in Russia? You mean the Russkies kidnaped him?"

"No, that'd be too far out in left field. Maybe a secret meeting about Red China."

"Doesn't add up, Gunther," Jones said. "Suppose the President did go to Moscow on some wild, supersecret mission. Do you think he would have remained silent this long? Do you think he could have allowed all this uncertainty and mystery without revealing the truth? It's been

145

two days since the crash. Or go a step further. Don't you think he would have told the Vice President where the hell he was going? Madigan may be a political lightweight, but I can't conceive of somebody like Jeremy Haines going out of the country and not telling anyone about it. And I mean anyone."

"If he went to Russia," Pitcher said, "then why the Air Force One trip to Palm Springs?"

"Decoy," Damon suggested. "Just to make everyone think he was heading to California. He might have taken another plane to Moscow. And *that*, Mr. Pitcher, is exactly where *you* can start digging."

"Huh?"

"Like finding out if any other transport planes left Andrews the night Haines was supposed to leave. Big, long-range planes."

Jones was still in a refuting mood. "A goose chase, Gunther. It's absolutely unthinkable that Haines wouldn't have revealed his whereabouts after the crash. Before the accident, yes, there could have been some reason for total secrecy. But not after that plane went down. He'd have to tell the country the truth. My God, look at all the crazy rumors. The stock market dive. I picked up one report in Arizona that SAC's been alerted. That's something Chet can check into."

"He could have gone off his rocker," DeVarian said. "Taken off for Russia on his own—a kind of Rudolf Hess flight, a peace mission dreamed up by a sick mind."

"No," Jones objected again. "If you're going to use the Hess analogy, that was strictly a one-man affair, a solo flight. The President of the United States couldn't pull anything like that off all by himself. He'd have to involve at least a certain number of persons. A pretty large chunk of the Air Force, for one thing. He'd have to clear that flight through God knows how many Air Defense Commands. And do you think he'd leave someone like General Coston totally in the dark?"

"I would think," Damon said slowly, "that the President of the United States could pull off any damned thing he wanted to, and in complete secrecy if the stakes were high enough."

"Granted," the White House reporter said. "But only up to a point. And the point where your logic falls apart is that plane crash. Assuming the existence of a secret flight to Moscow or someplace, by now he would have come forward and disclosed the whole thing. What stakes would be high enough to throw the whole world into a turmoil?"

The five men in DeVarian's tiny office fell silent, shuffling the mental cards of arguments and reasoning.

"There's one more possibility," DeVarian said finally. "Farfetched, I'll admit, but nothing seems too farfetched in this situation. Suppose he did get the same urge that prompted Hess to fly off to England, a half-baked peace mission. Only he didn't bother to tell the Russians about it first. So he has a jet take him over to the Soviet Union and is shot down. It stands to reason the Russians wouldn't be bragging about killing the President, even if it was justifiable."

"You're still on the insanity kick," Jones said. "He'd have to be out of his mind to invade Soviet airspace without any warning."

"Not insanity as such, Jonesy," DeVarian said. "More of a fixation like Hess had—the notion he could end the war by the sheer drama of flying to England unannounced. Haines could have had the same fixation, a sudden, dramatic peace mission would end the cold war just as Hess thought his flight would bring England and Germany together. If the Russians shot Haines down, that would explain why he hasn't revealed his whereabouts—he could be dead. And Moscow had a perfect out. The plane crashed in Arizona, a coincidence that took the Soviets off an embarrassing hook."

"I'll agree with one aspect of your hypothesis," Jones said.

"What's that?"

"Haines is dead. How or why—I can't even guess. But I think he's dead. Or he would have unbuttoned this whole rotten mess by now. I wish to God there could have been some mistake on that body identification. That, regardless of fingerprints and all that crud, it was Haines they found in that wreckage. And remember, they still might find his body, and the only mystery you'd have left is the identity of the extra passenger."

The White House reporter slumped wearily in his seat. Damon knew Jones must be exhausted, emotionally as well as physically. "Jonesy, why don't you go home and get

147

some sleep? That crash site must have been pretty hard to take."

"Hard doesn't describe it. It wouldn't have been so bad for Pitch, I imagine. He's seen what a busted-up airplane looks like. Me, I didn't believe what I saw. And not just the wreckage and bodies. The little things. Like the matchbook covers. God, how many times have I swiped those matchbooks off Air Force One so I could give them to friends as souvenirs? Or that shoe I found. The laces were still tied. And it was an elevated shoe. I remember when I picked it up, I was thinking about the frailty of human vanity. Somebody on that plane must have been selfconscious about being short and a hell of a lot of good it—Gunther, what's the matter?"

Damon's mouth was open, almost gaping like an impaled fish.

"What kind of a shoe did you say you found?" he breathed.

"An elevated shoe. It was built up to give added height. Why the—"

The White House reporter stopped, what he was about to say suddenly choked off by an alarm bell reverberating in his brain. "Jesus, an elevated shoe," he muttered.

"Yeh," said Damon. "An elevated shoe. Only it didn't belong to anybody with an inferiority complex about height. There *was* an impostor on that plane. Wearing shoes to make him as tall as Jeremy Haines."

Typically, it was DeVarian who took the opposite tack—that of trying to break down the symmetrical logic of the clue mainly because it was almost too good to be true.

"Let's not jump at conclusions," he said cautiously, yet unable to keep the eagerness out of his voice. "There were sixteen persons on the plane. Eliminating the woman secretary, that leaves fifteen who might have worn elevateds. We can't assume that shoe belonged to an impostor."

"No, we can't," Damon countered, "but it's a pretty good place to start. Maybe Colin here, could ferret out how tall all those crew members were. In that way we might find out if anyone outside the impostor might have been wearing built-up shoes. I'm sure it couldn't have been Admiral Philips—he was about six two. Ditto Phil Sabath. I've known Phil for years. He was almost a six-footer—

148

come to think of it, I've been swimming with him, and in his bare feet he was three or four inches taller than I. That leaves two security guards, the two stewards and the three Secret Service agents. I doubt if the guards or stewards would be wearing uplifts—they'd probably have GI shoes on their feet and I never heard of an elevated being standard GI equipment. The agents are another matter. I suppose a Secret Serviceman could have vanity like anyone else. We could find out the height requirements for agents—that might eliminate them."

Jones arose with the important air of a fictitious detective about to unveil the name of the murderer. "I don't think we have to check any of this out."

"Why not?" asked Damon.

"Because I think I know who the impostor was."

"Okay," Damon said. "Let us in on it."

"Think back. Gunther, you asked Pitch about the appearance of the man he thought was the President the night the plane took off. Think, now. Pitch said he not only looked like Haines but he walked like him. Doesn't that ring any bells?"

Damon shook his head but DeVarian whistled.

"Senator Haines," the bureau chief said quietly. "The President's brother. He walks exactly like Haines. Those short, quick steps."

"Wait a minute," Pitcher said. "I've seen the senator. He's got white hair. Haines had gray hair. The guy who boarded that plane had gray hair. Besides, the senator's in Maine fishing. He went to Boston the night of the crash."

"Yeh," Damon said. "But nobody's heard from him and nobody can find him. The hair would be easy to fix—just dye it gray. Pitch, can you find out from your airline buddies if Bert Haines actually flew to Boston?"

"Maybe, if he took an airline plane. I can check the passenger manifests. Let's see—he'd fly Eastern, American or Northeast. I'll do it first thing in the morning."

"You'll do it right now," Damon ordered. "Boy, I think we're on to something. Bert Haines is at least two inches shorter than the President. But put elevated shoes on him, dye his hair, give him that homburg Jeremy Haines always wears, add the similarity of their walk, and you've got the answer. At night, from where Pitch and the other reporters

149

were standing, you couldn't tell them apart. Pitch, get going."

Jones was thoughtful as he watched the aviation editor go out the door of DeVarian's office. "Even if we find out it was Bert Haines impersonating the President, we're still a long way from the truth."

"Sure," Damon agreed, "but we've got our foot in the door."

"I wonder if we should be walking in," the White House reporter said in a low voice.

"And what does that crack mean?" Damon demanded.

"Meaning we may be sticking our journalistic noses into something bigger than we can even imagine. Something maybe we shouldn't know about. That's what bothers me. If we find out that the senator never went to Maine, it's a copper-riveted cinch he was posing as the President. So the next question is, what in God's name prompted Jeremy Haines to arrange the switch?"

"Followed by another question," DeVarian said. "If Jeremy Haines deliberately planned this whole mess, why is he still hiding? He must know his brother is dead."

"More than that," Damon said. "He sent his own brother to his death. Along with Phil Sabath and everyone else on that plane. Accidentally, if we buy Pitch's explanation of the crash. But that doesn't mean they're less dead. And if Jeremy Haines is alive, I hope he has a motive strong enough to justify what's happened. Maybe you're right, Stan. Maybe he's just nuts."

"It's not inconceivable. The presidency is the loneliest job in the world. A man might crack wide open, particularly at this time. Wondering how to avoid World War III without giving up the country's underwear."

"If you're through with me, I'll get back to my many-sided mausoleum," Colin announced. "You still want me to check on those crew members?"

Damon pondered this for a moment. "No, let's wait and see what Pitch comes up with. I'll be in touch with you."

After Jones and Colin left, DeVarian lit his ninth cigarette of the meeting and blew smoke rings toward the ceiling. "You know, Gunther, Jonesy said something which we should consider."

"Jonesy said a lot. What in particular prompts this outburst of precaution?"

"That we could be sticking our noses into something too big for IPS or any wire service to handle. The situation, to put it mildly, is somewhat touchy."

"I know that, Stan. If it makes you feel any better, I promise to consult with you before we put anything out. But we might as well understand one thing right now. If Pitcher tells me Bertrand Haines wasn't on any flight to Boston, I'm going to run with it—to all twelve hundred and fifty-eight IPS clients."

It was one of Rod Pitcher's virtues as an aviation specialist that his field of acquaintances stretched far beyond airline public relations men. He also knew numerous pilots, stewardesses, crew schedulers, ramp personnel, salesmen, ticket agents, dispatchers and reservations clerks—often by their first names. He had cultivated many friendships among the industry's rank and file. He could walk into any airline operations office at National Airport, for example, and be greeted more like a colleague than a newspaperman.

Thus it was relatively easy for him to obtain the passenger manifests in question. At American, he merely phoned an assistant district traffic manager and found out where the manifests were kept.

"Just want to look through them for one particular night," he explained. "Checking to see if somebody I know was aboard any flights to Boston. Thanks, Jimmy. No, I won't have to take them out of the office. I'll look at them there."

American's manifests drew a blank. No sign of a "B. Haines" anywhere. He had a further hunch and went up to the airline's Admiral's Club at National Airport where he asked to see the registrations for that never-to-be-forgotten night. He figured that, being a United States senator, Haines probably belonged to this private club and might have stopped in for a drink before taking off. He did not ask the receptionist at the club if Haines was, indeed, a member because he did not want to tip his hand. But, again, he found no sign that the senator had visited the club on this occasion.

At Eastern the search was somewhat complicated by sheer numerics. Pitcher called on a passenger service representative he knew at the airport, again explaining in a casual, "it really isn't very important" tone that he just wanted to check the names of passengers boarding planes to Boston for this one day, up through the final scheduled flight.

"I'll show you where the manifests are located, Pitch," the PSR informed him, "provided they haven't been sent to our accounting office in New York. But there'll be quite a few names. We've got seven shuttle flights to Boston, plus another five regular flights."

"Do you have anything out of Dulles for Boston? Or Friendship Airport? Or would everything leave from National?"

"They all depart National. Here's the office."

Fortunately the manifests hadn't been transferred to New York yet. The PSR introduced Pitcher to the traffic clerk on duty and left him with a sheaf of manifests for the regular flights.

"I'll need the shuttle manifests too," Pitcher said.

"There aren't any manifests for the shuttles," the clerk said. "But I can let you see the individual boarding cards. Maybe you should go through those first. There are a helluva lot of them."

The reporter examined approximately five hundred boarding cards without success. Then he turned to the manifest sheets. His eyes were tired and he was worried that he might skip over "B. Haines" even if he saw the letters. But he was lucky as well as persevering. On the fifth and final manifest, marked "Flight 518, DCA-BOS, Scheduled Departure 9 P.M.," he found his B. Haines. Next to the name, in a small space under a column labeled Check-In, were the letters "N.S."

No show.

With difficulty, Pitcher suppressed his excitement. "I hate to bother you, but is 518 the last flight to Boston?"

"Last one," the clerk replied. "Nothing more until eight the next morning."

"I think I've found what I was looking for," Pitcher said.

CHAPTER NINE

Only Stan DeVarian's firm conservatism blocked Damon's intentions of breaking the Senator Haines story that Thursday night after Pitcher's report. The bureau chief and the news superintendent had a knockdown verbal battle before Damon surrendered to his superior's authority. In a wire service, the chain of command is as inviolate as in an army.

"You're throwing one hell of a beat into the ash can," Gunther protested in a last-ditch argumentative flurry.

"We're not throwing it away. We're just delaying it. Until we can check out a few more facts. I repeat what I told you at the start of this little donnybrook, Gunther. The brother didn't have to go to New England on a commercial plane. Pitch should check air taxi services. Haines might have even decided to take a train at the last minute. That could be the reason he didn't show at the airport. Train service is fast these days—five hours between Washington and Boston on that new Pennsy express. We can find out if he had a parlor car reservation. Let's keep our shirts on until we're sure."

"I'm sure now," Damon grumbled. "I'll bet you a dinner at the Press Club this thing'll pop wide open while we're doing a reasonable facsimile of the goddamned play-it-safe AP. Hell, I'll even bet Madigan will announce it at a press conference tomorrow."

"So the world won't come to an end. Better we miss on this than look silly if the senator's found fishing at some Maine lake. Do you want Pitch to keep checking tonight?"

Damon thought that over briefly. "No, it's too late for the night cycle. Besides, he's bushed. It'll take him another three or four hours to go through train reservations and air taxi stuff. There must be a half dozen air taxi outfits operating out of here. I'll put him back to work tomorrow morning."

DeVarian examined his subordinate with something akin to affection.

"Sore at me, Gunther?" he smiled.

"A little," Damon admitted. "I think you're being overly cautious. But what the hell, you're the boss. I may get drunk tonight—the inevitable sublimation for a frustrated newspaperman."

DeVarian's cold blue eyes narrowed. "You may have some more frustration in the future, Gunther."

"Oh?" The one word was more of a challenge than a question.

"Yeh. I may tell you to sit on this a while longer even if Pitch finds out Haines didn't go to New England on any means of public conveyance."

"Our little donnybrook, as you phrased it," Damon snapped, "seems far from over, I take it. Your move, Stan."

"Don't blow your blood vessels, my friend. I figure we might do some further detective work before we unload. For example, I have a hunch your secret-flight-to-Russia idea might be skirting pretty close to the truth. So I'll make a bargain with you. If Pitch finds out that some mystery plane left Andrews the same night as Air Force One, and we have this Senator Haines angle well coppered, I'll let you open fire."

"Mr. Pitcher is going to be a very busy young man," Damon said.

"We can put somebody else on the air taxi outfits and the railroad. Pitch'll do better concentrating at Andrews. You know our aviation editor—he wouldn't take a train from here to Baltimore. He'd regard it as unpatriotic."

Damon chuckled, his good humor restored. The more he thought about it, the more that Moscow flight made sense. They had evidence that Senator Haines did not go on a fishing trip. They had indications that it might have been the senator aboard the presidential aircraft. If they could establish the existence of a mystery departure from Andrews, it all added up to justification for a story even under DeVarian's boundary lines of caution. The departure angle was nebulous, admittedly, because Pitcher could never get confirmation that the President was aboard any departing flight. IPS would have to speculate that it *could* have involved the President on some secret mission. But even the mere speculation might force some official admissions—or maybe some interesting "no comments" which in themselves would add credence to the speculation. Of course there might be flat denials but that was the calculated risk any newspaperman took with a story based partially on circumstantial evidence and raising intriguing possibilities instead of presenting only hard-nosed facts. And now he had DeVarian's promise to let him break it.

"You've got a deal," he said. "And believe me, brother DeVarian, I'm gonna hold you to it. Tomorrow ought to be one hell of a day. Pitch'll be working on the plane angle and Jonesy can give us the poop on Camp David. Maybe we should have some one talk to Senator Haines's wife. It stands to reason she'd know if her husband actually went fishing."

"I doubt if it would do any good," DeVarian said. "If there was some kind of a plan to plant the senator on Air Force One instead of the President, she'd either be sworn to secrecy or she wouldn't have been let in on the plot in the first place. As for Jones, with all this arguing I forgot to tell you. He's already left for Camp David."

"He isn't wasting any time," Damon observed.

"Nope. He said he wanted to get it out of the way. Figured there might be too much popping tomorrow."

"That might be the understatement of the year. I only hope nobody else is on to what we are."

It was just as well for Gunther Damon's peace of mind and mental equilibrium that he did not know that Vice President Madigan, at this very moment, was phoning the director of the Federal Bureau of Investigation with the pointed question:

"Do you think it could have been the President's brother whose body was found on the plane?"

The FBI chief was the visual antithesis of predecessor J. Edgar Hoover—lean, scholarly-looking with his horn-rimmed glasses, and almost ascetic in appearance. He was soft-spoken to the point of seeming diffident, but his FBI associates knew only too well that Director Paul Reardon's personality was that of a marshmallow with a steel ball hidden inside.

The Vice President's abrupt question took him by surprise, and Reardon was a man who was seldom surprised by

155

anything. His answer was not an answer but a cautious probing.

"Sir, do you have any particular reason for asking that? Anything you've heard that might make you think the unknown body was that of Senator Haines?"

"Well," said Madigan a bit petulantly, as if the FBI Director was challenging his common sense, "I've been talking to Ruth Haines, the senator's wife. She hasn't heard a thing from her husband. She's a little worried because nobody's been able to find him. And it got me thinking. I just wondered if you knew or suspected something I haven't been told."

"Did Mrs. Haines call you or vice versa?" Reardon asked.

"I don't see where that makes any difference," Madigan bristled. "As a matter of fact, I called her. I'd like very much to talk to Bert Haines. He might be able to fill in some of these damned gaps. So I called her to ask if she had heard from him yet. She said no, and she sounded quite upset. Quite upset, Mr. Reardon."

"I can well understand that, Mr. Vice President," Reardon said sympathetically. He said nothing else. Madigan was left dangling on what the FBI chief evidently considered the end of the conversation.

The Vice President became miffed. "Well, how about it, Reardon? I asked you a simple question and I'd appreciate some kind of answer. I'll ask it again if you can't understand plain English. Was Bert Haines on Air Force One?"

"Mr. Vice-President," Reardon said with firm politeness, "we've already talked to Mrs. Haines. She drove her husband to National Airport that night, she put him on a nine o'clock non-stop flight to Boston and she waited until the plane took off."

Gunther Damon was at home, having just finished science's most magnificent contribution to the health and welfare of bachelors who can't cook—a frozen TV dinner. He had eaten it absent-mindedly, and by tomorrow morning he probably would not even remember what kind of a dinner he had put in the oven. He was one of those men who would not have been unhappy to have somebody invent a pill that could afford complete nourishment and satisfaction of hunger, because generally he considered both cooking and eating an unfair consumption of his valuable time.

He would admit to certain female friends, those who regarded his penchant for frozen dinners as a subconscious, lonely yearning for matrimony, that such repasts usually had all the culinary appeal of a glass of water. Actually, the TV meals were part of his rather systematic mind, a kind of timing mechanism. In the fifteen minutes it took to pre-heat the oven, and the subsequent twenty-five minutes for cooking, he knew he could mix and consume his nightly before-dinner quota of three martinis.

Damon opened the *Evening Star* to the radio-TV page, looking over the television schedule. It was one of those nights when not a single station had anything of interest, which was almost as annoying as those nights when there were excellent late movies on at least three channels. He wished he had a good book. He considered driving to the drugstore in a nearby shopping center to pick up a paper-back, then decided against it because he was anxious to hear from Jones on the Camp David trip. Maybe he'd call Janie. He abandoned this notion. Janie was the last girl he had bedded with and on his part it was a purely sexual relationship, one he could not bear repeating on two suc-cessive dates. If it was sex he wanted tonight, it would have to be with a different woman. The hell with it. He was tired, anyway.

And while he did not want to admit it, he was also bored. And lonely.

Vice President Frederick James Madigan was at home, re-counting to Hester the events of the day with what he hoped was appropriate modesty for a man imbued with a new spirit of aggressive confidence.

"Everyone's being real helpful," he assured his wife. "Naturally, it's a bit difficult because I'm literally only half a President. I wish they'd find out what happened to Haines. I'd like to be either in or out of office, not midway through the door."

"The body they found in the plane wreck," Hester asked, "what are they doing about identifying it?"

"The FBI is cross-checking the fingerprints, I suppose. But that involves going through millions of files. God knows how long it'll take to establish his identity—provided his fingerprints are on file."

"Most people are, aren't they?"

"Well, yes. If they were once in the military, or have had some kind of a security check or a criminal record. That covers most of the population. You know, Hester, I had a hunch it might have been Bert Haines on that plane instead of the President. But the FBI director told me they're convinced Bert went on that fishing trip."

"Did they check the fingerprints on that body? To see if they were Bert's?"

"I would assume they did or they wouldn't have been so positive. For the life of me, I can't figure out why it's taken so long to locate Bert."

"Maybe he didn't go on the fishing trip but couldn't tell Ruth," Hester said with a sly look.

"Why on earth would he do that?"

His wife cluck-clucked in mock exasperation. "Oh, come on now, Fred. If a man wanted to go away for a while and his motives weren't exactly honorable, what better excuse could he give than a phony fishing trip in a place nobody could find? I wouldn't be a bit surprised if Bert Haines were shacked up somewhere with a floozy under an assumed name."

The possibility had never occurred to Madigan, who with all his faults was at least faithful to the marriage vows— perhaps more from fear of Hester than from a moral sense. Actually, he was rather naïve about such matters and he was quite shocked that a United States senator could even be suspected of conducting an assignation.

"I can't conceive of Bert Haines doing anything like that," he declared.

"Why not? Just because he's a senator? It certainly would explain why nobody can find him in Maine, which isn't the biggest place in the United States. Fred, I'll bet he's even trying to get into Maine incognito so the state police can find him where he was supposed to be in the first place. No wonder he's still missing. He probably was too ashamed to come back to Washington from where he really was."

The Vice President gravely pondered this interesting conjecture. Come to think of it, he mused, this would explain why Reardon acted so unco-operative on the phone. The FBI probably knew where Bert Haines was—and who he was with, if the President's brother was indulging in some extramarital monkey business.

"I'll leave it to others to follow this line of inquiry," he told his wife. "I think it's beneath my dignity. This could be very embarrassing to Ruth. I certainly am not going to call her any more."

Which meant that Fred Madigan suspected his wife had solved the mystery of the missing senator.

Rod Pitcher was at home, his abused eyes feeling as if there were weights tied to their lids. He also had a monumental headache compounded by chagrin over what he considered Damon's cavalier treatment of his detective work.

The news superintendent had reacted to Pitcher's breathless phone call from the airport with surprising casualness. "Okay, Pitch, nice work. We're going to sit on it for tonight and I want you to check some more stuff out tomorrow. Be in as early as you can—like no later than eight-thirty. You'll have to go out to Andrews first thing."

Rod was complaining loudly to Nancy. "Three and a half cruddy hours of going through those manifests and shuttle boardings. Then he doesn't even use the story. I make like Ellery Queen and Damon says they're gonna sit on it. Nancy, we got any aspirin?"

She brought him the pills and a glass of water, perching on the arm of his chair while he gulped them down with a grimace and listening to him grumble some more. "I swear, Nance, I'm gonna quit this rat race and get a good job with an airline. Look how late I was for supper tonight, and your pot roast was ruined."

"I thought you said it was delicious," she chided him.

"It was very good," Pitcher amended hastily. "But not as good as the first time you cooked me a pot roast. Then it melted in my mouth. Tonight's was a wee bit overcooked."

"You're fibbing, beloved husband," she purred. "The pot roast was awful and you know it. Rod, you don't have to lie about my cooking. When I fix you something and you don't like it, tell me the truth. That's the only way I can be a better cook."

"You're a very good cook," he assured her. "Better than you claimed to be when I was courting you. Anyway, you're sensational in bed and that's even more important."

"Don't change the subject. Anyway, I have a slight suspicion you're more upset about getting home late than

159

about their not using your story. Do you think I'm mad at you?"

"Are you?"

She lowered herself into his lap and kissed him very gently, very softly, a fleeting caress that was electric in its unspoken tenderness. "Rod, when we started going together, remember all those times I had to break dates? Like when we were supposed to go to the Aviation Club dinner and I got stuck in Detroit in a blizzard? Or the airline Christmas dance when I was on reserve and had to take a trip out two hours before you were to pick me up? The time you had tickets to that hit play and we had a mechanical delay out of Chicago—so we missed the first act?"

"Yeh, I remember. I figured the only way a guy could get a stewardess to keep a date was to marry her. So I did. What's your point?"

"My point is that you always accepted those broken dates as part of the occupational hazards when you go with a stewardess. You never complained. You never got angry. That's one reason I fell in love with you. Then came a certain day when American asked you to speak to a stewardess meeting on air safety. You told the girls how important their jobs were, and how proud you'd be to have a daughter grow up to be a stewardess."

"So?"

"So in a way you were telling me in front of everyone I worked with that you were proud of me. That's the day I decided I was in love with you. Now the shoe's on the other foot, husband. I'm proud of you. I'm proud I married a newspaperman. Even one who comes home late and gripes about a big exclusive they didn't use and lies about my cooking just so my feelings won't be hurt. Don't be so oversolicitous, Rod. It's as bad for a marriage as being too inconsiderate. Do you read me?"

"I read you, Nancy," he said huskily. "I also love you."

"The feeling is mutual. Let's have an after-dinner brandy, followed by seduction."

"Who's gonna seduce who?"

"Pour the brandy while I think about it. Did Mr. Damon have anything else to say besides what you told me?"

Pitcher pushed his wife off his lap and went over to their small portable bar where he located a bottle of brandy. He poured some into a couple of tumblers and swished the contents around professionally. "Yep, he wants me to go out to Andrews tomorrow morning."

"Why, honey?"

"To check outgoing flights, I guess. Just between us, Nancy, Gunther's got a notion that the President secretly flew to Moscow on some kind of a screwy peace mission. That the Palm Springs trip was a cover-up."

"I guess I'm just a dumb ex-stew, but if a Moscow flight was secret, what does he expect you to find out? They won't tell you much at Andrews."

"Nope. I'll be looking for clues, mostly. The tower won't have anything down in black and white, like 'secret flight to Moscow,' but it'll have a list of departing planes and Gunther says I should see if any were long-range transports. I wonder."

"Wonder what, Rod?"

"I wonder," he said as he handed Nancy one of the brandy glasses, "what Gunther will do if I draw a blank."

Malcolm Jones was at home, his burly frame aching with fatigue in every seam and joint. Twice, on the way back from Camp David, he had nearly fallen asleep at the wheel and for the last fifteen miles he had driven with his window down, poking his head out every few minutes to catch the cold, crisp air on his face.

His wife was vastly displeased at his making the trip when he was so obviously exhausted from the Arizona assignment.

"You could have gone tomorrow just as well," she nodded. "Now look at you. You're an absolute wreck."

"Fix me a double scotch on the rocks," he said wearily. "And do me another favor, Anne—lay off. I'm too tired to argue and, believe me, I went tonight because I knew I'd be just as bushed tomorrow."

His wife looked at him and softened to sympathy instantly. After eighteen years of marriage, she sensed that these were symptoms of more than fatigue. He was upset about something and she knew him well enough not to ask him why. Sooner or later he would volunteer what was bugging him if he wanted to. Sometimes he did and sometimes he didn't. Tonight, she reckoned, he didn't. She merely went to get him the scotch.

Jones stretched out on the couch, uncomfortably aware

161

that his mind was racing even as his weary body sagged to a stop. His brain was an engine that persisted in running after the ignition key was turned off. He'd have insomnia tonight, Jones thought, with all his fatigue. He sipped the scotch his wife brought him and stared at the ceiling.

"Mal, why don't you go to bed?"

"I will. After I make a couple of phone calls."

"One's to the office, I suppose. Do you have to call the office tonight? Won't it wait until tomorrow?"

"Only take a minute. Then I'll go to bed. I promise."

"I know you, Mal. They'll want you to come in tonight and you'll go."

Jones shook his head. "Anne, I wouldn't go downtown tonight if Kim Novak was waiting for me in a transparent nightgown. But I do have to check in. I told Gunther I would."

He lurched to his feet with an effort, went into his den and closed the door. He dialed the IPS number. It rang only once before Bobby Andrews, the early night switchboard operator, chirped brightly, "IPS, Andrews."

"This is Mal Jones, Bobby. Has Mr. Damon gone home?"

"Yes, sir."

"Would you give me his home number? I have it here somewhere but I'm too tired to look it up."

"It's 365-2306, Mr. Jones."

"Thanks, Bobby. One more favor. Have you got that card index with all the unlisted numbers handy? The one that has the home phones of government officials. Good. Will you look up Reardon? Paul Reardon. The FBI director."

He waited until Andrews found Reardon's unlisted number and read it to him.

"Many thanks, Bobby. I'm home if anybody wants me, and if anybody wants me tonight, it had better be damned important. Like the end of the world."

He dialed Gunther's apartment, half hoping that the news superintendent would be out. But Damon answered almost immediately.

"Jonesy, Gunther. I'm back from Camp David. It's dark and it's dead. No sign of activity."

"I'm not surprised," Damon said. "My Moscow brain storm looks better and better."

162

"Maybe," Jones said with such curtness that Damon was mildly startled.

"Anything eating you, Jonesy?"

"No, Gunther. I didn't mean to snap. I'm just tired. Guess I'll hit the sack."

"Good idea. See you tomorrow. 'Night."

Jones hung up. His stubby fingers beat a tattoo on the battered, wobbly card table that served as his work desk. Not for another five minutes did he dial the second number Andrews had given him.

The continued failure to find the President's body and the mystery of the unknown passenger registered on the world's diplomatic and journalistic seismographs with the impact of a global emotional earthquake.

The British Prime Minister issued a statement assuring the Acting President of the United States "that the United Kingdom, even as it prays for the safety of President Haines, reaffirms its support for the principles of freedom to which our two great nations are pledged throughout eternity." Privately, the Prime Minister of Great Britain called Madigan on the transatlantic telephone, asking quietly but firmly, "What the devil's going on there?"

The British press asked the same question publicly, suggesting that the apparent disappearance of Jeremy Haines—coming only a few years after the assassination of President Kennedy—indicated that the United States Secret Service must be wallowing in inefficiency.

Peking Radio reacted as expected. First it said the entire incident, including the plane crash, was "a deliberate plot by the warmonger Haines to lay the blame for a kidnaping hoax on the People's Republic, so as to give this blood-seeking criminal an excuse to attack China." One hour later Peking Radio announced solution of the mystery. President Haines, it said, was not dead but in seclusion under heavy guard because he had gone insane from his futile attempts to "restrain the warmongers in the United States Defense Department from unleashing World War III." The third Peking version topped the first two in scope. Vice President Madigan, said this account, ordered the presidential plane shot down so he could seize power and commit America to war. It described Haines as a martyr.

The Soviet Union's *Pravda* was unusually restrained,

163

merely commenting that it "hopes the American people will remain calm until the unfortunate mystery is solved, not trying to incite harmful suspicion and making wild accusations concerning alleged 'Red' plots." It praised Haines as a "man of good intentions" and expressed hope for his safety.

In the United States press comment was comparable to the thoughts expressed by *Pravda*. Thursday's Washington *Star*, in an editorial, summed up the general press agreement that public calmness was needed—along with some fast and effective detective work by the FBI and CIA. Said the *Star*:

> Acting President Madigan's plea for reserved judgment must be accepted by every thoughtful American. It will take will power and self-discipline, for the very elements of this incredible mystery lend themselves to wild rumors and panicky speculation.
>
> In turn, it is incumbent on the Acting President to keep the public informed of all developments. Mature restraint can be kept alive only by frankness and a willingness to share with the American people the truth as it is pried out of the sun-crusted mud of an Arizona gorge, or perhaps out of a twisted mind that may have forged history's most fantastic plot.
>
> The quick, total solution of these twin tragedies of sudden death and mystery is essential, no matter what motives, reasons, explanations or even skeletons are unearthed in the process. Any attempt to hide or evade the truth will merely feed the seeds of unfounded suspicion and fan the flames of hatred in an atmosphere already reeking of a threatened atomic holocaust.
>
> This must be understood by the leaders of the people as well as the people themselves. The November 22, 1963, tragedy of Dallas at least had the one saving grace of finality, which helped preserve a nation's unity in a time of sorrow. John Kennedy was dead, and Lyndon Johnson was President. Now there is no finality, merely mystery and uncertainty, and both will test the courage and understanding of citizen and government official alike until the world gets the answer to the question: "Where is Jeremy Haines?"

The *Star*'s editorial was read too late by those lawmakers who had insisted on rushing into print with demands for special investigations, probes and, above all, immediate action. Among the measures quickly introduced were:

Seven bills calling for special joint Senate-House committees to investigate the entire affair.

One bill demanding that ultimatums be served on Red China and Russia pledging war "if either or both are proved responsible for this crime."

One resolution urging a special congressional investigation of the Amalgamated Condor, and another tossing in the Federal Aviation Administration and the Air Force along with the Condor.

Two bills seeking an outright ban on all flight operations "in or near thunderstorms, to include scheduled airline flights as well as military aircraft."

Neither the FBI nor CIA had time to ponder any congressional advice. Both were swamped with calls from citizens swearing they had seen President Haines on various occasions after the crash. The locations involved virtually every major city between California and New York. The specific sites varied from a brothel in New Orleans to a Catholic Church in Albuquerque where, the caller assured the FBI, "the President was weeping as he prayed."

Haines was reported having been seen registering at a Phoenix motel "with some flashy brunette" and also, on the same day, attending the Chicago Cubs-Los Angeles Dodgers game at Wrigley Field. It would not have surprised the FBI to have someone claim he saw the President playing second base in that game.

The stock market tobogganed, rallied, then faltered anew into a steady decline.

An angry audience in a Baltimore night club booed an alleged comedian off the stage when he cracked, "Everyone wants to know where President Haines is—hell, he's probably off fishing somewhere with Judge Crater."

A man jumped out of his room on the forty-eighth floor of a New York hotel. The suicide note he left behind read: "If the President had the courage to leave this sick world, so do I."

The television networks resumed their normal schedules for the first time since Air Force One was reported missing. But NBC judiciously canceled a variety show which included a comedy skit about a fictitious bachelor President being harassed by matrimony-bound women.

The American Committee for Truth about UFOs, duly noting the failure to find the President's body and the suspicion that he was not aboard Air Force One, issued another statement suggesting that Jeremy Haines was kidnaped by beings from another planet. It described this as "the only logical solution to the mystery," a claim which won quick acceptance from irreverent IPS deskman Sam Foley. "It figures," he remarked jauntily to Les Butler. "We should get a ransom message from outer space any time now. I even know what it'll say."

"Okay, I'll bite," said Butler, "what will the message from Mars say?"

" 'We've taken your leader,' " said Mr. Foley.

All the living ex-Presidents wired Madigan their assurances of support. A great many Americans went to church and shared anew their thoughts, their fears and their prayers for Jeremy Haines with the God each worshiped.

And at the bottom of a metal-littered gorge in the middle of an Arizona desert, the blistered hands of weary men continued to dig for a body they wanted to find, yet a body they were afraid to find, and a body they half suspected was not even there.

Rod Pitcher obtained clearance into the Andrews control tower Friday morning by the simple process of resorting to an occasionally necessary journalistic vice. He lied.

The prevarication was committed on the unsuspecting person of Charles Alexander. The FAA public information chief might have given Rod clearance anyway, but Pitcher was taking no chances on handing any government official an inkling that IPS was snooping into the Air Force One mystery.

"New York's suggested I do a feature story on the Andrews tower," he told Alexander on the phone. "Kinda get the feel and spirit of the place. What's the chances of my getting in there today?"

"Don't see why not," the FAA man said pleasantly. "Dennis Ripps is the tower chief on the day shift. I'll give him a buzz and tell him you're coming. What time can you make it?"

"Let's see, it's a quarter to nine now. I'll leave the office at nine and it'll take me about thirty minutes to drive out there."

"Okay, Pitch. Have fun and say hi to the Ripper for me."

"The who?"

"The Ripper. Ripps hates the name Dennis and everyone calls him Ripper. Personally, I have a strong idea he thinks it makes him sound like a sex fiend."

The tower chief turned out to resemble a sex fiend about as closely as Santa Claus. Dennis Ripps was a tall, gray-haired, grandfatherly type with friendly but tired eyes that carried indented circles underneath, so pronounced that they looked like the sun-protection lampblack worn by football players. He had the unruffled calm so emblematic of air traffic control men, with the God-given ability to keep tempers and emotions under a tight rein in the antiseptic pressure cookers where they labored. The Andrews facility was like all others Pitcher had seen, as spotlessly clean as an operating room but with the same quiet, hidden tensions that thicken the atmosphere of life-or-death surgery.

Ripps welcomed the reporter with such cordiality that Pitcher had a momentary pang of conscience. "Alexander told me you were coming. Glad to see you. This your first time in a control tower?"

"First time in Andrews. I've seen the one at National and I've been in the Dulles tower too."

"If you've seen one, you've seen them all," Ripps philosophized. "What exactly did you have in mind? Just wanna stand around and observe for a while, or do you have any specific questions?"

On the way out to the airport, Pitcher had composed what seemed to be a logical reason for examining the tower's departures logs for that memorable night. He knew he was tiptoeing close to security matters but the Andrews tower was operated by FAA, not the Air Force. He figured a civilian like Ripps would give him access to the logs with far less suspicion than a military man.

"Well, I'm interested mostly in doing a mood story . . . re-creating what the tower was like the night the President's plane disappeared. It'll be part of a layout we're doing on the Air Force One business—for example, what went on at the White House that night, what the Vice President was doing, that sort of stuff."

"Sounds interesting," Ripps said. "I don't know what I

can tell you; I wasn't on duty when the plane took off. It might be better for you to talk to the night tower chief."

"I thought I could do that later," Pitcher explained casually. "Right now, I was wondering what other kind of traffic you were handling before and after the take-off. This would let me do a kind of running play-by-play. Then I'd like to just watch you fellows work for a few minutes and get the feel of the operation . . . some of the dialogue and so forth."

"Well," the tower chief mused doubtfully, "I suppose I could show you the logs for that night. Pretty cut and dried, though. We just keep a list of the arrivals and departures. Time, Greenwich clock, of course, type of aircraft, aircraft serial numbers, where the plane's going or coming from. That what you want?"

"That'll be fine for a starter," Pitcher said, praying he was succeeding in corking up his eagerness.

"We keep two twenty-four-hour lists," Ripps said. "One for arrivals and the other for departures. They run from 7 A.M. one day to 7 A.M. the next. Which do you want first?"

"Oh, I guess the departures," Pitcher replied, again with a studied effort at assumed indifference.

The tower chief opened a filing cabinet sandwiched between two steel desks and brought out a folder. "Here's the date we want. Why don't you sit at one of these desks and go through this stuff at your leisure? I'll go back to work while you look it over. If you have any questions, just yell."

"Fine," the reporter said. Ripps walked away. Pitcher opened the folder and began reading the flight departure list. He took out a notebook and occasionally stopped to make an entry, strictly for camouflage purposes. If Ripps or anyone else in the tower should glance over, they would see him ostensibly at work on his "play-by-play."

Toward the bottom of the fourth departure sheet, he found a line that shot a chill through his backbone.

2202   AF-1   CONDOR N-20081   Palm Springs, Cal.

After that line, he found departure information on only eleven other planes. Five twin-engine Convairs, an Aero Commander, a couple of Constellations, an F-104 fighter and two jet trainers. No long-range jet equipment, Pitcher thought disappointedly. He again went over the departures preceding Air Force One. Nothing had left Andrews that entire day, night or early the following morning that remotely resembled an aircraft capable of a Moscow flight. The only possibility was a Boeing KC-135, a military version of the 707, but the Air Force used this jet as a tanker or a rather spartan transport. Its fuselage, in fact, was windowless and a President was hardly likely to fly all the way to Russia in such uncomfortable accommodations. Besides, Wright Patterson Field near Dayton, Ohio, was listed as the destination for this KC-135.

Maybe Haines took off for Moscow from some other area airport. Dulles? Baltimore's Friendship? That was too farfetched. The President wouldn't use a civil airport if he wanted secrecy. Andrews would provide the maximum security, and it had to be Andrews or nothing. It seemed to be nothing, Pitcher concluded, and Gunther was going to be one disconsolate news superintendent with his Moscow hunch fairly well shattered.

He removed the arrivals sheets from the folder, more to keep looking busy than in expectation of finding anything. He reflected ruefully that he was still going through the motions of make-believe research when the story he was really after had just gone flat.

Idly, with no enthusiasm and with a feeling of pointless boredom, he perused the arrivals. He was about to put the sheets back in the folder when his eye caught the final entry on the last sheet.

05:09   MATS SF 35   BOEING N-26000   Minneapolis

There was something about that aircraft serial number that rang an alarm bell of familiarity. Something that prodded the reflexes of his memory.

"Mr. Ripps, could you come over here a second?"

The tower chief obliged quickly.

"This line here, Mr. Ripps. N-26000. Why the hell would that number stick in my mind? Does it mean anything to you?"

Ripps chuckled. "It should. You covered presidential flights before?"

"Quite a few."

"That's why you remembered that number, Mr. Pitcher. N-26000 was the old Air Force One. Boeing 707. The predecessor of the Condor. It's still part of the presidential fleet. They use it for VIPs and various bigwigs. I think the Secretary of State flew it to Paris a couple of months ago. Could have been in Minnesota for fifty different reasons. Training flight, probably. That 'SF' stands for special flight and special could mean anything, like hauling a few congressmen around on a junket. Or training, like I said."

"The departure logs I just finished looking at, Mr. Ripps. Are they complete?"

"Complete? What do you mean, complete?"

"Do they list every plane that leaves Andrews? For example, suppose there was some kind of a top-security flight, one the Air Force was trying to keep strictly hush-hush. Would that be included on the list?" Pitcher realized he might be pushing Ripps far enough to make him distrustful, but it was a calculated risk that had to be taken.

The tower chief, however, apparently suspected nothing. "No, I've been here for thirteen years and I never heard of the Air Force putting any flight under a security wrap. Not even any presidential flight. The same thing's true of arrivals. When a plane lands or takes off at this base, we log it."

Pitcher replaced the arrivals logs in the folder. "I wish the President had been using N-26000 that night," he said. "Maybe the whole thing wouldn't have happened. Good plane, that 707."

Ripps nodded agreement. "Get what you needed out of the logs?"

"Well, as you said, they're pretty routine. Interesting, though. If you don't mind, I'll watch your crew operate for a little while."

The aviation editor stayed what he trusted was a convincing twenty minutes of observation, then thanked Ripps and left. Strike-out, he meditated. Yet what he had dug up on the Senator Haines angle still looked promising. Enough to earn him mention in the weekly IPS critique written and distributed by the New York bureau. It was a mimeographed competitive report on the previous week's major stories, praising or criticizing the other bureaus for their performances and tabulating how many newspapers used IPS on the bigger stories compared to UPI and AP.

The *IPS Deskman*, the report was called. Most IPS staffers considered it purely subjective, guilty of the worst possible grandstand quarterbacking, hindsight and second-guessing. Particularly when a bureau was being lambasted for losing the play to the opposition. Naturally, when New York was being complimentary, the *Deskman* assumed all the truthful and lofty aspects of the Bible.

Even as Rod Pitcher returned to Washington via the Suitland Parkway, he was thinking what the *Deskman* would say—provided Damon actually used his Haines story. Something along the lines of "Washington came up with the best beat of the week, a bell-ringing exclusive on the possibility that the unidentified body found aboard Air Force One was the President's brother. Great job of reporting and writing by WA's aviation expert, Rod Pitcher."

He thought about the proud moment when he could take a copy of this as yet unwritten but positive tribute to his journalistic prowess home to show Nancy, and he wallowed in the delicious self-hypnosis of daydreaming all the way downtown.

Malcolm Jones found himself thinking about the President as he entered the FBI headquarters at Ninth and Pennsylvania for his appointment with Reardon. It was his veneration toward Haines that had prompted his call to the FBI chief and, as he admitted this, he suffered a simultaneous confession of disloyalty to IPS. He hadn't even told Damon or DeVarian about this visit. He merely informed the switchboard that he had some important personal business to attend to and would be "out of pocket" for about an hour.

It was one minute before ten when he entered Reardon's outer office and gave his name to the receptionist.

It was forty-eight minutes later when he left the FBI Building and hailed a taxi for the White House. A rather harrowing forty-eight minutes, Jones thought. At times he had the impression that Reardon was examining him with the detached absorption of an entomologist peering at an impaled bug. Malcolm Jones was something of a glib talker, but in front of the FBI chief he had groped for words and phrases with all the uneasiness of an inarticulate suitor trying desperately to blurt forth a message of love.

Reardon had been pleasant enough, but it was a fragile Christmas-ornament kind of pleasantness that Jones knew could have been shattered with his first utterance of an unwisely chosen word or the wrong inflection.

The cabby wove skillfully through Washington's late morning traffic and decided to indulge in that form of editorial oratory aimed at captive audiences by such citizenry as taxi drivers, barbers and sports fans. "Look at all these goddamned cars. Everybody in this goddamned town tries to drive to lunch at this time of day. Why the hell can't they walk to a restaurant—or take a cab?"

Malcolm Jones wasn't listening. He still was mulling over the conclusion of his conference with Paul Reardon.

"Thank you very much for coming, Mr. Jones. It's possible we might have to take the course you suggest. By the way, are you married?"

"Yes, sir."

"Then I hope you don't talk in your sleep."

CHAPTER TEN

Gunther Damon had sent his aviation editor to Andrews that morning with the sublimely happy confidence of a horse player armed with a hot inside tip on a long shot.

When Pitcher returned to report failure, Damon's reaction also was identical to that of a horse player whose hot inside tip had run an ignominious last. He cursed, moped, paced and then suddenly snapped back into unbridled optimism, an emotional coil spring refusing to lose its resiliency.

"Well," he informed Pitcher, "I hope you're not discouraged because I'm not. I still think he left Andrews sometime during the night. That blasted control tower was probably ordered to keep it quiet."

"No dice, Gunther. The tower chief told me they log every flight."

"That doesn't mean there wasn't a secret flight. Those . . . those logs you were telling me about. The Air Force could have flown Haines out of there with a phony destination. Like advising the tower they were taking off for Hoboken or someplace. Strictly a cover-up. Then—okay, what's wrong with that?"

"I checked every type of aircraft listed in the departures. Nothing left Andrews that was capable of flying to Moscow. Except maybe a KC-135 and that's a tanker."

"So couldn't they modify a tanker into a transport?" Damon pressed. "What is a KC-135, anyway?"

"A version of the 707. Nuts, Gunther, it's just a big metal cylinder with wings and engines. No windows, even. Don't you think the Air Force has enough regular long-range transports without putting the President of the United States into a windowless tube for an eight-thousand-mile flight?"

"Yeh," Damon conceded reluctantly. "Well, we're sure

173

back where we started. Jonesy says Camp David was locked up tight. Deader than yesterday's newspaper. Got any ideas?"

Pitcher brightened. "There's always the Senator Haines yarn," he said eagerly. "That's still promising. We know he didn't go to Boston on that plane."

"You know it and I know it," Damon growled. "But DeVarian is playing it coy for a while. We've got Bob Johnson checking whether brother Bert could have chartered a plane or maybe taken the train. Stan wants to make sure."

The aviation writer's face wrinkled into the incredulous look of a man who had just been advised that Senator Bertrand Haines might have walked to Boston. "The train? Why the hell would he have taken a train?"

Damon laughed. "Oh, come on, flyboy. Lots of people still take trains."

"Not unless they have to," Pitcher snorted. "I'll lay five to one Johnson doesn't come up with anything more than I just did at Andrews."

"Your odds are lousy," Damon said. "I'd give you ten to one. Meanwhile, you got any brain storms on where we go next?"

Pitcher pondered this briefly. "Nope. Except that the brother angle should look pretty hot if Johnson whiffs on the train or charter plane."

"I'm inclined to agree. But Mr. DeVarian has donned his cloak of caution. Well, guess you can go back to your regular grind. I just thought of something."

The "something," it developed, was a phone call to Warner Goldberg of the IPS Senate staff. Damon gave him a quick briefing on what they knew—or didn't know—about Senator Haines and his fishing trip, and the shoe found at the crash site. He also told him that a query to the FBI on whether the mystery body could have been the senator had produced a suspiciously cryptic "No comment."

"What I'm getting at, Warner," he continued, "is whether you think you could get in to see Madigan at the White House. Privately, I mean. You've known him ever since he came to Congress and you've always been on pretty good terms with him, haven't you?"

"I guess so, Gunther. I used to drop in on him now and then. Felt kinda sorry for him. He seemed lonely. He's always been accessible, I'll say that for him. But he's the President now, or half-President anyway."

"Half-assed President," Damon cracked and was immediately sorry he had said it. The Hill reporters were peculiarly tolerant of members or ex-members of Congress, including the incompetents, the rabble-rousers and the occasional crooks. You could seldom get the average Hill newsman to say that any congressman was all bad, even if the lawmaker in question was known to be a hypocritical slob. Some of the reporters covering Joe McCarthy, for example, had liked the Wisconsin senator while they were simultaneously eyewitnesses to his incredible activities. Congressmen were their chief news sources, and they tended to protect them as a parent will defend ill-behaved children when they are criticized by others.

Goldberg's silence at the "half-assed" remark was confirmation of some resentment, and Gunther decided to make hurried amends. "Well, guess I shouldn't make cracks like that about a guy who's on a tough spot, Warner. But I'm trying to nail down this Haines trip business and I figured Madigan might know something. Something he'd be willing to tell a reporter who's been close to him and good to him, for that matter."

Goldberg was mollified, but also mystified. "I'm not sure he'd be able to tell me anything even if he knew it, Gunther. Furthermore, I'm not sure what you want me to ask him."

"Do I have to draw you a diagram? Ask him first: has the FBI or anybody else given him evidence that the unidentified body on Air Force One was that of the President's brother? Then sound him out on what he knows about that alleged fishing trip. It's a fairly good assumption that the authorities could have been checking up on the senator just as we are."

"Gunther," Goldberg pleaded, "Madigan's the Acting President. He may be a hack politician to you, but he's the Chief Executive to the rest of the nation. And to me too. Even if I get in to see him alone, he'll tell me to go fly a kite when I start pumping him about Haines or anything else connected with this crazy deal. And one more thing, boss man. If he knows we're snooping around, he's liable to blow the whistle on all of us."

This already had occurred to Damon. "There's always

175

that danger," he countered. "But we can sidestep it. Tell him everything he can give you is off the record. Tell him we've heard some rumors about Senator Haines and we wanted to check them out right at the top before we do anything with what we've gotten on our own. Make it seem more like a gesture of . . . of cooperation or—hell, make it patriotism."

"Well, okay," Goldberg said doubtfully. "But how much do you want me to tell *him?* How much should he know that we know?"

"Play it by ear. Start off by telling him we're pretty sure Senator Haines didn't get on any flight to Boston like he was supposed to. Then feel him out. I've got a feeling Madigan will open up. Keep me posted, pal."

Gunther put down the phone and mentally rubbed his hands in anticipatory glee. The arrival of reporter Bob Johnson, with the news that his own digging had produced a fat zero, added to the news superintendent's conviction that Bertrand Haines had indeed left Washington that night —not for New England, but for Palm Springs, California, aboard Air Force One.

Arranging a private interview with the Acting President was not as difficult as Warner Goldberg had feared.

Confronted with Goldberg's request, Madigan was at first inclined to reject it as politely as possible. Then he remembered that the IPS man had always been friendly to him when he was in Congress and later when he became Vice President. There also was a desire on Madigan's part to establish an image as a warm, friendly, thoroughly democratic Chief Executive who was willing to see anybody who had legitimate business.

This image fitted his self-portrait of a President who combined the humanistic qualities of Andrew Jackson and, of course, Harry Truman. That he was consciously trying to mold himself as a carbon copy of past Presidents was a yardstick of his own lack of stature. Frederick James Madigan, even when he was being decisive and forceful, merely was imitating. It never occurred to him that even in so minor a decision as whether to grant a newspaperman a solo interview he was more of an actor playing the role of how he imagined a President should act.

Madigan was well aware that, while an exclusive presidential interview made the reporter so honored most happy, it also suffused the rest of the White House press corps with the smoldering resentment of Captain Bligh's crew. But Goldberg had assured him, "I'm willing to settle for a completely off-the-record meeting if you'd prefer it that way," and this took the Vice President off the alienation hook. Anyway, Madigan reasoned, if other reporters complained, he'd just have to grant a series of exclusive interviews and keep all the boys happy.

Goldberg judiciously asked that he be admitted to the White House via an entrance that would avoid the lobby adjoining the White House press room. Madigan quickly consented, agreeable to any strategy capable of outflanking the hazard of favoritism charges.

He welcomed the IPS reporter with such excessive geniality that he came close to being patronizing. "Warner, my boy, it's good to see you. I really appreciate your coming to see me. This job of, uh, Acting President has kept me away from my old friends of the press. Why don't you sit right down there and we'll have a chat."

Goldberg lowered himself rather gingerly into a high-backed chair directly across from the Vice President who, he had to admit, looked surprisingly impressive behind the ponderous scrolled desk. Madigan, just by being in this hallowed room, had seemed to acquire a maturity and dignity so foreign to his normal personality that Goldberg was ill at ease. He had the uncomfortable feeling of a man who had just come unexpectedly face to face with his long-ago divorced wife and discovered she had assumed qualities of beauty and dignity he never knew existed. It still was the Vice President facing him, yet it was a different person.

Madigan broke into his thoughts. "Now, Warner, what did you want to see me about?"

Goldberg cleared his throat, conscious that never before had he been nervous in the presence of Fred Madigan. The reporter was a competent veteran of many a congressional session, a small person with a jaw shaped like a battleship prow but with narrow shoulders topping a spindly frame. The effect was like pasting the face of a prize fighter above the body of a concert violinist.

"Well, Mr. Vice President," he started out cautiously, "it's about this disappearance of the President and—"

"Just a minute, Warner," Madigan interrupted. "You

177

realize, of course, this isn't a subject I'm at liberty to discuss with any reporter—even an old friend like yourself."

"I know that, sir. That's why I told you on the phone I'd be willing to make this all off the record. You see, sir, I think we might have come across something which could be news to you."

Madigan was instantly interested. "I think I've been kept pretty well informed of all developments, but I'll be the first to admit you boys of the press are most astute. Most astute, Warner. So what exactly have you ascertained?"

Even at this ticklish moment, the thought flashed through Goldberg's mind that being Acting President had somehow ballooned Madigan's vocabulary. He never could remember his having used a word like "ascertained" before, and he almost had to stifle a chuckle. "Sir, we have reason to believe it was Senator Haines who was on Air Force One. Substituting for the President."

Madigan smiled, a superior, condescending smile that said the reporter's bombshell had landed with a dull thud. "That possibility has occurred to others, Warner, including myself, I might add. Before I comment on it, may I ask the basis of your, well, shall we call it a theory?"

Goldberg was determined to walk a tightrope of discretion in what he would tell the Vice President. "The senator was supposed to have taken a plane to Boston that night. We have evidence that he did not take the flight for which he had reservations, or any other flight. Or a train or chartered plane."

Madigan's face still wore that smile of superiority, but now it was a slightly diluted smile. "Would you care to provide me with the details of your evidence, Warner? All off the record, naturally."

"Sir, I guess you'd categorize it more as suspicion than evidence. We found out there was no record of his having picked up his reservation for his flight, no record of his being on any flight, and no record of his having gone to Boston or Maine by any other means unless he drove up there."

The smile was gone, replaced by a slight frown.

"That's very interesting," Madigan allowed. "It, uh, doesn't quite jibe with what I've been told on the highest authority. The highest authority, Warner."

"And what was that, Mr. Vice President?"

It was Madigan who was now choosing his words with defensive prudence. "I cannot emphasize too strongly, my boy, that this conversation *must* be off the record if we're to share a mutual confidence. Is that perfectly clear?"

"Perfectly, sir."

"Well then, the FBI has talked to Mrs. Haines. The senator's wife. She took him to National Airport that night, watched him board, and waited there until the plane took off for Boston. That's what I meant when I said your evidence didn't jibe with what I've been told by—well, Warner, strictly for your information, what I've been told by none other than FBI Director Reardon."

Goldberg permitted himself the indulgence of a low whistle. "That seems to tear it, sir. Except that I still don't understand it. We're convinced he didn't take that plane and yet his wife saw him board it."

"There is a certain, ah, discrepancy," Madigan acknowledged. "But it's not an unexplainable discrepancy. It's very possible the senator did not use his own name when he got on the plane. Incommunicado, so to speak."

Goldberg decided he would not bother to correct the use of "incommunicado" when Madigan meant to say "incognito." The improved vocabulary had sprung a leak, but the reporter had no desire to embarrass the Vice President. "What would be his reason for going, uh, for not using his own name, sir?"

"I don't know, Warner. Possibly Bert Haines is the type of person who doesn't want any fuss made over him. And you know the airlines—they'll roll out the proverbial red carpet for a dignitary like a United States senator. Why, I myself have flown several times incommunicado, for the express purpose of avoiding a lot of fuss and attention."

Goldberg had a strong hunch this professed modesty was pure malarkey, which it was. "That may be the explanation, sir, but there *was* a reservation made in his name for the 9 P.M. flight to Boston. If he made the reservation under his own name, why go to the trouble of traveling under an assumed name? Of making two reservations?"

Madigan shook his head in frank puzzlement. Unless— and the suspicion voiced by Hester suddenly popped into his mind—unless Bert Haines had some kind of ulterior motive in making two separate reservations. One under his

179

name which he did not claim, and another under a different name. How this could be part of an assignation plan he could not fathom, but he had no experience with assignations and maybe the twin reservations were just a male straying-from-the-straight-and-narrow technique.

"There's another possibility, or rather explanation," he finally said to Goldberg. "One I'm not at liberty to discuss, Warner, but one which I assure you is most logical and which has nothing whatsoever to do with the President's disappearance. It is rather a delicate matter, of an extremely personal nature, so just take my word for it."

This naturally piqued Goldberg's reportorial curiosity to an unbearable degree. "As you said, sir, this is all off the record. I'd appreciate anything you could tell me . . ."

"There's nothing to tell, really," Madigan said soothingly. "Look, Warner, we're men of the world. If Bert Haines had a reason for going to Boston under a different name, it must have been a very personal reason, so let's leave it at that, shall we?"

Man-of-the-world Goldberg got the idea but he was not about to leave it. "Am I correct then, Mr. Vice President, in assuming that the FBI is satisfied Senator Haines flew to Boston and presumably still is somewhere in Maine? And that the mystery of his whereabouts boils down to a question of delicacy?"

"Your assumption," Madigan sighed, "may not be correct but as far as I'm concerned it's a damned good possibility. After all, my boy, the FBI isn't going to lie to the Acting President of the United States. Reardon says Bert Haines was on that plane, period."

"Mrs. Haines says he was on that plane," Goldberg corrected him. "I think you said it was Mrs. Haines who told the FBI she saw him board and then take off."

"So what?" The Vice President shrugged. "Ruth Haines wouldn't have any reason for lying either. Certainly not to the FBI."

The reporter nodded in silent, almost reluctant agreement. His mind whirled with unanswered questions and nagging uncertainty. "What still bothers me, sir, is the fact that the senator stays missing when the whole world's in an uproar because his brother's missing too. It doesn't add up. You'd think Senator Haines would have heard about the mess by now."

"It would seem so," Madigan said. "But I suppose it would be easy for a man to lose himself in Maine if he wanted to—and not even have a radio with him."

Goldberg decided he had no choice but to play his trump card. "There's one more thing before I stop taking up your time, Mr. Vice President. Maybe you already knew it, but there was an elevated shoe found in the wreckage of Air Force One."

"An elevated shoe? Is that supposed to have some significance?"

"I don't know, sir. My boss thinks it may be significant. He thinks the shoe must have belonged to a man impersonating the President. That the unidentified body was that of a person shorter than President Haines, and the shoes were part of the disguise."

The thermometer of what had been Madigan's diminishing interest suddenly shot up again. "I didn't know about any shoe, Warner, but General Coston told me the unidentified body was that of a man somewhat shorter than Jeremy Haines. This business of the shoe makes sense. It certainly adds, ah, credence to the theory of an impostor."

"It does, sir. This is why the boss wanted me to talk to you. He was positive the President's brother was on Air Force One—because of his failure to show up for the Boston flight and the clue of the shoe."

"But the FBI has scotched that not-going-to-Boston business," Madigan reminded. "So while the elevated shoe apparently belonged to an impostor, the impostor could not have been Senator Haines. It also occurs to me, Warner, that the shoe could have been owned by one of the legitimate passengers or a crew member."

"I doubt it, Mr. Vice President. I didn't discuss this in any detail with my boss, but I got the impression he's convinced nobody on the plane wore such shoes. Anyway, there's one way to find out once and for all whether Senator Haines was on Air Force One."

"You tell me," the Vice President said curtly, irritated because he hadn't been advised of the shoe discovery.

"Sir, could you ask the FBI if the fingerprints on the mystery body were those of the senator? That should settle it once and for all."

Madigan stared at Goldberg. Then he decided that he'd finally better confirm this himself. He rang the intercom buzzer connected with Mrs. Hahn's desk. "You stay put, Warner. I'll get Reardon on the phone and—Mrs. Hahn, get the FBI director for me, will you? Tell him it's urgent."

The Vice President and the reporter sat in silence, waiting for the call to go through. They were so engrossed in their thoughts that both started when Mrs. Hahn's metallic and impersonal voice came over the intercom. "I have Mr. Reardon for you, Mr. Vice President. Line 2."

Madigan picked up the phone and charged straight to the point. "Mr. Reardon, has anyone thought to compare the fingerprints on that unidentified body with those of Senator Haines?"

Goldberg fervently wished he could hear what was being said at the other end. Madigan was frowning in open anger.

"Goddammit, Reardon, I asked you a question and I don't want questions in return. I want answers. Never mind why I want to know. It's sufficient that I asked. Now, how about those fingerprints?"

The Vice President, his face still peevish, listened while Goldberg strained to hear from four feet away. Madigan's fretful expression dimmed slowly into a look of disappointment strangely blended with relief. "Thank you, Mr. Reardon. I apologize for snapping at you. Afraid my nerves are a bit on edge. This is a terrible strain, you realize, I'm sure. Good-by."

Madigan hung up. He looked at Goldberg and shook his head. "I'm sorry, Warner, but you can go back and tell your boss he's way off base. Reardon says one of the first things they did was to compare Bert Haines's file prints with the fingerprints on that body. They didn't match."

Gunther Damon took the news glumly, his journalistic coup of the century falling apart like an overcooked turkey. De-Varian, Pitcher and Goldberg felt sorry for him, although Pitcher, it must be added, also was feeling sorry for himself. Exclusives were rare on the aviation beat. Pitcher's last supposed one had been several years ago when he wrote flatly, quoting the usual "well-informed sources," that Lockheed would win the supersonic transport design competition. The very next day the FAA announced that Boeing was the winner. Pitcher had expected to get fired.

"It's part of the game, Pitch," Gunther had reassured him. "Don't take it too hard. Maybe you'd just better cultivate some well-informed sources who are somewhat better informed. Who the hell did you get it from, Lockheed?"

"Somebody at FAA," Pitcher had said sorrowfully. "I won't trust that sonofabitch from now on if he tells me the sun rises in the east."

The memory of that black day still sat in Rod Pitcher's guts like the burning aftertaste of a Mexican dinner. Ever since then he had yearned for a chance to make amends to Damon, IPS and himself. The Senator Haines story had assumed all the mammoth proportions of retribution, revenge and requital, even though there was a tiny demon of conscience occasionally reminding him it was Damon's hunch that had sent him to the airline boarding lists in the first place.

Now, as the four men sat in DeVarian's office masticating the import of Goldberg's conference with the Vice President, the aviation editor decided that maybe it was time to stiffen Damon's spine.

"Look, Gunther, there's still something screwy about that Boston flight. No matter what Warner found out from Madigan, there are too many holes in it."

"Holes? What holes?" Damon rasped. "One, Haines's wife saw him take the plane. Two, even if he didn't, it wasn't him on Air Force One anyway. There goes our ballgame, Pitch. The only thing with holes is our lousy solution."

"I'll give you one hole," Pitcher insisted. "Haines caught that Eastern flight for which he had confirmed space, yet he was listed as a no-show. Why?"

"Warner explained that," DeVarian said. "Or rather, Madigan did. The Vice President figures he decided, probably at the last minute, to travel under an assumed name. He ignored his own reservation and used another."

"Why?" Pitcher repeated.

"Madigan has the idea that the senator was up to some shenanigans," Goldberg broke in. "Like a shack-up job with some babe. He didn't say this in so many words, but he sure implied it. His alternate explanation is that Haines didn't want the airline to fuss over him and he wanted to travel incognito."

"There's your other hole," Pitcher said.

Damon was beginning to feel the stirrings of reborn hope. "Elucidate, Pitch."

"If he was going off on some sin trip, what alibi would he have given his wife? She went to the airport with him. She saw him get on the plane. She watched it take off. What was she doing when he walked up to the ticket counter to claim a reservation under a different name?"

"Maybe she was in the ladies' room," Goldberg snickered.

"Maybe we should ask her," Damon suggested.

"Ask her if she was in the ladies' room?" DeVarian said. "I'm sorry, gentlemen, but I think we're grasping at proverbial straws. We started out with circumstantial evidence that an impostor was substituted for the President, and equally circumstantial evidence that the President's brother could have been the impostor. The former possibility still is very much alive, but the latter has been exploded. All this speculation about Bert Haines and the Boston flight is a pure waste of time—because even if we could prove he didn't go, we know now that he wasn't on Air Force One. I suggest we all get back to work."

"That's for me," Goldberg said. "My God, it's after two. My Senate colleagues will be ready to castrate me. Anything else, Gunther?"

"No. Thanks, Warner. Sorry I took up your time with a cruddy wild goose chase."

"Don't mention it, boss man. I liked playing detective. And it was quite an experience seeing Fred Madigan in the Oval Room. You know, he might not turn out to be such a bad President."

"Frederick James Madigan," Damon scowled, taking out his frustration on the absent Vice President, "has all the initiative and originality of a robot."

"That's not fair, Gunther," Goldberg protested. "You didn't observe him on the job like I just did. He was damned decisive. Boy, you should have heard him chew out Paul Reardon."

DeVarian was amused. "Madigan chewed out the FBI director? I'd sooner believe that he talked back to that Amazon wife of his."

"Chewed him out good, believe me."

"About what?" Damon asked.

"Well, I didn't hear both ends of the conversation. Only Madigan's. When he asked Reardon whether the fingerprints on the mystery body had been checked out as belonging to the President's brother, Reardon apparently didn't answer

184

him right away. He asked some question of his own, like why did Madigan want to know, and our Freddie nearly blew his head off. No, sir, Gunther, the Vice President can be tougher than you think."

"Tougher, maybe. But still stupid."

"History will tell," Goldberg said airily and left.

"Guess I'd better go over to the CAB," Pitcher announced in a resigned voice. "I haven't checked route applications for a couple of days."

"I know," Damon said. "We got two callbacks today. They're on the message spike. One says how come we missed Bonanza's filing for a Phoenix–Seattle route and I forgot the other."

Pitcher was properly indignant. "Hell, Gunther. It's not my fault I missed those. I was at Andrews—"

"I know, Pitch. I'm not blaming you. Stay in touch with the desk. Never know when we'll need you."

After the aviation writer departed, DeVarian rose and walked over to pat the crestfallen news superintendent on his shoulder. "Sorry, Gunther. And I honestly mean it. I'm sorry. I thought we had something hot too."

"Yeh," Damon said morosely. "Well, I suppose if we had a dollar for every story that didn't pan out, we could retire. Poor Pitch. I think he could smell the Pulitzer prize. He was really gung ho on that no-show angle."

"Good man, Pitch. A trifle insecure, isn't he?"

"Who isn't? Any guy who doesn't feel a twinge of insecurity at one time or another has the insensitivity of a Gestapo agent."

"That include you, Gunther? You're the most self-assured person I've ever known."

"That includes me, Stan. Some night I'll get bombed with you and I'll tell you all about my self-assurance. It's about as permanent and solid as ectoplasm."

"How about tonight? I'd be perfectly willing to tie one on tonight. Might do us both some good. You've been putting in a few eighteen-hour days and I'm not far behind you."

Damon was tempted, mainly because he was feeling sorry for himself. Then he decided he didn't want DeVarian's company tonight, even though he usually enjoyed the bureau chief's patient, calm appraisals of life's problems. "Thanks, Stan, but I'll cry on your shoulder some other time."

"Okay, Gunther. Any IPS matters you want to discuss?"

"Nope. And if there were, I'd rather discuss them tomorrow. I think I'll go back to my desk and contemplate my navel, like Buddha. They tell me it's good for the soul."

He strode into the noisy newsroom and reached the immediate conclusion that he would rather contemplate Lynx Grimes, who was wearing a V-necked white blouse and a tight-fitting skirt that seemed to mold itself to her slim thighs like cellophane wrap clinging to the top of a jar. His resolution never to socialize with female employees wavered, tottered and collapsed.

For the first time since That Night, the bureau's crisis-fed pace had slackened. It was the time of the day, partially. Midafternoon at IPS normally saw a slowing down of activity. Most congressional hearings are held in the morning, and staff concentration was shifting from the P.M. report for afternoon newspapers to the layout for the next morning's papers. And further, Damon realized, the Haines story itself had reached a strange kind of impasse, as if history had paused to catch its breath. It seemed incredible, but there was not a single story coming in on a dictation phone at this minute and Lynx Grimes had taken advantage of the lull to peruse the contents of the office bulletin board.

These consisted of the posted work schedules for the next two weeks, two Gunther Damon edicts on overenthusiastic expense accounts, a mimeographed notice from New York Personnel proclaiming that hospitalization insurance premiums were about to go up again, and a letter to DeVarian from an IPS regional sales manager in Denver extolling the performance of the Washington bureau on a House committee hearing two weeks ago involving the selection of a dam site in eastern Colorado.

". . . and as you know, Stan," the letter added, "the client who asked for good coverage has been threatening contract cancellation and this terrific response to his request probably saved our necks."

Gunther reread the letter over Miss Grimes's shoulder, thinking cynically that saving IPS's neck also saved the salesman's commission while contributing nothing to the financial well-being of the reporter who had covered the three-hour hearing against the competition of three AP and two UPI newsmen working in convenient relays. There would be other letters from the business side, Damon knew,

186

and they would not be complimentary. He had assigned most of his limited manpower to the various phases of the Haines story, deliberately ignoring coverage of news that was secondary to the President's disappearance but still major to individual newspapers.

Lynx turned around and smiled at him, a smile provocative in its faint touch of shyness. "I was just reading the bulletin board," she explained unnecessarily, as if she had to justify her being away from the bank of dictation phones.

"It's a quiet day, for a change," Gunther observed. "Haven't had a chance to talk to you much, Lynx. How's it going? How do you like your job?"

"I like it fine, Mr. Damon. It's certainly been exciting these past few days. Even being a dictationist, well, I felt I was part of it. It kept me from thinking about promotion to reporter, and that's quite an accomplishment."

She grinned as she said this, and Gunther liked her grin. It was spontaneous, completely natural and transformed her plain if regular features into the beauty of a happy child. If she'd only wear make-up and knew how to apply it, he thought, she'd be a veritable knockout. *Sans* any cosmetics, she still was damned attractive. All of a sudden he felt bashful, an affliction which not only surprised him but worried him. He was about to ask her for a date, and he should be the stern, paternalistic executive bestowing the favor of his attentions on a lowly dictationist. Instead, his heart was pounding in both anticipation and fear of being turned down.

"Uh, Lynx, I was wondering if, uh, you had any plans for this evening." Inwardly, he scolded himself for stammering out this first stage of the invitation, for his lack of glibness and smoothness when he wanted to be so casual and offhand.

She inspected him with the wary surprise of a deer trying to decide whether to eat from the outstretchced hand of a coaxing human. "No, no particular plans, Mr. Damon. I was just going home and—"

"I thought you might like to have a drink with me after work," he said hastily, afraid to let her utter any further word that might be stretched into a possible alibi for a refusal.

"I'd like to very much," she blurted with disarming frankness.

"Good." Gunther Damon felt like whistling. "Suppose you meet me in the lobby when you get off. What time is that—six?"

"Seven," she repeated in a voice that suddenly dipped a tone lower, as if feminine eagerness had just encountered feminine caution.

"Seven it is, Lynx. We'll go over to the Willard Room across the street. See you then."

He watched her move gracefully toward the dictationists' desks and then caught himself, hoping that nobody on the day desk had observed the brief session. He wondered if maybe he should tell her to meet him at the Willard instead so no IPS staffer would see them go out of the Press Building lobby together. No, he was being overprotective although he was not quite sure whom he was protecting— himself or Lynx. The hell with the staff and IPS and his own rules of professional vs. social conduct. He was, he admitted, expectantly happy and he also was uncomfortably aware that seven o'clock was one hour before his normal quitting time and about three hours earlier than his departure routine for the past few days.

"Mr. Damon." The voice of Mrs. Strotsky, the switch board operator, intruded on his cogitations. "Mr. Colin's calling you from the Pentagon."

He returned to his desk and picked up his phone. "Damon."

"Chet Colin here. Say, do you suppose you could shoot Rod Pitcher over here in a hurry?"

"He's at the CAB, Chet, or should be any minute now. What's up?"

"The Air Force says it'll announce at three-thirty its preliminary findings on the crash."

CHAPTER ELEVEN

At precisely three-thirty Rod Pitcher and approximately thirty other reporters were handed a mimeographed Air Force release, along with an announcement that General Coston would hold a briefing in fifteen minutes. That gave the press a scant quarter hour to digest the accident report, and their hasty scanning made them grateful that a briefing was scheduled. For those with little aeronautical background or knowledge, it made painful reading.

DEPARTMENT OF DEFENSE

Public Information Office   Release AF-10384
Department of the Air Force For Immediate Release

Investigation of the crash of the presidential aircraft near Winslow, Arizona, has proceeded to the point where preliminary findings may be made public.

Based on all the evidence to date, the Air Force Board of Inquiry has determined that the probable cause of the accident was the unfavorable interaction of severe vertical air drafts and large longitudinal control displacements resulting in a longitudinal upset from which a successful recovery was not made. The Bureau of Safety of the Department of Transportation concurs in this tentative finding.

The aircraft, an Amalgamated Condor was equipped with a Fairchild flight recorder. The recorder sustained some fire and impact damage, but data were obtained from a readout that still is in progress. Unfortunately, examination of the cockpit voice recorder, which was more severely damaged and burned, produced no information.

The flight recorder data indicate that the trip was routine up to the point when the aircraft was given permission to climb in order to avoid severe thunderstorm activity directly in its path. Its altitude at the moment it was cleared to climb was 43,000 feet. The flight recorder data show that, as the climb was begun, the aircraft was in light to moderate turbulence. Heavier turbulence was then encountered for approximately three minutes, followed by a sharp and abnormally rapid increase in the rate of climb to approximately 9,000 feet per minute until the altitude peaked at 47,285 feet.

In the next seven seconds, altitude was lost at an increasing rate accompanied by a shift from positive G forces to negative G forces until the aircraft struck the ground.

The main wreckage area was located at the bottom of a gorge twenty-two miles east of Winslow. Destruction from impact and subsequent fire was total and there were no survivors. The aircraft impacted almost vertically. A section of the tail containing one elevator was found approximately one and a half miles east of the principal wreckage area. Another elevator was located more than two miles east of that area. An inspection of the latter component and of the tail section, including the other elevator, gave positive evidence that structural failure of both elevators occurred. This was attributed to excessive loads exceeding their design strength.

Correlation of this failure with the data obtained from the flight recorder indicates that one elevator separated completely from the aircraft either just prior to the final dive or during the dive, presumably from excessive stresses as the pilot attempted to regain control and halt the rapid loss of altitude. The second elevator, while it did not separate from the aircraft, was found in a badly damaged condition due also to loads exceeding design capability. Examination by structural experts from the Amalgamated Aircraft Corporation, the Air Force and the Bureau of Safety disclosed that this elevator also failed to function due to stress failure of its hinge bolts only a few seconds after the other elevator departed entirely from the tail section.

All flight control systems have been carefully studied

for indications of possible control malfunctions. Absolute continuity of control linkages and cables could not be established because of the extensive damage. However, there was no evidence of any control system failure or malfunction except those associated with elevator stress failure.

There was no evidence of arcing, burning or electrical overload on any of the generators. All available wiring bundles were examined for evidence of electrical arcing or beading but none was found. There was no evidence of a lightning strike on any of the wreckage. The venting in both wings was unobstructed and showed no fire damage. There was no evidence of internal wing tank fires prior to ground impact. As far as could be determined, there was no evidence of hail damage found on the nose section or the leading edges of the wing, tail or engine cowlings.

Selected but numerous samples of the aircraft wreckage were flown to the Federal Bureau of Investigation laboratory. These included the tail section and both elevators. No explosive residues were found and there is no reason to believe the aircraft was sabotaged. Further tests relative to this aspect, however, are continuing.

Examination of the engines disclosed that all four power plants were developing full thrust just before impact. There was no indication of engine malfunction. There also was no indication of a collision with another aircraft or birds. As far as could be determined, all fire damage resulted from impact with no evidence of an in-flight fire which might have contributed to or caused the accident.

It is evident from the flight recorder traces that in the final stages of flight the aircraft climbed steeply, reaching a climb rate about three and a half times its normal rate, pitched nose down and then dove toward the ground at high air speed. The Board of Inquiry, therefore, has concentrated its investigation on the possible cause or causes of this final maneuver and whether the structural failure of empennage components was due in part or totally to (1) the actions of the crew, (2) in part or totally to the severe turbulence, or (3) to a combination of the pilot-weather factors.

The Board considers it significant that the flight recorder readout was remarkably similar to those obtained after several previous accidents involving loss of control of large turbine-powered transports that encountered abnormally severe turbulence. In the majority of these incidents, the aircraft was caught in powerful updrafts and forced into an excessive rate of climb, accompanied by a sharp nose-up attitude. Coincident with crew attempts to maintain control was the encountering of sudden and equally powerful downdrafts. The latter occurred just at the moment when the control input was directed to bringing the aircraft's nose down to a more level attitude in an effort to prevent a stall due to the excessive nose-up attitude and the subsequent loss of lift.

The introduction of a strong downdraft into a situation when the aircraft already was being trimmed to reduce altitude and to reverse nose-up attitude could have only one result—a sharp pitchdown and a subsequent dive challenging the skill and experience of any pilot in a recovery attempt.

The Board of Inquiry is convinced that this was the situation facing the crew of Air Force One, and such conviction is based not only on previous accidents occurring under similar circumstances, but on data furnished by the United States Weather Bureau which demonstrated beyond question that the turbulence encountered by the presidential aircraft was generated by a wind shear preceding a vicious line squall. Such wind shears usually involve violent, sharp gusts that can either be downdrafts, updrafts or a succession of both and with no warning when one might change to the other in a split second.

However, the Board has been unable to ascertain definitely whether elevator failure was due to turbulence alone. The flight recorder readout shows inconclusive but logical evidence that an unsuccessful attempt to recover control at least contributed to the structural disintegration and may have been the sole source of this failure. The violent pitchdown may have been the result of elevator separation following excessive gust stresses, but it is equally plausible to deduce that it also could have stemmed from the combination of updraft-downdraft conditions and the actions of the crew in combating this unexpected development.

In fact, the Board of Inquiry believes that the latter possibility is the more likely and logical probable cause of this accident. This belief should not be interpreted as criticism of the crew or the techniques followed. The Board, indeed, believes that the pilots were faced with hazardous circumstances which they were unprepared to meet.

The commander of Air Force One, Colonel Marcus Henderson, and the copilot, Major Samuel Foster, were veteran and able airmen who had demonstrated through numerous tests and check rides their unquestioned qualifications for the safe operation of an aircraft. Furthermore, both had extensive experience in flight operations involving severe turbulence.

In attempting an admittedly theoretical reconstruction of what events must have transpired in the cockpit of Air Force One, however, the Board investigated the background of these two fine officers. It was impressed by the fact that neither pilot had, as far as could be determined, any experience in operating a Condor under the severe turbulent conditions undoubtedly encountered by the presidential aircraft.

Because of the previous turbulence incidents involving swept-wing turbine equipment, there has been considerable emphasis placed by both the Air Force and the civil carriers on training crews to combat successfully even the most drastic conditions affecting aircraft control. The result has been a virtual cessation of loss of control incidents in recent years. Certainly, Colonel Henderson and Major Foster were exposed to this extensive training and the Board of Inquiry has been greatly concerned as to why such training apparently failed to prevent this accident.

In the course of this thus far brief but extensive investigation, the Board noted that Colonel Henderson and Major Foster were assigned to the presidential air fleet seven years ago when primary aircraft of that fleet was the Boeing 707-320, the long-range intercontinental model of the Boeing 707. Part of their qualifications for flying Air Force One was a six-week training curriculum at a major airline's Flight Training Center, under a contract the carrier held for instructing all Air Force One pilots in the operation of Boeing transport aircraft.

The curriculum included intensive sessions in a 707-320 simulator and the course placed particular emphasis on aircraft control techniques in severe turbulence. The utilization of a simulator enabled the instructors to re-create, almost as realistically as actual flight maneuvers, conditions identical to those encountered by Air Force One over Arizona. The Board of Inquiry further noted that, according to airline and Air Force records, Colonel Henderson and Major Foster had no difficulty in passing this or any other phase of the training program.

However, and the Board holds this to be of utmost importance, when the Air Force acquired the Amalgamated Condor for use in the presidential air fleet, no Condor simulator was available. All pilot qualification checks were conducted in the actual aircraft during actual flight. Only recently has a digital flight simulator been obtained for Condor crews, and there was no opportunity for either Colonel Henderson or Major Foster to receive simulator training before they were assigned to the flight which ended in disaster.

Subsequent to the accident, special tests were run in the new Condor simulator which approximated, as nearly as could be determined, the weather and turbulence conditions encountered by Air Force One. These disclosed a previously unsuspected instability which the pilots undergoing the tests described as an oversensitivity of controls and a tendency to permit hazardous overcontrol. Fifteen pilots were tested as to their handling of a Condor affected by first a severe updraft, then an equally severe downdraft, followed by a violent pitchdown and a high-speed dive. Of the fifteen pilots, eleven imposed such large control displacements as to theoretically cause failure of the elevators along with possible failure of other empennage structure when they attempted to recover from the dive.

Under these conditions, with heavy control column

194

forces presenting a difficult recovery problem, a pilot used to the normal sensitivity of the Condor's control system would have a natural tendency to attempt to override the elevator control column load and such overriding, at a critical stage of the recovery, could well lead to structural failure. Loss of elevator effectiveness during a high-speed dive is particularly characteristic of T-tail aircraft.

It seems evident that in the case of Air Force One the rapidly decreasing air speed even as the rate of climb increased sharply, combined with a high nose attitude, prompted the crew to take drastic action to prevent what would appear to be an impending stall. Acting on this concern, and quite probably while being subjected to severe vibrating accelerations from the turbulence, the pilots used full down elevator and aircraft nosedown stabilizer trim to change the aircraft's flight path.

Although these large control displacements would have the effects of arresting the speed decrease and high climb rate and would return the aircraft attitude to near level, they also would develop extremely high negative G forces approximating the weightlessness of a space flight. Such forces would result in a chaotic situation in the cockpit of any aircraft exposed to forces of this type and magnitude.

Besides the distraction of warning lights and ringing bells which were probably activated under the negative G conditions, loose items such as briefcases, charts, logbooks, etc., would be tossed around. The crew members would be forced upward against their belts and the average pilot unquestionably would have difficulty keeping his feet on the rudder pedals and his hands on the control yoke.

It was at this moment that Air Force One probably was exposed to a sudden and violent downdraft—at a time when control forces were reduced to zero or even reversed and the pilot's hands were off the yoke as a result of the high negative G effects. Under these circumstances, with the control column remaining in full forward or nosedown position, a steep dive was inevitable.

The Board of Inquiry feels justified to theorize that,

when the pilot managed to place his hands on the control yoke some eight seconds later, the aircraft was in a vertical dive and air speed was building up rapidly with an accompanying loss of elevator effectiveness.

The Board is convinced that a final recovery attempt was made at this precise moment, resulting in excessive loads on the elevator structure and failure due to inadvertent overapplication of the controls. Such overapplication, as the special simulator tests demonstrated, was most possible and even likely in an aircraft whose normal control forces were the most sensitive of any large transport aircraft built.

The Board of Inquiry at this stage of the investigation can find no reason to apply the verdict of pilot error to this tragedy or to attach any blame whatsoever to the crew. Rather, the Board believes that both crew and aircraft were exposed to a set of extremely hazardous circumstances which neither were equipped to handle, the pilots in terms of experience and the aircraft in terms of structural strength.

The Board also emphasizes, however, the tentative and preliminary nature of these findings. The investigation is continuing and a full report will be issued at a later date when evaluation and analysis of all available evidence is concluded.

General Coston held a news conference immediately after distribution of the Board of Inquiry report, and the wisdom of this decision was confirmed by the first question from a worried-looking Washington *Post* reporter.

"General Coston," he asked, "would you care to put the Board's verdict into language the layman can understand?"

"Just what don't you understand?" Coston said pleasantly.

"I refer, sir, to the second paragraph listing the probable cause of the accident. I quote: 'the unfavorable interaction of severe vertical air drafts and large longitudinal control displacements resulting in a longitudinal upset' and so forth. I wonder, General, if you could put this into plain English. Because frankly, sir, I don't know what the hell the Board's talking about."

"Well, it means that Air Force One went out of control in severe turbulence," Coston answered with a kind of resigned patience. "It went into a dive and, in attempting to recover from the dive, too much force was applied to the controls and the elevators failed."

"General, that seems to imply pilot error, doesn't it?" the Chicago *Sun-Times* man asked.

"No, it does not. The Board of Inquiry report makes it clear that the crew was blameless. Henderson was faced with a problem he couldn't solve. The problem was not of his making."

"Of whose making was the problem?" the AP pressed.

"The problem was a combination of many factors. I don't think you can boil them down and pinpoint the blame on any single factor."

"I'm not talking about blaming a factor, General," said the AP. "If you won't tag the crew with pilot error, what individuals would you blame? The people who built the Condor? Air Traffic Control? The Weather Bureau? The Air Force for accepting a plane with, let's see, the report referred to it as a 'previously unsuspected instability'?"

Coston took a firm grip on his self-control. "In an accident of this sort, there's really no single cause and therefore no single area of blame. It was the result of a chain of unfortunate circumstances. For example, I personally believe that if Colonel Henderson had had the advantage of simulator training in the Condor he would have been able to cope with the situation. The lack of simulator training was a matter of not being able to obtain the necessary hardware soon enough. The White House was anxious to utilize the Condor as a presidential aircraft and it was put into presidential service before a Condor simulator was built."

"Did Colonel Henderson or the other pilot ever express any concern about the Condor's handling characteristics in turbulence?" That one was fired by Pitcher.

"Colonel Henderson, I understand, preferred the old Air Force One. The Boeing 707. But it's natural for most pilots to prefer one aircraft over another. Most of his flight experience had been on Boeings and he liked the plane." Coston peered suspiciously at the questioner. He remembered Pitcher's probing from the first news conference.

"Well then, let me rephrase my question. What was the source of Colonel Henderson's preference for the 707, as opposed to the Condor?"

"Source? He just liked the Boeing better. You might like

a Lincoln better than a Cadillac, or a Chevvy more than a Plymouth. It's pretty difficult to spell out a pilot's likes and dislikes, just as it's hard for a driver to explain exactly why he prefers one car over another."

"General, you're evading—"

"I'm not evading anything, sir," the general snapped.

"—you're evading the question. I'll rephrase it again, General. Was Colonel Henderson's dislike for the Condor—"

"Just a minute. I never said he disliked the Condor. I said he would rather have flown the Boeing."

"I'll rephrase it for the third time," Pitcher persisted. "Was Colonel Henderson's preference for the 707 ever reflected in any official report to the Air Force? Did he ever complain to his superiors about the Condor?"

"Colonel Henderson made no official representations to the Air Force concerning the safety of the Condor."

"Did he ever make any unofficial representations?"

"In private conversations with other officers, I'm told, he expressed his preference for the Boeing."

"In those conversations, did he say why he'd rather fly the President around in a 707 instead of a Condor?"

"You're asking me to give hearsay evidence," Coston protested. "To quote Colonel Henderson secondhand. It seems more pertinent to me, as chief of the Air Force, that Henderson never submitted official complaints about the Condor. I think, sir, you might let others ask some questions."

"He's doing fine," someone in the back of the room said loud enough to paint a flush of anger on Coston's face. There was an embarrassed, uneasy pause before the New York *Times* put the next question.

"Is the Air Force going to obtain another Condor as a replacement?"

"I don't know. We'd have to ask Congress for the money. That decision hasn't been reached yet. I don't think it's even been discussed. Right now, we're going to use the Condor's predecessor as the primary presidential aircraft. Temporarily, of course."

"As chief of staff, would you recommend purchase of another Condor?" Pitcher would not let go.

"My feelings on this matter were expressed before we bought the Condor. I thought Air Force One should be a supersonic transport. Congress thought otherwise. I still believe the President's long-range aircraft should be an SST."

"That belief is based on your desire for a faster plane? Or is it based on how you feel about the Condor's safety?" The *Star* had taken up Pitcher's cudgels.

"It's based on the speed factor, not on safety," Coston replied testily.

"General, are there any plans to ground the Condor?" the UPI wanted to know.

"Negative."

"Well, in view of this accident," said the AP, "is the Air Force going to make any modifications in the plane? Or any changes in operating methods?"

The general seemed relieved at this question. "We've discussed with Amalgamated the possibility of strengthening the tail section, the horizontal stabilizer area, that is. Actually, although the Board of Inquiry report did not go into this in detail, the failure on Air Force One occurred at the place where it was anticipated failure might occur first from abnormal stress loads. At points where the Condor had the least reserve strength. Now, it's not definite whether these points can or should be beefed up. On an airplane, if you strengthen one component you may weaken another. In the case of the Condor, or so we're told by the manufacturer, beefing up the tail-fin components might make the wing the critical component and this would be equally unsatisfactory, of course. As for operating techniques, well, we're putting all Condor pilots through our newly acquired Condor simulators. We have every reason to believe that proper familiarization with the aircraft's handling characteristics in abnormally rough air will prevent a recurrence of this type of accident."

"General, to change the subject a bit," the Dallas *Times Herald* said, "could you tell us why Air Force One was flown into such turbulence? I would have assumed that the pilots of a plane carrying the President always would be on the supercautious side. They were warned of such weather, were they not?"

"They were aware of thunderstorm activity in their path. They were not expecting turbulence of such violent magnitude, or obviously they would have changed course, or even reversed course as an extra precaution."

His reply prompted UPI to go into the weather more thoroughly. "General Coston, the Board of Inquiry report did not mention the weather forecast available to the crew, either before take-off or while en route. Are you satisfied, sir, that their weather information was adequate?"

"It was inadequate, I'm sorry to say, but that's also a matter of hindsight. Unfortunately, weather forecasting remains a somewhat inexact science although it's improved considerably over the past decade."

"How do you—" The Scripps-Howard reporter tried to get in a question but Coston shook his head.

"Just a minute, please. I want to finish answering the previous question. Now, let me explain what I meant by the word 'inadequate.' I'm not trying to attach any blame to the weather forecasters. The weather briefing Colonel Henderson received before making out his flight plan did indicate thunderstorm activity, but not at the altitude he chose. That was his principal reason for selecting the altitude. He thought he'd be above the weather. Not until he was relatively close to the storm area did it become apparent that the adverse weather was at a much higher altitude than anyone expected. We've got to assume he figured he could climb above it. Again, we're second-guessing. We're Monday-morning quarterbacking a fine pilot and an excellent officer. He made a command decision based on his ability and knowledge. The decision turned out to be wrong, but only the good Lord above could have told him in advance what he was flying into."

Scripps-Howard managed to join Rod Pitcher on Coston's mental roll call of reporters who deserved a firing squad. "It seems to me, General, that the Air Force is going to great lengths to protect the reputation of the pilots, Colonel Henderson in particular. If I read the Board of Inquiry report correctly, sir, and I'll admit I'm no aeronautical authority, the elevator failure occurred because he tried to pull out of the dive too soon. Or because he applied too much pressure or too rapid pressure on the controls. Is that correct?"

"According to the Board's preliminary findings, that was the basic cause of the accident. That's what the language 'large longitudinal control displacements' means."

"Then how can you reconcile this verdict with both your

statement and the Board's report that no pilot error was involved?"

"I fail to see any discrepancy in the Board's findings," Coston growled.

"Any discrepancy? It's crawling with discrepancies. First the Air Force says the pilot used the wrong technique for pulling out of the dive. Second, you've just told us—or implied it, anyway—that Henderson made the wrong command decision. That he should have changed course or turned back. And you still say there was no pilot error involved? You can still defend his so-called command decision when he presumably had the life of the President of the United States in his hands? When he should have erred on the side of caution?"

The general's face again turned beet-red. "I suggest you read or reread the entire report. It deals in considerable detail with the principal reason why Colonel Henderson could not make a successful recovery from the dive. The reason, as far as I'm concerned, is unchallengeable. It might help to restate it. The Condor's controls, to begin with, are sensitive—they were deliberately designed that way to make an extremely heavy aircraft easier and safer to handle. But we know now that oversensitive controls can be a booby trap for a pilot exposed to turbulent conditions, a pilot who had never before flown a Condor into such severe conditions. I reiterate that if Colonel Henderson had received the benefit of simulator training, the same type as he received on the Boeing, I don't think this tragedy would have occurred. Does that answer your question?"

"No, sir, it does not. Not entirely. Getting away from the subject of the wrong recovery technique, I still would like to ask how the Air Force can justify the fact that the commander of Air Force One deliberately flew into an area of known severe turbulence, with the President on board. Or supposedly on board."

"We're not trying to justify anything, sir. We're trying to explain what happened. I'm not going to stand up here and libel the reputation of a man unable to defend himself. Let me put it this way, and I can't put it any stronger. If I had been piloting Air Force One that night, I probably would have continued on course just as Henderson did. Now, does *that* answer your question?"

"No, but I don't see any use in pursuing it any further.

You're just trying to protect your own. To cover up—"

"I agree with you, there's no point in pursuing this line of questioning," Coston said, anger still written on his features. "And I admit to protecting our own—against any attempt to read into the Board of Inquiry report blame which is not in that report. May I have another question, please?"

A correspondent for *Time* changed the subject. "General, the report says flatly there were no survivors. Does that mean the Air Force believes President Haines is dead?"

"I believe that at the press conference held the morning of the crash it was decided that all information on this aspect would come from the White House. No comment."

Rod Pitcher decided the door had been opened to his Senator Haines theory. "Well, the Air Force is in charge of the investigation. Couldn't you tell us what's being done to establish the identity of the unknown body?"

"Again, I must refer you to the White House. No comment."

"General," Pitcher asked, refusing to let the door slam shut, "how about giving us your own personal views on this? Do you think the President was on Air Force One?"

"My own personal views are unimportant. No comment."

"Are they still looking for the President's body at the crash site?" *Newsweek* asked.

"Yes."

"How long are they going to look?" UPI inquired.

"Until we're satisfied he was or was not on the plane."

"Then you think there's still a chance he was? That he's dead and not just disappeared?" the *Post* asked.

"No comment."

"In all your experiences with air crashes, have you ever heard of a case where you haven't accounted for all the people on board?" Pitcher's foot was still in the door. And Coston's answer left it there.

"No," the general said tersely.

"Then it's your opinion that failure to find the President's body means there's virtually no chance he was aboard?" *Time* was following the IPS line of attack.

"No comment."

"Oh, come on now, General," the *Star* insisted. "You must have an opinion."

"I've got one. I'll just keep it to myself."

"Would you give it to us off the record?" the *Times* asked.

"No."

"Don't you trust us?" said the AP plaintively, as several reporters laughed. Coston relaxed into a grin.

"As patriotic Americans, yes. As reporters exposed to temptation, no. And if I gave you my opinion, even on an off-the-record basis, I expect the temptation to leak it some way would be overwhelming. So let's drop it, shall we?"

"Sir, it's been less than a week since the crash occurred," the UPI noted. "Isn't it unusual for a Board of Inquiry report to be issued this fast?"

"Very unusual," Coston agreed. "But this is an unusual situation. We felt we owed it to the nation to make public what we know about the accident thus far. The findings are tentative, of course."

"Do you anticipate any revisions in the findings?" someone in the rear called out.

"Well, I don't want to go out on any limb. But I'd be surprised if there were major changes. The Board has done an exceptionally thorough job in a very short space of time. With the help, I might add, of the Bureau of Safety, the FBI, Amalgamated, and everyone else concerned with the investigation. Their cooperation has been superb."

"General Coston," a Hearst reporter said, "the report states there's no evidence of sabotage. Is this conclusion based partially on any investigation of the occupants aboard Air Force One?"

"It is."

"Well, it's been disclosed that one of the security guards was not a regular crew member. Was his background investigated?"

"You're referring to Sergeant Jervis. Yes, he was investigated. Complete bill of health. A fine non-com. I regret his death very much, just as I regret the deaths of all those aboard, crew and passengers alike."

"You said you feel that the replacement for the Condor as Air Force One should be an SST," Pitcher said. "In the interim, is the Air Force making any plans to refurbish one of its Condor cargo planes for use as a presidential plane?"

"No. We'll use the Boeing for the time being. Until we

see what happens to our SST appropriations request. I'll entertain one more question."

It was asked by Colin. "General, would you blame the fate of Air Force One primarily on the machine or the man?"

"That would be oversimplifying it," Coston said thoughtfully. "Few accidents, if any, have a single causal factor."

"I deliberately used the word 'primarily,' General."

"I know you did, Chet. Let me put it this way. I've known Marcus Henderson ever since he was a second lieutenant with a pair of brand-new wings. He was a fine pilot. He was a fine person. You asked me if I'd blame the man or the machine. All I know is that Colonel Marc Henderson didn't have any more to do with that accident than I did. Maybe less."

"Maybe less?"

"Less. After all, I made the final authorization for purchase of the Condor."

"Thank you, General Coston," said the AP.

Rod Pitcher was used to the reasonably new opulence of the FAA Building and the clean if rather spartan atmosphere of the Civil Aeronautics Board. The comparative dinginess of the Pentagon not only surprised but depressed him.

The press room from where he and Chet Colin had just dictated their accounts of the Board report and the Coston news conference came close to deserving the adjective "squalid." The room was large, but this was the kindest thing that could be said about it. It was also crowded, with ancient desks smothered under piles of old news releases, newspapers and military journals.

Pitcher suspected that some of the handouts must have dated back to World War II and he wondered if the regular Pentagon reporters had somehow acquired the pack-rat habits of misers. In these unkempt surroundings, the fastidious Mr. Colin seemed woefully ostentatious, a graceful willow blooming in the midst of gnarled cacti. His own desk was as bad as any of the others.

"How can you work in this mess?" Pitcher demanded. "Don't you ever throw any of these handouts away?"

"The desire to cling fondly to dead Defense Department releases," Colin explained, "is nothing but a disease afflicting anyone who works in this room for a period longer than three days. After all, the military never seems to discard anything so we've apparently absorbed this fine quality, by osmosis, so to speak."

"It's nothing but an unholy mess," Pitcher repeated. "My God, look at this handout. 'Release for Sunday AM's, March 28.' I wonder what year."

"It could be last year," Colin confessed. "I guess I could get rid of it but there's something about this place that seems to make discarding anything a crime. I don't defend it, God knows. I think Custer's plan of battle must have come out of this dungeon. Aside from your low opinion of my working environment, Pitch, what did you think of this afternoon's events?"

"The Board of Inquiry report didn't surprise me at all. What did surprise me was that they're still trying to find Haines's body."

"Why surprised? It could be there, in about fifty different pieces."

"Hardly," Pitcher scoffed. "Chet, everything in this entire snafu adds up to the President's not having been on that plane."

"They haven't identified all the bodies yet," Colin pointed out. "Like I said, Haines could be spread out over a couple of Arizona counties."

"Then how do you explain the one body they couldn't identify?"

"Just somebody who got on the plane, Lord knows how and why, without any of you observant gentlemen of the press noticing him the night they left."

"Baloney. Nobody sneaks aboard Air Force One—"

"Not even if the President himself figured out a way to do it?"

"Okay, then explain why he'd do it."

The Pentagon reporter shrugged. "There's no ready explanation, Pitch. Maybe if the President's ever found alive, he'd give us the answers."

"Hah!" Pitcher exclaimed triumphantly. "So you don't think he was on the plane, either. Now, I still figure that damned brother . . ."

"Pitch, I don't know what to think. And neither does anybody else in this five-sided monument to red tape. The only thing I've been able to get out of the Air Force is 'no

205

comment' or 'it wasn't pilot error.' Which reminds me, did you buy that whitewash job on Henderson?"

"It was no whitewash job," Pitcher said with a semblance of a glare. "For my dough, that Scripps-Howard guy deserves a good boot in the ass for that hatchet job he was trying."

"What hatchet job? He was trying to get at the facts."

"The hell he was. He was trying to read into the facts we were given some insinuations and accusations he had no business making. The only whitewash was on the plane itself. And Coston came damned close to admitting Henderson didn't think much of the Condor. In fact, I gathered that neither does Coston. That last remark he made—remember? And he was really ducking most of the questions about the plane. I got the idea he was trying to tag the Condor with all the guilt without ever actually saying so. Right?"

"I guess so. I also got the idea he was getting pretty sore at you. Anyway, I'm glad Gunther sent you over. I'm used to Pentagonese but I couldn't have handled that Board report alone without a degree in aeronautical engineering."

"You should see some of the CAB accident reports. This one was grammar school stuff. Well, I suppose I'd better get back or Mr. Damon will be climbing the walls, clutching callbacks to his bosom."

"Don't mention callbacks to me," Colin glowered. "I get ten a day—the AP has three guys here and UPI two, and then New York roasts me for not matching everything they file."

"Par for the course," Pitcher commented. "See you around, Chet."

He dialed the bureau and told Mrs. Strotsky he was returning to the office. By this time the CAB already had closed shop for the day. Pitcher figured he could just check in and then get home to Nancy.

He drove back to downtown Washington over the bewildering complex of Virginia's roads, pleasantly conscious of the ten cents a mile IPS granted for staffer automobiles used on company business. What with all the trips to Andrews and today's Pentagon assignment, he could turn in an expense account of at least twenty dollars.

The aviation editor walked into the bureau to be confronted with a Gunther Damon whose frown had a slim glimmer of triumph embedded in the wrinkles.

"Read this, Pitch." The news superintendent handed him a piece of copy torn from the A wire.

BULLETIN

WINSLOW, ARIZ. (IPS)—A FLASH FLOOD SWEPT THROUGH THE GORGE CONTAINING THE WRECKAGE OF AIR FORCE ONE TODAY, DROWNING TWO RESCUE WORKERS AND BURYING MOST OF THE DEBRIS UNDER AT LEAST THREE FEET OF WATER. OFFICIALS FEARED THAT THE FLOOD, WHICH MOVED SOME WRECKAGE AS FAR AWAY AS A MILE, WOULD MAKE FURTHER SEARCH FOR PRESIDENT HAINES'S BODY ALMOST IMPOSSIBLE.

"Holy cow," Pitcher breathed. "That's a tough break."

"Very tough," Damon agreed. "Particularly tough on our beloved Acting President."

"Huh?"

"Now he might wind up being Acting President until the next election."

CHAPTER TWELVE

Vice President Frederick J. Madigan, notified of the news from Arizona, immediately called a late afternoon Cabinet meeting. It was the second since the crash and caused several members to complain, only in the presence of their closest associates of course, that Madigan apparently was either lonesome or trying to run the government by committee. They were unprepared for his opening remarks.

"Well," he announced, "I must say this is one fine pickle we're in."

Secretary of State Sharkey looked sharply at the Vice President, shrewdly suspecting that Madigan had taken the flood development as a personal inconvenience.

"Pickle?" he ventured.

"Pickle, mess, snafu—whatever you want to call it. I don't mind telling you gentlemen, this status of Acting President has been something of a strain and now it appears both the status and the strain could go on indefinitely. Not that I have any ambition to be sworn in as President, I assure you. But I still feel more like a figurehead than a nation's leader under these circumstances."

"You shouldn't feel that way at all, Mr. Vice President," Sharkey said with as much sympathy as he could muster. "We all realize the difficulties of your position. There isn't much we can do about it at this point."

"That's exactly why I called this meeting," Madigan said. "And that's why I've also invited FBI Director Reardon, Mr. Packer of the CIA and General Geiger, chairman of the Joint Chiefs of Staff. Plus General Coston, of course, and the Chief Justice. It's my considered judgment that we can't continue this way forever. First, I'd appreciate an up-to-date briefing from our two generals, here, and the FBI and the CIA, on any developments in this mystery. Second,

I'd like to pick your brains, so to speak, on the advisability of declaring Jeremy Haines officially dead."

An uneasy silence from every man in the Cabinet Room greeted the Vice President's words. Madigan sensed unspoken reactions that ranged from disbelief to resentment, but he already had decided to plunge his foot into the ice water of probable resistance.

"Mind you," he added in a conciliatory tone, "I said advisability. I'm not saying we should declare him dead. But I do feel, rather strongly, that this distasteful subject should be discussed. Because of that damned flood, we may never find his body. And it seems to me, gentlemen, that we should be asking ourselves if there's any kind of a time limit for such a step. A sort of a legal minimum for a missing President, so to speak."

"The President," Sharkey reminded him, "may be missing for other reasons than inability to locate his body at the crash site. As we all know, it's not unlikely he wasn't even on the plane."

"True," Madigan said, "which is further justification for our pursuing this matter. If he wasn't aboard, then why hasn't he come forward? He may have gone insane. He may have been murdered. He may have committed suicide. I'm afraid, gentlemen, that in the absence of any clue as to his whereabouts we might as well start seriously considering the probability that he's dead. So again, I feel I must put this before you for discussion. And I'd like to ask the Attorney General for an opinion. And then the Chief Justice, if I may."

Attorney General Howard Kelly, a broad-shouldered man whose totally bald dome almost seemed to have reflective qualities, simply stared at the Vice President.

"I don't have any offhand opinion," he said slowly. "There's no real precedent. I suppose we'd have to follow the District of Columbia's statutes on when a D.C. resident can be declared dead. That's one year, I believe. I'd have to check into it."

"Mr. Chief Justice?" Madigan was feeling the intoxicating exhilaration of Authority and Command, now blissfully oblivious of the reason he had raised the issue. Namely, Hester had raised it herself when he called her to tell her about the flood.

209

The Chief Justice shook his head in a gesture that combined disapproval toward Madigan and a veto of Kelly's suggestion. "The President is not a legal resident of the District," he said. "He votes in and therefore is a resident of his home state. We would have to consult the authorities in Mr. Haines's own state on this matter. If they should be consulted, that is."

Secretary of State Sharkey could no longer hide his anger. "I would suggest, Mr. Vice President, that this entire discussion is unnecessary at this time. I assume we have many more important things to consider."

"And I would suggest, Mr. Secretary," Madigan said tautly, "there is hardly anything more important than telling the American people exactly how long they are to be without a President. A leader, I might say."

"They have a leader in the Acting President," Sharkey replied—suppressing a strong desire to add "I hope."

"I thank the Secretary of State for his expression of confidence," Madigan said with an attempt at a friendly smile that somehow wandered into a sneer. "As God is my witness, I'm merely trying to dispel the clouds of uncertainty that surely exist not only in this country but among our allies. I cannot emphasize too strongly, as God is my witness, that I do not want to be President of the United States. But we must face reality, gentlemen. We can't drag this thing on forever."

"Drag what on forever?" Sharkey asked with open rudeness. "If Haines were sick, unable to perform the duties of office, you'd carry on for him as long as necessary. You have the same responsibility in this case. He happens to be missing, not sick, and that's why we have an Acting President. Until we are positive he's dead, this subject is moot."

"I agree," the Vice President said, again with forced cordiality. "Except that everything seems to point to his being dead. Which is why I've brought the matter up. General Geiger, would you or General Coston have any enlightening information on this phase? The investigation, I mean."

The towering chairman of the Joint Chiefs crossed his long legs and nodded at the Air Force chief. "I'll let Bob answer that, Mr. Vice President."

Coston glanced at his superior reproachfully. He had

welcomed the summons to the Cabinet meeting with all the nervousness of a pilot ordered to land a B-58 supersonic bomber on the shortest runway at Washington National. He possessed the military man's inherent distrust and dislike of politicians and, having just been through the harrowing meat grinder of a press conference, he did not relish running the gamut of a Cabinet interrogation.

"I'm afraid, Mr. Vice President, I have nothing new to report," Coston said unhappily.

"Well," Madigan said, "perhaps you can brief us on the significance of this flood business. I gather from the news dispatches over the White House tickers that search operations have been suspended. Is that correct?"

"Correct, sir."

"For how long, General?"

"I wish I knew, Mr. Vice President. Water's still too deep for any digging. Depends on how fast things dry out. Even when we resume, Lord knows if we'd find much. The flash flood not only drowned wreckage but washed some of it maybe a mile or more away. It's sure delayed things, that's all I can tell you right now."

"General Coston," Madigan said, "I don't want to assign you to any limb, but I think we'd all appreciate your own thoughts on the prospects of finding the President's body. Assuming he was on the plane."

Coston gazed at the ceiling for a second and the Secretary of State, sitting only a few feet away, noticed that the airman's eyes were bloodshot. He wondered how much sleep Coston had been able to grab since that awful night, and he felt a throb of compassion for this dedicated officer.

The general hesitated. "In view of the preceding discussion," he answered dryly, "you're putting me on quite a spot."

"I realize that, General," Madigan said. "But I think the Cabinet would benefit from your considered opinion."

Coston lit a cigarette before replying, the act giving him time to compose his words carefully. "Okay, I'll tell you exactly how I feel. First off, I'm convinced the President wasn't on Air Force One. When we start digging again, I figure we'll be looking for the proverbial needle in the haystack, only it's a needle that wasn't there to begin with. You asked me, Mr. Vice President, to judge the situation if we could assume he was aboard. In that case, I'd have to say that we should have found some trace of him by now."

"That's in the category of pure theory, isn't it?" Secretary of Labor Gilbert put in. "Some bodies you haven't been able to identify. That of the President could . . ." He paused, as if unwilling to bring up the indelicate possibility of Jeremy Haines's body being dismembered. Coston grasped his embarrassment.

"Let me put it this way, sir. We've been unable to identify five bodies. Four of them were crew members and the fifth, well, that's our mystery man. But he has been identified, in a negative sense. In other words, we know he wasn't the President. However, when I use the word 'unidentified' I'm referring to our inability to point to any body or piece of a body and say, 'That's Colonel Henderson or that's part of Major Foster.' "

Someone at the end of the long, circular Cabinet table involuntarily sucked in his breath at Coston's blunt phrasing. The general continued in a matter-of-fact tone that was more chilling for its very impersonality. "Now, I said before I don't think we'll ever find Mr. Haines's body because I don't think he was on board. I base this, first, on the evidence that the unknown passenger probably was posing as the President. Second, we have found enough portions of bodies to add up to the four crew members—so many torsos, so many arms and legs, and so forth. I apologize for possibly indulging in some unpleasant language but we haven't found any, uh, leftover portions. Is my reasoning clear?"

"Only too clear," murmured Defense Secretary Tobin.

"Very clear," Madigan agreed. "And in support of my contention that the President is dead."

Sharkey tossed at the Vice President a look of utter disgust. "And just how did you reach that conclusion?" he asked.

"Simple. If he was on the plane, he had to be killed. If he wasn't on the plane, he would have come forth by now. I.e., he is dead."

"There are," the Secretary of State said slowly, coating each word with undisguised contempt, "a number of possible explanations of the President's disappearance and the reason or reasons for his silence. Until his death is verified beyond any doubt, I consider this entire discussion not only a waste of time but an insult to the President of the United States."

Sharkey had thrown down the gantlet. Frederick James Madigan picked it up.

"Perhaps," the Vice President said, "your feelings are indicative of unwillingness to serve in my Cabinet."

"This isn't your Cabinet, sir," Sharkey snapped. "We were appointed to serve at the will of Jeremy Haines. And I'll be damned if I'll resign."

"Just a minute, both of you," Defense Secretary Tobin interrupted. "This is no time for a family fight."

"The Secretary of State," Madigan intoned with pompous dignity, "has cast aspersions on my integrity. I think an apology is in order."

Secretary of Labor Gilbert, whose temper had a short fuse and whose vocabulary contained a residue from his early days as an automobile assembly line worker, slammed his fist on the table.

"I think you're full of crap, Madigan," he snarled. "Let's wait until we bury Haines before we swear you in."

Madigan flushed. Some of the false façade of courage instilled in him by his wife began to crumble. He realized now that the Cabinet's sympathy toward his difficult position could not be translated into automatic support. With the wavering of incisiveness came an instinctive decision to be Noble. He rose and put his hand out toward the Secretary of State. "Jim, I guess I'm the one to apologize. I'm sorry. I've been under a terrible strain. As God is my witness, I'm just trying to do what's right. What Jeremy would have wanted me to do."

Sharkey, surprised at the sudden surrender, accepted the handshake. "No apology is necessary, Mr. Vice President. We also want to do what the President would desire, and that includes giving you all the assistance possible. May I suggest we take up what you proposed at the start of this meeting? Namely, a report from the FBI and/or the CIA."

Madigan nodded in the direction of FBI Director Reardon, who got to his feet with the reluctance of an unprepared schoolboy called on to recite. The Cabinet seemed to let out its collective breath, relieved at the end of the quarrel.

"There has been some speculation that the unknown body on Air Force One was that of Senator Haines, the Presi-

213

dent's brother," Reardon began. "The FBI has investigated this possibility and is satisfied that the senator left Washington the night of the accident on a planned fishing trip in Maine. Now I—"

"Just a minute, Mr. Reardon," the Vice President said. "Perhaps you might phrase this in a different manner. Is the FBI satisfied that Senator Haines was not on the plane?"

"Yes, sir."

"You've already reported to me that the fingerprints of the mystery passenger did not match those of the senator's. I wanted the Cabinet apprised of this fact."

"Yes, sir. We haven't ascertained the ownership of the prints yet, but they definitely weren't those of Senator Haines. If I may proceed, Mr. Vice President?"

"Please do."

"The FBI, I regret to say, has been unable to determine the whereabouts of the President. We have checked hundreds of leads, reports, rumors, clues and possibilities. All efforts have had negative results. The investigation is continuing. At this time, that is all I have to report. I'm sorry."

"Mr. Reardon," Madigan said, "the Cabinet might be interested in the whereabouts of Senator Haines. I, for one, am at a loss to explain how a United States senator could remain out of touch this long, in this period of national crisis, and with his own brother missing and possibly dead."

"Frankly, Mr. Vice President," Reardon said earnestly, "so am I. The authorities in Maine have checked every lake, every fishing spot, in the state. There's absolutely no sign that the senator even went to Maine. We do know he went as far as Boston. There his trail ended. There was no reservation made in his name on any northbound flights leaving Boston, no indication that he rented a car in Boston or took a train north. Obviously, he still isn't in Boston or he would have heard about the President. But where he is, we don't know."

The Cabinet chewed over this admission briefly.

"Does the FBI think the disappearance of the senator has any connection with that of the President?" Tobin inquired.

"Not as far as we can determine," Reardon replied. "I would say we have two separate events with no apparent connection. But I hesitate to label the senator as a disappearance case, Mr. Secretary."

"There must be a connection," Tobin insisted. "Two brothers, one President and the other a senator, both disappear the same night and you call this a coincidence?"

"I didn't call it that, Mr. Secretary," the FBI chief remonstrated mildly. "I said there's no apparent connection at present. We're still looking into it."

"I'd like to ask the CIA's views on this," the Defense Secretary pressed. "Are there any indications of an international plot behind this whole affair?"

Director Julius Packer of the CIA took an enormous curved pipe out of his mouth and sleepily blinked his deepset eyes. His voice emerged from a huge chest in a kind of hoarse, gravelly rumble. "None whatsoever," he assured the Cabinet.

"You seem unusually confident about this," Madigan noted. "As you know, when all this started we put SAC on a twenty-four-hour alert in full expectation that Russia or Red China might start something, while we were in a confused state. Would the CIA recommend suspending or easing our alert?"

"That's a military decision," Packer answered, "and military decisions aren't in our province. We can only advise and—"

"We'd appreciate your advice," the Vice President told him.

"Well then," Packer said, "let me say that we've seen no signs of hostile or overt actions on the part of either China or the Soviet Union, and furthermore no evidence that their agents played any role in the events of the past few days. But if you want my personal opinion, I'd keep our bombers and missiles on an instant retaliatory basis. Until further notice."

"Precaution, hunch or suspicion?" Tobin asked.

"Precaution, mostly. A little bit of suspicion. Certainly no hunch on my part. It's just that, well . . ." The CIA official hesitated.

"Go ahead, Julius," Madigan urged.

"Well, just because we haven't been able to unearth anything pointing to a fine Commie hand in all this doesn't mean there isn't. I tend to agree with General Coston that the President wasn't even on Air Force One. And yet, if that's the case, I can't understand why he hasn't revealed his whereabouts. It doesn't make sense, it doesn't add up, and it worries me. We have a totally illogical situation here and maybe we shouldn't be looking for logical answers."

"If the Reds wanted to pull the trigger," Sharkey observed, "they could have done it in the first twenty-four hours when we were in a state of shock. As far as our Russian and Chinese desks at State are concerned, Peking and Moscow appear just as puzzled as we are."

"Their puzzlement," Packer said, "could be a cover-up. If they were instrumental in arranging the President's disappearance—or maybe his murder—they wouldn't be bragging about it openly. I'll say it again. Let's keep that alert in effect."

Madigan, not a little grateful for the altered atmosphere, looked around the table and found nods of approval. "I so order, General Geiger," he said.

The Cabinet meeting droned on to other matters, important items such as the latest Mars space probe and such unimportant items as Secretary of Transportation Harvey Brubaker's plan to bring the independent Civil Aeronautics Board into his own agency. He had been slapped down the first two times he had proposed it to Haines but decided he might spring it on Madigan. The Vice President liked Brubaker, possibly because Harvey was the only top official in Washington who was basically more incompetent than himself.

Unfortunately, Madigan's sensitivity was bleeding from every pore after Sharkey's attack and he was in no mood to support Brubaker's obvious attempt at empire-building. He was well aware that most of the Cabinet regarded the Transportation Secretary as Jeremy Haines's poorest appointment, one stemming from a combination of bad advice and political pressure.

Sharkey and Gilbert left the White House by the back door, the latter noting with unconcealed sarcasm that only Brubaker had departed via the lobby outside the press room so he could talk to reporters.

"I hope the stupid bastard remembers that Cabinet meetings are off the record," Gilbert growled. "I'd hate to have the country find out what went on at today's."

"It would be most unfortunate," Sharkey agreed. "Nels, do you think I was too rough on our Acting President?"

was about to fly his own aircraft up to Canada for some fishing. To make a long story short, he invited me to go along and I accepted. We went to his bachelor quarters in a Boston suburb, and later took off from Logan International Airport for Canada about 4 A.M. That would have been about a half hour before the news about my brother was made public. Well, that's about the whole story. I cannot find adequate words to express my sorrow for what has happened. I'm not conceited enough to claim that my presence in Washington would have made much difference, but at least it would have prevented some of the speculation I understand has existed because of my actions.

"Now, I'll be happy to answer any questions. Warner, I'll let you go first."

"Senator, we have reason to believe that Eastern listed you as a no-show on the nine o'clock flight to Boston. Yet your wife saw you off and you obviously went ahead with your travel plans. Could you clear this up?"

"Well, I'm afraid I have another habit which seems to have contributed to unnecessary confusion. I honestly don't like to fly under my own name. The airlines make a fuss about a senator, for which I don't blame them. But as a member of the Senate Aviation Subcommittee, I frequently travel incognito so I can observe things like cabin service, baggage handling and so forth. On this occasion, I had informed my secretary that I intended to take Eastern's nine o'clock flight to Boston. She naturally assumed I wanted a reservation and made one under my name. I didn't know this and unfortunately I failed to tell her I preferred to make my own for this particular trip, which I did. I went to National Airport that night with my wife and checked in under the name I sometimes use. No airline personnel recognized me and obviously Eastern figured I just didn't show up for the flight. The FBI, by the way, also was aware of this no-show business and I gave them the same explanation I've given you. My wife, by the way, was in the airport coffee shop while I was checking in and didn't know I wasn't traveling under my own name. Next?"

A Scripps-Howard reporter wanted to know when and how Haines learned of the crash.

"We had flown today from our fishing site to Montreal and I bought a newspaper. I saw a reference to the President's being missing. I phoned my wife immediately. She notified the Vice President, who contacted me at the Montreal airport and gave me all the known facts as of this hour. He made very quick arrangements for a Royal Canadian Air Force jet to fly me here. I'm most grateful to the Canadian government."

"Senator," asked the *Evening Star*, "you've indicated there have been some rumors to the effect that you were the so-called mystery passenger aboard Air Force One. Now that you've shown up, alive and healthy, I'm glad to say, do you have any idea about this unknown person?"

"None whatsoever. I don't have the foggiest notion."

"Do you believe the President is dead?" the New York *Times* asked.

"No, I don't. I—please hold your questions and let me finish—I don't believe it because I don't want to believe it. I have nothing on which to base this except sheer hope. And I suppose that's the best way to put it. I'm hopeful, rather than optimistic. Actually, I don't know any more about this entire situation than you do. As I said earlier, Vice President Madigan has been kind enough to brief me on what's known up to now. I can't speculate, guess or theorize any better than anyone else."

The Chicago *Tribune* got in the next one. "Senator, as the President's brother you were fairly close to him. Did he give you any clue or warning or the slightest indication of a planned disappearance?"

"He did not."

"Well, when was the last time you saw him?"

"The same night Air Force One left for Palm Springs. I went to the White House about eight o'clock to say good-by to him. We also discussed some personal matters."

"Did the personal matters involve the Palm Springs trip or anything that might throw some light on what happened?" asked the Washington *Post*.

"What we discussed was just what I said—personal. Nothing to do with the trip or international matters or anything like that. You might say it was a conversation between two brothers, rather than a President and a senator. I'd rather not comment beyond that."

"Did the President seem worried or upset or, uh, not himself?" This was from the AP.

"He was tired but cheerful. I thought myself he was a

little preoccupied, but that's standard for a President these days."

"He said nothing unusual? Nothing that might hint of something in the wind?"

"Absolutely nothing. As I told you, our conversation consisted of personal matters, you might say family matters."

Goldberg decided it was time to bring up what he figured Gunther Damon would want brought up.

"Senator, it's inconceivable to me, and maybe to the rest of us, that if the President were deliberately plotting some kind of a disappearance act, for what must have been vitally important reasons, that he wouldn't have taken his own brother into his confidence. I find it hard to believe, sir, that what you discussed that night was nothing but family matters. Any comment, Senator?"

Haines's tired eyes seemed to flash sparks of anger and then suddenly filled with tears.

"I don't really care what you find hard to believe, Warner. I've told you the truth. The President said nothing to me which could cast the faintest light on what's happened. I only wish to God he had." His voice cracked as he spoke the last seven words, and it was like the tinkle of breaking glass. Goldberg wished he hadn't challenged him.

"I'm sorry, Senator," the IPS reporter said. "I wasn't questioning your truthfulness, sir. The mystery's got us down, too, and we're just trying to get some answers."

The senator looked at him in a way that accepted the apology without words. Bertrand Haines started to speak, choked off a sob, and walked out of the room. The reporters were silent.

"He may say he's hopeful," the Los Angeles *Times* finally murmured, "but for my dough there's a guy who thinks his brother is dead."

Gunther Damon moved his chair back from the copy desk slot, stood up and let night editor Bill Utely take over this journalistic command post. The news superintendent glanced at the big electric clock on the wall. Nine forty-five, and the last takes on the Senator Haines story were clearing the A wire.

He felt tired and yet vaguely restless. Outside, the roar of Fourteenth Street traffic had dwindled to an occasional horn or a protesting screech of brakes. He walked to the window and aimlessly stared across the street at Garfinckel's corner display space, occupied as usual by an exquisite, original evening gown. For some reason he remembered the few times the department store had displayed something other than special women's apparel in that corner window at Fourteenth and F streets—such as on the occasions of FDR's and JFK's deaths, when large pictures of the two departed Chief Executives were draped in mourning black, illuminated by a single spotlight.

He wondered when Garfinckel's would get around to putting Jeremy Haines's picture in the window, with that dignified collar of Stygian hue. And this journey of thought took him back to the mystery, with its countless unanswered questions and frustrating labyrinth of contradictory clues and theories. Logic tortured by the implausible. Facts cruelly assaulted by the impossible. For every ready, easy explanation, a demolishing counterattack of irrefutable rebuttal.

Gunther Damon sighed wearily, and went over to Frank Jackson's overnight desk. "Frank, guess I don't have to tell you we should go heavy on connecting the senator's return with that unknown body. You know, blowing up the possibility that the brother was posing as the President."

Jackson was a pleasant-faced, gray-haired man with that inconsistent calm so inherent in many men who labor in the hectic snakepit of wire services. "Sure, Gunther. Say, you look bushed. Why don't you go home?"

"I suppose I should. I keep feeling the minute I leave, all hell will break loose again. And once I get home, I don't think a bulldozer could budge me out of that apartment tonight."

Jackson grinned. "So you're afraid to leave?"

"That's about it. You got any problems?"

"Nope. Layout's pretty well set. Thought I'd lead the main presidential story with the brother coming back. Chris Harmon's got a damned good overnighter on diplomatic sources worrying about Secretary Sharkey."

"Worrying about him? What's the angle?"

"Well, you know Haines wasn't one of those Presidents who tried to be his own Secretary of State. He leaned on Sharkey. He was a Midwesterner and he wasn't too savvy on international affairs when he took office. He learned fast,

222

but he learned from Sharkey and he never hid that fact. So the way Chris sees it, and the way Chris writes, the diplomatic corps expected Sharkey to pretty much take over and help Madigan with anything faintly resembling an international problem. Only he apparently hasn't done much at all. Not a single public statement since Air Force One went down Not one news conference."

"Interesting," Damon mused, "but not very conclusive. He may be doing a lot of advising on the q.t."

"Not according to Chris. He says in this story that Sharkey's even been avoiding every diplomat in Washington. No sign of any conferences or meetings. There's one paragraph that says flatly a couple of top ambassadors tried to see Sharkey and got shunted off to the lower echelons."

"Is Chris sure about all this? If he hasn't got this coppered, he's gonna have one hell of an angry Secretary of State."

"I talked to him after he phoned in the overnighter. He says he got the original tip from an Assistant Secretary who told him he hasn't even been able to contact Sharkey at home since the President disappeared."

"Well," Damon reasoned, "I suppose Sharkey's in the dark like the rest of the country. He probably didn't want to see anybody because he didn't have anything to tell them and he hated to admit it. Hell, the British papers are lambasting the Secret Service for letting the whole thing happen, including the crash. That reminds me, did Pitch do an overnighter on the accident report?"

"Yep. Good job. Little too technical but I did some paraphrasing in spots where it got too heavy. Pitch'll probably claim I screwed up the facts."

"Our prima donna division occasionally can't see the forest for the trees," Damon commented. "I wish I could get our Mr. Pitcher to write for the uninformed public instead of aiming his stuff at airline pilots."

"Rod," chuckled Jackson, "would rather have been an airline captain than a newspaperman."

"That's for sure," Damon agreed. "But he's not—and if he gives you any guff about spoiling his copy, lemme know. Well, guess I'll make a phone call before I go home. Maybe I won't have to go home."

"If you score," the overnight editor requested, "take

time out to let me know where I can interrupt you. Just in case."

"Naturally," Damon said ruefully. "Even my sex life is run by the IPS switchboard."

"Quit complaining, boss. On the overnight, you don't have a sex life. There are times when I wonder if I got my wife pregnant by osmosis."

"Or by the milkman," Damon laughed.

"Unfortunately for that libelous theory, I'm home when the milkman comes. Good night, Gunther. Oh, before you go, think we should play up that Cabinet meeting?"

"Nobody seems to know why Madigan called it. Brubaker was the only one who talked afterwards. As usual, he didn't say anything. Along about the fourth or fifth paragraph of the main lead should take care of it. Spellman told his briefing it was routine. You see Jonesy's story?"

"Yeh," Jackson said, lighting his fifteenth cigarette of the night. "I kept wondering how the devil any Cabinet meeting could be routine at a time like this. But with Frederick James, anything's possible. Well, good night again."

Damon merely grunted his farewell. He felt that restlessness again and he walked over to the switchboard where he asked Bobby Andrews, with assumed nonchalance, for the list of staff home numbers. Deliberately, he pretended to examine several numbers even as he surreptitiously memorized Lynx Grimes's.

He had apologized to her, rather gruffly, for breaking their date when the Board of Inquiry crash report, the flood story, the Cabinet meeting and the Senator Haines arrival had all popped loose, one after the other like a string of exploding Chinese firecrackers.

"I'm going back to my desk, Bobby," he said. "Give me an outside line."

He dialed her number. She answered after the second ring, her voice sounding lower on the phone than in person.

"Lynx? This is Gunther Damon. Did I wake you?"

"No, I was just watching TV."

"Sorry about tonight. Everything hit the fan at once."

"I understand. You've got a rain check when things settle down."

"They've settled down a little. I seem to be wound up like
224

a three-dollar watch. How about a quick nightcap at the Willard? I'll pick you up."

She hesitated. "It's a little late, Mr. Damon, I'm already in my pajamas and I have to be at work tomorrow."

"What time?"

"Well, I've got the eleven-to-eight shift tomorrow. I suppose one drink wouldn't hurt, but I hate to get all dressed again."

Damon briefly thought over that inevitable female obstacle course, and tried to hurdle it with an equally inevitable and totally unsatisfactory male solution. "Just slip into a skirt and sweater. Nothing fancy about the Willard."

"A skirt and sweater is not exactly my idea of the uniform of the day for a first drink with my boss. I'd invite you over here for a nightcap but my roommate is about ready for bed and we'd disturb her, talking."

Damon mentally cursed the rigid Washington rule that All-Attractive-Single-Girls-Seem-to-Have-Roommates-Who-Want-to-Sleep. He gave up, telling Lynx he would see her tomorrow. He waved good-by to Bill Utely, told the switchboard he could be reached at the Willard Room for the next hour or so, and left the Press Building. He entered the hotel at its F Street doors and descended the stairs leading to the elongated corridor known as Peacock Alley. "Hello, Steve," he greeted the maître d' in the Willard Room.

"Good evening, Mr. Damon. You're by yourself tonight?"

"Yes, unfortunately. How about this table in the corner?"

He ordered a whiskey sour from Mary Ann, his favorite waitress, and glanced around the big room, which was almost empty at this time of night. He always enjoyed the Willard Room. It was a quiet anachronism in Washington's world of glittering, spangled cocktail lounges, with its enormous high ceiling, green marble pillars and crystal chandeliers. A kind of oasis for the casual drinking that was part of serious talking or serious thinking.

Characteristically, Gunther Damon was thinking now—the events of another busy day, another twenty-four hours in which the mystery of Air Force One continued its defiance of reason and logic. Nothing added up. That crazy business of the supposed impostor. The failure of the President to reveal his whereabouts after the crash, provided he was alive. And if he were alive, why was he still in hiding and where? Why expose the nation and the free world to the vapid leadership of Fred Madigan? What was the overwhelmingly important crisis that could have generated a plot making the Gordian knot a simple bow by comparison? And was it important enough to warrant the creation of another crisis, one of indecision, uncertainty, confusion and fear?

The magnitude of a disappearance scheme, Damon knew, required accomplices. Not even the President of the United States could have accomplished it on his own, taking no one into his confidence and trusting not a single official either in his Administration or in the career services. So if there was a plan, who was in on it besides the President himself? Such top brass as Cabinet members? Or even Frederick J. Madigan? Or was the conspiracy carried out by relative small fry, a handful of minor characters sworn to secrecy and relied on for their loyalty toward Jeremy Haines and their patriotism toward their country?

Or, Damon also reflected sadly, was the intrigue born in the mind of the President at all? Was it Moscow- or Peking-made? Could it be a supercriminal kidnaping plot with a colossal ransom demand as yet unmade? That one, Damon admitted, was really on the wild side but it was hard to scoff at the most unthinkable explanation. At this point he was willing to concede the possibility that the President of the United States could have somehow been spirited away by invaders from outer space. He castigated himself for even dignifying this science fiction potboiler of an idea by including it in his reveries. Yet he had not been able to prevent it from strolling uninvited into his mind. My God, he thought, I'm really clutching at the proverbial straw.

He forced his thinking processes back to the more prosaic but likely theories. Who in the Official White House family would Haines have trusted the most? The senior Cabinet member, in terms of standing and prestige as well as close association, would be Secretary of State Sharkey. Wait a second. Chris Harmon's overnight story. Sharkey's unexplainable behavior, his lack of action during the past week. How much did the Secretary of State know? Was he avoiding everyone because he *did* know the answers? And couldn't tell anyone those answers?

Gunther Damon consulted his wristwatch. He strode rapidly down Peacock Alley toward the main lobby and found a phone booth. He dialed the office and asked Andrews to connect him with Chris Harmon's home.

"This is Gunther, Chris. That overnighter of yours on Sharkey—it gave me an idea. You got any way of finding out what Sharkey's been doing the past few nights? I hear you've been told he isn't reachable at home."

The State Department reporter was puzzled. "I'm not sure what you mean, Gunther. He has been leaving fairly early for him. About six or seven every night. Maybe he is going home and just doesn't want to be bothered. No social engagements that I know of, and anyway all the society fluff's been canceled since that plane crashed. What's the pitch? Has Drew Pearson got him involved in a sex scandal?"

"Chris, I don't think he's going home. I've got the goddamnedest hunch he's been seeing the President of the United States. And I don't mean Fred Madigan."

Christopher Harmon had a nasty case of ulcers and a thorough dislike for newspapermen who got excited, the latter undoubtedly explaining the former. He kept his emotions corked up like vintage wine to be opened on very special occasions, and such occasions were not only rare but virtually non-existent.

The first time he displayed the slightest agitation over a story was on December 7, 1941. In fact, that was the only time, until Gunther Damon presented him with this provocative hunch. His fertile mind automatically computed Damon's hypothesis, analyzing it for reasonableness and probability.

"I think," he said in a tone that for Chris Harmon was hysterical exuberance, "you might have something. But do you also have any great inspirations on how I'm supposed to get the honorable Secretary of State to admit it?"

"Chris, does Sharkey always use the same car on official business?"

"I imagine so. The Cadillac limo, I've never seen him ride in anything else."

"Okay. Can you get into the State Department garage? Isn't that where the car's kept?"

"Sure. What am I supposed to look for? Fingerprints of Jeremy Haines on the door handles?"

"Nope. Mileage."

"Mileage?"

"Mileage, dammit. Chris, go down to that garage first thing in the morning. Tell 'em you're doing a story on the use of government cars—how much they're driven every week, like compared to the average motorist. It may not work but there's just a chance you could find out how many miles that Caddie has been driven since the night of the crash."

"I might also find out what the inside of the District of Columbia jail looks like."

"Hell, no. Chances are those chauffeurs or mechanics or whoever's in charge of that car will be tickled pink to talk to a reporter. I don't have to write out a script for you, do I? Ask a bunch of questions about safe driving tips and crap like that. How it feels to have the honor of driving around a Cabinet officer. But above all, drag that mileage out of him or them."

"Gunther, I don't want to sound stupid, but what will we do with the mileage figure even if I get it?"

Damon chuckled, a low, triumphant, almost dirty chuckle. "Simple. We divide the total mileage accumulated on that car since Air Force One went down by the number of days that have elapsed. That gives us the approximate mileage per day. We divide that by two. Get it?"

"No, but that devious mind of yours fascinates me. Continue."

"Then after we take half that daily mileage, we take a ruler and we look at a road map of this area. We match the ruler against the map's scale of miles to an inch, and then maybe, just maybe we can find out where Mr. James Sharkey has been driving every night."

Harmon whistled in combined awe and admiration, but he was cautious. "Look, Gunther, you're assuming he's gone someplace but home every night. I just said—"

"I know what you said. I'm playing a hunch, Chris. But it's the strongest hunch I ever had."

"I've a hunch too, Gunther. That you're right."

"Based on what you know or heard?"

"Nope. My ulcer just started to hurt. Good night, Sherlock. I'll call you in the morning."

Damon returned to the Willard Room, his mind boiling with excited anticipation. He ordered a second whiskey sour. He realized he was skating on the thin ice of pure supposition but this was the way he operated best, and throughout his career he had been right more often than wrong. There had to be a link between Sharkey and the missing President. Harmon's story could be a foot in the closed door of the unknown. It wouldn't cast more than a sliver of light, but it was a beginning. A key card turned up in a game of solitaire, breaking a tantalizing log jam.

Tomorrow, he told himself, might bring the beginning of the end to the enigma of Air Force One.

CHAPTER THIRTEEN

It helped not a little that Chris Harmon was not unknown to the personnel in the State Department garage. He parked his own car there occasionally, one of the fringe prestige and convenience benefits that never appeared on the IPS payroll check.

A minor secretary in Sharkey's office had tipped him off when the Secretary arrived at his desk, as usual regarding Saturday as just another workday. Harmon made the request to her casually, explaining, "I'm working on a little project and I just want to be sure he's around in case I have to call him." When her confirming message came through, he called the IPS switchboard.

"This is Harmon. I'll be out of pocket for a little while. Is Damon in yet? Okay, just leave word with him that I'm looking at speedometers. No, speedometers. He'll understand."

He found the chauffeur in charge of Sharkey's limousine without trouble. The chauffeur was a handsome Negro in his fifties. He was polishing away at the hood with a chamois, humming some undecipherable tune which he broke off as Harmon approached.

"Good mornin', Mr. Harmon. What brings you down to our little motor pool?"

"Morning. Joseph, isn't it? I can't remember your last name."

"Hutchens, Mr. Harmon. Joseph Hutchens. Anything I can do for you, sir?"

"You might, Joseph. We're getting some material together on official cars. The ones used by the top men in government. I'm checking on your operations down here. Wondered how it feels to be driving a man like Secretary Sharkey around."

Hutchens beamed with such warm pride that Harmon felt like a Judas.

"Well, I'll tell you, Mr. Harmon, the Secretary's a fine man. A very fine man. Thoughtful. Always polite. Even when he's got a lot on his mind. And I guess he's got a lot on his mind these days. You fellas heard anything more about the President?"

"No. You might hear more than we do, Joseph, on your job."

It was a matter-of-fact statement, made in a tone of nonchalant innocence, but the Negro's demeanor altered instantly. Joseph Hutchens was nobody's fool. "Mr. Harmon, you just tryin' to sound me out? Pump me a little, maybe? You know better than that. I can't tell you anything. Believe me, man, when I'm drivin' this car I've got no ears at all. No, sir, no ears."

Harmon could have kicked himself for arousing suspicion. He was going to have one hell of a time worming a mileage estimate out of this boy. He decided to retreat. "So help me, Joseph, I'm not snooping. I honestly want to know something about how a Cabinet chauffeur works. The hours you have to put in. For a starter, how long have you been with State?"

The chauffeur was mollified but still apprehensive. "Can't see any harm in tellin' you that. Been here since Mr. Dulles was Secretary. Didn't drive him, though. Mr. Sharkey's the first Secretary I've had the honor of chauffeurin' and it's an honor. Yes, sir, a real honor."

"Have to take any special tests to rate this job?"

"No, sir. I kinda inherited it. Man before me, he retired. They asked me if I wanted to be the Secretary's chauffeur and I said sure. Closest I'll ever get to being a Cabinet man myself, I figured."

He chuckled and Harmon laughed with him, politely.

"I suppose you sometimes have to put in long hours?"

"Yes, sir. Real long. But I don't mind. Just my wife and me at home, and she understands. Our kids, they're all grown up and moved away. Got one son who's a doctor. You know, I'm mighty proud of him but he always tells me, 'Pop, I'm real proud of you.' So I don't mind drivin' around at night, sometimes. Like receptions and stuff like that, when the Secretary has to go someplace."

"Do you do all the driving, Joseph? Or does Mr. Sharkey

231

sometimes ask you if he can take the wheel? I wouldn't blame him. It's a beautiful car. Remember, some of our Presidents liked to drive themselves. Truman was one. And LBJ."

"Yep, I remember readin' about them." Hutchens grinned. "Seems to me they got in a mite of trouble doin' it, too. Didn't Mr. Truman get stopped for speeding, once? And Mr. Johnson, he was hell-bent for leather when he drove around that ranch of his."

"Truman was stopped on the Pennsylvania Turnpike, but that was after he left office, if I recall correctly. I suppose Mr. Sharkey isn't the speeding type."

"No, sir, he's not. To answer your question, Mr. Harmon, he never drives. Not this car. Matter fact, I don't know if he ever drives. When he wants to come down on a Sunday or holiday, he always calls me and I go pick him up in Chevy Chase. He's got a car in his garage but I think his wife's the only one who uses it. Nice car, too. White Ford convertible. Man, that's my dream in life. Older I get, Mr. Harmon, more I want a convertible."

"Does Mr. Sharkey do any back-seat driving? Tell you you're going too fast or too slow? Or what streets to take?"

"No, sir, like the Greyhound ad says, Mr. Harmon, he leaves the drivin' to us. He just sits back there and thinks. And I guess he's got a lotta thinkin' to do, these days."

"I guess he has," the reporter agreed. "But to change the subject, Joseph, does this car have any special maintenance? Is it greased or have oil changes more frequently than, say, the average private automobile?"

"Well," Hutchens said, "we pretty much follow the factory manual. One thing, I keep this baby a lot cleaner than most folks do their own cars. I make sure she's polished up a bit every day. Wash her myself, sometimes. Right after I bring the Secretary to work and I know he's not gonna be using it right away."

"It's interesting that you follow the factory manual," Harmon said. "Now on my car, my service station keeps telling me that twice-a-year lubrication and oil change every six thousand miles is for the birds. I change mine every three or four thousand. I guess if six thousand is good enough for the Secretary of State, it should be good enough for me."

"Well, I'll tell you, Mr. Harmon, personally I agree with

your service station. Now I got a little Plymouth. That Owner's Manual has same recommendations as yours. But I figure it's best to be on the safe side. And I'll let you in on a little secret, only don't print it. I kinda watch out for this Caddie too. I just changed the oil on her myself . . . let's see, now, it was the day after the President got lost. And there wasn't no six thousand miles between changes, either."

Bingo, thought Harmon. The hole's open. This is the luckiest line of questioning in journalism history. But play it cozy, chum. Don't get careless or he'll clam up. "Well, now you've got my motoring curiosity aroused, Joseph. Not my reporter's curiosity. What did you change it at—three thousand? Like I said, I've been doing it at three or four."

The Negro fell into the trap so eagerly that Harmon would have been sorry for him, except Chris was too busy mentally congratulating himself. "Well, let's take a look at the sticker, Mr. Harmon. I use stickers just like the regular garages. Let's see, now."

He opened the door on the driver's side of the big Cadillac and knelt to read the figures scrawled on the lubrication-oil change record. "No, sir, no six thousand miles here. Oil change before was 4100. Last one was at 7055. Just about three thousand, I'd say."

"Well I'll be darned," Harmon said with a make-believe, disarming enthusiasm that would have done justice to an Alfred Lunt. "And she looks like she just came off the assembly line. I didn't even figure she'd have that much mileage on her. You sure keep her up. What's the speedometer read now, anyway?" Swallow that bait, boy. Please, swallow it.

Joseph Hutchens swallowed it. He leaned into the car and examined the speedometer reading. "Exactly 7795 miles, Mr. Harmon. How about that?"

"Yes," said Christopher Harmon, inscribing two figures into his memory track. "How about that?"

Gunther Damon came to work early that Saturday morning, although he was five minutes too late to talk to Harmon in person. Mrs. Strotsky gave him the message that "Mr. Harmon says he's gonna look at speedometers. What's he talking about?"

"He's buying a used car," Damon explained. "You're

233

the nosiest switchboard operator east of the Mississippi and possibly west."

"If I wasn't nosy," Mrs. Strotsky announced in her well-modulated bellow, "I wouldn't know a damned thing about what's going on in this nuthouse."

Damon cheerfully chucked Mrs. Strotsky under the chin, waved laconically at Les Butler, and went right to his desk to give the overnight report its daily inspection. He merely glanced at most of the stories, but read Chris Harmon's speculative piece on Sharkey with renewed interest and more than normal concentration. Butler came over and had to say "Gunther" twice before the news superintendent looked up.

"Coffee flip time, Gunther. You in?"

"No," Damon said. "It's on me this time. I'll lose anyway. Here, give Custer this two bucks. Tell him to get some glazed doughnuts too."

"Doughnuts too? Boy, you're in a happy frame of mind. Tell you what, I'd like some ham and scrambled—"

"Doughnuts," repeated Damon. "Don't stretch your luck. I'm just feeling expansive."

"You're feeling more than expansive," Butler said wisely. "Something must be percolating on the Haines story."

"Correct."

"You care to confide in your day editor?"

"Not yet would I like to confide in my day editor."

"Your day editor is a quivering mass of curiosity, peerless leader."

"My day editor will have to curb his curiosity. I haven't got all the ducks lined up yet."

"I would be the last one to jeer at our peerless leader if any of his ducks flew away at the first shot. Perhaps you'd—"

"Perhaps I'll renege on the doughnuts if you keep asking me questions. You're the journalistic equivalent of a nagging wife. Go away. I'll fill you in later."

"I may sulk," Butler said. "There's nothing worse than a sulking day editor whose curiosity burns unsatisfied, like a frustrated virgin."

"There's one thing far worse. A sulking day editor who thinks up pornographic similes. I'm serious, Les. I don't want to say anything until I get a few things checked out. We got burned once on that mass of assumptions known as

234

the Senator Haines angle. And speaking of the Haines burning, our aviation editor has just arrived. An hour early, no less. He must have had a fight with Nancy."

"He probably wants to get off two hours early and is trying to impress you," Butler corrected. "Well, I shall retire to the slot and await Mr. Pitcher's wrath. It seems New York chopped his overnighter by about forty per cent. He'll blow his stack."

"I'll blow mine in unison," Damon said. "The preliminary crash report on Air Force One was no story to cut. Did you say anything to New York?"

"Jules Tamborello called a while ago about something else. I asked him how come the hatchet job on Pitcher and he said there was too much technical crap in it."

"Frank Jackson said it got a bit heavy but that he fixed it up. I'll give Tamborello a ring. I'm in such a good mood I might not even lose all of my temper. Look, Pitch is reading his story now, Les. He'll be over here steaming in two minutes."

Pitcher was over in one minute and twenty-seven seconds, his face seething with the glow of righteous anger. "Goddammit, Gunther, I'm no prima donna but that goddamned New York—"

Damon held up his hand. "Yeh, I know, Pitch. They butchered you. I'm gonna raise some hell about it. Give me a chance to read it over and take a look at the incoming report. Relax and I'll call you over when I get Jules baby on the horn."

Pitcher went to his own desk. Damon read his story, counted the lines and then walked to the day desk where he examined the original copy. It had, indeed, been emasculated with large chunks of the actual report cut out and even some quotes from the Coston press conference slashed by whole paragraphs. Damon briefly looked over the incoming copy from other bureaus, including a long story from New York on a wildcat subway strike that had hit the city during the last evening's rush hour. Now he was seething too.

He asked Mrs. Strotsky to get him Jules Tamborello on the New York tie line, returned to his desk and beckoned Pitcher. His phone rang just as the aviation editor sat down, expectantly.

"New York says the overnight editor has gone home," Mrs. Strotsky said. "Do you wanna talk to anybody else?"

"Yeh. Try Miles Burke." Burke was vice president and executive news editor. Pitcher looked both impressed and worried.

"Burke here."

"Gunther Damon, Miles. How are you this morning?"

"Fine, Gunther, just fine. But, heh-heh, you didn't waste IPS money to ask about my health, did you?"

"Nope, I'm spending IPS money to tell you New York should send its overnight desk back to journalism school."

"I gather, heh-heh, our overnight desk has committed a nefarious crime, Gunther?"

"If you can put stupidity in the category of crime, Tammorello deserves to be indicted. Look, Miles, we're busting our asses on this Haines business. Yesterday the Air Force puts out a preliminary report on why that plane crashed. Plus a press conference. Rod Pitcher did a helluva fine overnighter. His original copy ran about fifty-five lines. Your clowns cut it to twenty-eight. It was the President's plane that went down, Miles, not a goddamned Piper Cub flown by somebody's grandmother."

"Well, now, Gunther, you know that very few stories have to be told in more than three hundred words. Jules might have been a little overzealous but wire space is at a premium. You know that."

"Yeh, at a premium, Miles. But if wire space is so damned precious, how come New York let its overnighter on that two-bit subway strike run sixty-one lines? Six hundred words on a story that's of prime interest only to New York. And your Mr. Tamborello cuts the Air Force One crash report down to less than three hundred. That's not editing, Miles. It's inexcusable butchery."

"Now, Gunther, I—"

"You let me finish, Miles. This bureau is overworked, shorthanded and so damned tired the guys are walking around with their chins on the ground. We're bleeding out our guts on the biggest story in history and we won't put up with any incompetent slob at your end who wouldn't know a legitimate news story if it ran up his butt. Six hundred words for a goddamned lousy subway strike and you give me a wire space alibi. Jesus Christ, Miles!"

"Well now, Gunther, calm down. Tell you what. I'll talk to Jules myself later today after he's had some sleep. We work hard up here too, heh-heh, believe me."

"Why don't you call him in about an hour, after he's gone to sleep?" Damon suggested. "The knucklehead deserves to be jarred awake. And you can tell him if he wants to argue about his great news judgment I'll be delighted to discuss it with him."

"Gunther, I promise I'll talk to him. I'll let him know exactly how you feel."

"Miles, you don't have enough profanity in your vocabulary to let him know how I feel. You tell him for me to keep his clumsy hands off major Washington overnighters or I'll come up there and amputate them. Good-by, Miles. I hope I've spoiled your day. The stupid sonofabitch just spoiled mine."

He hung up, still boiling, and then had to grin at the startled expression of awe on Pitcher's face.

"I feel better," he relented.

"God, Gunther," Pitcher marveled, "that oughta do some good."

"Sure it will," Damon said. "For about three or four days. Then we'll have to fight the battle all over again. Ever meet Jules Tamborello?"

"No. He must be something."

"Actually," Damon chuckled, "he's a nice guy and a pretty good newspaperman. Being in New York is his main trouble. Bring him down here and we'd shape him up in about a week. You kind of lose perspective up there. Well, are you satisfied with my defense of your prose?"

"Eminently," Pitcher said happily. "Frankly, Gunther, I wouldn't have the nerve to talk to Miles Burke the way you did."

"That didn't take nerve, Pitch. In the first place, I can get away with that kind of insubordination. My severance pay would break this outfit. In the second place, I was right and he knew it. They shouldn't have mangled your story that way. Good yarn, by the way. You satisfied with the Board of Inquiry report? Think that's what really happened?"

"I am," Pitcher replied positively.

"No pilot error? Strictly the airplane?"

"Strictly. Funny thing, Gunther. I keep wondering how much of a mystery we'd have if Air Force One hadn't crashed. Assuming, of course, that the President wasn't on it."

Damon nodded, half meditatively and half in agreement. "Yep, assuming a lot of other things too. Such as there really being an impostor plot. Then you've got to speculate on whether Haines would have stayed missing this long if that plane hadn't gone down. Whether there's any connection between the accident and his hiding someplace."

"The tragedy," Pitcher commented, "is that the crash probably wouldn't have happened if any plane but the Condor had been used. That pilot had a hell of a lot of experience on the 707. Too bad Haines or whoever took his place didn't wait for the old Air Force One that came in later that night."

"History is written by the little words in our language," Damon said. "Like 'if.' Well, Pitch, I'll let you get back to work."

The aviation editor was five yards away before the delayed reaction, a mental double-take, struck Damon's brain with the impact of an anvil. "Pitch!"

Pitcher turned around and came back. Damon was eying him. "Something wrong, Gunther?"

"What you just said. Repeat it."

"Repeat what? I think I said they should have flown a 707 that—"

"No. You said something about the old Air Force One coming in the same night. Where did you get that tidbit?"

"At the Andrews tower when I was checking on all those departures. I looked at the arrivals too. The tower logged a landing for N-26000—that's the number of the Boeing 707 Kennedy and Johnson used. Haines too, until he got the Condor. I recognized it, the number, I mean."

"Pitch, where did it come in from?" Damon spoke very slowly and very distinctly.

"Let's see, I'm trying to remember. Minneapolis, I think. Yeh, Minneapolis. I wondered what it was doing in Minneapolis. I asked the tower chief and he said it was probably on a training flight. Or maybe hauling some junketing congressmen around. He didn't seem to attach any importance to it, Gunther. I—"

"What time did it land?"

"Hell, I can't remember that. Wait a sec, it was around 5 A.M. Or a few minutes after."

"Sure?"

"I'm sure. Five A.M. or thereabouts. But why—"

238

Damon already had picked up his phone and jiggled the hook three times to raise the switchboard.

"Mrs. Strotsky, get me our Minneapolis bureau on the double. I want to speak to the bureau manager. Make it person to person. What the hell's his name—here's the bureau directory. Memphis . . . Milwaukee . . . Minneapolis. Bureau manager Calvin Brenden. Brenden, Mrs. Strotsky. Calvin Brenden."

"I don't get it, Gunther," Pitcher fussed. "Should I have told you about that arrival before? You said to check departures. Long-range stuff. What's so significant about this one arrival?"

"I don't know," Damon muttered. "One of my hunches, maybe. It could be that we checked the wrong thing at Andrews. Departures instead of arrivals."

"Well, that made sense," Pitcher protested. "We were trying to find out where the President really might have gone. Like to Moscow. Who cares what came in that night?"

"Jeremy Haines, maybe," Damon said, almost in a whisper. "Jeremy Haines might have cared what came in that night. On the number two plane in the presidential air fleet."

"But, Gunther, the Air Force uses that plane for all sorts of purposes. It must land at Andrews fifty times a year. Why are you crawling all over this one landing? It could have been a normal operation. It probably was."

"A normal operation in normal times. But these aren't normal times. All I want to know is whether it actually flew from Minneapolis to Washington. If I find out that it didn't, even my suspicions are gonna have suspicions."

His phone rang.

"Damon. Put him on. This Brenden? This is Gunther Damon in Washington, Cal. Would you do some fast checking for us? It's damned important. Fine. Do you have any good contacts at your airport? The main one, I mean. Yeh, Minneapolis-St. Paul International, I guess that's what you call it. That's the only big one, isn't it? I thought so. No military air bases around your area, are there? Okay, this is what I need. Find out if the old Air Force One was in Minneapolis the day before the President's plane went down. The plane Kennedy and Johnson used to fly. See if

239

it was there, say, two or three days before. The plane's number is—what the hell is it, Pitch?"

"N-26000. It has the words 'United States of America' on the fuselage above the cabin windows."

"N as in Navy. Two-six-zero-zero-zero. Got it? No, I can't tell you what it's all about yet. I'm not sure myself. But get after it right away and call me collect. Don't put the answer on any message or trunk wire. Phone me person to person. If I'm out, give the information to Rod Pitcher. You know, our aviation editor. Oh, he says the plane has 'United States of America' on the fuselage, if that'll help. Cal, I appreciate this. I'll pay off in martinis first time you get to Washington. Phone me as soon as you can. So long."

Damon sat back, stroking his chin with thumb and forefinger. Pitcher shook his head. "You still don't get it, do you, Pitch?"

"No, I don't. I don't see what difference it makes whether that 707 landed at Andrews after Air Force One left. Or what it was doing in Minneapolis. What's important about Minneapolis?"

"Nothing's important about Minneapolis. Provided our former Air Force One actually was in Minneapolis. But I've got an idea it wasn't. That whatever you saw on those arrival logs was a phony. That's why I asked Brenden to check it out."

"Where do you think it came from?"

Damon did not answer immediately. He swiveled his chair around and concentrated his gaze on the Willard Hotel across the street. He suddenly swung back.

"Pitch, right now Chris Harmon's digging up something that might give us a lead to Haines's whereabouts. If he produces it, and Cal Brenden tells me that 707 hasn't been in Minneapolis, I'm going to put two and two together and I'm coming up with a very fascinating answer. Maybe a couple of answers."

"Where do you think it came from, Gunther?"

"Right now, I can only guess. And I'll keep my guesses to myself. My hunch is that we've been looking in the wrong direction. At where the President really flew to that night. Now we'd better start looking in the other direction. Come on, Mr. Harmon. Phone me, dammit, phone me. Pitch, go back to work. I want to think this out some more."

He waited impatiently for Harmon to call. He was only

momentarily disconcerted by the arrival of Lynx Grimes, who looked in his direction with a shy half-smile and received in turn a half-wave that was as much embarrassment as salutation. He would have liked to talk to her but Stan DeVarian came in and Damon disappeared immediately into the bureau chief's office to brief him. DeVarian was typically non-committal and outwardly unenthusiastic, which meant nothing. Damon knew that Stan, like Chris Harmon, usually consigned overly excitable reporters to the same niche in which adults place giggling adolescents.

"Well, let's just wait and see, Gunther," was DeVarian's reaction to his news superintendent's latest brain wave. It could have meant an indifferent "Boy, you're out of your mind" or an enthralled "Boy, you've got something."

It was mild torture for Damon to wait and he had to resist calling the State Department press room to inquire as to Harmon's progress or lack of it. Chris finally phoned him at eleven-twenty, apologetic for the delay.

"Sorry, Gunther, but I had to go through the motions of a legitimate interview. I got what you wanted in a hurry, but if I had left then the chauffeur might have smelled a rat and called Security. Hell, I had to ask him about everything but the color of his grandchildren's eyes and then—"

"Skip the details," Damon said impatiently. "What did you find out?"

"The mileage accumulated on the Secretary's car since you-know-who disappeared, as of nine-ten this morning, was precisely seven hundred and forty."

"Seven-four-oh," Damon repeated. "Thanks, Chris. It seems a bit high but maybe not."

"Maybe not for what?"

"Let you know. I've got a date with a road map."

Custer finally produced an oil company map from the rectangular burrow known as the copy boys' desk. It covered the District of Columbia, Delaware, Virginia and West Virginia and was definitely frayed around the edges. Damon noted its age with faint suspicion as he spread it across DeVarian's desk.

"I don't know how old the damned thing is," Gunther said, "but it'll serve our purpose."

"Old is no word for it," DeVarian grumbled. "Lee must have used this to find his way to Gettysburg. Okay, Gunther, where do we start?"

"We start with that mileage total. Seven hundred and forty. Divide it by two. That's, let's see, that's three hundred and seventy miles of one-way driving for four days. For each day, the one-way driving is ... just a minute, Stan, I'm trying to remember my division ... four goes into thirty-seven ... it comes out ninety-two-point-five. Let's say ninety-two miles is the one-way figure for whatever destination Sharkey was aiming at every night."

"It's too high," DeVarian said. "Doesn't he use the official limo to go to work and back? You have to take that mileage into consideration."

"Yeh, I suppose we should. The Secretary lives in Chevy Chase. Give or take a few miles, depending on the route he'd take, that's fifteen to twenty miles. We'll be on the safe side and say it's twenty. That cuts the nightly mystery trip down to about seventy miles. Okay, now we take the map. This one's scaled fifteen miles to the inch. Let's have the ruler, Stan. First we look for any military bases about seventy miles from Washington. What have we got to the south?"

"Wait a minute. Why military bases?"

"If Haines is holed up somewhere and Sharkey's seeing him every night, a military base provides the maximum security. Dammit, if you've got one inch equaling fifteen miles, how many inches is seventy miles?"

"You must have gotten great grades in arithmetic, Gunther. Seventy miles would be almost five inches."

"Five inches south of Washington. Not quite to Fredericksburg. Nothing remotely resembling a military installation in that direction."

"Try west—there's my phone, excuse me. DeVarian. Yes, he's right here. It's Minneapolis, Gunther."

He handed the phone to the news superintendent. "This is Mr. Damon. Yes, we'll accept charges. . . . Cal? This is Gunther Damon. Did you find out anything?"

DeVarian watched Damon's face assume the exultation of a sweepstakes winner being notified of his luck. "Thanks one hell of a lot, Cal. No, I can't tell you what it's all about. Not yet, anyway. Maybe you'll be reading something before long. You're right, it's the Haines story. That's all I can say. Thanks again, boy."

He put down the phone and faced DeVarian, but he suddenly was sober rather than beatific. "Brenden says nobody at the Minneapolis airport, including tower, has seen even a reasonable facsimile of an Air Force 707 for at least three weeks. Stan, the plane that came into Andrews seven hours after Air Force One took off had something to do with the plot, the plan, the mystery . . . whatever you want to call it. I know it, Stan. I'm sure of it."

"You mean you think Haines was aboard the old Air Force One? Coming from someplace instead of going someplace?"

"No. Somebody else was on that 707. Somebody Haines wanted to see, and in secret. So badly that he staged the whole crazy business. The phony flight to Palm Springs. The disappearance. It still doesn't add up, though. Why's the disappearing act still going on? Why has he stayed hidden this long?"

"You're assuming again, Gunther. There could be twenty reasons for that older plane landing at Andrews."

"Then why did the log Pitcher saw list the originating point as Minneapolis? Why would the Air Force phony up a flight plan? To cover up where the plane really was coming from, that's the only explanation. Let's get back to that road map again."

The two men bent over the map. "Try west," DeVarian suggested.

"No soap, Stan. And look, if we go east for seventy miles we run right into Chesapeake Bay."

"That's a possibility," DeVarian said. "If he's holding some kind of a secret conference, what better place than a boat anchored in the middle of a bay?"

"Could be. If I remember my history books, that's how President Cleveland got away with a secret cancer operation. Aboard some private yacht, because there was a financial crisis at the time and Cleveland wanted to avoid panic. But how the hell do we look for some boat? I don't suppose IPS would spring for a helicopter . . . ?"

"Maybe, but I doubt if it would do much good. We wouldn't know what kind of boat or ship we were looking for, Gunther. He would be on a big cabin cruiser or some Navy vessel. Let's go back to land. What's to the north? Five inches would take us just above Westminster, Maryland, Stan. I don't know of any military installation around there. Let me try northwest."

He moved the ruler slightly to the left. The five-inch mark

243

rested almost squarely on the word "Thurmont." Just to the left of this small Maryland town was a green area marked "Catoctin Mt. Pk." Damon and DeVarian looked at the three words and then at each other.

"Catoctin Mountain Park," DeVarian breathed. "Ring a bell?"

"A loud bell," Damon said. "Catoctin's where Camp David's located."

"It can't be Camp David. Jonesy checked that out."

"Let's add up the exact mileage. The figures between the little red stars on the map. Forty-four from the center of Washington to Frederick. Another sixteen to Thurmont. That's, uh, sixty. Add, say, five more from Thurmont to Camp David. Sixty-five."

"Sixty-five," DeVarian repeated. "That's awfully close to our hypothetical nightly drive of seventy miles. The extra five could be accounted for easily. Sharkey's certainly been using the car around town the past few days. Going from State to the White House would be just one example. And we don't know the exact distance from State to his house. Gunther, I wonder . . ."

Damon slammed the ruler down on the bureau chief's desk as if he had been been handling a hot poker. "I think I'm through assuming, Stan. I think I know."

"But Jonesy said Camp David's deserted. No sign of life. He wouldn't lie to us."

Damon shook his head, a gesture that was more one of sadness than disagreement. "He could have lied."

"You're crazy!" DeVarian's face was flushed. "There isn't a finer reporter on any staff, wire service or newspaper. What you're saying is that Malcolm Jones has known the President's whereabouts for God knows how long and kept it to himself. He couldn't pull that on us."

"Okay, let's give him the benefit of the doubt. We'll send him back to Camp David. When we tell him what we've learned, he'll be an old fire horse, smelling smoke."

DeVarian sat down heavily in his chair, as if the weight of Damon's words had been like an unbearable, invisible burden added to the bureau chief's body. "I almost hope he tells us we're full of prune juice."

"He won't. Haines is at Camp David. I'll bet the rest of my salary for the year on it. Want me to call Jones?"

"Yes," DeVarian sighed. "Can we spare him for a few hours? Who's at the White House?"

"Al Spartan's there. He can hold down the fort until we finish with Jonesy."

"Okay, Gunther. Go ahead."

"Right. Incidentally, there's a very bright, sterling-silver lining in all this."

"So cheer me up."

"If we find Haines alive and presumably well, Freddie baby will have to get the hell out of the White House."

At this precise moment the object of Gunther Damon's affections put down the blue volume titled "Assessment by the National Security Council of Communist China's Intentions." He had finally gotten around to reading it.

Frederick James Madigan was breathing heavily. He stared at the black letters stamped on the document. TOP SECRET—CLASSIFIED. The gears and cogs in his mind whirred and spun, then came to a halt of irrevocable decision. The Vice President pressed Mrs. Hahn's button with the force of a man pushing down a plunger hooked to buried dynamite.

"Mrs. Hahn, would you please call members of the Cabinet and advise them I want to see them at the White House . . . make it a 3 P.M. meeting. Also I want General Geiger present, and the CIA director. And tell Newt Spellman I want to see him immediately. And get me Frank Corris. I'm cancelling all my appointments for the rest of the day."

"Mal Jones, Evelyn," Damon said to Mrs. Strotsky over DeVarian's phone.

"He's not at the White House," she said. "He phoned in sick this morning. Or his wife did."

"Jonesy's sick," Damon informed DeVarian, cupping the phone with one hand. "I'd better call him at home."

"Yeh," DeVarian grumbled. "Goddammit, that leaves Al all alone there. Better . . ."

He waited until Damon finished asking the switchboard to raise Jones at his house. "Gunther, we shouldn't leave the White House staffed with one man. Anybody else we can send over?"

"We've staffed it before with one man. I don't have

anyone else, Stan. Pitcher, maybe, but the White House scares the piss out of him for some reason."

"How about Harmon?"

"That leaves State unmanned. I don't want to take that chance. Let's sit on it for a while. If Al needs help, we can do some shuffling. Maybe I can get Jonesy. . . ."

DeVarian's phone rang. "Take it, Gunther. It's probably Jones."

Damon picked it up. "Jonesy, this is Gunther. How—oh, Anne. Is Jonesy able to come to the phone? Anne, what's wrong? . . ."

He listened, his brows narrowing into an expression of alarm and surprise. "Have you called the doctor? . . . What did he say? . . . Well, look, Anne, don't worry. He's upset about something. Tell him to take it easy and keep in touch with me, will you? Fine. He'll be okay. I'll talk to you later. . . . No, I just wanted him to run up to Camp David again. But I'll make other arrangements."

He hung up and turned to DeVarian, a shadow of puzzled concern crossing his face.

"What was that all about?" DeVarian asked.

"Jonesy apparently cracked up. Anne says he got up in the middle of the night and wouldn't go back to bed. About 6 A.M., when she tried to talk to him, he started crying. She called their doctor and he said Jonesy's smack in the middle of a nervous breakdown. Fatigue, probably. Fatigue, hell. It's conscience. Stan, I'm going to Camp David myself. Right now."

"Gunther, you may not be able to get close to the place."

"If I can't that's about all the evidence I'll need. It's probably crawling with Marine sentries. I figure they'll stop me at the turnoff from Route 15. That's five miles away from the main camp site. I'll find a phone and call you. You can go ahead with the story."

"What story, Gunther? You don't have—"

"The hell I don't. Item one, Sharkey's been going there every night. Item two, we know a certain plane landed at Andrews seven hours after Air Force One left. We don't know who was on it but I'll bet that someone is with the President right now. Item three, if I run into a platoon of Marines I'll know they aren't there on maneuvers. So I'm gonna rub those three little items together and start the biggest fire this town has ever seen."

"You may be starting an explosion, not a fire," DeVarian warned. "Christ, Gunther, I told you before—we can't afford to play around with TNT."

"We've got a legitimate story, Stan, and we've got to use it. For all we know, this could involve World War III. They'll hand us the Pulitzer prize without bothering to look at another entry. We'll have AP and UPI clients knocking down our door for contracts."

"Gunther," DeVarian said with deliberate slowness, "assuming Haines is alive and at Camp David, there's a pretty damned good chance he doesn't want this story broken by IPS or anyone else."

Damon eyed him, cold fury replacing enthusiasm. "And you think that because a President of the United States doesn't want a particular story, a newspaperman should be a polite, obedient and patriotic little citizen and whine, 'Yes, sir, Mr. President'?"

"This particular story might justify self-censorship if it comes down to that."

"Nothing justifies censorship unless the country's at war. That's the trouble with this damned town. Too many reporters becoming friendly with their news sources, and the first thing you know they're protecting their friends instead of milking the sources."

"You wouldn't admit there could be extenuating circumstances short of being at war?"

"I might. Inevitably, government officials would use the phrase 'National security is at stake.' National security would justify censorship, self or imposed. But who defines national security? It's too often a convenient rug for covering up dirt or somebody's mistakes. Any official who doesn't want the public to know the truth can fall back on 'national security.' Sure, I'd kill a story if I thought it would harm the country. But I'd want to be the judge of that harm, not the guy who doesn't want the story used. Too many people pay lip service to freedom of the press. They're all for freedom until they think they're embarrassed or hurt."

"Gunther, just remember John Scali and the Cuban missile crisis. We could be in the same boat."

"Yeh, the ABC White House reporter. He was the go-between when the Russians wanted to plant a peace proposal with Kennedy. You think there's a parallel?"

"Isn't there? He knew all about the secret negotiations

247

and yet he kept quiet until everyone else had the story."

"Sure he did. A damned fine reporter and a patriot. But he didn't have any choice. The minute the Russians contacted him, he had to cease being a reporter. He became a part of negotiations between two governments about to go to war. I'm not taking anything away from Scali. I know a few newspapermen in this town who would have written what he had in his hip pocket and said the hell with the Kennedy Administration. But remember, Kennedy didn't ask him to stay quiet. He didn't have to. Scali made his own decision. He did what he knew he had to do because the circumstances left an honorable guy no alternative."

"And you still don't think there could be a parallel?"

"No, I don't. The Cuban crisis was black and white. We were either going to go to war with Russia or we weren't. And the latter hinged on the success of secret negotiations. There wasn't any real mystery about them. What do we have now? A screwball plot with no rhyme or reason. Maybe someday Haines can justify what he's done to the country, but it'll take a potful of arguments to convince me. Kennedy kept us from World War III. Haines, if he's alive, has contributed nothing so far but the most screwed-up, bizarre mess in history. Sixteen deaths—hell, eighteen deaths with the flood—millions of frightened Americans, a collection of bewildered allies wondering what the hell is going on, a tinhorn politician trying to imitate a President, and the press is supposed to sit back and wait for Daddy Haines to come out of the woodwork? Dammit, Stan, he deserves to have this story broken before he gets around to sugar-coating it himself."

"But you said this story might involve World War III. So did Scali's."

"I don't know what this story involves. Not yet. Dream up the wildest possibility in human imagination and it could come close to the truth. But I can't see how even the most farfetched explanation can be an alibi for what Haines has done. Whatever his reason, whatever his motive, whatever his excuse, the whole affair has been so obviously botched that it deserves to be laid right out in the open so every person in this country can see it. Every person in the world, for that matter. That's why we're digging on our own. And if we shoveled up scandal, betrayal, treason, insanity or even murder—so be it. That's our job. The press

248

didn't send Air Force One out to destruction on some phony vacation trip. The press didn't hide the President of the United States. The press didn't put the country and the rest of his mixed-up world into a state of shock. Jeremy Haines did. So let him explain what we find out. Let him supply the alibis."

DeVarian sat there quietly, shaken by the fire of Damon's impassioned arguments. "Just how would you handle the story?" he asked finally. "How would you write it? You don't have a helluva lot to go on . . ."

Damon's voice cracked like an angry whip. "The world's been asking for four days, 'Where is the President of the United States?' We've got enough to supply the answer. Not the whole answer, but part of it. Depending on what I find out at Camp David, our story will simply say IPS has strong evidence that President Haines is not only alive but at Camp David, for reasons as yet undisclosed. Then we'll bring in the stuff about the other plane landing at Andrews. We know that for an absolute fact. Our story will speculate that whoever arrived on that plane may be conferring with the President. Obviously an extremely vital conference, probably with international implications. Dammit, Stan, I love my country as much as you do. We aren't giving out the whole story. We don't even know the whole story. Only the President can give us that. And so help me God, it's time he did. What IPS will be carrying will force him into the open. And that will be for the good of the country."

DeVarian started to reply, stopped when his brain refused to dredge up any kind of a final counter-flurry, and surrendered. "Okay, Gunther. You win. Go to Camp David."

"Who was that on the phone?" Malcolm Jones asked his wife, dully.

"It was Gunther. He just wanted to know how you were."

"That's all he wanted?"

She hesitated. "Well, he said something about your going back to Camp David. What's that all about, Mal?"

He did not reply. He went into the den and dialed a number.

"Mr. Reardon's office," he said into the mouthpiece.

CHAPTER FOURTEEN

Secretary of State Sharkey was the last to arrive at the Cabinet meeting, two and a half minutes past the appointed time.

He circled the big table and walked in back of the chair where the Vice President was sitting, tapping a pencil impatiently like a teacher annoyed at a pupil's tardiness. James Sharkey was about to apologize, when both his brain and his eyes did a double-take.

Each member had his own chair in the Cabinet Room, his individual title inscribed on a tiny brass plate attached to the rear of the high-backed furniture. When he left office, he could take the chair with him as a memento of Cabinet service. Now, as Sharkey moved behind the Vice President, he saw the plate on Madigan's chair. He saw the words on the plate and he felt a little sick.

"The President."

He knew that Haines's personal chair had been moved discreetly to a far corner of the room at the first Cabinet session following the crash, to avoid the obvious symbolism of an empty seat with its overtones of death. That bastard Madigan, the Secretary of State realized, this time had switched chairs and to Sharkey it was an ominous omen. He wondered if anyone else had noticed it.

His eyes rested on the telltale plate only for a fraction of a second, but it was sufficient to let the Vice President know Sharkey had spotted this deliberate discarding of all humility. A remnant of his old insecurity brought a flush to Madigan's face, but he managed to drape this momentary jab of guilt by glowering at the Secretary of State. Sharkey's response was a glare of his own, their angry stares clashing like a pair of dueling swords. The Cabinet, not knowing what had prompted the silent but openly bitter exchange but sensing the antagonism as if it had an unpleasant odor, stirred uneasily. Madigan put down the pencil and folded his hands in front of him, leaning forward slightly and milking both drama and rapt attention out of the gesture. One elbow was resting on a large pamphlet with a blue cover and only Sharkey recognized it instantly. That classified NSC report on Red China. Madigan lifted his elbow, picked up the publication and waved it in front of him in the manner of a parade spectator brandishing a tiny flag.

"Gentlemen, I have just finished reading a most interesting document. The one I hold before you. So interesting I'm amazed my attention was not called to it the moment I took office. So interesting and, I might add, so frightening that I felt it imperative to have the Cabinet go into immediate session for the purpose of discussing its import."

"Your attention *was* called to it, a few minutes after you became Acting President," Sharkey said quietly but in a voice that dripped with hostility.

Madigan slammed his fist on the table, so hard that two Cabinet members jumped. "You dropped a whole pile of papers on my desk and told me it was some stuff I should read when I got the time," he retorted. "Well, Mr. Secretary, I found the time and I'm shocked. Literally and absolutely shocked that you did not advise me of what this document contained. The potential death warrant of our beloved country, gentlemen. A death warrant."

He paused for dramatic effect, and was pleased to observe that all but Sharkey were impressed.

"You're referring," Sharkey said, "to the Security Council's report on Red China's willingness to make war. May I remind you, Mr. Vice President, both the Secretary of Defense and myself were present at the Council meeting when that report was submitted to the President more than three weeks ago. You were filling a speaking engagement, if I recall."

"Correct." Madigan smirked. "And the President, unfortunately, did not see fit to brief me on these contents when I returned. Gentlemen, for the benefit of those in this room who also were not privileged to study the report in question, I'd like to give you the gist of its message. Only it is not a message, my friends. I repeat, it's a damned death warrant."

He paused again, the oratorical delay of a politician

251

instinctively waiting for murmurs of intense interest or maybe applause.

"Before you proceed," Sharkey interrupted, "I would like to inform the Cabinet that the President fully intended to discuss this matter with all of you upon his return from California. He delayed such discussion on my own advice. There were certain diplomatic considerations involved, considerations I felt were important enough to preclude the revelations of this report even to a closed Cabinet meeting. I say this in the way of an explanation, not an apology. And I might add that the Secretary of Defense concurred in this decision."

"If *I* had been consulted," the Vice President said importantly, "I would not have concurred. The contents are vital enough to be disclosed to the entire nation, let alone the Cabinet."

"But you weren't consulted," Sharkey prompted, "and I must remind you, sir, that President Haines agreed with our recommendation to keep the Security Council's report totally classified for the time being."

"That, sir," Madigan said ponderously but with such intense feeling that several members were impressed, "comes close to impugning the patriotism and judgment of the President's own official family. The men in this very room."

"That was not our intention, I assure you," Tobin said. "In addition to the diplomatic, uh, considerations which Jim mentioned, the President felt that the slightest leak to the public would result in panic."

"In other words," Madigan sneered, "Haines didn't trust anybody in this room to keep his mouth shut with the exception of yourself and the Secretary of State. Aside from—"

"Just a minute," Tobin protested, but the Vice President charged ahead.

"—aside from regarding that as an insult to myself, I also regard the President's attitude as an insult to the rest of the Cabinet. I, for one, trust the common sense and discretion of my Cabinet colleagues. And I intend to transmit to this body the gist of the Security Council report."

His eyes swept the room in a direct challenge. Sharkey opened his mouth, a gingerly, tentative step over the precipice of protest, then shut it.

"I'll proceed," Madigan said triumphantly. "Gentlemen, what the Security Council has issued is a flat prediction that Red China is determined to launch an attack on the United States. I won't go into the sordid details, but the Council refers to this attack as not only possible but eventually inevitable. I repeat those words, gentlemen. Not only possible but eventually inevitable. Now the reason I've called this meeting is to ask you what we should do about it."

Labor Secretary Gilbert cleared his throat nervously. "May I ask the Secretaries of State and Defense if what the Vice President has just said actually represents the essence of the Council's report?"

"Goddamnit!" Madigan snarled. "Do you doubt my word? Don't you think I can read?"

"You read very well," Sharkey said dryly. "Yes, Nelson, that's what the Council believes."

"Let me read a few of the more pertinent paragraphs from the report," Madigan chimed in. He had underlined several passages and proceeded to read these to the Cabinet. They drew mumbles of surprise and an occasional horrified expletive. Madigan laid down the document again. "Any comments, gentlemen?"

"Mr. Secretary," Gilbert addressed Sharkey. "What did the Security Council recommend to President Haines?"

"There was no specific recommendation," Sharkey answered. "It was more of a consensus . . . a meeting of the minds that we should stay on the alert and be ready for instant retaliation."

"A course," said Madigan, "which in my opinion amounted to drawing up the blueprints for a second Pearl Harbor." He was pleased to hear two or three murmurs of agreement.

"I couldn't tell from what you've read whether the Council considered an attack imminent," Harvey Brubaker said. "The time element seemed to be vague. Is 'imminent' too strong a word?"

"Imminent is apropos in the sense that China would strike the moment she thought she could win what amounted to an overnight war," Sharkey replied. "When that moment might occur is a matter for debate. Nobody's sure."

"Exactly!" explained the Vice President. "Nobody's sure. Now, what I want to know again is what the hell are we going to do about it? Sit on our fannies and wait for their missiles?"

"Just what do *you* propose doing about it?" Sharkey had dropped all pretense of formal protocol or even simple courtesy. He could not bring himself to say "sir" to the Vice President.

"Well, I'll tell you one thing," Madigan answered, "I don't propose to preside over a country decimated by atomic war. And I don't believe the oath of office I took said anything about letting this country sit helplessly by while our enemies choose their own sweet time for starting a war."

"I'll ask you again," the Secretary of State repeated. "What can we do other than what's already been done? SAC is on a war alert. We're ready for instant retaliation. So we'll sit on our fannies, as you so succinctly phrased it, and be ready for the worst. Do you have any alternative?"

"Yes," said Madigan.

The Cabinet froze, minds and tongues collectively chilled into realization and anticipation of what the Vice President was about to say.

"And your solution?" Sharkey asked the question, already knowing the answer.

"Preventive war, I believe, is the correct expression," said the Acting President of the United States.

Gunther Damon headed out Constitution Avenue, over the Theodore Roosevelt Bridge and up the George Washington Memorial Parkway. It was the same route he drove to and from work, so familiar that he could travel it almost automatically as if his car were on rails and his only task was to keep the accelerator pedal depressed. At this time of the afternoon there was relatively little traffic and he could indulge in some mental gymnastics. First he thought of Malcolm Jones and wondered if the White House reporter had, indeed, lied to him about finding Camp David deserted that night. Maybe. But there also was a chance Jones merely had not sniffed hard enough. He could have turned back too soon, without really trying to pierce the heavy security guard that Damon felt must be there if the President were in residence.

The news superintendent had been to Camp David once

before, for a stag picnic at the invitation of President Johnson shortly before LBJ left the White House. He remembered his first impression had been that of a series of drab wooden structures with all the individuality and warmth of barracks. The buildings were painted a dullish gray-green and only the restful beauty of their wooded surroundings saved them from the cold impersonality of a typical military installation.

Which figured, because Camp David was a military installation, administered by the Navy, staffed by Navy personnel and guarded by the Marine Corps. It had begun life as a Civilian Conservation Corps camp in the days of the New Deal, but was turned into a presidential retreat in 1942 when Franklin Roosevelt wanted a secluded place in which he could relax. The spot fitted FDR's needs eminently and was a happy choice as far as the Secret Service was concerned. Hyde Park was considered too far away for a wartime President and FDR supplied the substitute asylum with its first name, "Shangri-La," after James Hilton's Tibetan city of seclusion and peace. Truman used it under the sobriquet but Eisenhower renamed it Camp David after his grandson and his successors retained that name.

Damon recalled his first sight of the President's quarters, when he had walked over a small stone bridge that straddled a placid pond and led to the large building that bore the sign "Aspen Lodge." Johnson had shown the newsmen through the lodge and Damon remembered being impressed by the quiet simplicity of the place, particularly the huge picture window that overlooked the lush green Catoctin Valley.

It wouldn't be peaceful now, Damon reasoned. Not if his hunch was right. He could imagine and relish in advance the inevitable experience of being stopped by the sentries, businesslike carbines slung over their shoulders, probably commanded by no less than a captain or even a major. And that was all he needed for confirmation. A definite indication of activity, of stricter-than-normal security precautions. He had no idea how close he could get. But he didn't need to get too close.

His mind raced over the many intriguing possibilities that lay ahead, all pointing to the news beat of his career.

He was so occupied by this daydreaming that he nearly missed the turnoff from the parkway to the Washington Beltway. He crossed the Cabin John Bridge into Maryland and bore to the left on U.S. 70S as it branched off the beltway in a slight dogleg. He passed a road sign reading, "Frederick, 32 miles," and he murmured aloud, "Camp David and Mr. Haines, here I come."

A couple of jittery coughs provided the only break in the tense silence that followed the Vice President's pronouncement. It was the Secretary of State who finally bestirred himself.

"You can't mean that," Sharkey said. "You couldn't sell Congress or the American people on a preventive war, let alone this Cabinet. It's unthinkable. Diabolical."

"If the American people and Congress knew what was in this document," Madigan proclaimed, "they'd demand a preventive war. You asked me for an alternative. You supply *me* with one, Mr. Sharkey. You hand *me* an alternative to letting our enemies strike the first blow, destroy at least part of our capacity to retaliate, and kill hundreds of thousands of our fellow citizens in a surprise attack. Maybe millions. You tell *me* what choice this nation would make between certain victory and possible defeat."

"There is no such animal as a certain victor in an atomic war," Sharkey said. "There is no guarantee that our armed forces could destroy China in one surprise attack. There still would be great danger of her own retaliation."

"The bastards wouldn't be throwing as much at us if we did clobber them first," Madigan said curtly. "Dammit, all I'm saying is that if war's inevitable we must have the initiative or we could lose it. Isn't that so, General Geiger? You military boys agree with me, don't you?"

The chairman of the Joint Chiefs rose to his feet, impressive in stature and bearing, his gray hair reflecting like steel in the brightly lit room. "Mr. Vice President, while there are unquestionably high-ranking military personnel who'd buy the concept of a preventive war, I assure you, sir, I am unequivocally opposed to that concept as criminally insane. And I speak for the rest of the Joint Chiefs."

"It would be criminally insane to let the Communists hit first," Madigan insisted. "General, let me ask you . . .

haven't you already prepared a list of priority targets within the Chinese mainland?"

"Yes, sir."

"You have enough bombers and missiles to strike every one of these targets?"

"We might not have enough to wipe out both China and Russia."

"That's not what I asked you. We're talking about China, not Russia."

"You can't eliminate the Soviet Union," Sharkey broke in. "The first nation that pushes the button for a limited atomic war stands an excellent chance of starting World War III. If we jumped China, Russia might—"

"The Security Council says Russia probably would sit out a U.S.-Chinese war," Madigan interrupted. "It's down here right in this report."

"The Security Council's analysis," Sharkey said calmly, "is that Russia probably would remain aloof if China attacked us. It says nothing concerning the Soviet Union's intentions if the United States pulled the trigger against China."

"I would assume," the Vice President said positively, "that Russia's intentions would be identical in either case. So I'll ask General Geiger again, do we have enough hardware to hit every essential target in Red China in a single attack?"

"It would depend on many unknown factors," Geiger replied. "The efficiency of the Chinese anti-missile system, for example, of which we know comparatively little. If that system is halfway effective, we couldn't complete the job in one attack. And that would mean exposure to retaliation, not only from the Chinese but from the Russians if they—"

"Suppose you just give me a simple answer to a simple question, General," Madigan said peevishly. "Do we have sufficient force to destroy all these priority targets in China? Never mind the ifs and buts. I want a yes or no."

"I can't give you a yes or no reply," Geiger said.

"Please answer my question theoretically, then. In theory, provided all these supercautious, hypothetical factors you cited did not come to pass, could we knock out China with one attack?"

Geiger looked at Tobin, seeking support that was not

forthcoming. The Defense Secretary was frowning unhappily, as if the weight of Madigan's persistence was pressing down on his skull.

"Theoretically," the general said with sullen reluctance, "yes."

The Vice President leaned back in his chair with an air of total vindication. "I submit, gentlemen, that hitting our sworn enemies before they decide to hit us involves far less of a calculated risk than the prospect of having our own retaliatory power crippled before we ourselves can start punching. To put this in its simplest terms, we stand a far better chance of winning a war that's certain to come if we seize the initiative, than if we wait for the enemy to surprise us. A better chance, with fewer casualties and less damage to our own people and facilities."

"It makes sense," Harvey Brubaker said. He tossed a glance of admiration in Madigan's direction and was rewarded by the Vice President's tight, somewhat forced smile.

"It makes no sense," the Secretary of State said. "Mr. Vice President, assuming you'd call in the congressional leaders for consultation before deciding on such action, do you honestly believe you'd get their support?"

"I would certainly weigh their views with great care," Madigan said. "But in the end the decision must be that of the President, or should I say the Acting President. I would take full responsibility for that decision, Mr. Secretary. And I am confident that it would have the blessings of the American people."

"I am confident," Sharkey said, "that you would go down with Adolf Hitler as the most irresponsible official in the history of any government. For God's sake, man, you'd still have to get congressional approval for a declaration of war. And you can't—"

"As Commander-in-Chief of the armed forces," Madigan intoned, "I have the authority to take whatever action I deem necessary for the security and safety of the United States. I don't have to ask Congress for a declaration of war."

"You'd actually attack China without warning?" Sharkey asked incredulously.

"This document, which Haines apparently didn't think important enough for me to see, provides ample justification for our pulling the surprise instead of them. It's either them or us, Mr. Sharkey. And if I have anything to say about it, it's going to be them."

The car sped along U.S. 70S, past the Rockville and Gaithersburg exits. Damon found himself inspecting the landscape, a pleasant canvas of rolling farmland, gleaming white dairy farms and an occasional tacky housing development interrupting the placid rustic scene like warts on an otherwise smooth complexion. He came abeam of Frederick and picked up U.S. 15. A sign, "Thurmont, 16 miles," flashed by and Damon could not prevent his heart from pounding a little bit harder.

The road narrowed to three lanes and then dwindled to two ribbons of asphalt. Ten miles beyond Frederick the Catoctin Mountains hove into view. It was not a high range but the mountains looked bigger than they actually were because of their proximity to the highway. They were topographical fleabites compared to, say, the Blue Ridge chain south of Washington. But at this distance they provided a scenic illusion of surprising grandeur.

The car purred through the tiny town of Catoctin Furnace and Damon slowed down. He was almost to Thurmont when he spotted the road sign marked "State Rte 77." He turned right and a few hundred yards past the turnoff he crossed a one-lane wooden bridge, his tires producing a resounding "clump-clump-clump." This was where he expected to see the first Marine sentries, but there were none.

He continued up a bumpy, winding road furnished with sufficient curves and dips to satisfy an inveterate lover of rollercoasters. Now he was at a ranger station and he remembered the sign that said, "Visitor's Center." No activity here either, and the first splinter of doubt sliced into his thoughts. He turned sharply to the right and headed up a smaller, narrower but still paved road for two miles, breaking to a stop at another sign reading "Camp 4." Still no sentries. Hell, could Jonesy have been telling the truth?

Camp 4 was Camp David's general area, he knew. He turned right again, and through the foliage lining the gravel road, just beyond a posted warning, "Federal Property—No Trespassing," he could see three rows of barbed-wire fencing. Jones had once told him the wire was electrified, not enough to kill but capable of stunning an intruder.

259

There was the sentry box he remembered from that other visit, directly ahead of him. A small booth built out of logs, and alongside a long pole suspended above the road like a barrier at a railroad crossing. A lone Marine stepped out of the booth as Damon stopped the car and rolled down his window.

A corporal, Damon thought. One lousy young corporal when he was expecting practically a whole company of leathernecks to be on duty. His heart sank.

"Hi?" said the Marine with cautious friendliness. "What can I do for you?"

Damon suddenly realized he really had nothing to say, no explanation to offer. "I'm Damon of IPS. I . . . we got a tip something was cooking up here. Uh, something to do with President Haines. I came out to check."

"President Haines?" The corporal laughed. "Hell, buddy, there ain't nobody here but me and couple of Pfc's."

Damon looked around. A Marine Corps jeep was the only vehicle in sight. "The place seems a bit quiet," he said lamely. "You been on duty long?"

"Just came on. Sir, this area's restricted. You got any credentials?"

Damon produced his White House pass. The corporal merely glanced at it with the same enthusiasm he would have displayed if the newspaperman had shown him a membership card in a Chevy Chase garden club.

"Well, you'll still have to do an about-face," the Marine advised. "Sorry, mister, but those are my orders."

"Yeh," said Damon. "Say, when you came on duty, was there any activity around here? Helicopters, limousines, that kind of stuff?"

"Nope. Quiet as a church graveyard. Sorry, sir, but . . ."

"I know. So long."

He turned the car around and drove slowly down the road. Jonesy hadn't lied. Camp David was deserted. Some big exclusive. All that brilliant detective work, figuring out the mileage gimmick. Well, nothing left to do but find a phone and give DeVarian the bad news.

He turned into State Route 77, but stopped and peered back at the gravel road leading to Camp David. Sunlight splashed through the trees, the beams hazy like shafts of light filtered through stained glass. Graveyard-quiet as the Marine said, Gunther Damon mused. A very apt description. Because he now was convinced that Jeremy Haines was dead.

Madigan's blunt words were a catharsis for what had been the Cabinet's silence. Minds suddenly were linked to tongues and a torrent of babel filled the room until the Vice President hammered on the table.

"I'd like to poll the members for their sentiments," he announced.

"You can't settle a life-or-death matter like this after five minutes of discussion," Sharkey said furiously. "Let's talk about it some more, for the love of God."

"I'm willing to settle for a poll of preliminary sentiment," Madigan amended in a conciliatory tone. "It would be helpful if I knew where the Cabinet stands at this point."

"The Cabinet couldn't possibly know where it stands right now," the Secretary of State bristled. "You sprang this on us without any warning. I demand that we discuss this further."

"I'll let you discuss it further—after each man has his say on how he feels as of now," the Vice President said. "As for springing this report on you without warning, that's not my fault. If Haines didn't see fit to let his own Cabinet in on what amounts to a national crisis, let him accept the responsibility. If he's alive to accept responsibility, that is. Which I doubt."

"I'd like to propose a little poll of my own," Sharkey said. "I suggest that we wait for further developments on the President's whereabouts before we even move a toenail in the direction the Vice President wants to shove us."

"And just how long will that be?" Madigan inquired sarcastically. "Another week? A month? Six months? A year? While we're waiting for Mr. Haines or his corpse to show up, we could be getting the hell bombed out of us. No, sir, Mr. Secretary of State, not while I'm Acting President."

Sharkey's boiling emotions propelled him out of his seat. "I insist, sir, that you canvass the view of this body on delaying your blind blunderings into World War III until we find out what has happened to the President."

He sat down. Madigan gave him a jovial pat on the shoulder that conveyed more condescension than agreement. "Okay, Jim. We'll go ahead and see where all of us

261

stand. Starting with you as the ranking Cabinet member. I take it you want to wait."

"You're damned right I do. And so—"

"Your opinion is duly noted, Mr. Secretary. The Secretary of the Treasury?"

Secretary of the Treasury William Lagos, a handsome man of Greek extraction, said quietly, "A vote not to wait is a vote for war. I say wait."

"The Secretary of Defense?"

Tobin lowered his head and his voice accompanied the movement. "I'd like to abstain for the time being." Geiger and Sharkey stared at him in near shock.

"All right, Mike, we'll get back to you later," Madigan said. "The Attorney General?"

Howard Kelly looked imploringly at Sharkey. "I'm stunned by this report. And there's no telling when we'll learn the truth about the President. I've got to go along with the Acting President."

Madigan was keeping score on a scratch pad. Sharkey noticed with distaste that the pad bore the presidential seal. "The Postmaster General?" Madigan inquired.

This was Carl Herron, the first career postal official in history to be promoted to Cabinet rank. He had one thing in common with James Sharkey. He worshiped Jeremy Haines. "Wait," he said and Madigan frowned. The Secretary of State could not resist a kind of grim inner chuckle. He had the distinct notion that the Vice President, in addition to keeping score, was figuring out which Cabinet members should be asked to resign.

"The Secretary of Interior?"

The normally florid face of Wilford Binks, a man of irrepressible humor and good nature, was pallid. "I don't want war, but the Vice President has made some telling arguments. I don't see any other course."

"The Secretary of Agriculture?"

"Well," said the lanky, dour-featured Theodore Larson, "I'd like to ask first if there's anything new on the President?"

"Not a word," Madigan said.

Larson's long face seemed to stretch further, a flesh-covered rubber band. "Then I've got to go along with Kelly and Binks. To wait might be suicide."

"Thank you, Ted. The Secretary of Commerce?"

Edward Silverman, a mild-mannered Jewish industrialist who, like Herron, had been one of Haines's few non-political appointments, bit off the end of a cigar and lit it before answering. "Frankly," he said, "I think this whole discussion is asinine. But you asked for my opinion, Mr. Vice President, and I'll give it to you. If President Haines didn't want us to see that report for the time being, he must have had a damned good reason. And if he wasn't ready to start a war despite what it said, I'm not either."

Madigan's ball-point scribbled angrily on the pad. "The Secretary of Health, Education, Welfare?"

Donald Nickels, an affable former congressman, coughed as the smoke from Silverman's cigar wafted its pungent odor into his nostrils. "If we don't wait, it'll be suicide."

"The Secretary of Housing and Urban Development?"

Barney Littell looked first at Sharkey and then at Madigan, trying to dredge from their expressions some encouragement for what he was about to decide. His own kewpie face wrinkled into a reflection of tortured inner conflict, but he finally blurted, "Wait."

"The Secretary of Labor?"

Nelson Gilbert smiled slightly at the anxious look on Sharkey's face. "If I didn't trust Jeremy Haines's judgment, which I do, I'd trust that of our Secretary of State. Wait."

Scratch-scratch went Madigan's pen.

"The Secretary of Transportation?"

Harvey Brubaker's face was sober, but it was the phony solemnity of a man grieving at a funeral for someone he actually disliked. "I trust in the judgment, patriotism and wisdom of the Acting President of the United States," he orated. Sharkey winced.

Madigan examined his note pad. "There are six votes to wait and five to support me. I, of course, uh, would have to side with myself. That makes it six to six, gentlemen. Mike, you seem to have the deciding voice."

Tobin's face was a study in tortured indecision. "So help me God," he whispered, "I don't know what to do. I just don't know."

"Dammit, Mike," Sharkey exploded. "You saw that report before anyone else. You know the President didn't regard it as justification for a preventive war. What the hell are you stalling for?"

263

"Because," Tobin said simply, "I haven't been able to sleep very well since I read it."

"Wait or don't wait, Mr. Secretary?" Madigan persisted.

"I can't give you an answer now," Tobin muttered.

"Suppose," Sharkey suggested, "we take a brief recess. Some minds might change."

"Some minds might change if you hold your own caucus outside this room," the Vice President snarled. "If you're going to try to sway Tobin's vote, I want equal time, Sharkey."

"I'm not going to talk to the Secretary of Defense," Sharkey said. "General Geiger, I'd like to have a word with you outside and in private, if you please."

"Yes, sir." The chairman of the Joint Chiefs rose and walked out of the room, followed by the diminutive Secretary of State. Madigan stared after them, worrying whether the pair could be plotting against him and what form their strategy would take. He decided quickly to concentrate on the wavering, shaken Tobin.

"Now, Mike, I understand how . . ."

In the corridor outside the Cabinet Room, Sharkey and Geiger conversed in low tones.

"This is it," the Secretary said. "Tobin could go either way. And that sonofabitch Madigan is crazy enough to pull the trigger five minutes after the Cabinet meeting breaks up."

"Even if the Secretary of Defense votes to wait?"

"I'm afraid so. Fred Madigan is using that NSC report as a symbol of his resentment against the President. Consciously or subconsciously, he's jumped on it as a means of proving he's as strong and capable of difficult decisions as Haines. Good God, I didn't dream he could get the support within the Cabinet he did."

"I'm not really surprised," Geiger said thoughtfully. "The whole country's on the verge of panic. I can see it in the Pentagon every day. Mass jitters. The natural impulse to throw a blind punch and then rationalize that it's pure self-defense."

"You go back in. I've got some thinking to do. Madigan's probably pushed Tobin over the brink by now."

Geiger returned to the Cabinet Room and resumed his seat at the opposite end of the table from the Vice President who, as expected, was engaged in vigorous conversation with the Secretary of Defense. Behind them, a sardonic smile on his swarthy face, was Nelson Gilbert. The rest of the Cabinet had broken up into small groups, the members talking quietly but gesturing vigorously.

Peace or war, Geiger thought, being decided by this handful of well-meaning, frightened men. Or perhaps by one of them, the Acting President, with his hatred of Jeremy Haines poisoning his reason and common sense. Madigan was sitting down now, and Geiger tried to judge from his expression whether he had succeeded with Tobin. The general would not be surprised if he had. There would be no incongruity in the Defense Secretary's deciding for a preventive war that his own military chieftains opposed. The fact that Tobin was a civilian made no difference. Sometimes soldiers, knowing war, dreaded it more than those viewing it with only abstract experience. And Tobin's very job made him vulnerable. Next to the presidency itself, it was the most man-killing post in government—a daily exposure to fear of what a potential enemy can do and the facts to support that fear. One of the greatest Americans and the nation's first Secretary of Defense, James Forrestal, had cracked under the strain of the cold war, a victim of suicide. No, Geiger decided sadly, Michael Tobin was ready to be pushed and probably already had been pushed. Where was the Secretary of State?

The Vice President called the meeting back to order, commenting, "I see we have to wait for Mr. Sharkey again."

The Secretary of State re-entered the room even as Madigan spoke. Sharkey took his seat next to the Vice President and caught Geiger's eye, shaking his head almost imperceptibly.

"I thank the Secretary of State for suggesting the recess," Madigan said smugly. "His apparent decision not to discuss things with the Secretary of Defense was indicative of confidence that Mike Tobin could make up his own mind. Your confidence, Mr. Sharkey, was justified. The Secretary of Defense has, indeed, made up his own mind. He does not believe we should wait for a President who, God rest his soul, may never appear."

"Is that right, Mike?" Sharkey asked.

"I hope I'm doing the right thing," Tobin muttered.

"I hope we all are," Interior Secretary Binks added.

"Mr. Vice President," Sharkey said, "I implore you, sir, to consult with key members of Congress before making a final decision."

"I'll consider your suggestion," Madigan said.

"Consider it?" the Secretary of State demanded. "It's incumbent upon you to talk to them. They can't be left in the dark on a matter so important."

"The President left me in the dark," Madigan said craftily, "along with the majority of the Cabinet. Besides, congressmen are known to be poor secret-keepers. One of them could very well blab this to the press, and if that happens we might as well head for the bomb shelters. The surprise element would be destroyed. By the way, when you all leave, say nothing to the newspapermen, except that this was a routine meeting."

Sharkey looked around the table at his fellow Cabinet members. "Is this all the discussion we're going to have?" he cried desperately. "Have you searched your souls and your consciences for what you've just done?" All his disdain for the Vice President boiled unchecked to the surface, an erupting volcano spewing its emotional lava. "Are you going to let this power-mad little man take the United States into World War III?"

Not a man spoke. Madigan's face was white with rage but he kept his own voice down, instinctively sensing that to lose his temper might break the fragile strands of Cabinet support.

"Mr. Sharkey, I must remind you that I'm acting on the basis of what the National Security Council, the CIA concurring, has warned will be an inevitable attack by China on the United States. I would be derelict to my oath of office if I did not heed that warning. Your own opposition has solidified my determination to protect my country. For your information, Mr. Secretary, I've made my decision. I'm walking out of this room and I'm going to my office. There's a little red button on my desk. It's connected to the war room at the Pentagon. I'm going to push it."

"Wait a minute," Tobin said hurriedly. "Don't rush into it. You should meet with the Joint Chiefs first. You should—"

"The Joint Chiefs, I gather, would display the same indecisive, mealymouthed, pablum temperament that General Geiger seems to possess. I see no further use in pursuing this discussion, gentlemen. The Cabinet has given me a vote of confidence and—"

"It was a goddamned narrow vote," Gilbert said hoarsely.

The Vice President ignored him. He stood up. So did Sharkey. The tiny Secretary of State seemed about to restrain Madigan physically. The rest of the Cabinet remained sitting, unable to move, as if the tenseness had sapped the strength in their limbs.

"Get out of my way, Sharkey," Madigan said coldly.

"Only the President of the United States can do what you are about to do," the Secretary of State said in a whisper.

"I'm the President of the United States," said Frederick James Madigan. "Haines is dead."

"No," spoke a voice at the other end of the room. "He is not dead."

Necks swiveled toward the entrance to the Cabinet Room. Nelson Gilbert gasped.

"My God," said Michael Tobin.

In the open door of the Cabinet Room, his big frame almost filling the aperture, stood Jeremy Haines, thirty-seventh President of the United States.

CHAPTER FIFTEEN

The Secretary of State said nothing, but his mouth widened into a canyon of a grin.

General Geiger wore the look of a little boy who had just seen the U. S. Cavalry arrive in the last five minutes of a Saturday afternoon TV movie.

The Secretary of Labor merely breathed, "Thank God."

The Secretary of Transportation uttered a puzzled "I don't understand."

The Secretary of Defense shook his head in disbelief, then his face brightened like a patch of earth freed by sunlight from the shadow of a passing cloud.

The Secretary of the Treasury blurted, "Where the hell have you been?"

The Postmaster General resembled a man who had just seen visual proof of the Resurrection.

The long face of the Secretary of Agriculture contracted into a smile, wrinkles of delight appearing on the leathery skin like cracks in shattered safety glass.

The Secretary of Commerce, for the first time in twelve years, said a prayer in flawless Hebrew.

The Secretary of Interior froze into utter speechlessness, his jaw hanging like the unhinged prow of a landing craft.

The Secretary of HEW bore an idiotic expression, walking a facial tightrope between laughter and tears.

The Attorney General closed his eyes and then opened them, as if he expected the President should have disappeared with the blink.

The Secretary of Housing and Urban Development merely stared unbelievingly.

And across the face of Frederick J. Madigan flowed a rapidly shifting montage of shock, bewilderment, disappointment and a strange infinitesimal blending of fear and relief. His mouth opened, closed, then gaped open again to expel with unwilling force the two words that magically seemed to shrink his entire body, disintegrate his belligerence and strip him of his authority.

"Mr. President!" he exclaimed. As Jeremy Haines approached his end of the table, Madigan extended a trembling hand and the gesture was an alchemy of abject surrender and vaporized confidence. Haines grasped it briefly but warmly. "Fred," he said in a practical, matter-of-fact tone, "I think we'll need another chair."

Sharkey could have laughed as the Vice President scurried to the corner of the room where his own chair had been placed. Madigan, his face red, carried it back and put it down in its old spot, Haines sitting between the Secretary of State and the Vice President. Gilbert could not resist poking another needle into Madigan's already deflated hide. "You arrived in what might be termed the nick of time," he told Haines. "The Vice President was about to start World War III, with the acquiescence of the majority of his Cabinet. He was on the verge of contacting the war room."

Haines turned his head toward the Vice President. "What's Nelson talking about, Fred?"

All the long-festering, piquish bile in Madigan's system gushed forth, overflowing the dam of inferiority that had always blocked his loquacity in the President's presence.

"That damned Security Council report," he stuttered angrily. "I didn't even know about it until last night. I didn't want another Pearl Harbor. I didn't know where you were. If you had told me . . ."

Partial awareness dawned in the President's eyes. "Just what were you about to do, Fred?"

Sharkey surprisingly felt abrupt sympathy, even tolerance, toward the Vice President. "He was acting as he thought best, Mr. President. I think, sir, it would be helpful to all of us if you explained a few things. The things I knew, and General Geiger knew, but which we were unable to communicate to the Cabinet."

"Such as where you've been and what's it all about," Madigan flared again, acrimony still tainting his voice.

Haines nodded. He folded his big hands in front of him and began to talk.

"Gentlemen, I'll get to the most important item first. For the past four days I have been at Camp David with the

Premier of the Soviet Union, Mr. Alexei Bujesky. We have just concluded a unilateral mutual aid pact aimed at deterring China from what otherwise would be inevitable aggression. Its provisions are simple. If China attacks Russia, we'll go to the aid of the Soviet Union. If China attacks us, the Soviets will launch all-out war on Peking. We have every reason to believe this coalition will not only convince China of her certain destruction if she starts a war, but it also presages a new era of co-operation between the United States and the Soviet Union.

"You realize now, I'm sure, that the Palm Springs flight was a masquerade. A tragic masquerade, as it turned out, but a necessary one. It was absolutely essential that my actual whereabouts be kept secret during the negotiations with Premier Bujesky. The vacation trip was a ruse to make not only Washington but the country and the world believe I was nowhere near the White House.

"The genesis of this secret meeting was the Security Council report which, apparently, has been the subject of your meeting today. Or rather, it was partially the genesis. Approximately four weeks ago the ambassador of the Soviet Union asked Mr. Sharkey to arrange a private meeting with me. He emphasized the need for privacy, total secrecy, in fact. This was done. The ambassador came to the White House shortly before midnight. He reported to me that the Soviet Union, through its military intelligence, had received plausible reports of an impending surprise attack by Red China. The attack was to be against either the U.S. or Russia. If the Soviets had been convinced China would strike them, they would have launched a deterrent war of their own. But they were not sure of China's intended target.

"The Soviet ambassador conveyed to me the fears of Mr. Bujesky that if China succeeded in winning a quick war through an all-out surprise atomic attack on either the U.S. or Russia, the unattacked nation eventually would be the certain victim of similar aggression.

"With that in mind, the ambassador asked me if I would fly secretly to Moscow to discuss a pact aimed at deterring China. I pointed out to the ambassador that I doubted whether my flying to Moscow could be kept secret. There were too many security problems to overcome, and the very proximity of the Soviet Union to Red China would hardly be conducive to keeping my presence in Moscow a matter of strictest confidence.

"I suggested an alternate plan. Namely, that the Premier fly to Washington, also under the most rigid security arrangements. I told the Soviet ambassador it would be much easier to have a private meeting here, far removed from the possible presence of Red Chinese agents, than anywhere in Russia. And I guaranteed the privacy of the meeting. Even as we discussed the pros and cons of such an arrangement, I thought of the fake trip possibility. I had been toying with the idea of getting away for a rest anyway, and the Palm Springs ruse seemed to pop into my mind almost instantly. By ostensibly getting me out of Washington and affording a logical explanation for my absence from the White House, it also provided the necessary secrecy for my talks with Bujesky.

"The details for Mr. Bujesky's visit were worked out mostly via the hot line between Washington and Moscow. It was decided in the interest of secrecy that he should use an American aircraft. We figured there would be less chance of a leak, and certainly fewer problems in passing a plane through our various Air Defense Commands, if Air Force equipment were employed. Naturally, we did not want to bring such a personage as the Soviet Premier and certain of his most trusted advisers to the United States in just any plane. So we dispatched the former Air Force One to Moscow on what appeared to be a legitimate flight. It carried several State Department officials who happened to be Russian experts.

"In the event Chinese agents might start wondering about the presence of this aircraft in Russia, the Soviet Union ran in *Pravda* and *Izvestia* rather prominent stories to the effect that an American military transport was bringing to Moscow a number of DOS officials for preliminary conferences on a trade agreement. It was merely one more means we utilized to allay suspicion. And it further gave our radar warning units in Alaska and elsewhere no cause to make some embarrassing inquiries.

"The 707 arrived at Andrews approximately seven hours after Air Force One departed. Secretary of State Sharkey and I met the plane and we drove immediately to Camp David for our talks, confident that we had covered all our tracks. But then came the tragedy in Arizona. I was confronted with a terrible dilemma. I had given Bujesky my solemn word that our meeting would be in total secrecy. And, frankly, this was my desire as well as his. We each realized that if the Chinese were aware of what was going on they probably would pull the trigger immediately.

"At this point, I must apologize to the men in this room whom I had to deceive, along with the rest of my fellow Americans, and people throughout the world. Particularly I should apologize to the Vice President. Believe me, I wanted to take the Cabinet into my confidence. But please remember that the unexpected crash of Air Force One threatened the secrecy so essential to the success of the negotiations. I never dreamed that something would happen to the plane. When it did, I was tortured beyond belief by the knowledge that I was sentencing the nation to an indefinite period of confusion and perhaps panic. But I was powerless. To reveal my whereabouts would have revealed the plot, or enough of it for some well-educated guesses as to the motive behind the deception. We couldn't risk the slightest leak."

"Mr. President," Madigan said with a rare flurry of courage, "it's understandable why you didn't tell even the Cabinet before the California trip. But it was unfair to me, unfair to all of us, not to tell us after the plane went down. It's . . . it's as if you didn't trust us. I could have kept the secret. So would everyone in the Cabinet. Sharkey did."

Haines nodded understandingly. "I regret that very much, Fred. Perhaps it would help if I explained who was in on the plan from the start. The Secretary of State was the only top official. Phil Sabath, Judi Nance and Admiral Philips knew about the fake trip. They knew I wasn't on board Air Force One. The Secret Service had to be aware of everything because of the necessary security arrangements."

"Mr. President," Tobin asked, unable to suppress his curiosity another second, "who was the impostor? Who went in your place? He fooled everybody."

Jeremy Haines's face saddened. "An obscure first cousin from my home state. A bachelor with no family, fortunately. He was of approximately the same age and general physique as myself. He resembled me superficially. A slight difference in height was corrected by the use of elevated shoes. I hadn't seen him for some time but when this plan was first evolved I thought of him and decided he would make a perfect presidential impostor. That was the principal reason for a night departure. Darkness was essential to bring off the deception. I brought him to Washington secretly about three weeks ago when I briefed him on the mission. We even taught him to walk like me. He returned home and then was flown back to Washington the morning of the Palm Springs departure.

"Paul Reardon of the FBI was one of the few who knew the truth although not from the start. There seemed to be no need to bring the FBI into the picture if the deception had gone through as planned. But the crash changed this. Then it became necessary to brief Reardon on the real situation, or God knows what he would have been reporting to you, Fred. Remember, what proved to be embarrassing to the Vice President was the crash and my unexplained disappearance. This was not part of the original plan. I didn't expect tragedy to occur and the secrecy of my talks with Bujesky was the prime consideration. Each additional person told of the Palm Springs deception was a potential weak link in the security chain. As I said, originally the Secretary of State was the only top official cognizant of the vacation trip's real nature. It was the accident which forced us to let others in on it—if only to keep the investigation away from the truth for the time being. I was sorely tempted to notify Madigan and the rest of the Cabinet.

"I can only reiterate that the plane crash presented us with an unparalleled dilemma. In retrospect, I imagine I should have briefed the Vice President concerning the fake vacation. But again, I never dreamed anything would happen to Air Force One. Once that plane went down, it was too late to backtrack. The conference was in progress. If I made a mistake by keeping the facts from Fred, it was not telling him from the very beginning. I felt I couldn't tell you later, Fred, because the danger of a leak multiplied with each passing day and with each new person who was being admitted to the inner fold. For example, the chairman of the Joint Chiefs has been sitting in on the negotiations since the second day. We did not plan to have him until we found that Bujesky was accompanied by General Geiger's counterpart, along with some surprisingly complete data on the Soviet armed forces. We never did tell General Coston, although we seriously considered it. We almost told Secretary Tobin, too, but I figured Geiger could give us whatever military advice we needed.

"I'll grant you that we weren't exactly playing fair with such men as the Vice President and General Coston, not to mention the Cabinet, but in a sense this contributed to the success of the mission. I felt that if top-level officials like Fred Madigan and Mike Tobin showed obvious puzzlement and bewilderment through the whole situation, it added to the effectiveness of the deception."

"It sure did," Madigan said ruefully. "That's one of the things which kept throwing me. I couldn't figure out why, if you were still alive, you didn't make your whereabouts known after the crash. I found it impossible to imagine that you staged a deliberate disappearance without telling me. Or that, if you had staged it without my knowledge, you wouldn't have told me when the plane went down and that mystery body muddied all the water."

"My cousin's body presented some touchy problems," Haines said meditatively. "I was afraid there would be a slip-up and that somehow he might be identified as me. All I could think of was Fred Madigan actually being sworn in as President of the United States without knowing I still was alive. I couldn't let that take place, of course, yet the situation was precarious because if I had blocked a swearing-in ceremony the conference secrecy would have been demolished. That's when I insisted on confiding the truth to FBI Director Reardon. I told him to go ahead and let his agents investigate the identity of the unknown passenger but to make sure all their reports went straight to his desk. Sooner or later they would have found out about my cousin but the information could be bottlenecked on Reardon's desk until we were ready to explain everything."

"Mr. President," asked Tobin, "are you satisfied as to Russia's good faith?"

"Completely, Mike. They're as anxious to block China and prevent war as we are. Bear in mind that we had proof of their veracity right from the very beginning. While the preliminary plans were being made for my meeting with Bujesky, the Security Council report already had come to my attention. It verified what the Russian ambassador told me. It also confirmed what the Russians felt, namely that Peking would not expect either Russia or the U.S. to come to each other's aid.

"The one vital factor which our two espionage systems were unable to determine was the identity of the target nation. Mr. Bujesky was convinced, and I agreed, that we could not wait for China to make the choice. A mutual assistance pact at the earliest possible moment, negotiated in utmost secrecy, was the most effective deterrent. More effective and a hell of a lot safer than waging a preventive war."

Haines looked at Madigan as he spoke the last sentence. The Vice President said plaintively and defensively, "I didn't know all this. I didn't know about the negotiations. I wouldn't have considered a military solution if you had given me the facts to begin with."

"I know you wouldn't, Fred," the President said. "I'm truly sorry. The fact that you even considered the terrible course you were about to take is an indictment of my judgment. I ignored every lesson of history, every previous example of the necessity for establishing a close, trusting relationship between President and Vice President. And, Fred . . . all of you who were unwitting pawns . . . I can only express to you my fervent belief that the tragedy, the mistakes I made, the sorrow I caused, will someday be forgiven because of what has been achieved."

"When are you going to tell the press, Mr. President?" Sharkey inquired.

"Premier Bujesky will contact me via the hot line when he returns to Moscow. He's on his way now, using the same plane on which he came here. I've promised him the announcement of the pact will be held until we can release it simultaneously. As soon as I get the word on a joint time, I'll call a press conference. The word should come in a couple of hours."

"Didn't any of the newspaper boys see you come into the White House?" Madigan wondered.

"I took a helicopter from Camp David but we landed on the pad atop the FAA Building," Haines explained. "A car brought me over here and I slipped in via a back entrance. I might as well confess to you now, I was going to stay at Camp David until sometime tonight. But a certain newspaperman, whose name I can't divulge, tipped me off that his wire service had somehow traced me to Camp David and had a man en route to check. I decided I'd better get out in a hurry. All he had to see was the security arrangements around the place and he could have broken some kind of a story."

"You mean a newspaperman knew about the whole affair?" Brubaker asked.

"Not the whole plan. He merely suspected I was at Camp David. Fortunately, he confided his suspicions to the FBI instead of his own organization. Jim, what's the matter?"

The Secretary of State looked slightly ill. "I just happened to think how close we cut it. I tried to call you a few minutes ago. I wanted you to talk to the Vice President, or at least give me permission to tell the Cabinet you were alive. When I couldn't reach you, I knew you were on the way but I was afraid you wouldn't get here in time to stop what we were doing. If you hadn't . . ."

"I think you would have informed the Cabinet as a last resort." Haines smiled.

"I guess so," Sharkey said. "Frankly, I was ready to throw a punch at our Vice President. Fred, I want to apologize to you too. I called you a few names which I deeply regret. I hope you understand the spot I was on. Sworn to absolute secrecy."

"And I hope you understand the spot *I* was on," Madigan answered. "Mr. President . . . all of you . . . I would very much appreciate it if the events that transpired in this room today could be locked in our hearts. I . . . I don't want to go down in history as the man who nearly started World War III."

"It goes without saying," Haines said instantly. "I'm afraid that men like our Vice President, here, will have to be the unsung heroes. Or the unwitting heroes—such as the crew of Air Force One. Poor Phil Sabath. Luther Philips. Judi Nance. Or my poor cousin. I never did tell you his name, did I? For you and for the history books, it was Roger Boyer. A mild-mannered, inoffensive man who lived in obscurity because he wanted it that way, and who didn't even enjoy the dignity of dying under his own name because it had to be that way. He ran a little insurance agency in a small town out west. I always liked him. He never tried to trade on our relationship, as he well could have. He never approached me for a job, either. When I asked him to pose as me, he was as excited as a kid. He kept chortling that for at least a week or two he was going to be President of the United States and that nobody could ever take that away from him. I remember warning him that, if everything went off as planned, nobody would ever know that he was a make-believe President. You see, we intended to reveal the deception, eventually, but not the identity of the man who took my place. Roger just laughed. He said, 'I don't care if I don't go down in history. It's enough to know in my own heart that I was the President for a little while, and helped my country.' Well, my friends, I sent him to his death. And do you know, I'm going to arrange for his burial in Arlington National Cemetery. He never wore a uniform. He was medically unfit for military service. He told me he always regretted that. So I'm going to pay my last respects to Roger Boyer as if he had been a soldier who died in the service of his country. And I'll do the same for Phil Sabath and Judi Nance, if their families agree. All those who flew Air Force One that night will be laid to rest in Arlington."

The President's voice turned hoarse for the first time, the Cabinet could see his utter weariness, the lines of fatigue etched into his face as sharply as rivulets from a heavy rain can cut into soft soil.

"You couldn't have predicted the crash, Mr. President," Ed Silverman said softly. "Only God is omniscient."

"No," replied Jeremy Haines, "but that doesn't ease the guilt. I remember that when a handful of us began to plan the fake trip it almost seemed like a game to me. As if I were an author working out the plot of a complicated detective story, figuring out all the potential loopholes and weaknesses. Only I'm afraid the plot got away from me. I have much to answer for, to Judi Nance's parents, to Colonel Henderson's wife, to everyone who suffered a loss because of what seemed like such a clever little scheme."

The President rose. One by one, the members of the Cabinet stepped up to shake his hand. Madigan was the last and Haines said, "Stay behind a minute, Fred. I want to talk to you alone." The room emptied except for the man who was President of the United States and the man who thought he wanted to be.

"Tell me something, Fred," said Jeremy Haines. "Would you have pushed that button if I hadn't showed up?"

"I don't know," Madigan admitted. "Maybe, but I think I would have lost my nerve. I think the loneliness of the presidency would have overwhelmed me, caught up with me, at the last second. I was mad at Sharkey. I was mad at you. I actually thought I was President and I had this . . . this almost desperate desire to do something on my own."

"I understand," Haines said. "I let you down, Fred. Please forgive me for not trusting you. It will never happen again. You know, I've learned a lesson. From that crash. Our plan was perfect, but it didn't take into consideration the unexpected. It made no allowances for the unpredictable. And, in effect, that's been my attitude toward you. I haven't let you be a good Vice President because I somehow refused to admit the possibility that you might really have to replace me. I've paid only lip service to training you, preparing you for the presidency. Any mistakes you've made these past few days were my mistakes."

"Mr. President," said Frederick J. Madigan, "only a great man would have said what you just did. Now, would you tell me something?"

Haines nodded.

"Was it all worth while? The sixteen deaths on the plane? The chance you took, leaving the nation in the hands of . . . of me?"

Jeremy Haines looked through the Vice President rather than at him, his gray eyes burning as if with fever.

"Let me put it this way. If I *were* blessed with omniscience and could have foreseen the crash as an inevitable part of the tapestry we had to weave, I still would have dispatched Air Force One even to its certain fate. Not just as the President, but as the Commander-in-Chief of our armed forces would send a bomber on a vital suicide mission. The stakes were that high."

Jeremy Haines put his hand on the Vice President's shoulder. "And then, my friend, having done this, I would have sat in that oval room and cursed the day I ran for the presidency."

Deep in the bowels of the Pentagon a three-man communications team manned the two duplicate teletypes that formed the U.S. end of the Washington–Moscow hot line. A sergeant sat in front of each machine and behind them stood a major in civilian clothes, a Russian-language specialist.

"I wish to hell it would come," said one sergeant. "The suspense is murder."

"It'll come," the interpreter assured him. "A watched pot never boils or something like that."

"Is there a Russian equivalent for that little slogan?" asked the sergeant. "I'd rather—Jesus, here it is!" The machine in front of him clattered into life. So did the adjoining backup printer. The three men watched the Russian words march onto the teletypes. The interpreter looked at his watch and swore.

"Just the hourly test run," he said. "I think it's a quote from Gogol."

"I'll acknowledge and transmit our test," the sergeant sighed. He punched a few words in English, the message going onto a piece of half-inch tape in the form of a perforated code. He inserted the tape into a transmitter and shoved the sending key into the UP position. The tape moved through the transmitter at its fixed rate of sixty-six words a minute.

The three men relaxed. The teletypes chattered again.

"Return acknowledgment," murmured the second sergeant.

"Yes," said the interpreter. "I imagine—Wait a minute, that's not a test confirmation. It's . . . it says . . . 'FOR THE PRESIDENT.' . . . This is it!"

The printer keyboard danced, goaded by impulses sent over 4823 miles of cable at a speed of 186,000 miles per second. Three minutes later the transmission ceased and the machines fell silent as if exhausted from their quick surge of exertion. The major tore the paper from the printer. "It'll take me about five minutes to translate it," he said. "One of you guys get the White House on the horn. Tell 'em the Kremlin's coming in loud and clear!"

It was much later that night when Gunther Damon and Stan DeVarian found time to relax in the latter's office. They were relishing that first sip of hot, steaming coffee and for once Damon forgot to libel the coffee vending machine.

"Quite a day," he ventured.

"You said it," DeVarian agreed. "I thought our output looked pretty good, Gunther. You satisfied?"

"Reasonably. We logged a minute ahead of AP on the original break—Haines being alive. Even with UPI, according to New York. I don't know how we did on his press conference but I couldn't fault Al and Chris. They did a helluva job. We could have used Jonesy, dammit."

"I know. I think tomorrow I'll run out to his house and talk to him. A few reassuring words will get him straightened out. Funny how he went all to pieces. You suppose he got a guilty conscience—that he really did lie to us?"

"Yep. The night he went to Camp David, it must have been crawling with security. I'll bet he was stopped five miles away—the guards probably were told to use some excuse like secret construction work in the area, but Jonesy would have seen through that. Well, it doesn't make much difference now. God, how close we came to busting it wide open. I'll always wonder what we would have done if he had told us something was cooking at Camp David."

"I imagine," DeVarian said, "that's what hit Jonesy. He probably started wondering too. He must have had one hell of a tug of war tearing him apart—loyalty to us or loyalty to Haines when he suspected the President had to be alive. And maybe it's just as well we didn't bust it wide open, Gunther. A lot of history was made tonight. History that'll let all of us sleep better. I know I will. And none of us would have slept soundly if IPS had been the instrument for a premature disclosure that might have screwed up the works."

"We wouldn't have screwed up anything," Damon insisted. "We didn't have enough of the answers to cause any damage."

"Speaking of answers," DeVarian remarked, sidestepping a renewed debate, "there are a few I still don't have. For example, how the hell did Haines pull that impostor business on so many persons who had to have close contact with him that night? The security guards on the plane. The stewards. The helicopter pilots who flew him to Andrews."

"I guess you didn't read all the Q and A we carried tonight," Damon said. "A lot of the President's explanations got left out of the main lead. It seems Haines counted on both night and the power of suggestion. Those who knew someone was posing as him didn't matter. Those who didn't never expected the deception and it was easy for a man resembling the President to pass himself off. In other words, everyone expected to see Haines and so they assumed they did. That cousin was instructed to keep his hat over his eyes and his head down, from the time he boarded the helicopter until he was in the stateroom on Air Force One. Presumably he disappeared into the private quarters the moment he climbed aboard, just as he was ordered. Sabath, the secretary and the doctor were the only ones allowed to enter the compartment during the flight."

"And the intended arrival in Palm Springs also was to be at night," DeVarian observed. "But Haines was taking a hell of a lot of chances. How about that security guard on the helicopter? He must have been right on top of the impostor."

"Haines was asked that at the press conference," Damon explained. "The security guard wasn't a real Army man. They put a sergeant's uniform on a Secret Service agent. The Secret Service, naturally, was in on the whole affair."

"What about the deception at the other end? In Palm Springs? How was Haines going to work that if the plane had arrived like it was supposed to?"

"The President explained all that too. He personally told Tom Kendricks the vacation trip was a blind, although he didn't reveal why. Kendricks agreed to co-operate without asking a single question. The cousin was to stay at his residence until further notice. His servants were replaced by Secret Servicemen, which was logical because that's a normal security precaution for a presidential visit to a private residence. When the plane went down and all the mystery developed, Kendricks was one puzzled citizen. Haines was afraid he'd talk, so he had Jim Sharkey phone Kendricks and warn him not to say a damned word to anyone. Kendricks must have guessed that the President was alive, but he kept his mouth shut."

A copy boy came in and tossed a copy of the first edition of the Washington *Post* on DeVarian's desk. The two men glanced at the black headlines.

HAINES ALIVE
ANNOUNCES SECRET U.S.-RUSSIAN PEACE PACT
AND REVEALS FULL STORY BEHIND
DISAPPEARANCE MYSTERY

"I'd better clean up some work," Damon said. "Tell Jonesy hello for me."

"Sure."

The news superintendent walked into the newsroom, in time to see Lynx Grimes disappearing out the bureau door on the arm of a young man with peg trousers and hair that badly needed cutting. She was chattering away with happy, aimless animation and Damon heard her say, "Let's go over to the Willard and get a drink. I heard my boss say they've got a nice quiet cocktail lounge."

Damon turned morosely toward the desk of overnight editor Frank Jackson.

"Hi."

"Hi, Gunther."

"Frank, I think we could use a separate piece on the mystery. All the explanations and cover-up gimmicks that Haines concocted, combined in one package. Maybe we could tell it in the style of the last chapter of a murder mystery. Sort of tying up the loose ends."

"Good idea. I was figuring on a main lead, with sidebars on the pact itself and the diplomatic angles. New York's putting together a piece on world reaction. Any other suggestions?"

Damon did not answer. All of a sudden, he felt old and tired.

"Anything else, Gunther?" Jackson repeated.

Gunther Damon shook the cobwebs of self-pity out of his soul, as a wet dog rids himself of water. "Yeh. Be sure and get the President's addressing the nation on radio and TV tomorrow night up high in the main lead. No later than the third or fourth paragraph, I'd say. And, Frank, we should have a sidebar on . . ."

EPILOGUE...

Frederick James Madigan noted that the bevy of Secret Service agents in front of his apartment had dwindled to the usual two.

He inserted his key into the door. "Hester?" he called as he entered.

His wife came out from their bedroom and gave him a perfunctory kiss on the cheek. He tossed the final edition of the *Post* on the coffee table and slumped into his favorite lounging chair. Hester Madigan picked up the paper and read the eight-column headlines.

She pursed her full lips in displeasure. "The son of a bitch, keeping you in the dark the way he did."

"He apologized to me, Hester," Madigan said wistfully. "He told me personally it was the hardest decision of his life, but that he felt the country was in good hands while the negotiations were going on. Did you see me on television, at the press conference?"

"Yes, I saw you. You looked very good. He should have told you, Fred. It wasn't fair."

"Well, yes, but I want you to see his statement praising me. It's on page one. Right there, below the fold."

She gave the story a cursory examination and looked down at her husband. "He's still a bastard. How can you sit there and condone what he did to you? Conjuring up a wild plot like that and not telling the Vice President about it! It's humiliating, Fred. How does he think you must feel?"

Madigan expelled a sigh. "I know how I feel. I'm kind of glad it's all over. Let me tell you something, Hester. He's got a lousy job."

Malcolm Jones was feeling better. He had called DeVarian to get a certain confession out of his system and the bureau chief's sympathetic response seemed to dissolve the bowling ball that had been sitting in his guts. Then came a call from the White House. After he finished talking, he came into the living room with the first smile he had worn in five days.

"Who was it?" his wife asked.

"It was the President," he said, trying to keep the pride out of his voice. "He wanted to thank me for something. I'll tell you about it later when I feel more like talking. Meanwhile, Anne, he did say something I'd better tell you right now. He also called to offer me the job of assistant press secretary. He promoted Newt Spellman to the top spot."

"Oh, Mal—" she started to enthuse but stopped when Jones shook his head.

"I had to say no, Anne. It would smack too much of a pay-off."

She did not comprehend his words, but she still could fall back on the inevitable plea of an IPS wife. "You'd get some regular hours for a change."

Jones laughed. "Regular hours, working for the President of the United States? Don't kid yourself. You'd see less of me than you do now. I wouldn't take Spellman's job, for that matter. I guess I'll always be a newspaperman, Anne. You're stuck with a reporter for the rest of your life because that's what I want to be stuck with for the rest of my life."

She fired one more shot before surrendering. "It would only last as long as he was in office. Then who knows? Look at the wonderful positions press secretaries have gotten when they left the White House. Big salaries and . . ."

Malcolm Jones put his hand on her graying hair. "Covering number one man is all I ever want, Anne. Try to understand that."

Mrs. Marcus Henderson read for the fifth time the letter bearing the presidential seal, delivered by a special White House messenger that same night.

> . . . I know it offers you little solace that I have awarded Colonel Henderson the Distinguished Service Medal as a most inadequate token of my gratitude. No medal can compensate for the loss you feel. I can only pray that you, his widow, will someday put aside

your grief and come to the realization that he gave his life to the cause of peace, as surely as any soldier on a battlefield. The events of the past few weeks, I believe, will make this world a brighter one for all children, including your own, and your husband has earned the humble thanks of his President for the role he played in this achievement. Please accept my sincerest personal condolences, and may God grant you comforting strength in this hour of bereavement.

Jeremy Haines

She laid the letter down. As she stared with tear-filled but unblinking eyes at a picture of Marcus Henderson on the fireplace mantel, she felt the stirrings of the new life within her.

Rod Pitcher sat in front of his portable typewriter in the unused bedroom that passed as a den. He was not looking at it. He was glaring at a mortal enemy, inanimate but evil in its very silence.

Ostensibly, he was working on his novel, having recovered from the ignominious experience earlier that night when Damon had told him he wasn't needed on the Haines story. Now his usually fertile brain had dwindled to a trickle of halfhearted starts on sentences which he quickly X'd out. The absence of literary noise finally prompted Nancy to call out from the kitchen. "Having trouble, Rod?"

"I can't seem to get going," he complained. "Come in here and give me a kiss. Maybe it'll inspire me."

She complied but, while the kiss may have been adoring, it definitely did not achieve the status of inspiration. Pitcher patted her cheek, but glumly ripped the paper from the machine and wadded it into a ball.

"It's no use," he said. "Writing a novel about a Washington correspondent uncovering graft in the Senate has all the dramatic impact of a wet dishrag. All I can think of is the story I just helped cover."

"Who wouldn't?" she said softly.

"Maybe I should try a different plot. Something with an airline background."

"That would be nice. Then I could help you with the stewardess parts."

"Yeh. Hey, Nancy, I could have this airline captain accused of pilot error—that reminds me, I'd better remind Chet Colin tomorrow to goose the Air Force on when that final accident report is due."

"You can't stop thinking about it, can you?"

Rod Pitcher threw the wadded paper into his wastebasket. "No, I can't. It's hard to stop thinking about any crash, Nancy. When you love airplanes, something dies inside of you when a bird goes down. You don't even have to know the pilot. Fraternity of the air, I suppose you'd call it. I keep thinking about Marcus Henderson. Wondering what was going through his mind when he knew his elevators were gone and he couldn't pull out of that dive. Wondering if his last thoughts were of the President he assumed was on board, or his own family. Or maybe himself and that he was going to die. Jesus, what a way to go. Straight down to oblivion in a couple of minutes."

"Straight down to heaven," she said gently. "Or is that too corny?"

"No, it's not corny. Straight down to heaven. That would make a hell of a title for some book."

"Maybe the one you're going to write," said Nancy Pitcher.

The wind whistled through the lonely Arizona gorge, plucking with unseen fingers at the few pieces of metal left unclaimed in the muck. Occasionally a strong gust rattled the aluminum and the metallic sound slapped against the canyon walls.

A small coyote picked his way carefully through the remnants of muddy wreckage, pausing at intervals to sniff at pieces of yellow insulating material that had once lined the fuselage of a mighty aircraft. The thin gauze curtain of clouds that had been drifting over the desolate land suddenly parted and moonlight bathed the bottom of the gorge.

The coyote lifted his head and howled.

The forlorn sound echoed through the gorge, the desert's own requiem for the plane known as Air Force One.

AUTHOR'S ACKNOWLEDGMENTS:

Grateful appreciation for technical aid and advice is expressed to Captains William Bettwy, William Davenport, and Rod Coston of American Airlines; Alvin Spivak, White House correspondent for United Press International, and Louis Cassels, also of UPI.

An equal nod of gratitude to Grant Dillman, news editor, and Julius Frandsen, bureau manager, United Press International in Washington, treasured friends who exemplify the spirit of objectivity that is the lifeblood of the wire services.

A low bow in the direction of Susan Brown, who transcribed the manuscript while refraining from suggesting that I write it in longhand and type the corrections.

And finally, my thanks to the late Captain Frank Eberhart Haynes, Jr., United States Marine Corps—like the fictitious Marcus Henderson, a quiet hero.

Robert J. Serling
Washington, D.C.

All the terror and suspense of
ROSEMARY'S BABY . . .

THE SURVIVORS

A spellbinding novel
by Anne Edwards

A beautiful and lost girl . . . a man obsessed with learning the undiscovered truth about the shocking slaughter of an entire family . . . a high-speed journey along the razor edge of madness into the jaws of unimaginable horror . . .

A novel that grips the imagination like a vise until the final shattering turn of the screw . . .

"You'll be reading THE SURVIVORS right to the breathless end."
                                        —*Dallas Times Herald*

A DELL BOOK   95c

If you cannot obtain copies of this title at your local bookseller, just send the price (plus 10c per copy for handling and postage) to Dell Books, Box 2291, Grand Central Post Office, New York, N.Y. 10017. No postage or handling charge is required on any order of five or more books.